Bantam Books by

EMILY CARMICHAEL

The CAT'S MEOW

Emily Carmichael

BANTAM BOOKS

THE CAT'S MEOW
A Bantam Book / November 2004

Published by
Bantam Dell
A Division of Random House, Inc.
New York, New York

Bantam Books and the rooster colophon are registered trademarks of Random House, Inc.

ISBN 0-553-58634-3

Printed in the United States of America
Published simultaneously in Canada

OPM 10 9 8 7 6 5 4 3 2 1

This book is dedicated to my niece,
Kristen Bradshaw Mackenzie, my biggest fan,
my most active promoter, and a model for
more than one of my more zany characters

The
CAT'S
MEOW

chapter 1

MCKENNA WRIGHT looked up from her work to find the devil regarding her from her office doorway. The devil wore cowboy boots, a know-it-all grin, and a battered Stetson fringed with errant curls of sandy-colored hair.

"What the hell are you doing here?" Mckenna grumbled.

The grin widened. "Fine welcome."

Mckenna met him eye-to-eye. Her staff knew better than to disturb her when she was poring over a case, barricaded in the citadel of her office and enthroned at her desk. But her staff had left two hours ago.

"I knew I would find you here on a Friday night," the devil said. "Everyone else is out partying, or spending time with the family, or vegging in front of the tube. But not Mckenna Wright. She's hard at work for the firm, brow furrowed, mind focused, giving it her all for good old Bradner, Kelly, and Bolin."

Mckenna leaned back in her chair with a sigh. The *State of Arizona v. Todd Harmon* was going nowhere as long as Tom Markham, temptation personified, stood in her doorway. He couldn't come within sight of her without irritating, distracting, provoking, and otherwise tempting her to think about him rather than the work at hand.

"Okay, Cowboy, so you found me hard at work when I should be out partying. But I'm sure any hole in the party world is diligently being filled by your colleagues at the county attorney's office. After all, being on the government payroll means you aren't caught dead working after hours, right? We wouldn't want the taxpayers to get more than their money's worth, would we?"

He shook his head—a handsome head in spite of the too-long hair and cowboy hat. "You need to go out and have some fun once in a while, Mac. Then maybe you wouldn't be such a grouch."

Mckenna scowled. Of all her friends and acquaintances, Tom was the only one with the nerve to call her Mac. "Spare me the lecture," she said sharply. "Are you here for a reason, Cowboy, or is your idea of a Friday night party coming over here to needle me?"

His long, lean body lounged against the doorframe. A relaxed smile showed total unconcern with her annoyance. Tom Markham had always shown total unconcern for Mckenna's annoyance, even during the year he had worked for Bradner, Kelly, and Bolin. The fact that *her* nameplate was getting ready to add the title "Partner" while *he* barely even rated a nameplate hadn't intimidated him in the least.

But then, a man who had ridden bulls for a living before taking on law school might not regard a mere law firm almost-partner as intimidating, even one who cultivated a sharp tongue and an edgy temper.

"I *am* here to needle you," Tom admitted with an insouciant grin.

"Like I didn't know that?"

"And—believe it or not—I'm also here in an official capacity."

"Really," she drawled skeptically.

"Semiofficial. It is Friday night, after all. Want to go somewhere for a drink?"

She had to laugh. "You're asking me out?"

"Oh, no. Would I be so bold, after the last time?"

He would, Mckenna thought. Tom Markham's boldness knew no limits. If his boldness had been aimed at his work with BKB, he would have soared to the top, as Mckenna had done. But Tom Markham was bolder with bulls and women than with the law. Thus his current fate at the county attorney's office, stuck as a middle-class public servant, taking his revenge by being a thorn in Mckenna's side.

He answered her skeptical grimace with, "Nope! You don't have to worry about me takin' liberties, ma'am. You made yourself pretty clear on that score a long time ago, and I'm not a man to beat a dead horse. Actually, I want to talk to you about work. Nose-to-the-grindstone sort of woman that you are, you should appreciate that."

"Work," she echoed. "What work?"

"*State of Arizona* v. *Todd Harmon* ring a bell?"

The Harmon case was the last thing Mckenna wanted to discuss with anyone from the county attorney's office right then, especially sharp-eyed, sharp-eared Tom.

"I just thought, this being the beginning of the weekend and all, that music and maybe a little liquor could make the discussion more amiable."

Stuffing the file on her desk into her briefcase, Mckenna grimaced. "You're not going to give up and go away, are you?"

"Not a chance."

"All right, Cowboy. I'll give you an hour. After that I have to put my nose back to the grindstone. I have a ton of work waiting for me."

She insisted upon taking separate cars. No way would she cede a driver's seat to Tom. He led the way to the

Rainbow's End, a steak house and bar in a historic stage-coach stop on the western edge of Sedona. Almost everything in Sedona, Arizona, qualified as picturesque—from southwestern cowboy quaint to New Age kooky. But to go along with the ambiance, the Rainbow's End boasted the best margaritas in town.

The place also grilled the best steak in town, a reputation to which Tom paid tribute by ordering a huge New York strip, juicy rare, with a baked potato soaked in butter.

"I thought we were here for a quiet drink and legal talk."

"A man's gotta eat," he said, stabbing a near-raw hunk of steak and blissfully forking it into his mouth.

Dinner, caveman style. Mckenna contemplated throwing up. Her idea of a sensible meal was perhaps salad greens and a few slices of tomato. The closest she generally came to meat was opening a can of cat food for Nefertiti, her cat.

"You should weigh five hundred pounds, eating like that."

Tom swallowed a bite and answered cheerfully, "Just doing my part as top of the food chain. Nothing wrong with real food, Mac. You should try it some time. You're thin as a rail."

Regarding him sourly over the salted rim of her margarita, Mckenna said, "I like being thin as a rail. It's healthy." Not to mention elegant, fashionable, and sexy—three qualities that boosted any woman's career. It wasn't fair that dumpy and plain were usually fatal to a female seeking professional advancement, but that was the way the world worked. "That's just disgusting." Mckenna grimaced at Tom's steak. "Now that you're not battling bulls in the rodeo arena, you've decided to eat them?"

"Nothing better in this world than a good steak. And a good buttered potato. Mmmm. Lots of butter. And sour cream."

Mckenna took a cleansing sip of margarita just to drive

the notion of all that fat from her palate. "Can we get down to business, Tom? You did drag me here to do something more interesting than watch you drool over a dead cow, right?"

He grinned engagingly, showing white, straight teeth. "I could think of a number of more interesting things to do."

Mckenna skewered him with a glare.

"How's that boyfriend of yours?"

That caught her by surprise. "Adam?"

"Yeah, Adam. I heard he was quite the hot-shot attorney in Denver. The word is out that you two are planning to tie the knot."

"He is a hot-shot attorney, but the rest is rumor."

"Ah. Rumor. You can tell me. Is BKB going to lose its best attorney to matrimony?"

She gave him a superior smile. "Don't get your hopes up. My career is never going to take second place to matrimony. I'll be here to whip your ass in court for the foreseeable future."

He chuckled in acknowledgment that he'd been bested. Her answer to his question hadn't told him what he wanted to know, which was none of his business and he knew it. She didn't want to talk to Tom Markham about Adam Decker.

"And just what about the Harmon case did you bring me here to discuss?"

"Ah, Mac, you never relax a minute, do you?"

She scowled. "Not that it's any of your concern, but yes, I do take time to relax. In certain circles, in fact, I'm actually considered a fun person."

"Yeah, I know. When you take your cat to visit the hospital, the patients think you're a barrel of fun. Of course, considering the other stuff on a hospital agenda, their standards may be pretty low."

Mckenna set her glass on the table and whipped the

napkin from her lap. "I'm outta here." Even a good margarita wasn't worth being insulted.

"Whoa!" he commanded as she stood. "Wait!"

"Why? So I can waste time with this nonsense?"

"I do want to talk about Todd Harmon."

"Then get to it, Cowboy." Huffily, she sat. "What do we need to discuss about Todd Harmon, other than the fact that the county attorney and the bumbling Keystone Cops in the sheriff's office are targeting an innocent man simply because he's a high-profile celebrity?"

"Mac, if we wanted to target high-profile celebrities around here, we could drag half of Sedona to the station to get fingerprinted. This is a town full of celebrities."

"Sure. Artists, writers, a movie icon or two. But Todd Harmon is a genuine star. They don't come any bigger. America's boy next door. Mr. Country-Clean Living with a taste for occasional partying. So you just assume he's heavy into drugs."

"I know he's heavy into drugs. Not only doing drugs, but pushing them. Right here in the fair little town of Sedona."

"Bullshit," she said airily.

"I have witnesses."

"All of whom were snockered to the gills at the time of the alleged drug transaction. I'll rip them to pieces on the witness stand."

He waved a forkful of steak at her. "The stupid shit tried to sell coke to a police officer, for chrissakes!"

She answered with a superior smile. "Entrapment. I'll get it thrown out. The jury will never hear it. Besides, Todd thought it was a joke his buddies were playing on him."

Tom gave her a stern look. "Cut the defense attorney song and dance, Mac. You're not impressing a jury here. This is me. Your client is guilty as sin of both possession and selling, and we both know it. But to save the taxpayers money, the prosecution is willing to do a deal, because for all his money and worshipping fans, Todd Harmon is a small fish in a big, scummy pond. If he tells us who the big fish are and turns state's evidence when the time comes, we'll let him plead guilty to the lesser charge of possession. He'll get an abbreviated sentence, along with rehab, and before too long, he's back to wowing 'em on stage and making commercials for Pepsi."

Mckenna shook her head, but she did throw him a bone. "I'll talk to him, but he won't go for it. He knows you've got holes in your case, and he also knows he has the best defense attorney in the state on his side. I can kill you in court, Cowboy." Or at least she could if she somehow managed to make legal lemonade out of the bagful of lemons Todd Harmon had handed her. But she wasn't in the mood to give up the truth and watch Tom gloat. Not tonight. Not after the barbs he kept throwing her way.

"The truth has nothing to do with it, eh?"

More than he knew. But she put on her trademark confident smile and pulled out the standard lecture. "Right and wrong, true and false don't exist in a court of criminal law, only proving something beyond a reasonable doubt, and a jury can see reasonable doubt in something as small as a defendant's charming smile or the prosecutor's ugly tie. Hell, don't tell me you still believe in the law as a tool for righting the wrongs of society."

His smile twisted wryly. "Cynicism. It sounds so wrong coming from that angel's face of yours. Don't you ever get tired of sacrificing truth to ambition, Mac?"

She prayed for patience. Angel's face, indeed! The way Tom Markham often looked at her—as if she were some kind of ripe fruit waiting to be picked—never failed to muddle her brain, though she wouldn't in a million years let him know that. So she shot him a look that no one, not even Tom Markham, could call angelic.

"I'm not in the business of tilting at windmills, Cowboy. And realism isn't cynicism. I owe Todd Harmon the very best defense I can give him, because that's what the law says he deserves, whether he's a bum off the streets or a rock star. Everybody has the right to the best possible defense against eager-beaver prosecutors like you. So quit angling for me to hand you my client on a skewer."

He gave her a long, hard stare that she met head-on without a flinch. Tom Markham was an idealist, and he was not going to make her feel guilty about this, because everything she'd said was right. Idealists screwed up the world, not realists.

"Okay," he finally said, giving up on the stare. "Talk to Harmon, and think about it, Mac. Think about the greater good for a change."

She rolled her eyes as he pushed back his chair, slapped his Stetson onto his head, and stood up. "I'll get the bill."

"Never mind," she told him. "I wouldn't want the taxpayers to get stuck for that steak. My expense account is fatter than yours, I'm sure."

"The taxpayers won't be buying my steak." He grinned wickedly. "But I'll let you buy it with your fat expense account, if you insist. I'm outta here for the weekend. You'll be nose to the grindstone for BKB, right? But I'm spending the weekend on a pair of water skis at Canyon Lake. Call me Monday. We'll talk."

Mckenna stared into her glass while Tom disappeared out the door—just to prove to herself that she really had no desire to watch his butt as he walked away in those snug jeans. Then she smiled to herself. Like hell she didn't want to watch his butt. It was a supremely superior butt, as men's butts went, and she didn't have to buy the product just because she admired the packaging.

Waterskiing, eh? Skiing double, no doubt. She wondered who would be sharing the lake with him. Some "fun" honey with more boobs than brains, probably. Not that she cared. In fact, she totally didn't care. Tom had made his play for her when he worked for BKB, and she'd given him the cold shoulder for a host of reasons. She had lived at the top of the firm's ladder, while he had teetered on the bottom rung. Like that would have worked out? She didn't think so. Besides, an ex—rodeo cowboy wasn't even close to her type. That down-home drawl and stupid Stetson reeked of cowboy bars and country music. Mckenna preferred four-star restaurants and Mozart when she had time to indulge in such frivolities, which wasn't often.

She needed another margarita, Mckenna decided, and motioned to the waiter. From across the room he pointed to her glass with a questioning lift of a brow, and she nodded.

The office with its pile of work on her desk beckoned her to return, but she really did need this second drink. Tom Markham. What a pain. He had left BKB on the pretext of wanting to practice the kind of law that helped the community rather than pandered to wealthy clients. Mckenna snorted at the very thought. The man needed to grow up. Though he was no slouch when it came to the law. You didn't get away with much when Tom prosecuted a case. He was going to rake her over the coals Monday when she told him about the witness he didn't know about in the Harmon case. She had to tell him about it. No way around it. That was what she had told Todd Harmon that very afternoon when she had tried to get him to do the very thing Tom wanted him to do—take a plea bargain.

But damn, it was tempting to keep the whole thing under wraps.

"Mckenna!"

The hearty greeting came from a tall, almost skeletal fellow in an expensive gray suit and equally expensive blond toupee.

"Buddy!" She put on her professional smile. "Having dinner here?"

"Just finished. Was that our noble prosecuting attorney who just walked out?"

"Tom Markham. He's a good man."

Buddy's smile was cool to that notion—understandable, since he was Todd Harmon's agent, and Harmon was the man's bread and butter. "Frankly, I'd just as soon he were an incompetent bum. But we have the best attorney in the state on our side, right? Todd's not worried."

Todd should be worried, but Mckenna wasn't going to discuss the case with Buddy Morris just because he was her client's nosy agent. Morris and his superstar client had a peculiar relationship, with the agent pulling the strings that made the country-western star talk and move, or so it seemed to Mckenna. And while Mckenna frequently found Todd Harmon charming, Morris reminded her of a snake.

Her margarita had lost its taste, and she no longer wanted to wait for another. She looped her handbag strap over her shoulder and pushed back her chair. "Got to run, Buddy. Work is waiting at the office. Try one of the margaritas. They're good."

"I'll do that. Don't work too hard."

The tone sounded friendly, but the smile chilled. Mckenna felt his eyes on her back as she walked out the door.

In spite of her declared intention to go back to work, Mckenna gunned her BMW sports model right past the adobe office complex that housed, among other upscale offices, Bradner, Kelly, and Bolin. She had the mother of all headaches, and the very expensive house she had just acquired in Oak Creek Canyon beckoned with its comforts of Tylenol, a warm furry cat, and a soft bed. Damn Todd Harmon, anyway. She could almost feel her blood pressure rise at the thought of this afternoon's conversation in the living room of his multimillion-dollar home.

"Todd," she had said in a matter-of-fact, professional voice. "Maria Oranto's testimony is going to kill you. We need to make a deal."

Grimacing, he had refused to meet her eyes. "Maria won't testify."

"Maria *will* testify. I've already interviewed her. She doesn't want to testify, but she won't have a choice."

He merely shook his head, eyes lowered, wearing guilt like a tarnished halo. Mckenna tried not to second-guess clients who professed their innocence. But for sure, Todd's conscience smarted about something.

"Maria," he confessed, "is gone."

Mckenna had instantly leapt to the worst possible conclusion. "What do you mean, 'gone'?"

"Just gone. Back to Mexico. She was a wetback, and she was scared about all the hovering cops and lawyers. So she skedaddled home."

Mckenna's eyes narrowed. "Did you give her money to go home?"

"I owed her, Mckenna. She worked for me for over a year."

"Did you give her money past what you owed her?"

He had been silent, and she wasn't going to browbeat him into confessing that he'd bribed a witness. After all, she was the attorney for the *defense*, dammit!

Mckenna's head pounded harder as she thought about the sheer arrogant audacity of the man. Most of the time Todd came across as charming, down-to-earth, everybody's boyfriend, son, brother. But right then, Mckenna had wanted to shake him until he showed some common sense.

"Todd." She had mustered her most reasonable tone of voice. "I am required by law to tell the prosecution that there's another witness. I have to tell him that Maria has relevant testimony and I know pretty much where to find her."

He looked alarmed. "Shit, no, Mckenna! You don't have to tell anyone! Just leave Maria out of this. She doesn't speak good English, and she gets confused real easy about things. She could probably be talked into saying anything those cops want her to say, but it doesn't mean she'd be telling the real story."

"Todd, the law—"

"The law shouldn't ace out good sense. The cops didn't talk to Maria, so there's no way they'll ever know about her. Are we talking about justice here, or just blindly following a set of stupid rules?"

Her boss, Gilbert Bradner, had said much the same thing when she had hinted at her dilemma that afternoon after talking to Todd. She hadn't told him outright, of course. Gil would take the Harmon case away from her given a sliver of a chance. He didn't care for her having a high-profile, career-making case like this one, partly because she had always teed him off by refusing to toady, and partly because she was—sort of—the protégée of Sean Kelly, and Gil suspected the senior partner used her as his eyes and ears in the Sedona office. Since the partners played an endless game of "gotcha," that didn't go down too well.

She wasn't Sean's spy, really. But that was the kind of place BKB was. Tension upon tension. Gil would jump at any excuse to take the Harmon case from her and give it to an attorney who wasn't above being his little toady—Pat Carter.

So Mckenna hadn't consulted Gil outright, just hinted at a witness problem, and he'd warned her that losing a high-profile multimillionaire celebrity client certainly would add lead weights to the rising balloon of her career.

That was why she hadn't yet told Tom Markham about Maria, the housemaid who could have seen with her own eyes a ton of stuff that could get Harmon an all-expenses-paid visit to the big house, compliments of the State of Arizona. A wicked, evil, unprincipled part of her brain told her to consider the situation until Monday. After all, Harmon had a point. Maria was unavailable to testify, and finding her in Mexico would be like finding a needle in a haystack. Unfortunately for her defense case, when Mckenna had talked to the timid little maid, Maria had mentioned her family in a small town in Sonora. Knowing the name of that small town, how hard could it be to bring her back? The Mexican government would cooperate. They wouldn't want to make trouble over such a small thing.

But as things stood now, the prosecution didn't know about Maria. There was no hard testimony except from witnesses that Mckenna could blow out of the courtroom with one hand tied behind her back. She could win this case and be the darling of BKB and the media that would flock to the courtroom. Her career would soar; Gilbert Bradner be damned.

But the law said she had to tell the prosecution. Damn! Tom would jump on the girl's testimony. Unless Harmon did a plea deal, which would happen when hell started serving frozen daiquiris, America's country-western idol and his not-guilty plea would go down the river, and from his prison cell he would be composing new hits about stupid laws, injustice, and incompetent defense attorneys. And the firm would exact revenge by trashing any thought of making her a partner. Worse still, she would stay in Sedona, in this tiny satellite office two hours from a proper shopping mall and just as far removed from a chance to make a name for herself. That was if the partners were in a generous mood and didn't demote her to legal assistant. Sean Kelly wouldn't save her, even if he did like her.

Sheesh! No wonder her head pounded. Had she remembered to take her blood-pressure meds that morning? Just a few months ago her doctor had warned her to cool her jets or her heart was going to send blood rocketing through the top of her skull. That was happening now, if her headache gave a clue. Tears gathered in her eyes and made the road in front of her blur.

Even in daylight and seen through non-swimming eyes, the road winding through the canyon required close attention. Picturesque during the day, Oak Creek Canyon was damned dark at night. The stream tumbled through rocks and boulders on Mckenna's left, and towering cliff walls rose on her right. She squinted to see the pavement markings in the BMW's headlights, and that made her head hurt even more. Oh, man, but she needed a warm bath, a bottle of Tylenol, and a conversation with Titi, who, even if she didn't understand a word Mckenna said, at least never talked back. Or if she did, the backtalk came out as a cute little meow. Cats never had a problem with dilemmas like right versus expedient. Nope. Cats were always out for themselves.

Temptation returned. Mckenna could be out for herself, as well. Who would it hurt? Ethics or career advancement? Right or ... wrong? Was it wrong to want to get ahead? One more minor drug conviction in a world gone wild with drugs, violence, anger, and cheating. If Harmon had been selling, he'd been selling to his rich, jaded friends, who probably snorted coke as casually as drinking a beer. He hadn't been lurking around schoolyards, luring children into the drug culture. Todd Harmon was a nice guy. Self-centered, maybe. Self-indulgent. But he didn't deserve prison.

Besides, what difference would that one little conviction make? As Tom himself had pointed out, the state had bigger fish to fry than Todd Harmon.

All very well and good, but ethics countered with a body block. Damn, how could she even think such a thing? She was almost as bad as Miss Patricia Do-Anything-For-A-Win Carter. Cooler haircut, way better figure, and better sense of style, but almost as disgusting.

Damn, but Mckenna hated moral dilemmas. She hated it when what she had to do was the direct opposite of what she wanted to do. Really, really wanted to do. Her interview notes on Maria Oranto seemed to burn a hole through the file folder, the briefcase, and right into Mckenna's brain. Tell or don't tell? Be good or be smart? Back and forth, back and forth. Temptation and ethics.

The road ahead curved sharply. A white light exploded in front of Mckenna's eyes. The world spun out of control, then came up to smash her flat.

SHE WOKE to darkness. Darkness in her head, darkness behind her eyes, which stayed tightly closed. Fear prowled like a wolf through that darkness, but the fear didn't have a name. Just a general presence. She struggled to put a name to it, but the struggle made her weary. Weary and in trouble. She knew there was trouble somewhere. Danger, and the nameless fear. Best to stay in this darkness, behind closed eyes, where she might be safe. Safe until she remembered about the trouble, the danger. Safe until she remembered who she was, and why she was lying here in the darkness without a name to put to herself or the trouble that stalked her.

She took comfort from the darkness. Warm, quiet, soft. As long as the darkness provided refuge, she didn't have to open her eyes and let in the outside world. She didn't have to struggle to remember. Darkness soothed. It hid her from the world. No need to wrestle with who, what, and where.

So she floated in nothingness, drifting, sinking once again toward sleep. Content. Safe. Until murmurs stirred her precious darkness. Gentle touches disturbed her comfort, lured her upward toward the world and its danger, its struggle. She refused to open her eyes. Refused and refused. They would go away. She would outlast them. Then a weight landed rudely on her sternum, an insistent pressure that made breathing hard labor.

Near panic, she opened her eyes to find a yellow-eyed monster sitting on her chest.

No, not a monster. A cat. A cat the color of mink, with a baseball-sized head and two implacable eyes staring straight into hers.

Then the cat said, "Welcome back, Mckenna."

chapter 2

MCKENNA FIXED her eyes on the face that smiled down upon her. How could he smile when she wanted to scream, to shriek, to shout out her panic?

"Mckenna," he said gently. "Do you understand what I'm telling you?"

Richard Estrella, his white coat read, the lettering embroidered in sober black. Richard Estrella, M.D. A doctor of fit middle age, steel-gray hair, reassuring voice, and that damned understanding smile. But he didn't understand, because if he did, he for sure wouldn't be smiling. Not unless he had a sadistic streak.

The smile fell into a concerned frown. "Mckenna, can you speak?"

Hell no, she couldn't speak, because if she opened her mouth, all the feelings roiling inside her would escape in a cry that would bring down the ceiling.

"Mckenna?"

She swallowed, then made an Herculean effort at control. "Yes," she croaked.

"Yes, you can speak." He nodded with Hippocratic wisdom. "And yes, you understand?"

"Y . . . yes."

"Good. I'm sure you're full of questions, but try to just relax and listen for a few minutes. I know your head feels like someone set off a bomb inside it, but let me assure you that you're going to be fine, given just a little time. You have considerable trauma to the head from hitting the side window. That is responsible for the blood clot and contusions in the . . ."

He continued talking about lobes of the brain and the effect of trauma and bleeding in this area and that area. But she didn't care. She didn't want a medical discourse. She wanted to know why she was lying here like some blank sheet of paper, an adult woman who might as well have been born just minutes ago when she had surfaced from that warm, comforting darkness that still beckoned temptingly from some deep layer of her mind.

"But I have to tell you," Dr. Estrella continued, "that I strongly suspect that the accident is not entirely responsible for the trauma to your brain. Though they aren't totally conclusive, tests suggest that the initial blackout that caused you to lose control of your car might have been a symptom of a catastrophic event in your brain—what we call a transient ischemic attack, or TIA. Kind of like a stroke, but not so severe. It doesn't surprise me, young woman. Your blood pressure these past two years has been a catastrophe waiting to happen. I know you young people think, 'It can't happen to me,' but that certainly isn't the case. You backed yourself into a corner, Mckenna, where something just had to give."

Well, shame on her. Maybe she did, but she didn't remember. That was the hell of it. She didn't remember anything, not the car accident the doctor talked about, not her name, her age, or the faces of those women who had been in the room when she had awakened with that . . . oh, no, she didn't want to think about the cat. Not only did she have no identity and no past, but her poor injured brain was torturing her with hallucinations. She might have no memory, but she knew for damned sure that, in a normal world, a cat's vocabulary was limited to meow.

But Dr. Estrella had continued on with his discourse, his voice lowered in warning. "If I am correct, if you did experience a TIA, then it is a dire warning you should heed, young woman. Stress is a killer. You must manage it, be faithful in taking your blood-pressure medication, and take better care of yourself. Next time it will not be a TIA, it will be a full-blown stroke. In fact, I am going to treat you and speak to you as if it had been a real stroke, because sometime in the future, unless you do something positive to prevent it, that will be the case."

He pulled out a pen-sized light that he shone in each eye. "You're going to have a bad headache for a few days. And don't be alarmed if you have difficulty writing with your right hand or tap dancing with your right foot."

He straightened and smiled at the lame joke, apparently satisfied that her eyes were still in her head and her brain still resided somewhere behind them, however malfunctioning that brain might be.

"I'm going to set up a schedule of physical therapy for a few weeks. The disability isn't severe, and in no time you should be back in good form. And if you slow down a bit, worry less, get more sleep, and look into a bit of stress management, then there's a good chance this won't happen again."

Physical therapy? What about brain therapy? "But I . . . I can't remember anything."

"And I know that's upsetting, on the face of it, but I wouldn't let it alarm you too much. Temporary amnesia is very common in brain trauma. But the brain is a remarkable entity. Given time, it can recover from far worse traumas than yours. I feel very safe in predicting that your memory should return."

He felt safe. Just dandy. He wasn't the one lying here with a reformatted computer disk for a brain. "How long?" she demanded. "A day? A week? A goddamned year?"

He frowned at the rising pitch of her voice. "See now, Mckenna. That sort of stressing out about details is what you need to avoid. Just try to calm yourself. There's no telling how long the recovery process will take. Relaxing and letting time heal the damage is the best thing you can do right now."

She wanted to growl. He made the total loss of herself sound like a hangnail.

He took a clipboard from the foot of the bed and scribbled some notes. "The brain is very resilient, Mckenna. Once you're back in familiar surroundings with friends and family, things will come back."

"Is that a promise?"

"It's not a promise. As much as we'd like to congratulate ourselves on our understanding of the human body, what's inside our skulls still keeps a few secrets from us. Your gray matter got shook up a bit, but I think in the end you won't have lost much, if anything. Just try to be patient. You won't heal overnight."

"But I don't even remember where I live, or work, or, dammit, what I do!"

"I expect major things like that to come back in a few hours, a few days at worst." He gave her a look he might give an interesting lab rat. "Would you like me to set up an appointment with a psychiatrist?"

And have him find out that she had heard a cat talk, clear as she heard the good doctor here? She pictured a barred cell in the nearest locked ward. "I'll do without the psychiatrist, I think."

"If you prefer. We'll talk again tomorrow, and if your

memory hasn't shown some improvement by then, we'll look into getting you some help from psych. Okay?"

When hell froze over. "Fine."

Fine, indeed. She'd already found out a few things about her mysterious self. She had a low threshold for frustration, nearly nonexistent patience, and a distrust of any science beginning with the letters P-S-Y. Peachy.

JANE CONNOR and Nell Travis sprang up as Dr. Estrella came into the waiting room. He gave them a reassuring smile. "She's awake and feisty, though a bit confused. Probably the best treatment right now is attention from her friends."

Perched in Jane's arms, a plump sable cat meowed plaintively.

The doctor smiled. "And attention from her cat, also." He reached out and scratched Titi's neck above her little green therapy cat vest. "How's a puss?" he asked with total lack of proper medical dignity. "You going to take care of your mom?"

"So we can go in and see her?" Jane asked.

"You bet. But I should warn you, she's very muddled. Right now she doesn't remember much of anything, not only about the accident but about who she is. In my experience, this sort of amnesia is only temporary, but some of the loss may last a while. The best thing for her now is to be surrounded by familiar people and things. Has her family been notified?"

"Mckenna has never talked about her family," Nell said. "Though I know she has one somewhere in Denver."

"Well, if they can come down here and spend some time with her, that would probably help."

As the doctor left, Jane snorted, a sound Mckenna had always scolded her about. It made her sound like a horse, she'd said. A big, sloppy horse. Mckenna was into elegance.

"How does he expect us to notify Mckenna's family if she doesn't remember who they are?"

Nell, always the cheerful one, replied, "It couldn't be that bad. No one gets rid of family that easily. Besides, we're Mckenna's family. You, me, Titi, Piggy, Idaho, Dan, and Weed."

"Yeah, I guess you could say that."

When they got back to Mckenna's room, her stillness alarmed them. Deep purple shadows beneath her eyes were the only color on her face. Wisps of dark hair escaped the bandages wrapping her head, giving her the look of someone who styled her hair with a blender—certainly not the sleek Mckenna they had known these past several years.

Mckenna's appearance filled Jane with uneasiness. Somehow she had figured that once her friend regained consciousness, she would lose the wan, insubstantial vulnerability of the pale little twig of a person who lay beneath the sheets. But she still looked like a limp, bleached dishrag.

Not that Mckenna had ever been anything but a twig since Jane had first met her, back in the days when the three of them—or the six of them, if you counted their animals (which was only fair)—had started up the local animal therapy group. Jane had constantly ragged on Mckenna about her determination to stay a size three. The silly twit had kept herself skinny as some fashion model. But even with no meat on her bones, no one could call Mckenna insubstantial. She radiated energy, confidence, and a force field of ambition that often reached out and zapped anyone who got too close. But the person lying in the hospital bed couldn't zap a fly.

Titi meowed a feline demand, and Mckenna opened her eyes, which looked like two dark holes in the pallor of her face. Two dark holes that fixed them all with suspicious scrutiny.

"Hey there, Mckenna." Nell tried to sound hearty. "Doc says you're going to live. For a while you had us scared."

"Nah," Jane added. "Mckenna's too tough to let a little thing like plunging off a cliff stop her."

The eyes closed again. "Is that what I did?" she croaked.

"You did," Jane said. "Lucky for you there were trees in the way, or you would have ended up part of the dashboard, fifty feet down the slope."

"Jane!" Nell scolded.

"Well, she would have. Somebody upstairs likes you, I'd say." Jane put Titi on the bed. "Titi has missed you something awful."

Mckenna opened her eyes and gave the cat a wary look, but Titi just purred. She was, after all, an experienced therapy cat who knew exactly what to do for a hospital patient, whether that patient happened to be her mom or a perfect stranger. Her purring rumbled like comforting thunder, and she slid her plump, furry body between Mckenna's arm and her side.

"This is my cat?" Mckenna asked uncertainly.

"She's the love of your life. You've had her since she was eight weeks old. You really don't remember, do you?" Nell said quietly.

"I don't remember much of anything."

"Man!" Jane whistled. "That sucks."

Nell tried to sound encouraging. "Dr. Estrella says the amnesia's only temporary. So you shouldn't let it upset you. In the meantime, we'll just introduce ourselves. We're your best friends."

Titi interrupted her purring to meow.

"We're your best friends next to the cat," Jane corrected. "That's Nefertiti. Titi for short. She rules your household with an iron paw. I keep telling you to get a proper animal like a dog, but so far you've resisted."

Mckenna tried to smile, but it was obviously an effort.

"And I'm Jane, dog trainer extraordinaire and kennel owner. Don't let the fire-engine-red hair fool you. I'm sweet as a newborn lamb."

"And she's a liar, too," Nell said with a laugh. "She's about as sweet as a Rottweiler with an attitude. I'm Nell. I have a dog who's a millionaire—that's Piggy, and fortunately, she gives me an allowance to keep me fed and clothed. My husband Dan will be by later."

Mckenna looked at them as if they were alien escapees from Roswell.

"But most important," Jane said, "is you. You're Mckenna Wright, star player of Bradner, Kelly, and Bolin, and the slickest killer attorney in the whole state of Arizona. You're drop-dead gorgeous in spite of being thirty years old, have the best haircut in Sedona, not to mention the coolest clothes, and major attitude."

"Jane!" Nell chided.

"No harm there. Mckenna's proud of having attitude." And Jane wanted to see a bit more of it. Maybe voicing out loud who Mckenna was, would bring that person back.

Nell explained, "Jane doesn't mince words. But really, you two are the best of friends. You and I and Jane started the Hearts of Gold pet therapy group that works here at the hospital and the local nursing homes. And you're helping us expand the pet therapy services all over the north part of the state, with the help of Piggy's money."

Mckenna's dry lips twitched into a little smile. "Piggy the dog really has money?"

Nell smiled. "It's a long story. An old gentleman we used to visit left her a trust fund when he died."

"I don't suppose he left any to the cat, did he?"

Nell laughed. "You don't need to worry. You have a great job that pays tons of money, a dynamite house in Oak Creek Canyon, a cool BMW ..."

"Uh-uh," Jane reminded her. "Scratch the Beemer."

Mckenna let out her breath in a thready sigh. "I had a Beemer, eh? Wow."

"Very wow," Jane assured her. "Cool car. Its air bag saved your life."

"My head feels as if that air bag was made of concrete."

"Hi, hi! Mckenna!" A woman with hair almost as red as Jane's came through the door. "I heard you were awake. Hi, Nell, Jane, Titi."

"This is Diane," Jane told Mckenna. "Director of volunteers here at the medical center."

Diane looked puzzled.

"Mckenna has amnesia," Nell explained. "She doesn't know anything."

"I know lots," the patient insisted sharply.

There was a spark of the old Mckenna, Jane noted.

"I just don't know people, or ... well, other things. Temporarily."

"Oh, Mckenna, how awful!" Diane sympathized.

"Yes. Awful." Mckenna sighed, closed her eyes, and absently started stroking Titi, who purred even louder. When yet one more person walked into the room, she didn't even bother to open her eyes.

"What is going on in here?" the newcomer inquired sternly. The sternness went along with her nurse's uniform. "This room's beginning to look like Grand Central."

Diane waggled her fingers in a little wave. "I'd better go. Get well fast, Mckenna. You need to be visiting patients, not taking up a bed."

"We'd better go, too," Jane said. She lifted Titi from the bed. "I'm keeping Titi at the kennel until you go home, so don't worry about her."

"Don't worry about anything else, either," Nell said. "Your insurance agent is already working to get you a settlement for the car." She fished a piece of paper from her handbag and scribbled their phone numbers. "Here's in case you need anything. Just call. Tomorrow you'll feel better. I just know it."

Jane didn't say anything, but she doubted Nell's optimism. From the look in Mckenna's eyes—blank, confused, disheartened—she would guess some time would have to pass before Mckenna was herself again, if she ever was. She patted her sheet-draped ankle. "Take care, Mckenna. We'll be back."

She started to follow Nell out the door, but Mckenna's voice stopped her.

"Jane?"

"Yes?"

Mckenna looked more uncertain than Jane had ever seen her. "Is there . . . anything special about the cat?"

"Of course she's special. She's a therapy cat."

"Is that all?"

The cat and the woman in the bed exchanged a long look.

"What are you asking?"

Mckenna sighed. "Nothing. Forget it."

Jane could have sworn that Titi smiled. If cats could smile. Which of course they couldn't. Dogs could smile, but dogs were about as near-human as an animal could get. And cats were just, well, cats.

TODD HARMON sat at a window table in Oaxaca, nursing a seven and seven while Buddy Morris sipped a margarita and read the local rag.

"Poor Mckenna," Buddy said. "Hard to believe. Happened Friday, it says here. I saw her that night in the Rainbow's End."

"Yeah?" Todd said, reaching for a tortilla chip.

"Yes. She looked fine. The paper says the cause of the accident was a stroke. Imagine! At her age!"

Todd tapped his chip absently against the salsa bowl. "So Mckenna had a stroke and wrecked her car. Is she going to be all right?"

Buddy shrugged and handed over the *Red Rock News*. "Read it for yourself."

Todd read, frowning. "Jesus! She went off right on that curve where the drop-off is at least fifty feet. Lucky she wasn't killed. I can't believe she had a stroke. Mckenna's too tough for that."

"She has a high-pressure job defending villains like you. And apparently she didn't resort to the kind of stress relievers that you did."

"Quit nagging me about the coke," Todd objected in a low voice. "You're like an old woman. Worse, you're like a goddamned mother. Everybody does it. The government doesn't have any right to tell people what they can and can't eat, drink, and snort through the nose."

"The guys who write the laws think differently," Buddy reminded him. "And personally, big guy, I don't care if you snort an elephant up your nose, as long as it doesn't interfere with your concert or recording schedule. And getting thrown into the slammer is going to do that. I can't picture you finishing your next album from the exercise yard of the state pen."

"Hell, Buddy, it's not going to come to that and you know it. This is no big deal."

"You're fooling yourself. Just think for a change, will you? When the paparazzi get on this story, they're going to have a field day. Mr. Country-Clean slapped with possession and selling. Mr. Nice Guy is unmasked as a drug-snorting fraud who's been lying to the faithful fans who've turned all those albums into gold. So far we've managed to keep this low profile, but soon it's going to be a circus, Todd, and the media are going to chew on your bones. If you don't get yourself exonerated and somehow boosted back up on that pedestal, you could well be finished."

An olive-skinned waitress with a long black ponytail arrived with their dinner—a rib-eye steak for Todd and the enchilada plate for Buddy. As she set the plates in front of them, her cheeks darkened to a deep rose color and she gave Todd a shy smile.

In broken English she said, "*Señor* Harmon, I"—she pressed hands to her heart—"*muy, muy...* uh... love." She thrust her order pad toward him with a pleading look.

Todd knew what to do. He'd signed autographs for adoring fans on everything from napkins to various parts of the female anatomy. With a smile he knew would send the little waitress's heart soaring, he took the pen she offered, declared his love and admiration on the order pad, then signed his name in bold sweeps of ink. She took it back and pressed it to her heart, her eyes wide with joy.

"*Gracias! Gracias!*"

Buddy watched her go. "Suppose that'll do for a tip?"

"Not if you ever want to come back to this place, you cheap bastard."

Buddy chuckled. "I suppose." Then he sobered. "In any case, looks like you'll be needing a new lawyer. It's a damned shame."

The tone struck Todd as odd, and he gave Buddy a suspicious look. "You don't have to sound so happy about it. I sort of like Mckenna Wright."

Buddy shrugged. "You like anything with two X chromosomes."

"The fact that she's hot has nothing to do with it. I don't see the hurry to get a new lawyer. Mckenna's one of the top attorneys in the state. She's a pit bull in court."

"She can't do you much good in court if she's in the hospital. After an accident like that, and a stroke, you think she's going to bounce back to her office and resume work just so she can keep your ass out of the pen?"

Todd slapped the newspaper. "It says here she's in good

condition. She has plenty of time to recover. We don't even have a date for the preliminary hearing yet."

Buddy gave him his 'you're as dumb as a rock and why do I put up with you?' look. Todd hated that look.

"Todd, my boy, when are you going to learn to think beyond broads, booze, and banjo tuning? This accident is a perfect excuse to get someone better on your defense team. Mckenna's good, all right, but she's a little too smart for her own good, or yours. You tried to slip Maria past her, and it didn't work. So she's a loose cannon."

"The thing with Maria is no big deal. I can control Mckenna."

"Right," Buddy sneered. "Mckenna Wright is not one of those groupies who swoon at your songs and hang on your every word, boy. And word is that Tom Markham, the sonofabitch prosecuting this case, is a legal shark underneath that country-boy drawl and that golly-shucks-gee-whiz act of his. You're so used to everyone between Nashville and Hollywood kissing up to you that you've lost sight of the down and dirty real world. Tom Markham doesn't give a rat's ass if your last two albums went platinum. And Mckenna Wright isn't nearly as flexible as she might be about bending a few rules and getting creative with the law."

"How do you know?"

"I can name you a long list of cases where Markham has gotten the book thrown at some poor slob caught selling. I research, kid. It's my job to know everything that affects you and your career. That's what agents are for."

Todd made a rude sound. Buddy Morris had plucked him out of nowhere when Todd was a green, banjo-playing kid singing his songs at county fairs and local dives where he hardly made enough to keep his car in gas. The agent had set himself the task of making Todd a star, and now Todd Harmon was on top of the country-western charts, with a few good crossover hits, as well. He had two Grammy awards sitting on his mantel, two luxury houses—in Nashville, of course, and in Sedona—a ranch in Montana, a condo on the beach in San Diego, three cars, his own recording company, and a twin Beech out at the airport.

And Buddy took credit for all this since he managed the business end. He never let Todd forget that he had known him when Todd was just a punk kid with little more than a banjo and a beat-up truck, that he knew what was best for Todd better than Todd did, that Todd should just focus on music and superstardom and let Buddy manage the rest of his world, as he had always done.

But after ten years of letting Buddy pull the strings, Todd had begun to feel like a puppet. Maybe it was time for him to start running his own life, make his own decisions.

"I want to stick with Mckenna," Todd insisted. He pointed a tortilla chip at Buddy. "You never believe I know what I'm doing, but I do this time. Mckenna won't make a stink about Maria. She's not going to tell the prosecution or anybody else, and I'll tell you why. Bradner, Kelly, and Bolin have a rep that brings in the high rollers, the celebs, the people who can afford to blow a fortune on legal fees. What do you think would happen to their reputation if she blew my case when she didn't need to, just to follow some stupid set of hidebound rules? What do you think their other high-rolling clients would think if they let Todd Harmon go to jail for something as minor as selling a little coke to his friends?

"Hell, Mckenna's not stupid, Buddy. She's too smart to cook the goose that lays the golden egg."

Buddy let his boy have the last word. When Todd was in one of his independent moods, believing he could think for himself, the smartest thing to do was just to let his little flood of rebellion run its course.

And Buddy always did the smart thing. He was a man who could handle people, handle situations. Yessir. Buddy Morris was far too smart to stand by and see that banjo-playing, ballad-singing golden goose get himself cooked. Not if he could help it.

chapter 3

TOM MARKHAM liked being an attorney. He especially liked being an attorney in pursuit of putting the bad guys in a place where they couldn't hurt innocent people. Working in the county attorney's office, he got to do that very thing all day long, five days a week, and occasionally on weekends. Prosecuting cases for the county wasn't as exciting as cowboying around the rodeo circuit, which he'd done for six wild years, and it wasn't as lucrative as working for an outfit like Bradner, Kelly, and Bolin, which he had tried for a year. But unlike cowboying, lawyering didn't earn him broken bones and a yearly ration of stitches. And unlike BKB, working for the county made him proud as well as financially solvent. Not nearly as solvent as BKB would have made him. But hey! Pride counted for something.

Yes, indeed, Tom liked his job just fine. So Monday mornings didn't get him down like they did some folks. In fact, on this Monday morning, he marched into his office in Prescott whistling an old George Strait tune and looking forward to the day.

One of the legal clerks looked up as he passed her desk. "You're mighty cheerful this morning."

He gave her a smile. She was cute. Not quite as cute as the blonde pixie he'd spent the weekend with at Canyon Lake, but cute just the same.

"I'm always cheerful," he claimed. "What's not to be cheerful about? I had a great weekend waterskiing. The weather outside is gorgeous. And this very afternoon I'm having a state-of-the-art satellite dish installed to go with my new state-of-the-art television set. I'll be able to tune in to every football game the NFL ever thought of playing. Life is great!"

"Hmph!" was her comment on the NFL. "Waterskiing, eh? Did you take Clara?"

"Of course I took Clara. She's crazy for water. Can't keep her out of it."

A secretary with a pile of files cradled in her arms joined them. "Who's this Clara? I thought you were dating Trudy down in Phoenix."

"I'm not dating anyone."

The legal clerk sent the secretary one of those woman looks that no man could understand. "Clara's his Labrador retriever," she said.

"Well, then," the secretary queried. "Was Trudy at the lake, too?"

Tom laughed. "Does everyone in this big, bureaucratic government building keep track of my private life?"

"Only the women," the clerk admitted. "You're the only bachelor in this office, so you're the only entertainment available."

"Nice to know." He moved to take the pile of files from the secretary. "Let me have these, Cheryl. You look like you bit off a bigger piece of the filing cabinet than you can chew. Where are you taking them?"

"Up to Mr. Donovan's office."

John Donovan, county attorney, politically ambitious,

very anxious that none of the cases under the jurisdiction of his office made him look the fool.

"Okay," Tom said. "Up to Mr. Donovan, then."

"Perfect," said another attorney who strolled into the clerical section and caught the conversation. "Donovan wants to see you, Tom." He grinned evilly. "Happy Monday."

"Same to you, Clyde." He took the secretary's burden and, still whistling, walked toward the elevator to the second floor, where lurked the boss of this little bureaucracy.

When Tom walked out of Donovan's office ten minutes later, he no longer whistled. But neither did his expression match his boss's scowl. Tom knew the county attorney fretted about the Harmon case. Tom worried, too. The case should have been easy. The man had tried to sell coke to two undercover agents. They had him dead to rights. But Mckenna Wright was arguing the defense, and where Mckenna was involved, the prosecution should never get complacent. Sharp as a newly honed knife, that gal didn't know how to do anything other than win. Every thread she had picked loose from his case during their conversation the Friday before had been something he himself worried about. With Mckenna, you couldn't let anything slide.

Except he had a gut feeling that on the Harmon case, Mckenna wasn't quite as confident as she put on. She presented a good front, but he could read her. Somehow he had always been able to read her, from the first day they had met. He had walked into the luxurious offices of Bradner, Kelly, and Bolin for his first day of work, and there she'd been, beautiful, as sleek as a cat, a perfect combination of expensive fashion and professionalism. Way above him in the firm's hierarchy, of course. And looking down her perfect nose from her very lofty position. The Ice Queen.

But he had known from the first that beneath the flawless combination of *Cosmo* model and slick attorney was something human. At least that was what he'd told himself. The mystery of what lay beneath the smooth veneer had intrigued him.

Or maybe his interest had been a simple case of lusting after what he couldn't have. Since he'd been old enough to exchange diapers for junior Jockeys, the seemingly unattainable, whatever it was, had posed a personal challenge to him. All the paraphernalia he had won riding the rodeo circuit bore witness to that. His top grades in law school—another improbable achievement—testified to the same thing.

But Mckenna had proved a harder creature to conquer than the bulls he once rode. In fact, through his entire play for her, she had stayed very consistently uninterested, looking down her refined nose and letting him know that a newly minted junior attorney was far beneath her notice. Her disdain had been constant enough to make him give up, eventually—a humbling experience for a man who believed anything was within his reach if he just worked hard enough at it.

Ah, well, Tom thought. The world probably owed him a humbling experience or two. Life was a lot like a rodeo, in a way. Overconfidence just gave the bulls a better chance of stomping you into the dirt. Mckenna had done a pretty good job of stomping.

Still, when he sat down at his government-issue desk and picked up the phone to call BKB, his pulse began to race and an anticipatory smile curled his lips. Dueling it out with Mckenna, in the courtroom or out, was never boring. Dangerous as hell, but never boring.

Mckenna's secretary answered the phone.

"Hi, Peggy. This is Tom Markham."

Her professional tone immediately melted into a warm hello. When Tom had been at BKB, Peggy had been mother hen to his lost chick. "Tom, how the heck are you? Thanks for the birthday card, by the way."

"Was it a good birthday? I hope you partied it up."

"At my age, birthdays are never described as 'good.' But it was fun. I went skydiving."

"Peggy!"

"Sixty is not too old to try something for the first time. When you get to be my age, you young sprout, you'll realize that every once in a while you have to do something wild just to keep your heart pumping."

He laughed. "Is Her Highness in?"

Peggy immediately sobered. "You didn't hear?"

"Hear what?"

"Ah. That's right. I forget that you people across the mountain in Prescott don't read the Sedona rags. Mckenna crashed that little BMW of hers Friday night. She's in the hospital. They say she had something like a stroke, but not quite."

Tom felt like a horse had just kicked him in the head. He opened his mouth to say something, but nothing came out.

Peggy continued. "You wouldn't think that someone that young could suffer from something like that, but if anyone could have a stroke at thirty, it would be her. She doesn't know what relaxation is."

"I saw her Friday night," Tom said through a tightened throat. "Probably right before she drove off and had her accident. How bad is she?" An unexpected thrill of fear surprised him as he waited for the answer.

"I think she'll be all right. I visited her in the hospital yesterday. The air bag saved her from being really hurt, but I guess she hit her head pretty hard. She's pretty confused. She didn't know me."

Peggy sounded hurt, Tom thought.

"I had to tell her who I was, kind of introduce myself, you know? I must have looked a little put off, because she apologized for not knowing who I was."

Silence cracked on the phone line.

"Mckenna apologized?"

"Yeah. Amazing, huh?"

Mckenna apologizing to someone for bruised feelings. What a concept! That wasn't the Mckenna he knew, the Mckenna who pushed her way through every day like a bulldozer in high gear. "It *is* amazing."

"And she's got some problems with her right side that she has to see a physical therapist for. I guess she's making good progress with that, though."

The clutch of fear began to loosen. "That sounds pretty good, then."

"I'm surprised this is the first you've heard of it. I know the little Sedona newspapers don't make it over the mountain to Prescott, but I would have thought someone in your office would have heard about it."

"I was gone all weekend—waterskiing down at Canyon Lake. And since I got into the office this morning, I've been closeted with Donovan. Uh...when do you think Mckenna will be back to work?"

"No telling, hon. Knowing Mckenna, she'll probably be back tomorrow unless someone ties her to a hospital bed. You know what I mean?"

"I know what you mean. Thanks for the info, Peggy. I think I'll run over to the hospital and see if I can't cheer her up."

"Oh, yeah, Tom. Seeing you will really cheer her up. If you're lucky, she won't remember who you are."

They both laughed.

Minutes later, when he called the hospital, he learned that Mckenna had been discharged that very morning.

MCKENNA'S JAW dropped when she first caught sight of her house. "Wow! This is *my* house? I own it?"

"You believe in living in style," Jane told her.

"I'll say!"

The house was one of the exclusive dwellings in Oak Creek Canyon. A sturdy wrought-iron gate blocked the entrance to the asphalt driveway, but both Jane and Nell possessed a key to the gate, which told Mckenna these two very dissimilar women were indeed her good friends. She might not remember much about herself, but she did know that nobody with two brain cells let casual acquaintances have free access to a house like this one.

Once Jane had opened the gate, they drove in Nell's minivan down to a bridge across Oak Creek, which burbled its merry way through a thicket of birch and pine. The minivan rattled across the uneven concrete of the bridge and then climbed to the house, whose front half-rose above the stream bank on sturdy pillars.

"This is a fantastic place!" Mckenna enthused. "My gosh! My whole life has become like a kid opening packages on Christmas morning. Everything I learn about who I am, where I live, what I do, is like a gift. A surprise. And this one's a doozy. Am I rich?"

Nell laughed. "Let's just say that you don't have to worry about paying the mortagage and buying the groceries."

Nell parked in front of the two-car garage, where they climbed out—accompanied by Jane's border collie and Nell's fat little Welsh corgi. Apparently neither of these two women went anywhere without an animal in tow. Mckenna walked, or rather limped—her legs were still very shaky—around the place and gawked. Because of the steep terrain, the house had two levels in front and one in back, a contemporary design constructed of logs and glass. Lots of glass. The garage comprised most of the first level, and a daunting flight of steps climbed to a huge front deck overlooking the stream with its lush green growth of birch, juniper, pine, and wild grasses. A rear deck led onto a level field of natural grass and shrubs, and behind the field, the precipitous wall of the canyon rose almost high enough to block the sky.

"I'm in awe," Mckenna declared.

"Yeah," Jane agreed wryly. "So were we when you bought the place."

Mckenna stared at the house. "The funny thing is, it just doesn't evoke any memories at all. You would think a person's home would at least feel familiar, even if that person's brain has been bounced around inside her skull."

They climbed up to the front deck—Mckenna more slowly than her friends—and Nell unlocked the front door. Apparently these two had access to just about everything in her life. Too bad they didn't have keys to her memory. "You haven't lived here very long. You moved in just a few weeks ago."

"Where did I live before that?"

"A slick condo in Sedona," Jane told her.

The inside of the house had been decorated in quiet good taste. From the harmonious blend of Southwestern art, wall colors, very expensive-looking furniture, Mckenna concluded that she was quite the sophisticate. "Did I do this?"

Jane laughed. "Are you kidding? Like you would have time. A decorator from Sedona did it."

"He did a beautiful job, though," Nell commented.

The dogs trotted into the house as if they owned it. Titi came down the stairs to greet them, looking every bit like a queen making a grand entrance. She politely touched noses with both dogs and then fixed Mckenna with a speaking look. Mckenna tensed, but the cat remained silent.

"Don't believe her," Jane warned. "I fed her when I dropped her off this morning."

"Did she say something? Did you understand her?" The anxious questions left her mouth before Mckenna could think better of it.

"Of course I understood her," Jane replied.

Nell snickered. "It's a safe bet that every time Titi opens her mouth or even looks your way, she's expecting food. Piggy is the same way." She gave the pudgy little corgi a fond smile, and the dog replied with an indignant glare that was eerily human.

Nell and Jane stayed in the kitchen to brew a batch of iced tea when Mckenna took herself on a tour of her house.

"Poor kid," Nell commented to Jane. "She seems totally overwhelmed. I wish there were more we could do to help."

Jane put the kettle on the stove to heat. "She'll survive. Mckenna's tougher than she looks."

"Oh, I know she'll survive. But I can't imagine what it would be like to lose your memory, your sense of self, your knowledge of how you fit into the world, who you can count on, who you love."

Jane grimaced. "Speaking of that..."

"Speaking of what?" Nell asked as she filled three glasses with ice.

"Who you love. Or rather, who Mckenna loves. Or maybe plays around at loving. Should we tell her about, uh, you know who?"

Nell's eyes widened. "Oh...him. Now there's a question."

A hint of distaste twisted Jane's lips. "Not that she's told us that much about him."

"Or that we know his address."

"Or phone number."

"Or even his last name. Do you remember his last name?"

"I don't recall Mckenna mentioning it. It was like she didn't really take the whole thing seriously. At least not seriously enough to involve us."

Jane chuckled. "Right. And if she had been serious, of course she would have had to tell us."

Their eyes locked, and over the exchanged look came a silent agreement.

"I guess if he's truly important, she'll remember him on her own, along with everything else," Nell said.

Jane nodded sagely. "And if she doesn't, if he deserves our Mckenna"—and her expression made clear that he didn't—"he'll be on the phone to her today or tomorrow and take the first plane coming this direction."

"Right," Nell said. "What was his name again?"

Jane looked innocent. "Can't say as I remember."

Nell smiled. "Me either."

WHILE NELL and Jane conspired in the kitchen, Mckenna explored her house as if it were the first time she had seen it. Everything in the house had a decorator's touch, but no personal clutter told her anything about the woman who lived here—maybe because she hadn't lived here very long. No family pictures hung on the walls, and the only books were tomes of law in the den. After finishing her tour, Mckenna felt more than ever like she had somehow stepped into a stranger's life.

"I've got just what you need," Nell declared when Mckenna wandered into the huge living room to claim her tea. "Photo albums. This stuff is bound to set off some sparks in your memory cells."

She had a pile of them. "Are those all yours?" Mckenna asked incredulously. "What are you, a photographer?"

"Journalist," Nell explained. "But I like taking pictures. And Dan is good enough with a camera that he once had me believing he was a professional photographer."

"He wasn't," Jane told Mckenna. "He was a sneaky, lying private eye. But you don't need that story right now."

Mckenna lifted a brow. "You married this guy?"

"I sure did," Nell said with a dreamy smile. Then she got

back to business. "Come on over here, Mckenna. This is going to be your life in Kodacolor."

There she was in a host of different poses, wearing the same face Mckenna saw when she looked in a mirror, only different somehow, not only because of the bruises currently marring her looks. The woman in the photos smiled confidently, the expression of someone who knows she's in charge. Even in the most casual photos she had the air of a fashion model. Always put together. In a painfully candid shot of her and Jane rocketing down the watery chute of Oak Creek at Slide Rock State Park, Mckenna looked in control, while Jane had arms and legs flying and her mouth open wide to shout something.

"Yuck!" Jane grimaced at the picture. "I haven't seen that one."

"We had fun that day," Nell said.

"Yeah. Even though we had to practically hog-tie Mckenna to get her out of her office. Some folks just don't know what weekends are for."

Other photos showed all three of them walking in what looked like a parade along with a few other people and dogs. One of the pictures showed Titi enthroned in a wagon pulled by Jane's border collie. Piggy marched beside Nell, her disgruntled expression obvious even in a four by six photo.

"Hearts of Gold," Jane said by way of explanation.

"What?"

"The pet therapy group," Nell added. "We sometimes march in parades just to let people know what services we provide."

"It's fun," Nell insisted.

"Are you sure I was having fun there?" Mckenna asked dubiously. "Look at the expression on my face."

"You loved it," Nell assured her as she turned to the next page.

Jane just snorted.

A photo on the second page immediately caught Mckenna's eye. "Who is that?"

Nell looked surprised. "You don't even remember Tom Markham?"

The photo showed a tall, whipcord sort of fellow leaning nonchalantly against the pipe railing of what appeared to be a horse paddock. If his face had been a bit craggier and he'd had a smoke hanging from his lips, he could have posed for one of those old cowboy cigarette commercials. But his mouth sported no cigarette, and his face, though it had a few years on it, looked more boyish than weathered. His battered cowboy hat, worn as if it might be a permanent fixture, joined with boots, boot-cut jeans, and a huge gaudy belt buckle to make the guy the perfect embodiment of an Old West that refused to die. The only jarring note was a T-shirt that sported a photo of the Labrador retriever that sat beside him, looking into the camera with a happy, loll-tongued grin.

That T-shirt did a nice job of showing off broad shoulders and a nicely sculpted chest.

"I know him?" Mckenna asked hopefully.

"Oh, yeah!" Jane assured her. "He used to work for your outfit, BKB, which pretty much means that he was your underling junior-attorney slave boy. He had the hots for you for a long time."

Mckenna smiled. Now that was intriguing.

"You weren't having any of that, though," Nell told her.

"I wasn't?" Mckenna tried not to sound disappointed.

"Froze him out completely," Jane said. "Stupid move, if you ask me. He's a great guy."

"I must have had a reason."

"He wasn't your type," Nell informed her.

"And you said it was inappropriate for a person in your position to get cozy with a junior associate."

Mckenna flinched at Jane's tone. "Did I say it like that? Like I had a broom stuck you know where?"

"No," Nell denied.

"Yes," Jane confirmed at the same time.

"Of course you didn't!" Nell gave Jane a quelling look. "Tom is a great guy, but he's sort of a casual type who doesn't give a fig for appearances or who's who or anything like that."

"He took his dog through one of my obedience courses," Jane said in a tone that implied such a feat did indeed make him a great guy.

"You know," Mckenna said wonderingly, "I am beginning to feel like I remember him. No details, exactly, but... well, his face makes me want to smile."

"You didn't do much smiling around him, that's for sure," Jane said.

"Maybe it's just my imagination, then."

They spent an hour looking at photos, and many of them did fire small sparks of recognition.

"That's Dan," Mckenna exclaimed, pointing to a photo.

"Yeah." Jane chuckled. "Imagine that. The man standing beside Nell in her wedding photo is her husband, Dan."

"It might have been someone else," Nell said. "I think it's wonderful that she remembered his name."

"Your dog is there? Heaven! What is she wearing?"

"It's a little bridesmaid's veil. That woman with her is Amy, Piggy's first owner. Piggy was a bridesmaid in Amy's wedding, so that gave me the idea to have her in our wedding, as well. After all, she played a starring role in getting Dan and me together."

"You mean, in trying to keep you apart," Jane said wryly.

Nell smiled. "She came to her senses, and so she got to be in the wedding."

"A dog as a bridesmaid..." Mckenna tried not to sound judgmental, but she thought to herself that with friends like Nell and Jane, it was no wonder she was the kind of person who would hallucinate about a talking cat.

Nell and Jane were about to leave when the doorbell rang. When Mckenna opened the front door, a bland fellow in a gray suit gave her a professional smile. "Mckenna Wright?"

"So I'm told," Mckenna replied.

He paused, frowning.

She relented. "Yes, I'm Mckenna Wright." Obviously the guy had no sense of humor. She wondered if she herself did—one of the many things she couldn't remember about herself. "What can I do for you?"

"I'm Henry Cass."

He clearly expected her to recognize the name.

"Uh..."

"Your insurance agent, Henry Cass. We've done all our talking on the phone. I haven't had the pleasure of meeting you face-to-face."

"Ah. Well, hello, Henry. Sorry I didn't recognize your name. The accident still has me a bit scrambled."

"Understandable."

"Come in, please."

"No, thank you. I just came by to drop off the items recovered from the inside of your car. We towed it on Saturday. It's totaled, of course."

A BMW sports model. Mckenna wished she could remember—the color, the smell of supple leather seats, the purr of a powerful engine. A car like that would be worth remembering.

"A check from the company will be in the mail very shortly. In the meantime, I thought you should have these odds and ends that survived the crash." He indicated a sizeable box at his feet—flotsam that had survived a crash she didn't remember.

Survived along with Mckenna herself. "Well, Mr. Cass, thank you. Sure you won't come in?"

"I have to be on my way. When you buy another car, I hope you'll remember us for your insurance needs."

"Sure I will."

"Sure you will," Jane echoed as Henry Cass got in his Lexus and carefully negotiated his way down the driveway, across the bridge, and back up to the highway. "And they'll jack up your rates sky-high because you had an accident." She nudged the box with her toe. "All that's left of the BMW, eh?"

"Stuff from the inside. Apparently there isn't anything left of the poor BMW."

"Don't you lift it," Jane chided as Mckenna tried to do just that. But her right hand and arm were still weak. Jane easily lifted the box and took it inside. "Where do you want it?"

"I must have a storeroom somewhere."

"Off the garage," Nell said. "Don't you want to see what's in the box?"

"Later. I'm famished. You guys will stay for lunch, won't you?"

Piggy the corgi took the invitation to heart, trotting toward the kitchen with an eager little grin on her foxy face.

"Piggy!" Nell scolded. "Where are you going?"

Jane answered for the corgi. "She's headed toward the food, of course. What did you expect?" Jane's border collie Idaho had stayed very properly at Jane's side, though longing brown eyes showed perfect willingness to share in a meal. But Titi had beaten everyone to the kitchen. Her round little head peeked around the doorway to see what was holding everyone up. She and Piggy both looked more than ready to tie on the bibs.

Nell laughed. "Dream on, Pig. We can't stay. We're in the middle of packing for our move to Tucson, and if I don't get back soon, Dan will just be throwing everything together in boxes without labeling anything."

"And I have to get back to the kennel," Jane said.

"I'll bring Mel over tonight," Nell said, "and you can use him as long as you need to."

That gave Mckenna a start. "I beg your pardon?"

"Mel is the VW Bug she said she'd loan you," Jane explained. She rolled her eyes. "Named after Mel Gibson."

Yes, indeed. Talking cats wouldn't make these girls bat an eyelash, Mckenna thought.

"You're sure that you're okay to drive?" Nell asked.

"Dr. Estrella said that driving was okay. Like riding a bicycle, he said. Muscle memory, or something like that."

Jane clucked in concern. "Yes, and he wanted you to stay in the hospital another couple of days, as well, didn't he?"

"He relented, obviously. I'm fine," Mckenna insisted. "This wasn't a real stroke, you know. I feel a lot stronger today than I did yesterday."

Nell still looked worried. "Well, you have our phone numbers. Promise to call if you need any help."

"Promise," Mckenna confirmed. She just wished someone could wave a magic wand and help her remember who she was.

When Nell and Jane had left, Mckenna stood in the spacious entranceway and felt a world of silence settle around her. She felt like an interloper in someone else's home. When Jane and Nell had been here, they had filled up the house with conversation and laughter, pushing back the shadows of strangeness. Now the unfamiliar house pressed in upon Mckenna's soul. She felt small. She felt alone. She felt like an imposter dressed up in someone else's skin.

Lunch suddenly didn't seem so attractive, though Titi still waited by the kitchen counter with her appetite plain on her face.

So she wasn't alone, Mckenna reminded herself. She

had her friend the cat. The cat who had given her the fright of her life just a few days ago.

"Imagine my thinking you could talk," she told Titi. "My brain really did get bounced around in my head. At least that foolishness is cleared up. You're a very fine-looking cat, and I'm sure we're the best of friends. Everyone else in my crowd seems to be hand in paw with some animal. But no more hallucinations, please. Cats don't talk."

"Of course cats talk," Titi replied. "People just aren't smart enough to listen."

chapter 4

MCKENNA SHRIEKED, jumped back, and banged into the hall tree that stood in the corner by the front door. The hall tree fell with a mighty crash, sending a windbreaker, a trendy beret, and a dilapidated sun hat sliding over the ceramic tile floor.

"Clumsy" was Titi's comment.

Eyes wide, Mckenna stared at the sable-furred creature. She opened her mouth, but only astonishment came out.

Titi simply gazed at her with condescending patience.

"This is a hallucination," Mckenna declared out loud. "I should go back to the hospital right now and check myself in. My brain has bigger problems than just a missing memory."

"Such hissing!" The cat paused to scratch behind an ear, then she jumped nimbly to the hall table without so much as a brush against the expensive Zuni pottery that sat there. "Problem here. You hiss and squall about everything instead of letting things come. Should learn from a cat. Watch me. I know how to live."

She was going to hyperventilate, Mckenna thought

with a touch of panic. Then she would pass out and lie on this cold tile floor until Nell came back with Mel Gibson. And maybe she could persuade Nell to take her back to the hospital.

"The cat is not talking," she told herself firmly, trying to force reality in to her misbehaving brain. "The cat is not talking. The stupid cat is absolutely not talking, dammit."

" 'Stupid'? Who's 'stupid'?" Titi's tail whipped back and forth a time or two before settling down. "Of course I talk. People don't hear because they only listen to themselves."

"That's absolutely preposterous."

The cat's whiskers flicked back, giving the impression of a smile. "Maybe your brain getting batted like a toy mouse makes you hear. You're very lucky."

Mckenna tried to breathe. "I'm talking to my cat. I'm really talking to my cat, having a conversation. I've got to sit down."

She escaped to the living room, where a leather sofa/love seat set offered respite. Titi followed and jumped onto the back of the sofa, assuming a sphinxlike pose and bringing her face almost level with Mckenna's. Instinctively, Mckenna's hand reached out to stroke the silky head, but when she realized what she did, she jumped as if burned.

"Oh, heaven!"

Titi just purred.

"I need a drink. The stronger the better. There's bound to be liquor somewhere in this house!" She went into the kitchen and headed for a likely cupboard—then remembered. Liquor and medication didn't mix. The doctor had warned her.

Medication! That was it! The medication she still took for head pain was doing this to her. What a relief! She'd thought insanity had set in, but it was just the side effects of her painkillers.

But wait. She hadn't taken the medication this morning

because the drug made her subject to motion sickness, and the drive up the canyon would have been a really long one if she'd spent the time tossing her cookies in the back-seat.

Damn! It wasn't the meds. "I give up." She braced her hands on the counter and thumped her head against a cupboard door. "Ship me off to Bedlam."

"Where's that?"

"The loony bin." She stopped thumping and rubbed her head. "Where they take people who talk to cats."

"Very special place, eh? We could go. Vacations are good."

"I could for sure use a vacation from..." She caught herself and gave the cat a narrow-eyed scrutiny. "You're really talking?"

"I've always talked. You didn't hear."

"Cats are supposed to say 'meow.'"

Titi sniffed disdainfully. "Shows what you know. I give good advice. If you had listened, you might not be in this fix."

"Which of my fixes would that be?"

"Not remembering."

"Oh, yeah." She sighed. "That one. The docs say everything should come back, given a little time."

"You'll do it again. Next time your brain will make you fall down the stairs. Broken necks are bad. Or your mouth will open to talk and nothing will come out, because the brain will be mush."

"Wonderful image," Mckenna said with a roll of her eyes. "For a cat, you have a way with words."

Titi preened. "Thank you."

Mckenna slumped into a kitchen chair. "I don't believe it. I'm talking to a cat as if it's the most normal thing in the world. Why on earth is this happening to me?"

"You're just lucky."

"Lucky!" Mckenna scoffed.

"Very lucky. Cats are smart. Cats are mellow. Cats are harmonious. Learn from me, and you'll live a happy life with no mush in the brain."

Mckenna continued to stare at the ceiling. "My cat is lecturing me on a healthy lifestyle. God help me!"

"He already did. He gave you me, didn't He?"

Mckenna's gaze snapped back to Titi and rested there with intense suspicion. "Are you telling me that you're some kind of angel in disguise?"

"No angel. I'm a cat."

Mckenna remained suspicious. "Some people get guardian angels. I get a cat?"

Titi blinked, all feline innocence. "You're a lucky girl. If you want to see a disguise, watch the dog."

"What dog?"

"The short pudgy one."

"Nell's Piggy?"

"That's the one. Dogs can't be trusted, because they're dogs. But Piggy . . . well, you asked about disguises."

"Are you telling me that Piggy isn't really a dog?"

Titi's tail twitched. "You didn't hear it from me."

Mckenna slumped deeper into the sofa. "I don't think I can take anymore."

"There's catnip in the pantry," Titi offered brightly. "I would share."

Instead, Mckenna went looking once again for vodka. Or at least wine. She couldn't blame this insanity on drugs, but at least she could lose herself in liquor.

She had just unearthed a six-pack of beer when the doorbell chimed. Nell with her little car, Mckenna thought. Just in time. Getting out of the house, and away from the cat, would serve even better than beer.

But the door opened not on perky blonde Nell, but on tall, lean, blue-eyed . . .

"Tom Markham!"

Her obvious excitement earned her a wary look from

the man, but the instant recognition at the sight of him heartened her so much that she said it again, with relish. "Tom Markham."

"I don't think you've ever been so glad to see me, Mckenna. Is this some kind of a trap?"

"A trap? Of course not. Why would you think that?"

"Past experience."

He looked just as he did in the photo Nell and Jane had shown her—battered cowboy hat, jeans that hugged lean hips, boots that had seen a good deal of wear. But today he wore a denim western-cut shirt instead of a T-shirt with a picture of his dog. And the live version of Tom Markham possessed a life and vitality—even just standing there on her front deck—that no photograph could convey.

"I just heard about your accident. Since I was in Sedona to take a deposition, I decided to come by and see for myself that you're still in one piece."

"That's so nice of you!" Mckenna Wright, whoever she was, certainly had caring friends. First Jane and Nell, and now this good-looking hunk of cowboy. "Come in."

"Well . . ."

Titi strolled through the open doorway and wove herself between his ankles, purring mightily. "Hey there, cat." He leaned down to scratch the furry ears.

For one moment Mckenna feared the cat would greet him back, in English. But Titi simply purred.

"I guess I could come in for a few minutes. You don't look much the worse for wear, Mac, except for that dressing on your head."

She touched the square of gauze that still covered her left temple.

"If that's all you got from driving off a fifty-foot drop, then I'd say you're incredibly lucky."

"Yes. You're not the first to say that."

As he walked through the door, Titi gave her a meaningful

look. Very meaningful. Except that Mckenna didn't know the meaning.

"These are your new digs, eh?" He went to the panoramic living-room windows that looked out over Oak Creek. "Not bad."

She would have offered to give him a tour of the place, but as unfamiliar as her own home was to her, she might have gotten lost.

He cocked his head wonderingly at her silence. "That knock on the head must have rattled your brain. Where's your usual line about 'If you hadn't quit BKB to work for the county, you, too, could be living like a queen'?"

So...she was a materialistic snob? "In your case, wouldn't it be living like a king?"

He looked around at the vaulted ceilings, native stone fireplace, and oak paneling. "Yeah, it definitely would be living like a king."

"Would you like something to drink?"

"Sure. You got a beer?"

"I do, if you don't mind warm beer." While she retrieved the beer she had discovered in the pantry, he opened the refrigerator.

"You saving these cold brews for something special?"

"What? Oh. Uh...no."

He chuckled and handed her one of the cold bottles. "I should have guessed the beer in your fridge would be designer beer." Untwisting the cap, he read the label. "Oak Creek Brewery. Honey brown ale." He took a drink. "Good stuff."

"Right. My favorite." Or so she gathered. "Make yourself comfortable in the living room. I'll get us some glasses."

She searched the kitchen for mugs, and found them—of course—in the freezer.

When she closed the freezer door and turned around, there sat Titi, regarding her with warm approval.

"Nice catch," the cat said. "Tomcat."

"Could you just maybe cool it for a while?"

" 'Cool it'?"

"Shut up. While the gentleman is here."

"Is he your boyfriend? I wouldn't know about boyfriends. Surgery."

"Trust me, they're more trouble than they're worth." Mckenna blinked. Now where had that little piece of cynicism come from?

"So you always say."

"I do?"

"You do."

Mckenna heaved a tortured sigh. "Listen, Titi. Just shut up for a while, okay? As a favor to me?"

"He doesn't hear," Titi said.

"Shut up anyway."

"Rude," the cat said archly.

Feeling as if she were in the middle of a very strange dream, she escaped into the living room.

"Were you saying something in there?" Tom asked.

"No. Nothing."

"Talking to the cat, eh?"

Mckenna froze.

"I do that with my dog all the time. Good old Clara. She always looks so interested." He grinned. "Sometimes I think she's the only one who really listens to what I have to say."

Mckenna let out her breath. "Right. Animals are great. I don't know what I'd do without that cat."

They sat together in the living room, drinking their beer, admiring the view, talking about the weather and other equally impersonal subjects. Titi wandered in and jumped onto the love seat to lie beside Tom, her feet tucked neatly beneath her and her tail curled alongside her body. She looked back and forth between Tom and Mckenna with catlike inscrutability.

As long as the furbag kept quiet, Mckenna thought, that was all she asked.

Tom looked at his hands with an oddly guilty expression. "I suppose that great Beemer of yours was totaled, eh?"

"Totally," she admitted. Had she ever subjected him to a lecture along the line of 'If you hadn't quit BKB to work for the county, you, too, could be driving a forty-thousand-dollar car'?

He sympathized. "That sucks."

Mckenna wondered what Tom drove. She pictured a pickup truck. A big noisy macho diesel. Memory? Or did he just give the impression of a guy who would drive a diesel?

She shrugged. "That's what one has insurance for, I guess."

He gave her a surprised look. "You're being very philosophical for someone who was bonded to a car like a mother to a child."

"Oh, well...yes. A person has to be philosophical." And she didn't really remember the car, but she wasn't going to tell him that. Revealing her loss of memory to any but her closest friends seemed like hanging out her dirty laundry in public.

But maybe Tom was a close friend. No. Jane and Nell had definitely classed him as rejected suitor. Rejectees seldom turned into anything besides someone who loved to see the rejecter fall flat on her face. Likely Tom Markham had come calling merely as a courtesy to an acquaintance who had been hurt.

"You want another beer?" she asked.

"No. I can't stay long. Have to get back to work. The county likes to get its money's worth."

He looked as if he expected some snide remark from her about his job, but she couldn't think of one.

"Listen, Mac." He paused, a bit painfully it seemed, and

gave her a searching look. "Word is you had a stroke or something that sent you off the road Friday night."

"That's what the doc suspects, but he's not sure."

"Uh . . . well, I'm feeling a bit guilty here, thinking that tense little exchange we had right before you got in your car and started up the canyon might have had something to do with you busting a blood vessel in your head."

She hesitated. "Exchange?"

"In the Rainbow's End. About Harmon."

He was speaking Greek as far as Mckenna was concerned. She sighed. "I'm a little bit fuzzy about Friday."

That was when Titi chimed in. "Cats are fuzzy. Mice are fuzzy. You are clueless."

Mckenna froze, waiting for Tom's reaction. He simply gave the cat a couple of long, gentle strokes along her back and continued to speak.

"That doesn't make me feel any better. Hell, it makes me feel worse. I really went after you Friday night—not that you didn't give as good as you got. And not that you're not used to our little battles. But I don't usually call your basic integrity into question."

He searched her face for reaction, but she didn't know how to react. "My basic integrity? That bad, was it?"

"Mckenna?"

"Yes?"

"You're very not yourself today."

She flushed. "What do you expect? I drove my car off a cliff, spent sixteen hours unconscious in the hospital, and . . . and . . ."

Titi completed the thought. "And now you can't remember where the cat food is kept?"

"Oh, shut up!"

He raised a brow. "Now that's more like the Mckenna we all know and love."

"Not you. The cat."

He smiled down at Titi, who purred up at him with fe-line benevolence. "She does talk a lot, doesn't she."

"She does," Mckenna agreed cautiously. "You...you don't hear anything unusual in that, do you?"

"Unusual?"

"You know. Unusual." How could he not understand the cat when she spoke so plainly? Somehow it would be less daunting to have the only cat in the world who spoke English than to be the only person in the world who could speak Cat.

"She sounds okay to me. Do you think she's sick?"

Titi wasn't the one who was sick.

"She sure likes attention, doesn't she? I'm not a cat man myself, but if they were all like Titi here, I could be. Clara might object, though. She thinks cats are an inferior species."

Titi gave him an indignant look. "What do you expect of a stupid dog?"

"She does like to talk, doesn't she? Makes you wonder what she's saying."

Titi regarded him complacently. "Told you he can't hear. Nice muscles, though."

Mckenna tried not to grind her teeth.

"Mckenna," Titi warned. "Mellow is good."

"Mckenna, are you all right?"

She unlocked her jaw. "Of course."

His eyes narrowed suspiciously. "Are you fuzzy just about Friday?"

"Lying is a sin," Titi reminded her.

"I...I..."

"You do remember the Harmon case, don't you?"

"Of course I do. Harmon..." The name was familiar, the memory just beyond her reach. It must have been something very important. She closed her eyes, trying.

"Crying in a bucket! You don't, do you? You have some kind of amnesia!"

Busted. Mckenna groaned. "Just about total, for now."

"But you knew who I was," Tom remembered with a confused frown.

"I confess. Jane and Nell just showed me some photos. You were in some of them."

"Damn! Mckenna, what does the doctor say about this?"

She sighed. "He says it should all come back. Probably. Soon, I hope."

"For sure?"

"Dammit, nothing is for sure. Don't you think I'd like an ironclad guarantee that all of this is going to go away?" Self-consciously, she touched the gauze at her temple.

"I'm sure it will go away," he said gently. "Mckenna, I'm so sorry. I can't help but feel that I caused some of this, at least."

Titi observed, "Such a gentleman."

This time Mckenna refrained from snapping at her, but just barely.

"As much as I'm in the mood to blame someone— someone besides myself, that is—I can't really think that anything you might have said to me would have made the least difference, Tom. To tell the truth, right now I don't remember all that much about who I am, but from all accounts, I give grief rather than take it."

Tom nodded. "Well, there's some truth to that."

"Besides, my doctor said he'd been scolding me about my stressed-out lifestyle just about forever. He told me to get into some stress management or else."

Titi sniffed. "All you need is to listen to the cat."

Tom smiled. He still stroked an appreciative Titi, who arched herself under his hand. "Well, I guess that makes me feel better."

"I'm glad one of us feels better," she said wryly.

He got up, picking up his empty beer bottle. "Do you recycle?"

"Got me. Just put it in the kitchen."

Titi meowed after him. "Come back. I'm not through being petted." Mckenna gave the cat a look and followed Tom into the kitchen.

"So I guess you're going to take a leave from work until all this works out."

She hadn't thought that far ahead, but suddenly the thought of showing up at her office and demonstrating how little she presently knew about the law seemed very unwise.

"Not that I wouldn't love to meet you in court in your current condition, but I figure I can trounce you on the Harmon case even once you get your marbles back in order." He smiled wickedly, and Mckenna's heart skipped a beat. She shot back what she imagined the old Mckenna might say.

"That sounds like wishful thinking to me, even in my current state of ignorance. Do you often trounce me in court?"

"I have to confess, not as often as my boss would like." He moved toward the front door. "Thanks for the beer, Mac. And listen, you take care of yourself. Okay?"

"Oh, sure."

"Let me know if there's anything you need. Anything I can do."

She followed him through the front door and onto the deck, and they both paused awkwardly, looking at each other. Then unexpectedly he took her gently by the shoulders and dropped a light kiss onto her cheek. Momentarily the scent of him—soap, a light aftershave, and man—surrounded her as his slightly rough cheek brushed hers.

"Take care," he said.

Before she could react, he was gone, walking down the stairs from the deck to the ground. She had been right.

Parked in front of the garage was a white Dodge Ram pickup, a diesel.

"I rejected *him?*" she murmured to herself.

Titi, who had strolled onto the deck and jumped onto one of the built-in redwood benches, offered her opinion. "You don't have the sense God gave a mouse when it comes to men."

TITI SETTLED comfortably onto a bench, soaking up the midday sun, and watched the man named Tom drive away. And then she watched Mckenna, her chief provider and servant, walk back into the house. Humans were strange, illogical creatures. They cared about meaningless things. They got their tails in a twist over unimportant matters. They simply did not know how to live their lives. But then, what did one expect of creatures who weren't cats?

Take Mckenna, for example. Titi had very generously decided to teach her some basic tricks for good living— things that the youngest kitten would know. And was the woman properly grateful? Did she listen? Or follow Titi's example?

No, she didn't. She acted as if someone had set her tail on fire. Silly girl. She was lucky that Titi didn't just hold her peace and let her steer her own frazzled way to yet another disaster.

But she couldn't do that. For one thing, if Mckenna drove herself to an early end, Titi would probably have to move in with Jane or Nell and put up with their dogs. Titi wasn't at all sure she could put up with the smug Miss Piggy on a full-time house-sharing basis. The two brown-nosing suckups who shadowed Jane's every move were even worse.

And more important, Titi was very fond of Mckenna. They had been together a long time, and sometimes people came to seem like actual family, even if they were merely human.

Still, Mckenna was going to be a tough patient, even for an experienced therapy cat like Titi. She had always taken her therapy duties very seriously, whether visiting hospital patients, schoolkids, or old folks. Usually, a touch of the nose or a gentle purr was enough to make someone happy, to shine light into someone's day. But this situation was more of a challenge, a twenty-four-hour-a-day challenge. This patient called for strong measures.

The task was daunting, and the temptation to hide beneath the bedcovers and sleep until the problem resolved itself, one way or another, nearly overwhelmed her. Then Titi thought of Piggy, the ridiculous little Welsh corgi, so smug about her adventures, taking credit for three successful romances and the downfall of numerous villains. Braggart dog. Titi suspected few of her tales were true. And even if they were, a cat could do better. Just being a cat gave Titi an almost unfair advantage in topping the accomplishments of any dog.

So she would take on the challenge, even though her patient showed every sign of being uncooperative. She would save Mckenna's health, possibly her life, and—she slid a glance to where Tom Markham had just closed the gate across the driveway and climbed back into his truck—maybe she would throw in a little romance, as well.

And just see Piggy top that!

NEXT MORNING, when Mckenna hung up the phone after talking to her secretary, she reflected on how nice it was to be near the top of the workplace ladder. She had found her office number in her address book, which she discovered in the desk in her home office, just the logical place for it to be kept. The book had also yielded the name of her secretary—Peggy Watson. The name rang a bell, not from her pre-accident life, but because the woman had visited her in the hospital—a very sweet person.

Since Mckenna was a big fish in the BKB pond, at least in Sedona, no one had questioned her announcement that she needed two weeks of sick leave. Peggy had been all concern when Mckenna had first phoned, and then she connected her to the Big Boss of the Sedona office, who that week just happened to be in the main office in Phoenix. Fortunately, Peggy had mentioned his name—Gilbert Bradner, the Bradner third of Bradner, Kelly, and Bolin. Mr. Bradner had oozed sympathy about the accident.

"Are you all right?" he had wanted to know.

"I'm fine," she had lied. "Just shaken up and achy, and the doc insisted I take it real easy for a little while."

"Well, you relax, then. And just so you don't get bored, I'll have someone deliver the Harmon files to your house. We wouldn't want you to have nothing to do, would we?"

Harmon again, the same case Tom Markham had mentioned. She didn't have the guts to tell her boss that Mr. Harmon had flown right out of her mind. As it was, his tone didn't strike her as sympathetic as his words. Something sharp resided just beneath the surface to inspire a half-remembered caution where Gil Bradner was concerned.

She had started to remember some things, though, and to feel more at home in her world. Her address book had yielded up several names that sounded downright familiar. She had recognized her parents' names right off, which encouraged her that she wasn't completely around the bend. For a moment she was tempted to phone her parents and wail out the litany of her misfortunes, but a caution rose from somewhere inside her and made her suspect that such a call might not be wise. Maybe once she remembered a few more details about them...Maybe then she would call.

Mckenna also found a sister and her husband, and without prompting from the book remembered that she had a teenaged niece and nephew. Digging deep in her heart, she found no feelings good or bad about her sister. Again she was tempted to pick up the phone and call, to have her hand stayed by reluctance. It seemed to her that family feelings should have survived in her heart, even though the memories were hidden away in her brain. The fact that they hadn't was scary.

Nevertheless, she had family, and she knew their names. Her parents lived in Denver. Her sister and brother-in-law and their children lived in Washington State, if her address book could be believed. Progress. She was getting there.

Moreover, Mckenna knew the name of the president of the United States. She didn't remember Arizona's senators or congressmen, but then, probably few Arizonans without the excuse of amnesia knew them. She knew what year it was, how to get to the closest grocery store, and which brand of cat food Titi preferred (of course, Titi had told her about five times, so Mckenna couldn't really take credit for remembering that).

Driving a car had come back to her the minute she slid into the front seat of Nell's little antique VW Bug. She had wondered if being behind the wheel again would make her nervous. It didn't. And really, why should it? She didn't remember her accident, so she didn't have to suffer through any postaccident jitters. Good thing, because she had to drive to the hospital every day to endure a session with the physical therapist. Her right hand and leg would be back to normal in no time, the therapist had assured her.

If only she had such assurances about her brain.

Two weeks of sick leave passed surprisingly fast. Her right-side coordination and strength did improve, just as her therapist promised. Titi pelted her with advice on how to de-stress (including naps on the sofa, daily indulgences—ice cream for Mckenna, catnip for Titi—naps on the bed, staring at a wall to empty the mind, naps on the living-room carpet, fly-watching). Talking to a cat ceased to be strange, which was rather frightening in itself. She took long walks beside Oak Creek—about her only opportunity to escape cat advice, because Titi flatly refused to go beyond the front deck.

"Things out there eat cats," she told Mckenna in a grave tone. "Also snakes and bugs and grass over my head and dirt and mud. Dogs like that stuff. Cats are smarter."

So Mckenna walked alone. She read the newspapers, which told her of things she just as soon wouldn't have remembered, and she watched television. Tom called three times during the two weeks, to check on how she was feeling and ask if she needed anything. Each time, Mckenna felt more lonely when they broke the connection. She wasn't really alone, though, because both Nell and Jane visited most days, sometimes together, sometimes by themselves. The animals came, as well—Piggy, Jane's border collie Idaho, and an adolescent golden retriever named Shadow. And once Nell's husband, Dan—a major hunk—brought his funny little dog named Weed for a visit. Titi had not been pleased. Weed was a bit too playful for her taste.

Yet with all the care and attention from her friends, Mckenna still felt alone. She was a stranger to herself, and that made her even lonelier. She consoled herself with the discovery that she could recall every convoluted plot and character from the daytime soaps she watched. So her memory actually worked just fine. It just didn't go back very far.

For instance, though she found her law diploma from Harvard—very impressive!—she remembered almost nothing about attending the school or what she had learned. She glanced through the law books on the shelves of her home office, but little seemed familiar. It would all come back with time, she told herself. But how long? On the last day of her two-week leave, the temptation to call her office and tell them she needed more time off almost had her picking up the phone. But she didn't. How much time would BKB allow her before demanding an explanation, or even booting her from her job? She didn't want to take the chance.

Mckenna could only hope that immersion in work would spark that part of her brain that held three years' worth of law school and years of experience as an attorney. It had to.

If it didn't, she was in deep trouble.

chapter 5

MCKENNA INSTANTLY recognized the building where she worked—one story, Southwestern-style adobe, with false vigas protruding from the front to give it that Santa Fe Spanish look. The faces she encountered inside also were familiar. Some of them even brought names to mind.

Mckenna could have danced with delight. Obviously this office was her real home, because it felt so much more familiar than the log-and-glass house in Oak Creek Canyon. This was real progress in the memory department.

The receptionist in the front office greeted her. "Good morning, Ms. Wright."

"Good morning." Mckenna glanced surreptitiously at the name displayed on the desk. "Good morning, Sherry."

An unfamiliar face came out of a room riding a wave of coffee aroma. Mckenna assumed it was the coffee room. It didn't spark any memories. Probably because a hot-shot attorney in a prestigious law firm seldom had to fetch her own coffee, guessing from the huge cup the girl was bringing her way.

"Welcome back, ma'am," the girl said as she handed her the steaming mug. Gold letters on the ceramic spelled out Mckenna's name. Handy, Mckenna thought, if she were to forget it again.

"Thank you . . ."

At Mckenna's slight hesitation, the girl provided her name. "Sandy. I started working in the file room right before your accident."

Well, at least she had an excuse to not remember that one.

"Sandy. Of course. How are you getting along, Sandy?"

"Absolutely great, thank you. I really like working here."

"Excellent. Thank you for the coffee."

Sherry the receptionist gave her an odd little look. Maybe she didn't usually thank the underlings who did things like bring her coffee.

"Mr. Bradner wants to see you first thing," Sandy told her. "He's in his office."

As if she knew where that was. In fact, Mckenna suddenly realized, she wasn't sure how to find her own office. So much for progress. But a woman in a charcoal power suit came around the corner and saved her from embarrassment.

"Mckenna! It is so good to see you!"

"Pat." Pat Carter. She immediately remembered the woman's name, and also recalled a certain animosity.

"You look as if you've been through the wringer!"

Good of her to mention it. Mckenna self-consciously touched the still livid bruise at her temple.

"How are you feeling?"

"Just dandy. How have things been here?"

"Fine. I'm handling the DeVries lawsuit, you know. That one is going to bring in a bundle. And the *State* v. *Tolleson* prelim went very well."

Pat drifted down the hallway as she talked, and Mckenna drifted with her, hoping they were going toward the office where Gilbert Bradner (Oh, joy! She remembered his first name!) waited to see her.

"Buddy Morris must have called Gil every day since your accident," Pat told her.

Who the hell was Buddy Morris?

"He wants a meeting as soon as you're back, but Peggy will fill you in on that, I'm sure." She tittered. "Peggy is such a gem. I tried to steal her away from you while you were gone, but she's loyal as a dog, I swear."

Good for Peggy.

"Mckenna, aren't you going in to see Gil?"

"What? Oh, yes."

Pat waved her hand toward the brass nameplate beside the door they had just passed. "Earth to Mckenna."

Mckenna smiled. "Coffee hasn't kicked in yet, obviously."

"Vacations do that to you, you know. Send you right down into low gear. That's why I stay away from them." She chuckled, but Mckenna sensed she wasn't really joking.

"Seems you're right."

"Why don't we have lunch today? I can fill you in on all the gossip you've missed."

What a thrill. The woman reminded Mckenna of a cobra. But she could do with an update on what was going on. "Let's do that. Come down to my office when you get hungry." An arrangement that spared Mckenna from trying to find hers.

Mckenna remembered Gilbert Bradner well enough even before she stepped into his office. Caution warnings clanged in her brain. But he greeted her genially, rising from his chair in welcome and running a rather pudgy hand over his bald head, brushing back a mop of nonexistent hair in a habit that Mckenna found very annoying. And she remembered that she'd always found it annoying. More progress.

"Mckenna, Mckenna!" His voice boomed with false

heartiness. "How are you feeling, my dear? God, look at that bruise! You're lucky to be alive."

His eyes probed. Searching for a weakness, Mckenna sensed. Did anything in this office not have undercurrents of hostility?

"It's good to have you back, my dear. Everyone here has missed you."

"It's very good to be back, sir."

He gave her a lordly smile. The same lordly smile that he'd given her ever since he'd moved up here to take over the Sedona office—after she had laid all the groundwork in getting it up and running. Sean Kelly—another name and face from her memory!—had promised her a partnership if she would get this branch of BKB off the ground. Then Gil had decided to head up the office in some sort of power play among the senior partners.

Mckenna remembered! She did remember! Too bad the memories weren't pleasant ones. Gil had never liked her, had thought her Sean Kelly's stoolie in Sedona. The promised partnership had never materialized, despite her success here. Gil's doing? He wore his jaundiced regard of her on his florid face, even though he tried to don a mask of geniality.

"Did you enjoy your trip to Phoenix, sir?"

He had been in the city when she had called after her accident. Who had been running the show here in Sedona? she wondered. Pat Carter?

"I did enjoy it. Played some golf with Sean and Dex. They send their regards, by the way. But the pollution down there, and the traffic! Makes one appreciate living up here, I tell you. Sedona is paradise. I don't understand why you've been wanting to move back down to Phoenix."

She did?

"Just not a small-town girl, eh?" he said with a chuckle. "I tell you, though, my girl, that I'd trade you Phoenix for

Sedona any day of the week. It's a rat race down there, and there's big money to be made up here, as we've proven.

"But down to business, I'm glad you're back, Mckenna. The workload has suffered. Vacations, leaves—necessary, I suppose, but difficult. Oh, I'm not twigging you for taking a rest. No doubt you needed it after your accident. But I'm afraid things have piled up."

She managed to fake her way through the rest of the conversation. Bradner did most of the talking, and all Mckenna needed to do was agree with him. He talked about several cases that were pending, including the Harmon case—the one in which Tom had offered to clean her clock.

"Did you get the files I sent over to your place?" Bradner asked.

"No, sir. They were never delivered. I assumed you had changed your mind."

He frowned. No, it was actually more of a pout than a frown, Mckenna decided.

"I told Pat to send them to you. It's not like her to forget. But you're here now. Ask Pat if anything significant has come up while you were gone. This case is too high profile to let slip."

Mckenna refused to panic. Reviewing the files should bring her up to speed, she reasoned. No need to panic. She could pull this off until her brain caught up with her life.

In a perfect world, she would explain the difficulty and ask for more leave, but Gil was obviously not open to the notion of giving her more time off. This office was like a pool full of sharks, and pity any wounded thing that bled into the water. That came not only from the morning's observation, Mckenna realized, but from memory. Progress. Depressing, but progress just the same.

The rest of the morning did not go well. She scarcely had time to glance through the stack of files on the

Harmon case before her secretary announced that Buddy Morris had shown up demanding to see both her and Gil Bradner.

Peggy Watson, Mckenna's secretary, proved to be the bright point of the day. Cheerful, friendly, almost motherly, she made Mckenna feel as if she had at least one real friend in the office.

"He must have been very concerned for you," Peggy said of Morris. "I swear he's called every day to find out how you were doing and when you were coming back to work. Not that I could tell him anything, or would have told him anything. He even had the nerve to ask for your home number. Of course I didn't give it to him. Strange sort of fellow, if you ask me."

Mckenna's quick look at the Harmon files had told her that Buddy Morris was Todd Harmon's agent and business manager all in one. Apparently, Harmon trusted the man to take care of just about everything in his life, because Morris had taken a very active part in arranging Harmon's defense. More active than Harmon himself, it seemed to Mckenna.

"Are these files over here everything on this case?" she asked Peggy.

"As far as I know."

Something nagged at Mckenna's mind, but the details eluded her, like just about everything else these days. "It seems to me there should be something else."

"Unless you took something home," Peggy suggested. "Sometimes I think you do as much work after hours as most people here do from nine to five." She looked sympathetic, and Mckenna wondered if Peggy sensed what the problem was. But she was the sort of loyal person who would keep the information to herself.

"I don't think I have anything at home or I would have seen it. After all, except to go to physical therapy at the hospital, I've hardly been out of that house for two solid weeks. It's probably just my imagination. Serves me right for being away from the case for so long."

"Your absence was hardly your fault," Peggy replied.

Bradner and Morris were not so generous. They both obviously expected her to be up to speed. Fighting back panic, she told herself that she could carry this off. Then she could bust her butt combing through these files until she knew the case backward and forward.

"Let's review what we have here," Bradner said once they were all three seated in the conference room. "I'm not going to be directly involved with Todd's defense. In fact, I'll be headed back to the Phoenix office next week, and I'll be there on and off for a while, tending to that police brutality case. But I wanted to sit in on this meeting, just in case I or any of the other partners need to have some input. It's a shame that Todd himself couldn't be here, but we understand how busy his schedule is. I want you to know, Mr. Morris, how important this case is to us. Your client is going to get the very best we have."

"Damned straight he is," Morris asserted. "What's at stake here is not just a few months in the slammer for some ordinary little nobody. Todd Harmon has built a music empire not only around his talent and style, but his reputation as a straight-shooting, clean-living example of true country-western values. His fans are not going to like it if he ends up doing time for drug possession and selling."

"We understand, of course," Bradner assured him.

"Those cops had it in for my boy," Morris told them. "This whole thing is a setup, if you ask me, and I'm not going to let Todd be punished for it."

Gil raised an eyebrow in Mckenna's direction.

"Mr. Harmon authorized us to deal with Mr. Morris just as if we were dealing with him directly," she assured him. How fortunate that she'd at least gotten a quick look at the files. "As you noted, Todd has a very busy schedule and knew there would be times when Mr. Morris would have to speak for him."

"Ah. Very good, then. Where are we?"

Mckenna had very little notion, really, but she successfully covered that up by reading from the files. The charges. The prosecution's case—so far, at least. The judge they had drawn, and the pros and cons of requesting a jury trial over a trial by judge. Having more time to review the case would have helped. Had Pat Carter deliberately not sent the files to make her look bad? Mckenna wondered.

"I'm worried that Tom Markham is prosecuting this one," Bradner said. "The man is sharp, a legal shark. And he thinks he's on some kind of mission to clean up Dodge. You can't make a mistake around him. If you do, he'll rip you to pieces. He can twist a jury—especially a predominantly female jury—around his damned little finger with that down-home country charm he puts on. Damned bad luck, drawing Tom."

Mckenna had thought Tom was joking when he mentioned trouncing her in court on the Harmon case. He certainly hadn't seemed like a shark. On the contrary, he had been charming. Down-home, country charming, as Gil Bradner had put it. Had the purpose of his visit been more to bring encouragement to a friend, or to check out the damage to an opponent? The cutthroat atmosphere around this office made the latter seem more likely.

The louse.

"We don't have a preliminary hearing date yet, do we, Mckenna?"

She glanced down at the file. "No, sir. If Todd wants to speed things along, he could waive his right to a hearing and we could go right into setting a trial date. The more quickly we proceed, the less likely the media will hook onto the story and create a circus."

Was that part of her legal education coming back, or

had she gotten that tidbit from watching *Law and Order* on television the night before?

"We're not waiving anything," Morris scoffed. "We want every damned hearing we can get. If there's such a thing as justice, the case will get thrown out of court. This was entrapment, pure and simple. And probably a plant, as well."

"I'm sure Mckenna is on top of things, Mr. Morris." But Bradner didn't look as if he quite believed his own words.

The phone intercom buzzed and Bradner's secretary informed him that Mr. Bolin was on line two.

"I'll take the call in my office, Marge."

Bradner got up. "I'm sure you two can carry on from here."

Mckenna didn't see much to carry on with. The meeting had accomplished little besides letting Buddy Morris blow off some steam, but she supposed if Todd Harmon wanted to pay BKB's exorbitant rates to let his agent rant, he was entitled.

"Do we have anything else to cover, Mr. Morris?"

He smiled. "What happened to Buddy?"

"I beg your pardon?"

"You've always called me Buddy. Let's not get all formal now."

She bit her lip and tried to act composed. "Ah, yes, well, here in the office, we like to maintain a certain professional attitude."

"Oh, yeah. Well . . ." He fixed her with a searching look that made her very uncomfortable. "Glad to see you're back in the saddle again. I read about your accident. Terrible. Must have been terrifying."

"To tell the truth, I don't remember much about the accident."

"No kidding? Well, I guess that happens sometimes. Maybe better that way. But, back to my boy's little problem, here. Do you see any particular problems cropping up?"

Again with the armor-piercing stare. What did he want her to say? she wondered. She took the safe road. "I never tell a client there won't be problems, Buddy. Too much can happen during the prosecution of a case like this."

"But anything specific? Any potential killing blows?"

What was he getting at? "If I come across any insurmountable problems that we can't deal with, I'll be certain you're the first to know."

"Good."

"Right after Todd."

"Yeah, well, good luck catching him. He's trying to finish an album, and then his concert tour is going to keep him running for the next three months. But I'll stay in touch."

This just wasn't going well, Mckenna acknowledged once Buddy Morris had left. She didn't know if she could do it. Was it fair to trust that her acumen would return before she did her client irreparable harm? Did she dare ask for more leave? She opted to spend the day poring over the Harmon files before deciding.

When noon rolled around, Pat suggested they eat lunch at Spices, a nearby restaurant. In the office parking lot, she looked at Mckenna's little loaner Volkswagen and laughed. "Tell me that's not your new car."

"A friend of mine is letting me use it. I think it's cute." Mckenna didn't introduce Mel by name. Somehow she didn't think Pat would see the humor.

"When are you going to buy a real car?"

"When the insurance check for the Beemer gets here. But I like the Bug, actually. It gets me around."

"Zero to sixty in ten minutes?"

"Actually, I haven't had it above forty-five. I think Nell said that fifty-five is about its top speed."

Pat laughed. "Beemer to Bug. Poor Mckenna." Then she offered to drive them to lunch in her Lincoln Navigator.

The moment Mckenna walked through the front door

of Spices, she knew that she came to this restaurant often. Familiar scents, familiar décor. She even remembered which table she preferred, one by the window so she could keep an eye on her precious Beemer.

Today, however, they sat in the corner beneath a basket overflowing with some leafy plant.

"This is just about your favorite lunch place, isn't it?" Pat asked. "The food is good, but I've never understood the décor. Why would you do Midwest down-home country with chintz curtains and old farm implements in Sedona, of all places, where the total theme everywhere else is Mexican, Native American, and Southwest?"

"I guess they want to be different."

Pat ordered a vodka rocks. Mckenna stuck with wine. They went through the motions of girl chat and office gossip. Mostly, Pat chatted and Mckenna listened.

Pat sang praises for Gil Bradner's strategies on the police brutality lawsuit the firm was handling in Phoenix.

"He's brilliant, you know. We are so lucky to work for him, even if at times he is a total pig. Would you believe that yesterday he asked *me* to get his coffee? I told him, 'Mr. Bradner, I'm a U of A graduate in law, third in my entire class. If you want to sue Starbucks, then I'm your girl. But I don't fetch coffee.'"

Mckenna laughed.

"But I got it for him anyway," Pat said morosely. "It pays to keep the man happy, no matter how you do it."

Business wasn't their only topic of conversation. Mckenna learned about the 1965 Corsair that Pat's husband was restoring. "According to Duane, Ralph Nader is the Antichrist. How could anyone write a whole book dissing such a cute little car? Of course, Duane doesn't call it cute. He goes on and on about the engine, the engineering innovations. Boring stuff. You know, you should let him help you shop for a new car, Mckenna. He really knows cars from the inside out."

She might have been mistaken about Pat Carter, Mckenna decided. The woman certainly acted as if they were friends, talking easily about her family, her pet peeves, and office news. She listened well, also, but Mckenna tried to be cautious in what she said, limiting her conversation to her accident, the tragedy of a trashed Beemer, the boredom of two weeks at home with no work to keep her busy.

Picking up on Mckenna's no-work comment, Pat apologized profusely. "I don't know how it slipped my mind to send you those files. It just got so busy, you know."

Mckenna reserved judgment.

A second glass of wine along with her excellent London broil might have influenced the warm feeling inside Mckenna as she sat there with the bright sunshine pouring through the window, talking and laughing with a colleague, eating good food and drinking excellent wine.

"I don't think I've ever seen you order anything other than a salad," Pat said. "Are you off your perpetual diet?"

Perpetual diet? How depressing. She shrugged. "A good meal now and then never hurt anyone."

Lord, but she was tired of this charade, the little shuffle and dance to fix missteps and hide her weak underbelly.

"I've always admired your diet discipline," Pat said with a smile. "If I could get rid of fifteen pounds or so, Duane might spend more time with me than his stupid cars."

The temptation to confide in this friendly woman became an actual pressure in Mckenna's chest. She just couldn't keep up the act much longer.

Don't do it, a voice inside cautioned.

"Of course," Pat continued, "I've always thought you carried the diet thing to the extreme, always counting calories, eating rabbit food, obsessing over grams of fat." She shook her head with a sigh. "But you do look great in your clothes."

How could she have forgotten something as basic as

eating habits? Mckenna wondered. The London broil tasted mighty good. When she returned to being herself—strange thought—no doubt she would go back to dining on lettuce and fat-free yogurt. What an unappetizing prospect! In a spate of rebellion at deprivation to come, she ordered a piece of pecan pie for dessert—with whipped cream!

Pat gave her a puzzled frown. "I think that accident did something to your mind. Or maybe your stomach."

Little did she know, Mckenna thought as she savored the first bite of rich, sugary pie. "Well, it did teach me that life is too uncertain to ever miss a chance at eating a good dessert."

With dessert—Pat had ordered apple cobbler—the conversation turned, unfortunately, to work.

"I hear you had a meeting with Buddy Morris this morning," Pat observed. "Some welcome back for your first morning. That man gives me the creeps."

"Uh-huh," Mckenna agreed. The pie had most of her attention.

"How did it go?"

"With Morris? Okay, I guess."

"Now if Todd Harmon came in every once in a while to discuss his own defense, I'd be green with envy. I adore his music. And he's not bad-looking, either. Have you seen his last video? 'Pipe Dreams'?"

Had she? Mckenna doubted it. From what little she knew about herself, country-western didn't seem to be her style. "Haven't seen it."

"He's going to get another Grammy for that one. Mark my words."

"Hm."

"How's his case going? You're going to save his gorgeous ass, right?"

"Of course." Such confidence was probably obligatory.

"You're going for the not-guilty plea rather than a plea deal with Terrible Tom?"

Terrible Tom, who had trotted out to her house, full of concern, simply to find out if she was still capable of wielding a legal sword in Todd Harmon's defense.

She wasn't capable, her inner voice told her. "Well . . ."

"You know, anything other than a not guilty is going to severely damage Mr. Squeaky Clean's image and cost him fans."

"Uh . . . we haven't decided yet exactly what strategy to use."

"You haven't decided?" Pat exclaimed. "What was all that talk about entrapment, discredited witnesses, and flattening Tom Markham like roadkill in the courtroom?"

She had said that? Threatening to flatten a man like Tom certainly seemed the pinnacle of overconfidence.

Pat went on to offer her own legal opinion, citing precedents, court rulings, rules of evidence, and her own rather pithy observations on the record of the judge who had drawn the case. Mckenna stayed silent, figuring that opening her mouth in this situation would only prove her own ignorance. She concentrated on trying to look knowledgeable and intelligent.

From Pat's narrow regard, Mckenna suspected her effort didn't work.

"Girl, what has happened to you? You've got this blank look on your face, like you don't know what the hell I'm talking about, and you didn't even get me for talking dirt about old Finkel. You always totally chew on anyone who dishes a judge in public. It didn't even get a rise from you. You know, you seem like a completely different person."

Suddenly the pecan pie turned to concrete in her stomach. "Rest-room run," she told Pat. "I'll be right back."

Alone at last, her arms braced against a sink and her forehead resting against the cool glass of the mirror, Mckenna tried deep breathing to calm the roiling in her stomach. Was all that unaccustomed rich food making her stomach want to heave, or was it the realization that she really couldn't do this? Even if she could manage to fool everyone, and that was doubtful, she couldn't provide her clients with the legal services they deserved. How had she ever thought to pull it off? She didn't know a habeas corpus from a mea culpa.

She lifted her head and regarded herself in the mirror. The sculpted dark brown hair showed the need of a trim. The bruise on her temple had congealed to yellow-green. All in all, just the slightest unraveling in the smooth, professional image Mckenna Wright presented to the world. If people only knew the smooth and sophisticated Ms. Wright had unraveled down to the very core.

"It'll come back," she told the image in the mirror. "Be patient. It's in your brain, and soon, very soon, it'll all come back."

Mckenna sighed. She would ask Bradner for a longer leave, explain the problem in the most optimistic terms possible. Maybe he would understand. He had to understand.

But that could wait until tomorrow.

WHILE MCKENNA talked to herself in the bathroom, Pat Carter dug her cell phone from her handbag and dialed the office.

"Marge, this is Pat. I need to talk to Mr. Bradner."

While she waited, Pat tapped a manicured fingernail against the tablecloth and smiled.

chapter 6

MCKENNA LASTED at the office just an hour after lunch before going home. She took the Harmon files with her, determined to concentrate on her notes, the police reports, and witness interviews until the legal education in her brain started to flow forth. She knew it was there.

But maybe it wasn't there. That was the scenario she feared the most: this situation wasn't a temporary loss, but permanent damage. Forevermore, her life would begin with waking in that hospital bed, most of her past a closed book. Her childhood, education, family memories—everything gone, wiped out by a bursting blood vessel and a fifty-foot cliff.

Sitting in her home office, surrounded by her expensive oak furniture and her personal law library, she squeezed her eyes tightly shut, as if the dire possibilities might disappear, as if the encyclopedic information stored on her shelves might somehow start trickling into her brain, if only she could concentrate hard enough. But when she opened her eyes, the dire possibilities were still there, and the ins and outs of the law were still a mystery. She reached for the phone.

Fifteen minutes later, Dr. Estrella returned her call. "Mckenna. What can I do for you?"

She bit her lip. "Hey, Doc. I don't mean to be bugging you. But I'm getting a bit concerned. My memory isn't coming back."

His reply was a mysterious medical "Hm. It's been—what?—a couple of weeks now?"

"Two weeks and three days."

"Nothing has come back? Not at all?"

"Well . . ."

"No familiar faces or places pop out at you?"

She had known Tom Markham, but then, she had seen a photograph. Still, something about Tom had sparked recognition beyond the photo. She had even known Pat Carter by name. Gil Bradner had inspired a few unpleasant recollections, and she remembered the way to the grocery store, had remembered her office, and her secretary had definitely been familiar. "Okay, some things are coming back. But a lot isn't. My education . . ."

"Can you add, subtract, and multiply?"

"Of course."

"Do you know who Abraham Lincoln was?"

"Well, yes. But I can no longer quote case law on possession and sale of illegal drugs, or anything else, for that matter."

"Mckenna, be patient. Long-term memories—the things you learned during your childhood—often return before more recent memory. If you can just relax a bit, things will come back."

Easy for him to say.

"Your physical therapist says your right side is nearly back to one hundred percent, and that's an amazing speed of recovery, even though the disability was slight. I have every reason to believe the rest of you will recover as well. How are the headaches?"

"Better," she admitted.

"Would you like me to refer you to a psychiatrist?"

Who would certainly raise his or her brows if Mckenna admitted having conversations with a cat. And if she had to lie to her psychiatrist, then what good was seeing one? "No shrink, thank you."

"I see we have a follow-up appointment next week. Would you like to come in sooner?"

"No," she said with a sigh.

"Okay, then. Try to take it as easy as you can. Hang out with friends. Go to familiar places. Relax and don't try to force it. The brain works in mysterious ways, and we don't yet understand as much as we would like to understand. Forcing an issue with memory sometimes just drives things deeper into hiding."

When she hung up the phone, Mckenna didn't feel re-assured. Her law books loomed above her on the shelves, guardians of something she once possessed but had no more.

"Worry, worry, worry," Titi commented from where she reposed on the armchair. "So serious. Such a frown."

"If you were in my place, you would worry, too!" Mckenna snapped.

Still seeking comfort, Mckenna picked up the phone once again, this time to call Nell. Unlike Jane, who seemed to be the "suck it up and quit complaining" type, Nell was quick to offer reassurance.

"Nell," Mckenna greeted her friend. "It's Mckenna."

"Mckenna! Hi. I've meant to call, but I got so busy packing..."

"Don't apologize. You're not my nursemaid."

"It's not that. I just wanted to check in and find out how you're doing. Did you go back to work yet?"

"Yes, I did. And it was pretty much a disaster. I felt like

I was walking around in someone else's life. Minor stuff is coming back, but not the important things."

"Like the law," Nell guessed.

"Like the law."

She heard Nell's quiet sigh through the momentary silence. Then, "You know, Mckenna, do you think there's a chance, just a chance, that in your deepest secret heart, part of you doesn't want to remember that part of your life?"

What a notion! "No! Of course I want to remember!"

"The reason I ask is, about a year back I wrote a piece for the local rags on a very successful hypnotist in Sedona."

"One of the Sedona swamis."

"See, there, you remembered that. That's what you always called the set of Sedona folks who depart a bit from the mainstream. But this guy is very legit. Degrees plaster his walls. Maybe hypnosis . . ."

"Thanks for the suggestion, Nell. But no thanks. The very idea gives me the creeps. Dr. Estrella wants me to see a shrink, and now you pull a Svengali out of the hat. I'm desperate, but not that desperate."

"Okay. That's what I thought you'd say. But keep it in the back of your mind. Really, though, I'm sure things will come back eventually. Two weeks isn't such a long time. You've never been the patient sort. . . ."

"I'm beginning to realize that."

"Yes, well, on a more cheerful note, Dan and I are going for pizza tonight. Want to join us?"

Mckenna smiled. "Maybe. I'll think about it and call you later. Thanks for the invite."

Mckenna hung up the phone and dropped back in her chair. Hypnotist, indeed! She could just picture some droning swami with a swinging watch fob waiting for her to fall under his spell. Not likely.

"The phone said patience," Titi said. "You need patience."

"You heard the other side of the conversation?"

Titi's ears twitched. "I hear everything. That's what ears are for. I don't understand why a talking cat surprises you so much. The phone talks to you almost every day, and it's not even alive."

"The phone doesn't talk . . ." she began, then gave up. "You're right; I need patience. That doesn't come easily to me."

"You remember."

Mckenna grimaced. "No. I observe."

"Lying in the warm sun will make you feel better. This time of day the sun comes in best through the living-room windows. It hits the love seat just right."

That almost sounded good. "Maybe a nice hot bath would have the same effect."

The cat growled. "Water! Hot or cold, water is good only for drinking."

"That just shows that cats don't know absolutely everything," Mckenna told her in a superior tone.

"Everything worth knowing."

Mckenna merely snorted.

Before Mckenna could go take that relaxing bath, however, the phone rang.

"How ya doing?" Tom Markham asked when Mckenna picked up the receiver. Mckenna had come to look forward to their phone conversations during the past two weeks. She had even caught herself wishing they could have another face-to-face conversation, but that was before she had put two and two together and come up with a very nasty four.

"You'll be sorry to hear," she told him in an icy tone, "that I'm recovering quite nicely."

His frown came right through the phone line. "What do you mean by that?"

"I figured it out, Markham. My memory cells may be in hibernation, but the rest of my brain is perking along just fine. You came over here not out of concern for a friend, but to find out if I still can give you a run for your money in court. Does the Harmon case ring a bell?"

Silence—guilty silence, she thought—met her accusation. Then, surprisingly, he chuckled. "You think I'm afraid of you in court, on the Harmon case, of all things?"

"What? I'm not competent enough to pose a challenge to you?"

Her ire was growing by the moment. The entire frustrating day—the uncertainties, the worry, the near hopelessness, the feeling that she was an impostor walking around in someone else's clothes, invading someone else's life—coalesced into resentment of Tom Markham's attitude.

"Of course you're competent enough to challenge me." He paused. "When you're yourself."

"And that's why the visit and the oh-so-concerned calls, isn't it? You're watching to see if I stay the lamebrain with the blanked-out mind, hoping I don't recover my lost wits."

Now an edge sharpened his voice. "From what I'm hearing right now, I'd judge that you're getting back to being the old Mckenna pretty fast."

"Too bad if that bothers you."

"I sort of liked the new version of Mckenna."

"Because you thought you could trounce her in court."

The phone exploded with his snort. "Honey lamb, New Mckenna or Old Mckenna—neither one has a leg to stand on in getting Todd Harmon off the hook."

"We'll see about that."

"I guess we will."

"Fine."

"Fine by me, as well."

When Mckenna slammed down the receiver, Titi

jumped, then gave her a reproachful look. "Now you're mad at the phone."

Mckenna replied with a word probably not in the cat's vocabulary. "Phones do not... Oh, never mind!" With a frustrated groan, Mckenna picked up a leather beanbag paperweight and threw it. Even though she would have liked to throw it at the cat, she settled for targeting the wastebasket in the corner, which crashed to its side and shot papers onto the floor.

"Shit! Damn! Shit!"

Titi managed a feline version of "tsk, tsk," which inspired Mckenna to even stronger words. What the hell was she going to do? After throwing the gauntlet in Tom Markham's face, she couldn't ask for more leave. She was just going to have to force her brain back into action. Without picking up the mess, she got up and stomped out of her office. So much for relaxation.

"You're not relaxing," Titi called after her.

Another shrill ring of the phone spoiled Mckenna's dramatic exit.

"Goddammit to hell!" She detoured to the kitchen and picked up the wall phone by the refrigerator. "What is it?" she demanded, thinking this a return call from Tom, either to apologize or try to get even further ahead in the game of trading barbs.

"Mckenna?" Gilbert Bradner's voice asked dubiously.

Only a remnant of self-preservation kept her from cussing into the phone. Mckenna Wright, she concluded, had quite a temper.

"Mr. Bradner. Sorry. I just had a nuisance call, and I thought he was calling back."

"Ah, well, yes. Those can be quite annoying."

He didn't sound mollified, Mckenna thought.

"I had a talk this afternoon with Pat Carter. I have to assure you that she was very reluctant to come to me. But she is concerned that your accident has consequences that will be detrimental to the firm."

Mckenna suffered a sudden chill. "What do you mean?" As if she didn't know.

"She said you were very unfocused, seemed to positively flounder in any legal discussion, and overall seemed to be suffering an entire lack of acumen. I suspected as much in our meeting with Buddy Morris."

"Well..." Mckenna began, flogging her brain for something to say. So much for Pat Carter and her chatty girl talk. She should have been more careful. She should have known better.

"Mckenna, what's going on?"

"I'm just... I'm just..." Now would be the time to ask for more leave. But her challenge to Tom kept her mouth clamped shut on the words, even as she called herself all kinds of a fool.

Titi sauntered into the kitchen and gave her a baleful glare. "Bad phone. Don't talk to it."

Damned cat. "Sir, the truth is, I'm not quite myself since the accident." An understatement. "I have a touch of temporary, partial, really minor amnesia. But it's fading fast."

"I'm glad to hear it."

She heard implacability in his voice, along with a certain satisfaction. The jackass was enjoying this, she thought, and recalled her earlier revelation about his hostility.

"Mckenna, Pat just verified what I observed in our meeting with Buddy Morris. You've lost your edge, your grasp of legal strategy...."

And a good deal more, but Mckenna wasn't about to go into details.

"This is very tough for me, my dear. But the good of the firm must come first. So I've made the decision to put you on leave until your recovery is complete."

" 'On leave'!" Panic blossomed. "For how long?"

"Until you can demonstrate to us that you've regained the legal shrewdness and untiring energy that made you such a valuable asset to the company. I feel for you, Mckenna. I am not unsympathetic to your situation. This isn't your fault. But on the other hand, it isn't our fault, either. My priority has to be the good of the firm, and an aggressive law practice like Bradner, Kelly, and Bolin cannot afford to carry dead weight, especially dead weight in the top salary echelon. You can talk to human resources about applying for some sort of disability."

"Disability? You're firing me!" She still couldn't believe it, even though it had buzzed around her head with the other dire possibilities that cost her sleep at night. "Gil... after all I've done for the firm, how can you fire me?"

"Now, Mckenna, don't get all childish on me. Firing is such a harsh word. But if you would prefer termination to the uncertainties of indefinite leave, we can do things your way."

He must be a great attorney, Mckenna reflected. Only one of the very best could twist this conversation into doing things "her way."

"If you prefer termination, we'll give you severance pay. And once you're back to being yourself, we would be glad to consider your coming on board once again, depending on our case load and requirements of the moment."

Mckenna closed her eyes. This wasn't happening.

"If you could clean out your office as soon as possible, my dear, we would appreciate it."

Scraping together her last ounce of pride, she managed somehow to keep her voice steady. "It would be my pleasure, sir." *You miserable old lizard.*

As she replaced the receiver gently, so gently, refusing to surrender to the urge to slam it down on its cradle, Mckenna looked at Titi. The cat gazed back disapprovingly.

"Bad phone. Throw it out."

"You don't know how tempting that is." She massaged her brow with her fingers, chasing the headache that had begun to pound, pound, pound, and trying hard to hold together. A deep breath in, then out, then in again.

She concentrated on taking deep, therapeutic breaths, but the air moving in and out of her lungs couldn't calm the fountain of panic and anger that rose inside her. How dare they! How dare they be so uncaring, so callous, so ungrateful. She should sue. That would show them.

Right, a little voice in her head mocked. *Sue away. Hold up your sudden helplessness and plummeting brainpower for the whole legal community to snicker at.* And they would snicker, Mckenna suspected. Snicker, and sneer, and laugh knowingly. One day spent at BKB had taught her that a person in her position had mostly rivals, not colleagues. Did she really want to hold herself up to their ridicule?

No, she didn't. Maybe later, she decided—when she got back her legal skills. And she would get those skills back, along with everything else she had lost. She just didn't know how.

She sighed, trying to expel the hurt and uncertainty along with the air. It didn't work.

"You'll be glad to know," she informed Titi, "that from now on I'll be doing a lot of relaxing, whether I want to or not."

TWO DAYS later, Mckenna lay in bed, pillow over her head, dutifully trying to relax, when Jane barged into her house and ruined her effort. Titi—the traitor cat—and Idaho the border collie sat calmly by and watched as Jane pulled Mckenna out of her rumpled bed.

"It's nine o'clock in the morning, you slugabed!"

"Aaagh! Let go! Don't you know that you're supposed to handle the disabled with respect!"

"Disabled, my foot! Look at you! You're a mess."

Mckenna dared to glance into the full-length mirror on her bedroom wall. Her hair stood on end. The bruised puffiness of her eyes told the tale of two days spent in useless weeping. And the extra large T-shirt she had worn to bed—the one that boasted "Cats are Purrfect"—bore a line of ice-cream drips from last night's chocolate binge.

"What the hell are you doing to yourself?" Jane demanded.

Mckenna lifted her chin. "I'm relaxing. Doctor's orders."

"You've never in your life known how to relax, and you still don't. This"—she waved her arm at the cluttered bedroom, the litter of unwashed coffee cups, the crusted ice-cream bowl, the strewn clothes—"is not relaxing. You have fifteen minutes to take a shower and make yourself presentable. We're going to the hospital."

"I don't need to go to any damned hospital."

"Not for you, Your Highness. For the patients. You and Titi," Jane said grimly, "are going to spread some goddamned cheer."

By the time they arrived at the Verde Valley Medical Center, Mckenna had to admit that she did feel a bit better, probably due to her first shower in two days and the boiled egg and tea that Jane had forced her to eat. But her mood still hovered like a black cloud.

"I don't see why you had to barge in and interrupt a perfectly wonderful wallow in depression," she groused to Jane as they pulled into a parking spot.

"Self-pity isn't your style, kiddo. Trust me."

"I think I was doing a pretty good job of it."

"More like it was doing a job on you."

Mckenna sniffed indignantly. "How did you find out I lost my job? I didn't tell anyone."

"I called your office yesterday to ask if you wanted to have lunch. Peggy told me. She's pretty upset, by the way.

Had some pretty choice things to say about Gil Bradner and his loyal sidekick Pat 'The Bitch' Carter."

"Peggy had better watch out, or she'll find herself out on the street, like me."

Jane chuckled. "Not likely. Good secretaries are hard to find."

"And good lawyers aren't?" Then she remembered. "But I'm not exactly a good lawyer anymore."

"Geez! Quit your whining."

They signed the volunteer roster at the outpatient desk. Mckenna had actually remembered where the roster was located, a small victory on a dismal day.

"I'm not going to remember how to do this," she complained. "Just like I don't remember anything else."

"Poor you."

Stung by her friend's lack of sympathy, Mckenna snapped. "Well, how would you like it if *your* history started three weeks ago, if your cool car, which you don't even remember, was totaled, if your profession was down the tubes, if you had no income, no memory of family or friends, and no goddamned reason to get out of bed in the morning?"

"Maybe you should be grateful that you're alive," Jane snapped back, "which you wouldn't be if not for a couple of well-placed trees and a good air bag. Maybe there was a purpose for those trees being there, and for that air bag working the way it was supposed to. Maybe you're still expected to do something in this life, and for sure, that something isn't lying around in bed, eating ice cream and feeling sorry for yourself."

The tone wasn't quite as harsh as the words, but Mckenna flinched anyway. And Jane's border collie looked every bit as disapproving as his mistress, almost mirroring her expression.

It was almost too much. Mckenna pouted. "Are you sure that we're friends?"

"You saw the photos." Jane's half-smile eased the tension. "Listen, why don't you take Titi to see a few patients? There's nothing like visiting someone hooked up to a heart monitor to put your own problems in perspective."

"Let's go," Titi chimed in. "Patients need me."

Jane beamed. "See. Titi agrees. That was a 'let's get to work' meow if I've ever heard one."

"She's scary," Mckenna commented as Jane walked down the hall, her fiery red hair seeming to trail sparks in the wake of her purposeful strides. God help any patient who didn't obediently heal under the ministrations of Jane and Idaho.

"Very scary," Titi replied. "She's a dog person."

"Are you sure she doesn't understand you?"

Titi looked offended. "She speaks Dog. I speak Cat." With that, she marched indignantly off. Mckenna pretty much had to follow.

For an animal whose idea of a good time was lying in the sun, Titi exhibited a surprising work ethic as she did her rounds in the hospital. The cat knew exactly what to do, even if Mckenna didn't. In the Critical Care Unit, she obligingly invited the staff's attention by rolling onto her back in front of the nurse's station, then purring loudly when the staff took turns tickling her stomach. "Nurses need cat petting, too," she informed Mckenna as she rolled back to her feet. "Petting a cat is good for the heart."

"Doesn't she have a cute little meow?" one of the nurses said. "We're so glad to see her back. We've really missed her." Then, as if an afterthought, "You, too, Mckenna. How's the head?"

With a businesslike expression on her face, Titi led Mckenna from room to room. In one room she cuddled up to a bypass patient. In the next she entertained a toddler with a tumor, and Mom, who looked as if she hadn't laughed in quite a while, laughed right along with her little daughter. Then Titi played footsies with an elderly lady who swore to Mckenna that her cat did the very same thing. "My Pidge died a year ago," she told them. "I think she looked down from Heaven and told your Titi exactly what to do."

And at the end of an hour, Mckenna found herself smiling, her black mood lightened. She allowed herself to be dragged to Jane's place for lunch. The Bark Park Kennel, Jane's home and business both, sat on a hill overlooking the confluence of Oak Creek and the Verde River. The location was a prime site, but the kennel buildings, herding arena, and Jane's double-wide trailer house stood in isolated splendor—no other homes in sight. The rowdy greeting they got from Jane's "clients"—her boarding dogs—might have explained the lack of neighbors.

Titi trotted to the living-room sofa and made herself at home as soon as they walked into the house. At the same time, a golden retriever shot out of the bedroom at light speed, circled the living room several times in a yellow blur, and then pulled up in front of Jane in a perfect, expectant sit.

"Nice, Shadow," Jane told the dog, laughing. "If you would ever grow out of being such a rowdy, you could visit the hospital, too. You probably don't remember much about Shadow, Mckenna, but when he was a puppy, you two hit it off quite nicely."

Mckenna gave the dog an obligatory pat on the head, bemused by Jane's easy acceptance of her not remembering much of anything about, well, anything. She treated amnesia as if it were of no more concern than a sprained ankle or a bee sting.

"Tuna sandwich all right?" Jane asked, throwing Idaho's leash on the counter that divided the living-room area from the kitchen.

"Do I like tuna?"

"You used to love it. Of course, you liked anything that was low-fat."

With some concern, Mckenna watched Idaho and Shadow launch themselves into a race around the living room. "They won't chase Titi, will they?"

Jane bellowed out a guffaw. "Chase that cat? They'll be lucky if she doesn't chase them."

Titi merely eyed the dogs with feline disdain. "Dogs are dopes."

"I swear that cat has the cutest meow I've ever heard," Jane said.

If she only knew, Mckenna thought.

"So," Jane said as she opened a can of tuna. "Do you feel better now that you've seen some people with real problems?"

"Like my problem isn't real?" Mckenna groused. Actually, Mckenna did feel a bit better, but she wasn't about to admit it to bossy Jane.

Jane emptied the tuna into a bowl and put the can on the floor, where it was instantly knocked into a corner by a sable streak of fur. The dogs stood at a respectful distance while Titi cleaned out the can and then batted it around the kitchen floor. "The can is too small for big sloppy dog tongues," Jane explained. "But cat tongues are made for tuna cans."

Mckenna would not be diverted. "Why don't you think I have a real problem? How would you like to be in my situation?"

"I think it would be very annoying." She slopped a large spoonful of mayonnaise into the bowl of tuna, glancing at Mckenna out of the corner of her eye as she began to stir the mixture. "But it could also be taken as an opportunity."

"Some opportunity!"

"It is an opportunity! Look at it this way." She slapped the tuna onto four slices of wheat bread. "All of us have certain potential. We have a body, mind, spirit, and soul with certain qualities. But those qualities are always modified by the experiences and people that surround us as we grow up. We acquire fears, prejudices, and bad habits that hold us back and sometimes channel us into directions we shouldn't go."

"How philosophical."

"I minored in philosophy in college."

"You're kidding."

"Do I sound as if I'm kidding?"

"No."

"Well, there you are, then. Have you ever wondered what you would be if you could cleanse yourself of all the garbage that warped you while you were growing up?"

Mckenna just looked at her. Titi, also, sat in the middle of the kitchen floor and fixed her with a curious gaze.

"You think I'm warped, huh?"

"No," Jane replied carefully. "No more than anyone else. We all have our acquired baggage."

Mckenna pulled out a chair at the kitchen table as Jane set a sandwich in front of her. "Still, you make me sound like a mass of raw human material."

"You make it sound gross. I think you're free to find out who you really are without the burden of preconceived ideas imposed upon your innocent young psyche. Do you remember your parents?"

Mckenna searched her mostly blank mind. "Not really."

"See? That's good. Parents always screw us up. I know mine did, and I'll bet yours sent you off with some awful neuroses."

"You think I have neuroses?"

"Everyone has neuroses."

"Not cats," Titi added, sitting at their feet.

"No more tuna," Jane told her sternly. "Quit begging or I'll put you in a kennel with a pit bull."

Titi hissed and walked away, tail an indignant flagpole.

"You'll remember your parents, or you'll go off to reacquaint yourself with them, but maybe by that time you will have become someone unaffected by their parenting mistakes."

"Hm." Mckenna took a bite of her sandwich. "Good tuna."

"That's because I used real mayo. Before the accident you would have thrown a fit the moment you saw that mayo jar. You would have shrieked about too much fat."

"I couldn't have been that bad."

"Oh, yeah. Fat always sent you into a tizzy. But now you're someone else, you see. We're seeing the real you without the silly notion that you have to fit into a size three to keep people's respect."

"Did I think that?"

"You did. Why else would a sensible, intelligent woman starve herself into a twig? Now you're free of whatever prejudice made you think that, because you don't remember it. You're still yourself, with brains, spirit, compassion, humor, and great looks—though truthfully, your hair could use a trim."

Mckenna self-consciously brushed her bangs out of her eyes.

"But now you can find out who the basic, wonderful, uncorrupted Mckenna Wright really is. Which is a good thing, because your old self was killing you, living like you did. Eating lettuce for dinner. Working twelve or thirteen hours a day, and weekends, too."

"Well, I was doing something right. I have a dynamite house, which I am now going to lose. And a super car."

"Which you crashed when your blood pressure shot clean through the top of your skull. You know, Mckenna, your memories will come back, eventually, and maybe then you can get back your fast-track job and your luxury house and buy another forty-thousand-dollar car. If you still think those things are important. But if you take this opportunity to find out who the real you is, maybe you'll be grateful someday that all this happened."

Mckenna couldn't help but smile. "Jane, you're a unique individual with a really different perspective on life."

"You've told me that before, but the language wasn't nearly as polite. See, already you're a new person. Want a piece of cherry pie?"

chapter 7

THE HOUSE on Oak Creek went up for rent. Mckenna couldn't bear to sell it. Sale seemed so permanent, symbolic that she had given up on ever getting her life back. Within a week, she had leased the place for a year to a middle-aged accounting executive and his wife. They had two children, a terrier, and enough money to pay the outrageous rent that Mckenna demanded. It had to be outrageous. Her first look at her mortgage coupons had nearly given her a heart attack, and the rent had to cover the monthly mortgage plus put money aside for maintenance and repair.

Nell offered Mckenna her very nice house in Cottonwood, a stucco ranch-style home with a gorgeous wraparound porch and an acre of lawn. Since Nell planned to move to Tucson to be with her husband Dan, who had just started law school, she wouldn't be using it.

"I'm not going to sell the place, so this is perfect," Nell told Mckenna. "I'll be going down to Tucson about the time that you have to be out of the Oak Creek house. And I'd really rather you live there than renting it to strangers.

Heaven knows, with Piggy's trust fund, I don't need to charge you rent. You can live there as long as you want, until you get back on your feet. You'd actually be doing me a favor by taking care of it."

But Mckenna had made a discovery about herself. Seeping through the cracks in her depression, anger, and frustration, a sort of stubborn pride had taken hold of her. Maybe it was Jane's challenge to discover the real Mckenna Wright. Maybe it was something that had been there all along. But she wanted to stand on her own two feet. As Jane had said, this bothersome situation presented a rare opportunity to mold herself into the person of her choice. And the person of Mckenna's choice wouldn't be living rent-free on the charity of a rich friend.

But she did wonder if the old Mckenna had appreciated Jane and Nell quite enough for the generous and caring friends they were.

Nell accepted Mckenna's "no, thank you" with understanding, and the three of them teamed up to find a rental that would stretch Mckenna's severance pay as far as possible. They spent three discouraging days looking at houses with leaking roofs, weed-tangled yards, faulty plumbing, or odors that spoke of former animal residents with questionable house manners.

Mckenna was having second thoughts about the offer of Nell's house when Jane called with a prospect in Cornville, only a mile away from the Bark Park.

"I drive past the place every day," Jane said. "It's not bad on the outside, and the 'for rent' sign went up just this morning, I think."

"How much do they want for it?"

"I don't know, but it's worth a look."

Mckenna the Miser. She didn't think she'd had to play that role before.

The rental in Cornville sat on an acre of scrubby desert with a view to the east of Sedona's red cliffs and to the west of Mingus Mountain. A single-wide trailer home boasted a covered front patio and a garage with a tiny guest room built on. The small fenced yard was landscaped in the remnants of a lawn, and weeds bloomed in the raised flower beds.

"It has potential," Nell commented generously.

The inside of the trailer home proved to be more roomy than Mckenna expected in a space that measured fourteen by seventy. Someone had kept it very clean. A large kitchen with a bay window, a small but serviceable living room, a dark hallway leading to two bedrooms—one closet-sized—and a large bathroom. In an alcove off the bathroom sat an elf-size washer and dryer.

"This is bigger than the trailer I used to live in," Nell told her, "and with the fenced yard in front, you could even get a dog. Out in the middle of nowhere like this, you might need a dog for protection."

"Oh, come on!" Jane objected. "She won't need protection. I've lived out here for years with no problem."

Nell replied with a wry smile. "But any creep who bothered you, whether or not you had a dog around, would find a nasty surprise in store."

Jane huffed. "What do you mean by that?"

"I mean, that red hair of yours doesn't shelter a calm temperament within, and that black belt folded in your drawer isn't a fashion accessory."

"You're a black belt?" Mckenna asked, impressed.

"I haven't studied or practiced for a couple of years. Trust me, you won't need a black belt to defend yourself out here. It's very quiet. The only marauders you'll have to worry about are skunks, coyotes, and javalina." As an afterthought she added, "Though it's never a bad idea to get a dog."

Mckenna could just imagine how that idea would go down with Titi.

She took the rental. By the end of October, she had sold

most of her furniture, packed what was left of her belongings into a rental truck, and driven away from the last remnant of her old life. It was just Mckenna and Jane on moving day, because Nell and Piggy had left for Tucson the day before. Nell had given Mckenna a hug and warned her to take care. "You'll e-mail and let me know how things are going, right? And if you change your mind about the hypnotherapy idea, I still have the guy's phone number."

Mckenna laughed. "Not that desperate yet. But thanks. I'll bet Dan will be glad to see you. Tell him 'Hello' for me."

"Dan is so busy with classes that I'm sure he doesn't miss me at all. But I sure do miss him. Who knew that men could be so addictive?"

"Addictive, eh?" Mckenna's mind surprised her by conjuring up an image of Tom Markham standing on her front deck, brushing her cheek with a kiss. She pushed it away. "If I had to have an addiction," she said sourly, "I'd take drugs or ice cream over men."

Nell laughed. Actually, Nell laughed a lot, Mckenna noted. She radiated happiness just about everytime Mckenna saw her, and that happiness didn't seem to have anything to do with her fortune—technically, Piggy's fortune. Or her professional accomplishments—meager, as far as Mckenna could tell. Or her style (she had little)—or figure (size eight, at least). Maybe she had found the "true self" that Jane had advised Mckenna to search out. Maybe Nell had even done it without the help of amnesia.

"Ice cream?" Nell said through her laughter. "Tempting. But believe me, Mckenna, when you find the right guy, ice cream can't compete. Even walnut maple swirl."

Mckenna just smiled. There was something she certainly didn't need in her complicated life. Men.

So Nell had left, and Mckenna and Jane hauled what was left of Mckenna's household goods, along with a sullen Titi, to their new home in the wilds of Cornville. Titi was not pleased.

"I liked the other house," she said when Mckenna carried her into the trailer's living room and set her on the mustard-colored carpet. "I knew all the sunny spots in the other house."

"This house has sunny spots. And as soon as Jane and I unload the truck, it will have a bed and a sofa and food—all your favorite things."

"I want the other house." So plaintive, it almost sounded like a meow.

"I thought you were supposed to be a comfort to me, a guide to de-stressing, not a pain in the ass."

"Easier to mellow in the other house. The other house had a Jacuzzi tub."

"You don't like water."

"I liked to sit on the stool and watch the water go round and round. Especially when that rubber duck went around with it. Rubber ducks are good for stress. Go back to the other house."

"I brought the rubber duck with us."

"Not the same."

Mckenna sighed. "Nothing ever will be. I'm beginning to learn that."

Titi jumped onto the kitchen counter, tail twitching, and looked around disdainfully. "I don't like it."

"Chill out," Mckenna chided.

Titi wasn't the only cranky creature by the end of the day. Hours of loading, unloading, and unpacking left both Mckenna and Jane exhausted and ill-humored.

"We should have enlisted guy help," Jane complained. "I hate to admit it, but men have their uses."

"I don't know any guys to ask for help."

"What about Tom?"

"Tom Markham?"

"He's always been sweet on you. He would have helped."

Mckenna shook her head. "I'm pretty sure he's not sweet on me anymore."

Strange how Tom Markham kept crossing her path, in thought if nothing else.

She sighed. "Well, we got it done, anyway." She looked around her at the jumble of boxes, the sofa she had bought at a Goodwill store, the bedraggled curtains that looked like someone's cat—certainly not Titi, but some other, less-dignified cat—had used them as a swing. The shoddiness of it almost overwhelmed her, and she found herself agreeing with Titi. She wanted the other house. "Six weeks almost to the day from my brain exploding, and I don't have a job, I live in a broken-down mobile home, and my jeans are getting too tight. What a life."

The next day Mckenna borrowed Jane's van—a very utilitarian vehicle smelling of both sheep and dogs—to shop for a car for herself. The insurance check for the trashed BMW had arrived, and Nell had taken her little Bug with her to Tucson, so the time had come to get her own set of wheels.

"A used car," she told the salesman at the first car deal-ership.

The totaled BMW had paid out at over twenty thou-sand dollars, but much of that needed to go toward inci-dental items such as rent and food.

The salesman sized her up with a keen eye. Mckenna wondered what he saw. Her once stylish haircut had be-come ragged. She had thrown on jeans and a T-shirt—not wanting to subject any of her designer slacks and high-end blouses (her wardrobe didn't offer much in the way of grubby casual clothes) to the interior of Jane's van. Not to mention that her size-three slacks were getting just a bit snug.

"I have a nice 2002 Fiero you might like."

Apparently, she still looked like fast-car material.

"Something a little more used and a little less expensive, please."

Unfortunately, nothing a little more used and a little less expensive caught her eye. As she walked through the lot, however, a flashy red Infiniti reached out and dragged her over for a look. Mckenna couldn't resist at least a look. She suspected that her true self just wasn't a sensible used-car sort of person. But for now she would have to be.

Just temporary, she told herself. Someday she would get her old life back, along with a hot car.

She settled for a new Plymouth Neon, a current year model benefiting from an end-of-model-year price slash. With November just around the corner, the dealership really wanted to boot the poor little car out the door. But even the reduced price took a bigger chunk of Mckenna's insurance check than she had bargained for. After taxes and license fees, very little money remained to add to her stash of BKB's severance pay. And that measly stash had been alarmingly diminished by moving expenses, first and last month's rent plus deposit, and a hefty payment she had made to extend her health insurance, a benefit of employment to which she had never given much thought.

Life was expensive. Too bad she no longer had that fat BKB salary to pay for it. And too bad she wasn't the sort of person to put money away for a rainy day—another thing Mckenna had discovered about herself when she had examined her check ledger. Yes, her salary had been enough to make the IRS rub its hands together in greedy anticipation, but her tastes had been high maintenance. Her account had hemorrhaged for the cause of designer clothes, a palace in Oak Creek Canyon, and a very fancy car that had suffered a bad end.

Right at the moment, besides her rapidly shrinking checking account, all she possessed in the way of ready cash was a savings account that would scarcely pay for a month's groceries. A file of statements from a brokerage firm detailed her long-term investments, which were impressive. In the long term they might make her financially secure. But rain was falling in the short term, now, and she had no fiscal umbrella to keep her from getting soaked.

"So get a job," Jane told her when Mckenna complained. They sat in the all-purpose utility room of Jane's kennel. Or rather, Mckenna sat while Jane worked on the matted coat of a giant schnauzer who stood patiently on the grooming table.

"I just got the heave-ho from one firm. I doubt any other law firm would be eager to snap me up. Especially since my Harvard education is still on vacation."

As usual, Jane lacked sympathy. "Lots of people without a Harvard law degree go to work every day, kiddo."

"Well, sure, as doctors, real estate agents, teachers"— she waved a hand toward Jane and the giant schnauzer— "dog trainers. A person has to be qualified in some line of work."

"Nope," Jane denied. "Lots of people barge right into the work force with no training at all, and they generally get by."

Mckenna scoffed. "And what kind of jobs do they get?"

"Probably the kind of job you'll get," Jane said with a chuckle, then took in the expression on Mckenna's face and softened a bit. "Hey, girl, it's only temporary—for you at least. Your old brain is going to start ticking again, and then you'll snap up an even better job than BKB. Hell, you were killing yourself for them, anyway. You'll get a better job, for more money, with nicer people—if there are any lawyers out there who can qualify as nice people."

Mckenna huffed indignantly, picked up a dirty grooming towel to throw at her abuser, then glanced at the dog and thought better of it. "Dog," she told the hundred-pound black monster, "get her."

The dog obeyed, turning its big head to give Jane a

swipe with its washrag-sized tongue. Cats weren't the only animals she could talk to, Mckenna concluded.

So all right. She had to get a job doing something she knew nothing about, probably for minimum wage. As Mckenna drove her new Neon toward Cottonwood to start her job hunt, she searched her feelings. Resentment, embarrassment, chagrin—they were clouds on the edge of her mind, stirrings of remembered prejudices. They couldn't cast a shadow on the illogical excitement brewing inside her. This was a new adventure, a safari to hunt for the true Mckenna Wright. Not Old Mckenna, as she had started to think of her pre-accident self, but the true Mckenna that Jane had advised her to find. Maybe she would learn something valuable by working at a grunt job for a while. Working with the masses. She could even get enthused about the prospect.

Until she found that even "grunt" jobs with the masses have certain standards. The personnel manager at Wal-Mart looked at Mckenna's resume and laughed. Maybe she should have left off her Harvard law degree.

She walked into the Safeway grocery store armed with toned-down expectations.

"Have you ever worked a cash register?" asked the interviewer.

"No."

"Scanner?"

"No."

"Stocked shelves?"

"No."

"Done any customer service work at all?"

"No."

"Well, what work experience do you have?"

If she had told them the truth, they would have laughed as hard as Wal-Mart. Safeway took a pass on the opportunity to add her to their employment roster. Feeling about an inch tall, she headed home to her little trailer in Cornville.

Titi gave her a lecture from her new favorite spot on top of the television. "Your whiskers are drooping to the ground. Worry, worry. Worry won't buy cat food. Don't worry. Work. Good, easy, mellow job."

Mckenna collapsed onto the sofa. "You go out there and try to find a job!"

"Cats don't work. People work."

"I thought you were supposed to be teaching me to relax."

"I am. How do we relax, starving in a cold, dark tin house?"

Obviously, the cat had not yet forgiven her for moving to the low-rent district.

"We're not going to starve. Though we might both end up eating cat food."

The cat's ears came up to alert. "You need to work. I don't want to share."

"Oh, fine! Why don't you just tell me how to find work, then."

"Confidence."

"What?"

"No one tells a cat no. A cat has confidence. Watch." Titi stretched, jumped to the floor, then strutted across the little living room with tail held high, a little swagger in her rear. She paused, sat, and looked over her shoulder with eyes half-lidded, the epitome of a superior creature barely tolerant of everything around her. "Say no to this?"

"Try that at the grocery store and see how far it gets you. Besides, being a brain-dead ex-attorney has leached the confidence right out of me."

Titi yawned. "Whine, whine. Like you were a dog left at a shelter. Learn from the cat. Don't lie around complaining. Do something useful. Make yourself feel better."

"Like what?"

"Lie in the sun." Titi's favorite. "Jump on clean laundry. Roll in a patch of grass. Dirt will do, too. Then tomorrow go work. We don't have enough cat food to share."

Mckenna dropped her head into her hands. "Some people," she muttered, "get a guardian angel when their lives fall apart. I get a cat."

The next day she answered a Help Wanted ad from a Sedona animal hospital. She and animals were good together, she reasoned. How many other people carried on conversations with cats? Unfortunately, the front-office job required computer skills, as well. Mckenna had great experience with E-mail and cruising the Internet, but accounting and word-processing programs might as well have been Greek. In her old life, secretaries and accountants had dealt with those things.

For her next dose of rejection she inquired about a teacher's aide position at the elementary school. How hard could it be, after all, to manage a pack of kids that were half her size? She had second thoughts, though, after an interview that took place in a room crowded with the little devils doing what elementary kids did—whispering, giggling, indulging in kicking contests beneath their little elementary-size desks. A paper airplane flew into the back of her head just as she was extemporizing to the interviewer why elementary education was so important in a student's overall education. But she sucked it up, smiled, and tried to imitate Titi's version of confident.

When she landed the job, Mckenna thought her luck had turned. The first day of work proved otherwise. At the end of the day, after the pint-sized savages had rushed out of the classroom to visit their special kind of chaos on the hapless school-bus drivers, the keen-eyed teacher who was Mckenna's boss gave her a sympathetic look.

"Kids make you crazy, huh?"

Mckenna, smudged with paint, aching through and through, with an obscenity scrawled across her arm in ink (how that got there she didn't even know), sighed disconsolately. "I think I'll go in tomorrow and have my tubes tied."

So much for that job.

At the end of five days of searching, Mckenna had learned a new language, the language of Help Wanted:

Enterprising (or enthusiastic, energetic, motivated) worker wanted. Translation: You'll be putting in twelve-hour days with no overtime pay.

Competitive pay. Translation: Minimum wage (or below, if we can swing it).

Good benefits. Translation: No vacation the first year, five measly days thereafter. Group health (you pay the premium). Sick leave only if you're on your deathbed.

How, Mckenna began to wonder, did anyone in this world make a living?

Then at the end of the week, Mckenna hit pay dirt: the Cottonwood McDonald's. How hard could it be to work at McDonald's? Clueless teenagers worked at McDonald's. Senior citizens who could barely remember their names worked at McDonald's. The company prided itself on hiring people with disabilities.

She had a disability, Mckenna figured. As far as she could tell, she was unemployable. That was a hell of a disability. So McDonald's should love her.

She got the job.

Her first day of work was a Monday, a quiet day in the fast-food business. Not like Saturday, Rick the manager told her, when the place was a zoo. Saturdays were really busy, he assured her. Just wait until she saw the crowds and lines on Saturday.

If Rick didn't think Monday's crowd was a "zoo," Mckenna dreaded the promised activity on Saturday. The line at her register was constant. It never let up. One person after another. As soon as she got rid of one, another hungry face appeared.

Of course, that might have had something to do with Mckenna. Funny thing about fast-food customers: They expected their food fast, and they got growly if they had to wait a bit while Mckenna tried to find the proper key on her register. Then there were the folks who wanted custom-built hamburgers. Without cheese. Without onions. Extra mayo. No tomatoes. Hold the sauce. And their drink wasn't filled to the brim, or the cup didn't have enough ice, or she'd given them Dr. Pepper instead of Coke. How the hell was she supposed to know which was which? They were the same color, after all.

"Don't let it get to you," said Charlotte, Mckenna's trainer. Charlotte was a slender, smiling girl who couldn't have been older than seventeen. How she maintained her beautiful smile in the face of working the counter was a secret that Mckenna would never know. "Everybody's first day is tough, you know? But things get easier. By Saturday, you'll feel like an old hand at this."

Mckenna already felt old. Was that half the battle to feeling like an old hand?

"I really appreciate your patience," she told Charlotte the third time she showed her how to operate the coffeemaker. She couldn't even blame her ineptitude on her stroke, since her physical therapist just the week before had declared her as close to one hundred percent as any person had a right to be.

"It's all right." Charlotte laughed. "Someday you'll be helping a trainee who's just as much of a klutzoid as you are, and you'll think back to today and laugh. We all kind of work together here, you know?"

Mckenna couldn't help but compare the patience and understanding she got from Charlotte, Rick, and most of the other cheerful workers at McDonald's to the knife she'd gotten from Pat Carter and Gil Bradner. The firm of Bradner, Kelly, and Bolin had been a wolf pack. The eight-to-four shift at McDonald's acted more like a family—

even when Mckenna dropped the French-fry basket, sending hot grease and sliced potatoes all over the floor, and when she almost caused the microwave to blow up.

"Tomorrow will be better," Rick assured her at the end of the day, smiling sympathetically.

Tomorrow had to be better, Mckenna thought as she crawled into the Neon and headed home. She couldn't survive another day like today.

At home, she dropped onto the sofa without bothering to change from the grease-spattered McDonald's polo shirt. She yanked off the McDonald's ball cap and threw it into a corner.

"I can't believe a person can work so hard for a miserable six bucks an hour and change," she groaned.

Titi jumped onto the sofa and rubbed against her appreciatively. "Smells good" came out between purrs.

"Hamburger grease," Mckenna told her. "Not to mention French-fry grease, and that spot there is vanilla yogurt, and that smear came from a hot apple pie that I dropped because the box was just a little too hot."

Titi's jaw dropped open. "Now that's a perfect job! Meat, grease, yogurt! Do they need a therapy cat?"

Mckenna smiled wryly and rubbed her aching head. "It's a possibility, considering the number of customers I put in a temper today."

"You get to spend all day around that food? They pay you for that?"

"They don't pay me much," Mckenna said.

She thought of Rick, the store manager in his midthirties, making more money than the worker bees, of course, but still spending all his days dealing with demanding customers, incompetent workers like herself, and all the little crises that accompanied the restaurant business. She thought of Charlotte, who had a one-year-old little boy at home being cared for by her mother, no husband in the picture, no education to speak of, yet still cheerful and willing to give a newcomer a helping hand. Then there was Mandy, another young jack-of-all-McDonald's-trades, who squirreled away her wages to save for college. At minimum wage, that would take a long time.

People worked in such places for years, day after day, scraping by. From what she'd seen on her job hunt, McDonald's actually seemed like a prime place to work, for someone like Mckenna, whose effective education, skills, and experience totaled pretty close to zero. She was lucky to get the job.

But lord in heaven, she didn't want to keep it. Come hell or high water, she had to regain her wits, her old job, and her old life. She might have been stressed to the max at BKB, but she had driven a dynamite car, lived in palatial digs, had money to burn, and hadn't come home from work smelling like hamburger.

That had been the life!

chapter 8

TOM MARKHAM doodled in the margin of a yellow legal pad while listening to Mckenna's phone ring. And ring and ring. At least the other times he had tried to call, her message machine had picked up. Not that she'd returned his calls. Could be that she punched ERASE the minute she heard his voice. But at least he had gotten to talk to a machine.

This time all he got was ring, ring, ring, ring. And more rings. Then finally, the line clicked.

"We're sorry," a mechanical voice apologized. "The number you are calling has been disconnected."

Disconnected? What the hell? Had she changed her phone number just to get rid of him? He drew an exclamation point on the legal pad and laughed at himself. No, Mckenna hadn't changed her number just to get rid of him. Tom Markham didn't command that kind of importance in her life, even as an annoyance. She was irked at him, true. She wouldn't return his calls, probably didn't even listen to the messages he left. But he didn't rate something drastic like a change of phone numbers.

So why had her number been disconnected? Damn!

He picked up the phone again and punched BKB's number. If Mckenna had already gone back to work, then she was a fool. She should still be taking leave. He remembered the ugly bruise at her temple, the air of confused distress when he'd last seen her. That was before she had come up with the idiot idea that he had visited just to spy out how badly she was damaged, hoping for some kind of an advantage in the Harmon case. If she'd had her head on straight, she would have known that such a stunt was in her bag of tricks, not his.

But then, she didn't have her head on straight. That was why she should still be on leave. Or at least she still *should* be on leave.

The receptionist at BKB picked up with a cheery greeting.

"Hi, Sherry. This is Tom Markham over at the county attorney's office.

"Good morning, Mr. Markham."

"I need to speak to Mckenna Wright, if she's there."

A small, awkward silence. "Ms. Wright is no longer associated with BKB, Mr. Markham. I'll transfer you to Pat Carter. She's taken on Ms. Wright's caseload."

Before he could tell her not to bother, the line clicked over, and another phone rang.

She had quit BKB? What the hell happened? BKB had been Mckenna's life, her alpha and omega, food and drink for her soul. Rumor said the firm was about to make her a partner. His gut tightened. Nothing but disaster could have prompted her to leave.

"Hello, Tom," Pat Carter greeted him. "I was meaning to call you on the prelim hearing date the judge set for Todd Harmon. Since I took over this case, I—"

He rudely interrupted. "Pat, I didn't call about that. Where's Mckenna? What happened?"

Again the small, awkward silence. "You know, Tom, I

can't really say. What goes on internally here at BKB isn't something we talk about publicly. That would be violating Mckenna's privacy."

"Is she all right?"

"Listen, if you want to talk about the case, let's talk. The cops should be ashamed of the way they handled this. They might be able to get away with treating Joe Yokel like this, but Harmon is one of country music's most popular stars. You cross him at your peril. Your professional peril, that is."

"I'm shivering in my boots, Pat. Sorry to bother you. I was looking for Mckenna. If you talk to her, ask her to call me, would you?"

He set the phone down in a very controlled manner, resisting the need to slam it into its cradle. When a girl from the secretarial pool stuck her head in his office, she halted, hesitated, and looked as if she wanted to run.

"Bad day already, Tom?"

He smoothed out his scowl. "No. Everything's fine."

"I've got those McBride depositions ready."

"Good work. Put them over there on the filing cabinet. I'll get to them later. Was there any coffee left in the pot when you passed it?"

"Yes. Would you like me to bring you a cup?"

"Don't bother, Jan. I can get it myself." He walked with her down the hall. "I thought you ladies didn't fetch coffee anymore."

Jan chuckled. "Only for people we like. Besides, you looked as if you were in the middle of something important."

"Not important as much as confusing. Sometimes life is very confusing."

"You got it."

When he got back to his office with a cup of sludge that passed for coffee, his phone was buzzing. When he picked up, Peggy Watson's voice greeted him.

"Hey, Peggy. What's up?"

"Oh, Tom. Everything's up. Or down, depending on how you look at it. I'm on my break, outside, calling from my cell phone because I didn't dare talk to you at my desk. It's about Mckenna. Sherry told me you called."

His gut clenched. "Pat Carter said that Mckenna's no longer with BKB. What happened?"

Peggy snorted her disdain. "She got fired. That's what happened. That witch Carter put a knife in her back, and Gilbert Bradner twisted it home. Pat went to lunch with her, all buddy-buddy like, and from what I gather from the office gossip, she called Bradner from the restaurant to tell him that Mckenna was confused and no longer competent in the law."

As far as it went, that much was true. Or at least it had been last time Tom had seen Mckenna. It didn't surprise him a bit that some enterprising soul had used Mckenna's temporary disability to get her out of the way. After all, a vacancy at the top left more room for advancement of those below. Not only that, but the snitch got a juicy reward. The Harmon case must look like manna from heaven to someone who would just love to spend time in the national spotlight.

On the whole, this was good news for Tom. Pat Carter was a good attorney, but even on her best day she was no match for Mckenna Wright. Having Pat defend the case gave Tom his best chance to nail Todd Harmon on a narcotics charge.

So why did he want to go to the BKB office and hang Pat out to dry?

He sighed. "Peggy, when did all this go down?"

"Almost a month ago. They put it to her the very day she came back to work. The official story is that she resigned for health reasons, but that's a load of bull. Bradner jumped at the chance to get her out of here. He's never liked her because she was Sean Kelly's golden girl, you know. Bradner and Kelly are hardly friends. But do you think Kelly would move himself to defend poor Mckenna when he heard about this? No! Of course not. I tell you, Tom, some days this place just makes me want to come to work wearing shark repellent."

Tom sighed. "Do you know where she is now? I've called her at home, but her phone's been disconnected."

"I know, and I've been very worried. I've been trying to contact Mckenna, because the witch who put the knife in her back thinks there's something missing from the Harmon files. I got the disconnected message at her old number, and I tried the other law firms in town, thinking she might have hired on with one of them. It's like she's disappeared into thin air—which is one of the reasons I wanted to talk to you. I know you and she didn't always get along, but it seemed to me that underneath it all, you were friends. You would want to help her out."

Damn! He would, if he could find her. "Listen, Peggy, Mckenna was a bit confused. Whatever happened in the accident, whether it was a stroke or just a hard knock on the head, gave her amnesia. The doctor told her she needed to take time and relax, that eventually things would right themselves, but you know Mckenna..."

"Oh, I know that girl, all right. She doesn't have a patient bone in her entire body."

"Well, that makes me even more concerned. We really need to find her. Could you ask around the office—discreetly, of course—to find out if anyone knows anything?"

"Sure I will, Tom. And if I learn anything, I'll give you a call right away."

Tom hung up, then cussed. He reminded himself that Mckenna Wright was a grown woman, that her Swiss cheese memory didn't mean she wasn't competent to handle her own life, and that she didn't need him riding to the rescue. In fact, she wouldn't want him riding to the rescue.

The contrary woman didn't even like him. Even when he tried to be nice, she accused him of playing the villain.

None of his reasoning worked, though. He wanted to know where she was and if she was all right. He was contemplating the advantages of talking to a detective acquaintance when he remembered Mckenna's girlfriends. Those three were thick as thieves. If anyone knew where Mckenna was hiding out, they would.

Except he knew neither their phone numbers nor their last names. One of them ran the training class where he'd taken his dog Clara. He had just opened the phone book to look through the Yellow Pages when his intercom buzzed.

"Mr. Markham, Peggy Watson from BKB is on line three."

That was fast, he thought as he picked up the phone. "Hey, Peggy! Do you happen to know how to get hold of Mckenna's friends, Jane Something and Nell Something?"

"Yes, I have their phone numbers. Goodness! Why didn't I think of that myself? But listen, I have a piece of curious information for you."

"What?"

"It's so unlikely that I hesitate to pass it along, really."

Where Mckenna was concerned, lately, "unlikely" was the norm. "Unlikely information is better than no information at all."

"One of the legal clerks swore she saw Mckenna yesterday afternoon in Cottonwood." Peggy hesitated. Tom could almost see her chewing her lip. "And the curious part is, she says Mckenna was working at McDonald's. The one over on Highway 260. Not eating lunch there, mind you. That would be strange enough for Mckenna, because I've never known her to approach within ten yards of fat. But *working* there? Doesn't that just beat all?"

"That is unlikely," Tom admitted. "But thanks. It's

worth checking out. And if she's not there, well hey, I can get myself a Big Mac and chocolate shake."

An hour later, Tom walked into McDonald's, not really expecting to find Mckenna behind the counter. As Peggy had noted, the Mckenna they both knew confronted fat wielding a cross and a string of garlic.

But there she was, indeed, looking like a teenager in her McDonald's uniform, filling trays with hamburgers, chicken sandwiches, drinks, and hot apple pies. She looked harried, her brow creased in concentration as she glared at her register. A tendril of hair had escaped the confines of her cap and hung unattended near her eye— very un-Mckenna-like.

As Tom watched, a man crowded into the front of Mckenna's line and thrust a soft drink up to her face. Even from where Tom stood, he could see her color up at whatever it was the customer said to her. Then she took a deep breath, put on an apologetic smile, dumped the soft drink, and gave him another. Meanwhile, the hungry people waiting in her line looked close to turning into an angry mob.

Poor Mckenna. She looked as out of place as caviar in a Happy Meal. But maybe just to Tom's eyes, which were accustomed to seeing her battling in a far different arena.

She hadn't noticed him when he walked in, so Tom got into line behind a weary-looking woman with three children who wanted one of everything on the menu, or so it seemed to Tom. Mckenna labored to keep the order straight, succeeding only on the third try while the mother rolled her eyes and the children bounced up and down, changing their minds every few seconds about drinks and whether or not they wanted fries. Finally they left, tray piled high, and Mckenna faced Tom across the counter.

"Omigod! Tom!" Her face turned beet-red.

"Guilty as charged. Howdy, Mckenna. I was beginning to think you'd dropped off the face of the earth."

"You were hoping, maybe. No such luck. What do you want?"

"Well, mostly I wanted to confirm that you're still alive."

She glared. "Obviously, I am. Now, what do you want?" She pointed at the menu suspended above them. "To eat."

"Uh...Big Mac with cheese, large fries, chocolate shake."

Avoiding his eyes, she rang it up and took his money.

"Eat lunch with me?"

"I can't. I'm working."

"You can't spare thirty minutes?"

"No."

"What is this, a sweat shop?"

"It's a place of business that expects its employees to put in a full day's work, unlike government offices where *some* people work." She gave him a pointed look.

He tsked. "The Mckenna we all know and love is coming back, I see. Where's the manager?"

She shoved a tray toward him. "Tom, go eat your hamburger."

But Rick had overheard his question. "I'm the manager," he said with long-suffering geniality. "Is there a problem?"

Tom flashed his ID. "No problem. I'm from the county attorney's office, and I'd like to talk to Ms. Wright for a few minutes. Is that all right?"

As he'd known it would, the words "county attorney" inspired instant cooperation.

"Of course it's all right," Rick said, throwing a curious look toward Mckenna. "Take as long as you need."

Mckenna was less impressed, and therefore less cooperative. She didn't openly rebel as he led her to a table in the least-occupied corner of the seating area, but she did freeze him with a glacial glare.

"You can lose the indignation," he told her. "I do need

to talk to you. No one knows where to find you, you know. Peggy Watson is worried, and so was I. What's going on?"

"Is it your business?"

"You bet it is. You don't keep friends dangling just because you're too lazy to pick up a phone and give us your new number."

"Friends. Right!" Her tone dripped sarcasm. "We're friends."

"We are friends, Mac."

She merely snorted. "Well, *friend*, I don't have a phone right now."

He gave her a long, thoughtful look. "Okay. Spill it, Mckenna. What's going on?"

"I got fired."

"I knew that."

"That should make you happy. Now you don't have to worry about me getting my wits back and making a fool of you on the Harmon case."

He chuckled. "You still think that's what I'm concerned about? Believe me, I would have trounced you in court, even if you got your wits back with interest added. Facing you in court on the Harmon case hasn't given me a moment's worry." A lie, but too small to send him to hell, Tom figured. "But a disconnected phone and a friend disappearing from the face of the earth makes me downright fretful."

She eyed him cautiously, then gave him a half-smile. "Really?"

In that moment, she looked so like the Mckenna he'd always suspected lay beneath the ice queen armor that he almost choked on a French fry.

"Really," he managed to cough out.

She gazed at him thoughtfully for a moment. Then her eyes dropped to his hamburger. "Are you going to eat that entire Big Mac?"

"Uh . . . you want half?"

"You *are* taking up my lunch break."

"I guess that's fair." He cut the hamburger in two and watched curiously while she dug in. "I don't believe you're eating that."

"It's good. A person can't work here without developing a taste for a nicely done hamburger."

"Mckenna Wright, eating like a normal person—it's a miracle."

"And did I mention that I get a discount? It's one of the many perks of the job. The fries are good, too. Are you going to eat those? I could help."

"Go right ahead."

She had put on a few pounds, Tom observed. He wasn't surprised, the way she made his lunch disappear. He didn't blame her. She had years of noneating to make up for. The extra weight looked good on her. Good, indeed! She looked like a woman instead of a twig. Her hair looked different as well—less sculpted, softer. No more Corporate Barbie. Mckenna had joined the human race.

"Why are you looking at me like that?" She eyed him suspiciously.

"Just thinking you look good in that McDonald's shirt."

"You like the dab of vanilla shake on the sleeve?"

"Nice accessory."

"I thought so."

Tom shook his head at her mocking tone. Mocking with an undertone of good humor. "Mckenna, what the hell are you doing, working here?"

She popped a fry into her mouth. "I told you. I got fired."

"So Bradner fired you. But McDonald's?"

With a crosswise look, she explained. "Tom, I don't remember the law, which, as it turns out, is my only qualification to do anything. Right now I don't know a habeas corpus from a Corpus Christi. You'd be surprised at the number of potential employers who passed on the opportunity to snap me up. Safeway grocery, Wal-Mart, the school district..."

It wasn't his business, but he had to ask. "Are you getting by?"

Her mouth tightened, telling him more than her words would. She wasn't nearly as cool with the situation as she might have him believe.

"I'm getting along fine, so you don't need to waste your time worrying about poor little Mckenna. I rented my house on Oak Creek and moved to a very funky little place in Cornville. The Oak Creek property was too big for me, anyway. And"—she fingered the dark lock that fell to fall into her face—"I see you've noticed my new style. Did you know that my hairdresser charges eighty dollars just for a trim? Or I should say charged, in the past tense, because obviously I can't spend two days' pay just to patronize Georges. I found him by looking at my check register. Styles by Georges. His clientele reads like a Who's Who of Sedona. I don't think he has a last name. Everyone just calls him *Georges* in sort of an awestruck, worshipful tone."

Which was way more than Tom needed to know. Mckenna excelled at distracting from the real issue. She used to pull that stunt in the courtroom, to great advantage. "Mckenna, you'll get it all back, you know. In the meantime, don't you have family?..."

"Oh, sure," she snapped. "They're in Denver. I looked them up in my address book, to make sure, but I did sort of remember them. I'm thirty years old, Tom. I'm not running back to Mom and Dad. I can stand on my own two feet without depending on anyone's charity."

"When it's family and friends helping out, Mckenna, that doesn't count as charity. That's love and friendship."

"Love and friendship, eh?" Her eyes narrowed. "Just how close were we before my accident?"

He grinned and lied. "Pretty damned close."

Her look dissected him. "I think you're full of horseshit." Then, apparently satisfied with her own level of discernment, she smiled. "But hey, Tom, I appreciate the concern. Don't worry about me. One of these days you'll see me in court again, and I'll flatten you like roadkill. So don't get used to the free ride with the likes of Pat Carter. Oops! Look at that line. I really have to go."

She got up, leaned over the table, and unexpectedly bussed his cheek.

"Thanks for the hamburger, Cowboy."

A bit stunned, he watched her thread her way through the lunch crowd. She had called him Cowboy and not even noticed it. That was the name she had pinned on him when she found out he had ridden the rodeo circuit. Her memory was coming back in ways she didn't even notice.

Tom grinned. Cowboy. Always before, the name had come off her lips sounding like a slur. Not today. Today it had sounded almost sweet. And she had kissed him. His cheek tingled warmly from the casual brush of her lips.

Damned if the woman hadn't warmed his heart, as well.

Fifteen minutes later, he pulled into the driveway of the Bark Park, whose address he had looked up in the pay phone Yellow Pages just outside of McDonald's. He had a pile of work waiting for him at his office in Prescott, an hour's drive away, but there was something he had to do first.

When he walked in, Jane Connor looked up from her desk behind the counter. Her brows lifted. "Tom?"

"Hi, Jane."

She got up and walked around the counter to greet him. "What the hell are you doing here?"

"Nice welcome."

A border collie and golden retriever both wriggled from beneath Jane's desk and shot out to join them. "Don't bite him, boys," Jane warned the dogs. "You'll end up in court." The two gamboled around his feet, bowing and squirming for attention. They didn't jump up, though they both obviously wanted to.

"I wish my Clara behaved this well. How do you train a dog not to jump?"

"You should know, Counselor. You took Clara through my obedience class. But something tells me that's not why you're here."

"Something tells you right."

"Okay, then why *are* you here?"

"I just had a chat with Mckenna. Do you know where she's working?"

"She found a job? Great! Good for her. We haven't talked in a week or so."

"Jane, she's working at McDonald's!"

"All right! I wonder if she'd give me a discount on a Big Mac?" She chuckled. "Mckenna flipping burgers at McDonald's. Now there's a picture I never would have imagined."

"I don't think they're letting her do anything as dangerous as flipping burgers. There would likely be half-cooked meat ending up in someone's face."

Jane chuckled. "I can picture that, too."

"Jane! This isn't funny. Mckenna doesn't belong there."

"What's wrong with McDonald's? Lots of honest people work at McDonald's."

"Very few of them Harvard-educated attorneys."

Jane grinned. "Considering the way people sue at the drop of a hat, I wouldn't be surprised if they have an attorney or two on staff."

"You know what I mean. What kind of friend are you— hell, what kind of friends are *we*, to let her slave all day saying, 'You want fries with that?' for minimum wage?"

"Hey, working at McDonald's isn't the end of the world, you know. You're talking to someone who picks up dog poop for a living, among other things. Besides, I remember a time not too far back when you would have crowed a bit to see Miss High-and-Mighty pay a visit to the real world. Don't deny it."

How could he deny it? Ever since they first met, Mckenna had both fascinated and annoyed him. She was driven, a professional perfectionist, and her world had revolved around getting to the top. He had fantasized more than once about giving her a dose of reality. Although where Mckenna was concerned, that certainly wasn't the only thing he had fantasized about.

Now she was suffering a dose of reality far beyond anything Tom could have imagined, and it didn't set well with him. Heaven knew he should be crowing, but he wasn't. Seeing her struggle with the fast-food crowd made him want to reach out and snatch her away from there.

As these thoughts ran through his head, Jane regarded him astutely. "Doesn't feel as good as you might have thought, seeing her brought down off her high horse?"

He grimaced and nodded.

"So you think we ought to fix things, huh?" She sighed. "Well, I guess there's been a time or two that I might have wanted to shake that woman until her teeth rattled, but you're right. Mckenna shouldn't be working at Mickey D's. For one thing, she's probably screwing up the service but good."

"You're right about that," Tom admitted.

Jane nodded. "Mckenna's a kick-ass lawyer and a great gal, but practically speaking, she's not good at much of anything besides getting her hair done. You're right. We ought to help. Have any ideas, hot shot?"

Tom grinned. "As a matter of fact, I do."

MCKENNA HAD Saturday off, and she had never been so glad to see the end of a workweek. How anyone survived doing this sort of work for months, or heaven forbid, for years, was beyond her. Her feet sported blisters, her back ached, her voice had all but disappeared, hoarse from "Large fry or small?" or "Sorry, sir or ma'am, no breakfast after ten-thirty in the morning."

Some parts of the job weren't all that bad. The people were nice, both the crew and the customers—for the most part. Except for Rick the manager, the crew averaged at least ten years younger than her. But they included her in their conversation, laughed at her jokes, helped her out when she faltered—which was about ninety-five percent of the time—and generally disproved the common complaint that Generation X (or Y or Z, whichever they belonged to) cared for no one but themselves.

The customers, on the other hand, could be cranky. They objected to lukewarm sandwiches, and they didn't care much for getting a regular Coke when they ordered diet.

If she stuck at it long enough, someday Mckenna might get it right. But lord, she didn't want to stick with the job that long. The days she had spent on the fast-food assembly line had convinced her that she had to do something—anything!—to get her life back. Drudgery, she had discovered, just wasn't her thing. But what was she going to do about it? Right then, she didn't have a clue.

But on this bright November Saturday morning, she wouldn't worry about that. Today she didn't have to don the uniform and take up arms in the hamburger battle. Today was just for her. Her and Titi.

And they spent it doing something Mckenna thought she would never enjoy—yard work. A week before she had thrown seed onto the dirt in front of the trailer, euphemistically known as the yard, since the growing season in the Verde Valley really wasn't over until December. And now tiny green blades were springing up everywhere, along with not so tiny weeds. So Mckenna was actually on hands and knees in the dirt to pull the offending interlopers from her newborn lawn. Titi lay placidly at her side, supervising.

"Dirt-digging—good," the cat insisted. "Sand better. Dig lots, no stress. Flower beds grow catnip? Cats need catnip."

Shortly after their move, Mckenna had noticed Titi's conversation growing less articulate. At first she had been alarmed, thinking the cat might be sick. And then she had realized that Titi talked just as much. Mckenna's brain had just grown less facile in translation. She hoped that meant the old gray matter was healing.

Still, the prospect of someday not hearing Titi's lectures, officious observations, and unsolicited advice saddened her. At first annoying, not to mention alarming, the cat's verbosity had become part of Mckenna's life.

Not that she would ever let the hairball dictator know how much comfort she brought. The cat already thought she was God's gift to humankind.

Mckenna ignored the catnip slipping into the conversation. "What do you know about stress, anyway?" she inquired with a snort of disbelief. "What possible stress could a cat have?"

"Lots, living with you. Stay at work hours and hours. No one here to open cat food."

"You have kitty kibble out all day long."

Titi made a rude noise, something she was surprisingly good at for a cat. "You eat kitty kibble. See how much you like."

In the middle of this discussion, Jane's van drove up, followed by a Dodge Ram diesel truck. Mckenna rocked back on her heels and swiped a dirty hand across her brow, leaving a streak of dirt so thick she could feel it.

Jane got out of her van, took in the bucolic little scene, and laughed in delight. "I don't believe you're doing that. Are you actually putting in a lawn? You, yourself, with your own two hands?"

"Well, right now I can't afford to hire any other hands to do it for me. Besides, someone told me that scratching in the dirt is good for the soul." She glanced down at Titi, who had gotten up, stretched, then lay back down in the exact same spot.

Tom walked up behind Jane. He took in Mckenna's dirty jeans and smudged face with an amused smile. "You're just full of all sorts of energy."

That smile of his tickled something inside her, but she didn't know if it was annoyance or a contrary sort of excitement. "What's it to you, Cowboy?"

"It's a good thing," Tom told her as he and Jane came through the gate. "Because Jane and I both have ideas for all that energy." He grinned as he looked down at her still sitting in the dirt. "We come bearing propositions."

chapter 9

TODD HARMON fretted in one of the plush chairs of BKB's lobby. He didn't have time to come back from Nashville to deal with this mess. He had two more songs to record before his current album would be finished, and Hal Davis, his producer, was breathing down his neck about staying on schedule. He'd cancelled a cover photo shoot to fly to Arizona and twiddle his thumbs in some lawyer's office. As if he—Nashville's hottest star—had to jump at these people's beck and call. He didn't see why Buddy couldn't take care of these things. Didn't this new attorney know what kind of schedule a major star like Todd Harmon kept? Hell, in two weeks, his concert tour started in Kansas City. Then he'd be off to St. Louis, Chicago, Atlanta, Salt Lake City, Seattle, and Phoenix. He had to finish the album before all that started, and just how was he going to do that sitting around talking to some lawyer? Or worse still, sitting in the lobby waiting, as he was doing right now.

Buddy should have been handling it. Or at least Buddy should have been there so Todd could have someone to vent on. He had nerve breaking his leg and ending up in the hospital. Men Buddy's age shouldn't play tennis. *And major Nashville stars shouldn't get their ass caught in a wringer with the law,* said the voice inside his head that never did believe he could amount to anything more than a banjo-playing bum. Forget old guys making fools of themselves playing tennis. How about young stupid guys making fools of themselves by throwing away a fantastic career?

You're scared, the voice taunted. *First you were stupid. Now you're scared.*

The giggly receptionist put down the phone and blushed prettily. "Mr. Harmon, Ms. Carter will be right out."

The girl's obvious adoration quieted the taunting inner voice. "Thank you, ma'am." He touched the brim of his hat in a gentlemanly salute. The women loved that—old-fashioned country manners. And Todd liked to please his fans. He made money one fan at a time.

The girl had been blushing since he walked through the door. These days, he didn't run into many people who weren't fans of Todd Harmon. Too bad the Yavapai county attorney couldn't be counted among them.

Pat Carter strutted into the lobby with a big welcoming smile on her face. "Todd!" She held out a manicured hand in greeting. "Thank you for interrupting your busy schedule to make time for this. I'm sorry I had to keep you waiting."

Sure she was. Like he couldn't recognize a power play for what it was.

"But come into my office. It's more comfortable than the conference room. Would you like another cup of coffee? Or I can send Sherry out for something else. Anything you like."

"No thanks. Let's just get down to business and get this

over with. I'm finishing up an album, and I'd like to be back in Nashville tomorrow."

"Of course. I'm a big fan, you know. Goodness, I've followed you since the beginning of your career."

"That's nice, Ms.? . . ."

"Carter. Pat Carter. And I'm so sorry we had to switch attorneys on you, Todd, but at least it's early in the case, and the change won't be to your disadvantage, I assure you."

Todd wasn't so sure. He had liked Mckenna Wright. She was a no-nonsense sort of woman, oozing confidence, who gave the impression that she ate prosecuting attorneys for lunch. She hadn't been all that impressed with Todd's status as a major star, and he liked that. He didn't like it in anyone else he had to deal with, but he did like having a no-holds-barred attorney who wasn't easily impressed.

On the other hand, as Buddy had warned him, Mckenna was *too* smart at times. She had found out about Maria before he sent the girl out of range of dangerous questions. Eventually, of course, he would have convinced Mckenna that Maria wasn't important, that there was no sense in sharing her existence with the county attorney's people, since they would never find out on their own. Eventually he would have won her over, but the lady did have a stubborn streak.

Todd hoped that Pat Carter was the flexible sort who realized that rules didn't always need to be followed to the last letter, especially when a man's career was at stake. So maybe the attorney change wasn't a bad idea. Buddy had celebrated when he read the law firm's letter informing Todd that another attorney would be handling the case. But then, Buddy Morris and Mckenna Wright had rubbed each other wrong from the very first.

Pat led him to a spacious office where Gil Bradner waited for them. The partner stood and offered a hand.

"Todd! You look great, boy! Sorry we had to get you down here, but with the change in attorneys . . ."

"Yeah, I know. Let's just get on with it."

But Bradner wanted to chitchat for a few minutes before he left them to their business. Todd guessed the man just wanted to be able to say that he directly supervised Todd Harmon's escape from the looming possibility of prison.

Prison. Todd shied away from the thought.

"Well," Pat said after Bradner had left. "Here we are. Down to business, then. I think, just so we're on the same page, you should run through everything that happened on that night that you allegedly sold the cocaine to the undercover police officers."

"I didn't sell anything to anyone," he insisted. "It was a joke, for chrissakes. Don't these people have any sense of humor?"

She smiled. "Law officers seldom have a sense of humor. Neither does the county attorney. He's very interested in running for governor, and he wants to make a name for himself as being a tough, no-nonsense kind of guy. But I wouldn't worry too much. We regularly take on his minions and make mincemeat of them."

Her confidence smoothed some of Todd's ruffled feathers. "Yeah, well, that better be the way it works. I don't want some minor-league politician making hash out of my career just so he can add to his reputation."

"Not going to happen. So, down to business. How many people were at your home the evening all this went down?"

"A hundred. Maybe more. My parties tend to grow, you know?"

"Were there drugs in use at the party?"

Todd shrugged. "Probably. It was a real jumping party, and there were a lot of heavy hitters there. NFL stars. A couple of Hollywood types—Matt Severs from *Bad Boys.* He got the Emmy last year, you know."

"I remember."

"Yeah, well, Ben Affleck dropped by for a while, and Julia, and Britney—they just flew into the airport, stayed a little while, then flew out again. And there was a whole mob of Nashville people there. My producer, a load of studio musicians, backup singers, technical guys. Clint Black came for a while. Anyway, I'm not saying that any of those guys are users, but the whole entertainment gig isn't as uptight and straitlaced as, you know, people who aren't a part of that scene. So there was some dope going around, I guess. Probably some coke here and there. I wouldn't be surprised. Not to mention booze. Nothing illegal about booze. When I give a party, there's fountains of it. Everyone, including me, was drinking like a fish. We were feeling no pain, you know?"

"So you were drunk?"

"I'm not sure I would call it drunk."

She raised a brow.

"Okay, I was drunk, if you want to get technical. Nothing illegal about that. And then these two guys ask me if I could sell them a little coke. Hell, I thought it was a joke."

"They asked you? Directly asked you?"

"Sure they asked me."

"You're sure about that, because that doesn't jibe with the police report."

"Well, I think that's what happened. Like I said, I was drinking a lot. But the whole thing with the coke was a joke. Hell, like I need to sell drugs to make a living?"

She made him go over the scenario again, pounding him on the details. Who had seen the alleged transaction? What did he know about the stash the police found in the back of his dresser drawer in the bedroom?

"Planted?" he guessed. "Or one of the guests hid his stash for safekeeping. I don't know."

He waited for her to bring up Maria, because Mckenna had claimed that she had questioned the maid and taken notes. Those notes had to be somewhere in the files.

Hell, Maria could make the prosecution's case, for sure. Lucky for Todd that Maria liked him. She didn't want to make trouble, and her dearest wish had been to return to her family in Mexico with enough money to get them out of the shack where they lived. If Mckenna hadn't talked to the girl before she'd gone—but she had.

Pat *hmmmed* a bit while leafing through the pages in front of her. "Is there anything that comes to mind that we haven't covered, Todd? It seems to me that something is missing here. Mckenna was a stickler for organization. She always numbered her files sequentially, and a couple of numbers are missing."

"I've told you everything I told her." That wasn't strictly a lie, because Todd hadn't told Mckenna about Maria. She'd found out on her own.

"Well, I'll just have to talk to Mckenna and ask her what she did with the rest of this pile."

The rest of the pile. Todd's heart sank. Were Mckenna's notes on Maria in the missing "rest of the pile"?

He tried to sound casual as he asked, "How is Mckenna, anyway? I read about her accident in the newspaper. Hell, she must have a whole troop of angels watching over her. I know that place in the road where she went over, and man! She's lucky to be alive."

"Yes, she is. But she got shaken up a good deal."

"Mckenna's a hell of a tough lady. Good lawyer, too."

Her smile acquired an edge. "So am I, Todd. Don't worry. You're in good hands."

"Yeah. I didn't mean to sound like ... uh ... Did Mckenna go to another law firm?"

Pat looked a bit uneasy. "No. She didn't. Since you're so concerned, I guess I can tell you that Mckenna had some brain damage from the accident."

The flood of relief that washed over Todd made him ashamed. He liked Mckenna. He should be horrified at the news. "Brain damage. Damn! That sucks."

"Yes, well, we can all hope for her recovery. Mckenna didn't handle stress all that well, in my opinion, and this work involves a lot of stress. The word is that she had a stroke, and that's what made her lose control of her car. Blood pressure, and all that. But in your business, you must know all about stress."

A stroke. Another wave of relief. The newspaper had been right. Brain damage and a stroke. Todd Harmon and Maria would be the last thing on Mckenna's mind.

"Don't you?" Pat prompted.

"Uh ... sorry. What?"

"Know all about what stress can do to a person."

"You got that right."

The smile she gave him was almost a smirk. "For my part, I'd rather give stress than keep it. I consider it my job to give prosecuting attorneys as much stress as possible. And in the case of *State of Arizona* v. *Harmon*, I think we can do that. Together.

"So ... now let's talk about the preliminary hearing. ..."

She went on for another half hour, talking about legal strategies, evidence, lack of evidence, and so on and so forth, to Todd's utter boredom and lack of understanding. Never once did she ask him to confirm the absolute truth of the very creative account he had given her of the night he had been arrested. Probably she didn't care. Truth, he knew, had very little to do with guilty or not-guilty verdicts in criminal trials.

Before he left, Todd asked for Mckenna's address. "I'd like to send her some flowers," he told Pat. "And a copy of my new album, once it comes out. Just to let her know I haven't forgotten about her."

"That's sweet," Pat said. "But I think she's moved from where she lived when she worked here. You might stop at

Peggy Watson's desk on your way out. She used to be Mckenna's secretary, and she might have the new address."

Todd did just that, and got what he needed after signing his autograph on a napkin for Peggy. "Thank you, ma'am," he said, oozing boyish charm. He did love to make the older ladies blush. "I'm going to send Mckenna a big bunch of roses, and darned if I won't make my grouchy manager do the same. She's one special lady."

He left BKB's offices with a spring in his step that hadn't been there when he had walked in. Things were definitely looking up. Maria apparently wasn't in the files Mckenna had left for Pat, and if the girl and her whereabouts had been in Mckenna's brain, likely they were gone, disappeared in a burst of blood pressure. He felt bad for Mckenna, but this was great news for Todd Harmon. If the notes on Maria had truly gone missing—maybe destroyed in the car accident—then he might be home free. Buddy would order a magnum of champagne to celebrate. This had almost been worth the trip from Nashville.

Todd folded his lanky frame into his Mercedes sports convertible, whistled a tune that might someday be a new hit single, and took out his phone to dial Buddy's cell. When Buddy answered, he couldn't help but needle a bit.

"Hey, Bud. How're the nurses treating you?"

"Go screw yourself" was Buddy's reply.

Todd chuckled. "Maybe I should ask how you're treating the poor nurses." Buddy was a great manager and agent, but his impatience with adversity was legend.

"Cut the crap, Todd. How did it go with Carter?"

"Great. She's a fan."

"Whoop-de-doo. I mean legally."

"I know what you meant, Bud. Just pulling your chain. It went great. She doesn't know about Maria. Mckenna's got her brains scrambled from that stroke that sent her off the cliff. I sort of gathered that BKB let her go because she wasn't the sharp tack she used to be."

"Maria's not in the files?"

"Nope. Carter said a few might be missing. She thinks Mckenna might have them, but maybe if they were with her in the car, they got trashed in the accident."

Thoughtful silence from Buddy, then, "When I talked to Mckenna after the accident, she seemed real vague. I pushed her on the subject of problems in the defense, and she didn't say a thing. So maybe her head is scrambled. I just hope those files, if they exist, don't turn up."

"Carter didn't seem too worried about them. She did mention something about calling Mckenna to ask about them, but I think she just threw that out there. Anyway, I changed the subject real fast, so maybe she'll forget."

"Aren't you clever?"

Todd ground his teeth at the sarcasm. Buddy had made him. Literally made him. But the man had never given him credit for owning half a brain.

"I got Mckenna's new address," he told Buddy. "I'm going to send a heap of roses."

"That's sweet," Buddy said mockingly.

"I thought so. Hell, Buddy, none of this is Mckenna's fault. Her brains are scrambled, she lost her job, and she lost her nice house, too. This address is in the middle of nowhere over by Cornville."

"You'd just better hope that she lost those interview notes that she told you about."

Todd grimaced. "Yeah. You're right. Do you want the address? Or do you want me to put your name on the card with mine?"

Buddy was silent for a moment, then, "Give me the address. I'll send her something. I surely will."

MCKENNA LOOKED down the long row of Bark Park kennels, feeling very much as though this had been a bad idea. There were ten kennels along this aisle, five on each side, big six-foot-square pens bounded by chain link six feet tall on the sides and stretched over the top so that the jumpers couldn't escape their confinement. A dog door in each kennel led to the outdoor part of the run, where the "guests" could breathe fresh air, watch birds wheeling overhead, and hopefully, tend to their business on the gravel outdoors rather than the concrete indoors.

What Mckenna could see of the kennels confirmed that things didn't always happen that way, the polite, mannerly way. Dogs will be dogs, after all.

An aisle of ten big pens, and two more identical aisles in other wings of the kennel building made thirty big kennels in all. And up front were the cages for the little dogs, and the cat room. One couldn't forget the cat room, each cat condominium with its litter box that required daily cleaning.

"Go to it, kiddo," Jane said cheerfully. "This job doesn't require a lot of training. But be careful of the Rottweiler in kennel eight. He's a bit grouchy when you first go in to clean."

A grouchy Rottweiler? Jane hadn't said anything about grouchy hundred-pound Rottweilers when she had proposed this idea of hers. Mckenna should have known better. She should have told both Jane and Tom thank you very much, but one job was all she could handle. And here they wanted to pile on two more—only one of which involved getting paid.

But she needed the extra income. In her former life, when she had been living in her log-and-glass palace and wearing designer suits to her designer job, had she ever understood the concept of scraping by? Mckenna thought not. A few days at McDonald's had taught her that hard, honest work didn't necessarily mean you earned a living wage.

And speaking of hard, honest work... Mckenna grimaced as Jane handed her the pooper-scooper. "Did I ever do this in my former life?"

Jane knit her brows. "I think you helped me out once or twice."

"Did I like it?"

"Sure you did."

"You're certain about that?"

"Well, you must have survived. You're here. But wait. Maybe you watched the front office while Nell and I worked back here. I don't remember."

Mckenna's eyes narrowed.

"You'll be fine," Jane said with airy assurance. "I'll be next door in aisle two if you need me. Just yell if you have a problem."

"Right."

Jane left her alone with the scoop and pail, alone with only Titi for company. The cat sat sphinxlike on a shelf beside a pile of dog-food bags.

"Bad idea," the cat warned. "Too many dogs."

"And cats," Mckenna reminded her. "Don't forget the cats."

"Snots," Titi proclaimed. "Hissy snots."

"I take it you said 'Hello' and they didn't appreciate it."

"Snots," Titi repeated. "Rude."

Mckenna sighed. "I don't know if I can do this."

The education she had taken for granted had made all the difference between living well and barely living. First McDonald's, and now this. With every bag of fries she served at Mickey D's, she swore that if she ever regained that precious education, she would appreciate it every day of her life. Every floor she mopped, every table she wiped, added to her determination to do something to turn the light back on in that part of her brain.

That was the reason she had given in to Jane and Tom's mad plan. Working at the kennel as well as the restaurant would give her enough income to at least survive, and the other part of the plan...

Well, the kennels in front of her were scary enough. She didn't even want to think about Tom's part of the scheme.

The dogs in the pens looked at her intently, seeming to dare her to just make their day. Mckenna shook her head. "I can't do this."

"You can," Titi told her. "Now is survival time. Tell dogs we're in charge. Me, too, right?"

"You probably have more authority with these creatures than I have."

"Good. With dogs, stand straight. Talk low. Act tough. Dogs stupid. They'll believe."

"And the snotty cats?"

"Puff up. Says you're one bad cat."

"Right. Okay. Sure thing." She gathered her courage. "Here goes."

By the end of thirty minutes, she had cleaned one side of the aisle. The Rottweiler in kennel eight had given her a puzzled look when she had gotten her signals confused and tried to puff up like a cat, then he had retreated to a corner and let her go about her business. Other dogs had been friendly, bored, barky, whining, or anxious for attention. Much to her surprise, Mckenna found herself almost having fun, petting dogs on the head, having silly conversations with them. Going from dog to dog, kennel to kennel, would have been a picnic if not for her primary purpose with the scoop and the pail. As it was, the sheer volume that some of these furballs could produce astonished her. Her delicate sensibilities soon took a hike, simply out of sheer necessity.

Okay, cleaning kennels wasn't quite the hell she had thought it would be. But the law had to be better. Someday...Someday soon, she hoped.

Mckenna drew herself up and regarded her furry

charges with a serious mien. "Ladies and gentlemen of the jury."

Her audience watched attentively, tails wagging.

"Regard this poor defendant." With sweeping drama, she gestured toward Titi, who hunkered beside a bag of dog food and glared. "A cat. Wrongfully accused of"—she thought for a few seconds, then grabbed a rubber bone sitting on the shelf—"accused of pilfering this valuable, uh, bone, a suspect mainly because of her unfortunate, uh, felineness. I ask you, good people..."

Her opening argument faltered at the sound of Jane's chuckle.

"Your client wouldn't have a chance with these guys as a jury."

Mckenna's face grew hot.

"Not bad, though. Tom will have you talking to human juries again in no time. Is this as far as you've gotten?"

"I thought I was doing well."

Jane laughed. "Maybe for a first-timer."

"You said I'd done this before," Mckenna said suspiciously.

"I remember now, for sure. You watched the office. Yep. Let's get busy. I'll help. Remember, we still have all the outside sections to clean."

"Oh, joy."

"So, if your jury will excuse us..."

Mckenna discovered that the work went faster when she had someone to talk to, maybe because she didn't focus so much on the details of what she was doing.

"You're going to Tom's tonight, right?" Jane asked as they got to work on the outside runs.

"Yes. First tutoring session." Her stomach lurched when she thought about it.

"You don't sound too happy about it."

Mckenna hesitated, then confessed. "I'm scared, I guess. What if I try really, really hard and get nowhere? If I can't wake up that part of my brain, I don't think I want to know." Only the loom of McDonald's in her future—or some other similar job—kept her from phoning Tom and calling the whole thing off.

The loom of McDonald's—and, Mckenna admitted to herself, a certain allure in the prospect of spending an evening looking across a desk at Tom Markham. "I think Tom's doing this because he feels guilty," she speculated. "He seems to think that he hassled me to the edge of my brain exploding."

"Could be. Whenever you and he were together, I did notice your face getting red. I don't know if that was because he annoyed you, or he got your blood running, if you know what I mean."

" 'Got my blood running'? You mean, like turned me on? You said I gave him the old kiss-off."

"Yeah, well, that doesn't mean you didn't harbor secret yearnings. Sometimes you had peculiar reasons for doing what you did. I never claimed to understand what made you tick."

"Hm."

After a few minutes in which the only sound was the conversations of the dogs and the scrape of the scoopers, Jane added. "I don't think Tom offered law tutoring out of guilt. Though that's maybe what he's telling himself."

"Why, then?"

"Stupid question, Counselor. That man has always had the hots for you. You should have seen him when he stormed over to my place after finding you at McDonald's. We just couldn't stand by and watch you work your fingers to the bone, he said. Or yelled. He almost yelled."

"So you thought it would help to pile on two more jobs?"

"Well, it seemed like a good idea at the time. After all, you can use the extra cash, can't you?"

"Only if I want to pay my rent every month."

"That's what we figured. I tell you, the man has a thing for you."

Mckenna made a rude sound. Tom Markham could probably have just about any woman he wanted. What woman wouldn't fall for that down-home drawl and those kind blue eyes? Yes, Mckenna decided, his eyes were kind even when he was cracking a joke at her expense. Could he truly be carrying a torch for her, in spite of their tarnished history?

"That's a peculiar smile on your face," Jane noted. "You really like scooping, eh? I told you it wasn't that bad."

"No." Mckenna laughed. "I was thinking about Tom."

"Ah. That explains it."

"No. Nothing like what you're thinking in that romantic imagination of yours."

"Not a shred of romance in me," Jane assured her.

"I was just thinking that I don't exactly know what to think about Tom, because I don't remember our history, and . . . and I don't really remember myself, if you know what I mean."

They had reached the end of the row of pens. Jane put aside the tools of her trade, leaned against the wall, and regarded Mckenna with crossed arms. "Like I said before, Mckenna, at this point you can be whomever you want to be. Just go for it."

"Go for it," Mckenna said with a sigh.

"Tom might be just your type now."

"And he wasn't before."

Jane shrugged. "You fancied yourself as pretty sophisticated, a real dyed-in-the-wool yuppie. You only dated guys who wore clothes as expensive as yours."

"You make me sound pretty shallow."

"You weren't shallow. Under those designer clothes and world-class ambitions, you had—have, rather—a warm and unselfish heart. You would give a friend the shirt off your back, and everyone at the hospital loves you and Titi.

You were just too busy to pay much attention to a man who might actually require more of you than your good looks and perfect clothes."

"Like Tom?"

Jane nodded. "Like Tom. But anyway, don't take your current self so seriously, and quit beating up your former self. You were a good person. Just relax and let things play out. And don't be nervous about Tom."

" 'Nervous' is kind of an understatement."

Jane chuckled. "It's a good sign. A hell of an improvement over the indifference you used to pretend. Nell and I used to laugh about that. It was so obviously a put-on."

"Why?"

"Because no woman with blood in her veins could be indifferent to Tom Markham."

"Ha! I thought you had not a shred of romance in you."

"I don't. But that doesn't mean I'm a dried-up prune. I can tell USDA Prime when I see it. Come on." She led the way back toward the office. "We can finish up here later. I want to show you how to do the books. Did I tell you that I'm going to let you watch the kennel for a whole week while I take Shadow to Tucson for the obedience trials?"

"No, you didn't," Mckenna said with an edge in her voice.

"By that time you'll have the operation down flat."

"You're sure about that."

"Don't be grumpy. You need the cash, and Shadow's ready to score some High in Trial awards and start earning some points toward his obedience championship. You helping out here gives me a great opportunity to do some traveling with him."

Mckenna began to wonder if Jane didn't need a new self more than she did. "Don't you do anything that doesn't involve the dogs, Jane? You board dogs, groom dogs, train dogs, and show dogs. You have sheep, but they're only here for Idaho to get his herding fix. Before long, you're going to start barking like a dog."

Jane merely laughed. "Hell, it beats having to wear high heels and makeup to work."

"But look at this place."

They came through the door from the kennel to the office, which was clean but strictly utilitarian. Jane's gray steel desk came from Goodwill and matched the nondescript shade of her filing cabinet. The only hint of décor in the office was framed photos on the wall: Jane's dogs, of course, playing, sleeping, sitting primly beside Jane as some judge presented an award.

"Look at this place," Mckenna repeated. " 'Stark' is the only word I can think of."

"I like stark," Jane claimed. "It's refreshing. Besides, I don't have money for any froufrou décor."

"Gad! You work here twenty-four hours a day, with only dogs to talk to...."

"Cats, too," Titi reminded her. The cat had enthroned herself on the counter that separated the entrance from Jane's "office." "No better company than a cat."

Mckenna ignored her. "Every day you must get howled at, growled at"—she cut a look toward Titi—"hissed at, clawed, and slurped. All for this!" She spread her arms in a gesture that took in the entire Bark Park. "Plus, you're pretty and smart, but you don't date, or go to concerts, or out to eat, or anything other than work, go to stupid obedience trials, go to the hospital, and ... and that's it. Don't you get tired of living that way?"

Jane dropped down heavily into the chair behind the desk and gave Mckenna a jaundiced look. "Okay, I've been giving you a truckload of lectures, so I suppose that turnabout is fair play. But, Mckenna, this is a shoestring operation here. I can't afford a restaurant much more expensive than McDonald's or Taco Bell. And as for working all the time, I can't afford to hire help—except maybe Suzy, who comes in when I absolutely have to be gone."

"What about me? You hired me."

"At what I'm paying, you hardly count."

With a wry expression, Mckenna agreed. "I'm beginning to tumble to that fact in any number of ways."

Jane ignored Mckenna's lead-in to a whine. "I like what I do," she insisted, looking around at the plain office, then out the window at the training yard, the three wings of kennels. "No, I love what I do, and that's much more important than money. I like my life just the way it is."

Mckenna felt a familiar sense of contempt rise up from somewhere inside her—contempt for the edge of poverty lifestyle, the bare-bones house and kennel, and Jane's utter satisfaction with such a narrow existence. The feeling wasn't a positive one. Had the old Mckenna attached such importance to things, to status? And was that Old Mckenna trying to surface at last?

"Hey, Mckenna, you're remembering more and more."

"What?"

"How else did you know I didn't date or go out or anything? You and I used to go around about that a lot. I made fun of your perpetual diet and your fancy house and car, and you called me Plain Jane and a nun in a canine convent."

Mckenna's jaw dropped. "I said that? How rude!"

Jane got up, took her by the shoulder, and gave her a quick hug. "Don't worry, kid. You, me, and Nell—we needle one another like squabbling sisters, but we love one another like sisters, too. And that's not going to change." She grinned impishly. "The new you or the old you—you're stuck with us."

chapter 10

TOM MARKHAM lived in a smallish home set on a very large tract of land. Nature's own landscaping surrounded the house with juniper, mesquite, and scrub grasses. Off to one side a little barn sat well back in the trees, and two horses gazed curiously at Mckenna from the little attached paddock.

Of course Tom owned horses, Mckenna thought as she got out of her little Neon and looked around. He'd ridden the rodeo circuit before going to law school. Had she remembered that, or had someone told her? Bits and pieces of her life floated into her brain, unsummoned, every day. Unimportant stuff, mostly, like the names of her two cousins in Colorado (perhaps not unimportant to the cousins) and the fact that she liked diced green chiles on scrambled eggs. She also remembered that her scrambled eggs used to be the yolkless low-fat variety that came in a carton. How she had put up with that, Mckenna couldn't fathom. In her current incarnation, she liked eggs fresh from the shell and cooked in butter.

And that was why her size-three jeans no longer would

zip. Her new jeans, purchased that very day at Wal-Mart, were a whopping size six. Which was a good thing, really, because Wal-Mart didn't carry anything smaller.

You're stalling, a voice inside her head chided. *Sooner or later, you're going to have to walk up that flagstone path and knock on that door.*

Why was she so nervous? Mckenna wondered. This was just Tom waiting for her. Jane and Nell had told her that she'd closed the door in the man's face, metaphorically speaking, long ago, so probably the guy had no romantic designs. He felt guilty, and that had prompted him to offer help, to wake up the part of her brain that held the law under lock and key. These tutoring sessions wouldn't last long. Probably they would both discover that her education and skills would return in their own sweet time—if at all. Sitting in Tom's home office once a week, staring at case histories and law books, wouldn't bring them back any sooner.

And yes, that was exactly what she feared. She took a deep breath, gathered her courage, and rang the bell.

Tom opened the door in jeans and a T-shirt that bragged about cowboys doing it with a lot of bull. He looked less like an attorney than anyone Mckenna had ever seen. A tail-wagging yellow Lab was at his side.

"Hey, Mac. Right on time. Come on in. This is Clara. Don't let her get you dirty. She likes to jump on people to say 'Hello.' "

The house seemed to be bigger on the inside than on the outside, with an open, airy floor plan and big windows that took maximum advantage of the beautiful setting. The décor was Southwestern, of course. Artwork on the walls could have jumped out of a John Wayne Western. In one corner, an ornate roping saddle sat on its stand, covered by a colorful saddle blanket. A bridle—glittering with enough silver to finance a small mortgage—hung from the saddle horn.

Tom noticed her attention. "That rig is just for parades. All that fancy stuff isn't much use when you get down and dirty tending to real business."

Suddenly Mckenna wondered if Tom had considered her analogous to "all that fancy stuff," her and her fancy car and prestigious law firm and Ivy League law degree. All the fancy stuff that used to be. Had she had his respect as an attorney? Did it matter?

"This is a nice room," she commented truthfully. "Those trophies above the fireplace—I suppose they're yours."

"Hell yes. I busted my butt to win those. Busted, literally."

She took a closer look. Champion bulldogger. First place, team roping. National champion Brahma bullrider. Framed photos made a backdrop for the trophies. Some had apparently been taken by Tom, because he wasn't in them. One showed an ugly black-haired fellow about Tom's age leaning on a fence rail, toasting the camera with a beer. A palomino horse hung its head over the same fence rail and looked ready to take a sip of the fellow's beer for himself.

"That's my friend Owen. We call him Gimp. Best damned bulldogger in Colorado at one time. Maybe in the whole West."

Other photos featured Tom himself. One showed him riding a huge bull.

"You look like you're about to hit the dirt in this one."

"You're right about that. Dislocated my left arm and broke two fingers in that spill. That mean sonofabitch nearly stomped me for good measure before the clown drew him off."

"Really unexciting compared to being a lawyer, was it?"

"Ah, sarcasm. But you know, working in the county attorney's office sometimes comes close, except you don't get as many broken bones. Maybe someday I'll try something really dangerous and run for public office."

She laughed. "Politics would probably make bullriding seem like a walk in the park."

Tom got them each a Michelob, and they settled in to work at a hastily cleared table in his home office, a book-lined room with a scarred-up oak desk and a couple of framed awards from the University of Arizona law school.

"Okay," he began. "My idea is that working through some case histories and maybe digging through the books researching points of law is going to break loose your law education from wherever it's gone to ground. So, let's start with a review of some of the things you do recall. As I remember, your forte was criminal law. We'll begin with some really simple questions."

None of which she was able to answer. Ten minutes later, Tom seemed to realize he might as well try to get the rules of evidence out of a kindergarten pupil. Mckenna found that failure did not sit well with her. Even though she had known her skills had taken a sabbatical, sitting there in Tom's little office having to say "I don't know" to questions that would have been obvious to any first-year law student plunged her mood into the seventh level of the Inferno.

"Okay," Tom said with a sigh. "Let's move to something a little more recent. How about the Harmon case?"

Her head shot up, eyes narrowed with suspicion.

"Don't look like I just asked you to hack into a national defense computer. Believe me, I know everything you know about the case, and vice versa. And why would that be?"

Mckenna drew a blank. "Because we had spies in each other's offices?"

"No," he said patiently. "Because of discovery. The prosecution is required to share with the defense all evidence revealed during their investigation, and same with the defense. If you had uncovered some piece of information that affected the case, you would have shared with the prosecution. It's the law. So don't worry about breaking any confidentiality."

She wasn't quite convinced. Her pride stung painfully, and a good shouting match would have served as a balm.

"What does confidentiality apply to?"

Mckenna ground her teeth. "I don't know."

"Only to facts revealed by the client directly to counsel. So if Harmon had confided to you—say, the fact that he had killed someone and left the body in the trunk of his Lexus—you couldn't tell me that."

"That's not what Harmon is accused of."

Tom grinned. "Well, you remembered that all right."

"I read the files." Mckenna rolled her eyes. "Did you bring me here to grill me about Todd Harmon?" She got up and pushed back her chair. "I think I should go."

"Mckenna," Tom said calmly. "We already discussed why that's not so. There's no secrets you can tell me. And if something confidential is hidden in that brain of yours, you wouldn't tell me. That's such a basic instinct with attorneys that it would take more than a little knock on the head to rid you of that."

She didn't want to stay. What was the point in more humiliation?

"Mckenna, sit down."

His voice held a quiet authority that made it tough to argue. She sat.

"I didn't say this was going to be easy."

Giving in to embarrassment, she leaned her elbows on the table and buried her face in her hands. She wanted to dive into a hole somewhere. He saw through her so easily. "It hurts," she admitted. "Being this stupid hurts."

"This doesn't have anything to do with stupidity."

"Easy for you to say. Your brain isn't in tatters." Still, hearing the words made her feel marginally better. "Have

I always suffered from this much pride?" she asked with a bit of chagrin.

"That and more."

"What if I have to spend the rest of my life working the window at McDonald's and picking up dog messes for Jane?"

"You won't. I know you, Mac. Nothing's going to keep you down for very long."

She took her face out of hiding and met his eyes.

"Whatever you were before your accident, you weren't a quitter. And I don't think you're a quitter now."

"Whatever I was? Just what was I before the accident? I've heard different stories from Nell, from Jane, from my ex-boss." And from her cat, but she wasn't about to tell him that.

A little smile curved his lips as he leaned back in his chair and folded his arms across his chest. "It must be interesting, seeing the person you used to be from everyone else's perspective."

"Interesting isn't quite the word I would use."

"Instructive, then?"

"So you think I needed instruction on how to live my life?"

He tsked. "One thing you haven't lost is your touchiness."

"Well, maybe that's because in addition to half my brain being in neutral, people keep telling me how lucky I am to be starting over. Was the old me such a loser?"

"No." He wore a thoughtful expression that softened into a smile. "Mckenna Wright was a definite winner, not a loser."

Surprised, she gave him a questioning look. Then he came out with the big *But*, of course.

"But I think what concerned your friends was how much you wanted to win."

She went on the defensive. "What's wrong with being driven to win?"

" 'Driven' is the operative word there."

"Success requires hard work. I remember that, at least."

"Yes, but enjoying success requires reserving part of your life for something other than work."

"Are you saying I was a workaholic?"

"That's a very mild description of what you were. You not only were a workaholic, but you couldn't understand anyone not being a workaholic. Anyone who refused to live for their work was simply lazy, or unmotivated, or both. Anyone who took a pass on the race to the top rung—of work, of life, of wealth—you dismissed as a slacker."

Her eyes narrowed. "Are we talking about you?"

"Me? To tell the truth, Mac, I never gave a damn about what you thought. I've always lived my life according to what I thought."

"That isn't what my friends tell me." The best defense, Mckenna knew, was a good offense.

"Really? What do your nosy friends tell you?"

"That you came on to me and I slapped you down."

He laughed, and the laughter twisted the knife of her frustration.

"I suppose that's one way to look at it."

"Well, then, you did give a damn, didn't you?" she said.

"Not after I decided that you were so set on making yourself miserable that there was no helping you."

"Maybe I didn't need help. Maybe I was fine just the way I was."

He merely smiled, refusing to be provoked, as if he knew the deep-down uncertainties that prodded her to go on the attack. The compassion in his eyes made her even angrier. She didn't want to be the object of anyone's compassion.

"Maybe it was *you* that didn't have it right. You discovered that you didn't have the drive and dedication to work for a firm like BKB."

His smile grew broader. Infuriating.

"And because of that you ended up in a dead-end job working for the county."

He raised a brow. "Corralling life's bad guys is hardly a dead-end job."

"Well, there's nothing wrong with defending people who are suffering under the tyranny of overzealous law officers, either!"

Tom chuckled. "There's the old Mckenna."

"The old Mckenna!" She got up and starting pacing around the small room. The heels of her loafers clicked against the oak floor in time to her rising annoyance, causing Clara, who lay under Tom's desk, to raise her head and look at Mckenna in concern. "The old Mckenna! Everyone rolls their eyes about the old Mckenna, and I'm tired of it. And I'm tired of living in a piece-of-shit trailer and working at a place swimming in hamburger grease and picking up dog shit and listening to Jane talk about finding my damned true self. I want my old life back, dammit!"

She had finally gotten Tom's goat, and Mckenna stepped back to put a little more distance between herself and the expression on his face.

"You want your old life back, do you? Well, I'm sure you'll get it back, because everytime I see you, a little more of that Old Mckenna seeps through. You'll have to work for it, though. That should come naturally. All you knew how to do was work. BKB was your home, your family, your master, your reason for living. You spent a few hours every week taking your cat to visit the hospital, but other than that, your nose was so glued to the grindstone it's a miracle you didn't wear your face down flat."

She felt as if he'd hit her a physical blow. "Why did it matter to you if my life wasn't your stupid idea of perfect,

Tom Markham? It was my life. I didn't expect you to live it."

"Yes, you did," he countered. "Those months I was with BKB, you were the big cheese there, and you expected everyone there to manacle themselves to their desks, divorce their spouses, and foster out their kids so they could devote themselves full-time, without distraction, to the betterment of BKB and BKB's clients. Anyone who wouldn't do that was not only not worth his paycheck, he wasn't worth the tiniest bit of your regard."

She sneered. "Are we talking about you now?"

He laughed sourly. "Oh, no. You wanted me to stay. You even talked Gil into offering me a raise. When I work at something, I don't settle for second best. It just took me a while to understand that status and money don't necessarily translate into 'best.'"

Which was a fancy way of saying that she was a piece of shit, Mckenna decided. "I couldn't have been that bad."

"By your own lights, I'm sure you were very, very good. It was just other folks that had problems when you were around."

That was it. Mckenna slung her pocketbook over her shoulder and headed toward the front door. "In that case, I won't cause you any more problems, Mr. Markham." Even as she marched huffily through the front room, she felt his measuring eyes on her, oddly calculating. She wondered for a moment if his anger was real or feigned, because she sensed none of the heat of his words in his gaze.

Before she reached the door, he veered onto another tack. "And by the way, Mac, working for the county attorney is a great job. Any job that lets me send a punk like Todd Harmon up the river is a job worth doing."

Without even thinking about it, she whirled about and answered. "Todd Harmon is not a punk. And you're not sending him up the river."

"Really?"

"Harmon is a spoiled brat, but deep down he's got heart, which is something that you probably can't recognize, being the self-righteous know-it-all crusader that you are. Why he ..." She trailed off as the thought faded out through and around her words. Something about Todd Harmon. Something he had done, which had saddened her. Whatever it was, it had fled back into hiding.

"Coming back, isn't it?"

This time his tone was calm. Had the anger ever been there for real?

"Get you mad enough, you might just remember the whole thing."

He stepped close, into the tension-filled aura that surrounded her, tension born of anger, confusion, frustration, and the surprisingly mixed emotions that accompanied the sudden flash of memory, gone almost as soon as it appeared. Part of her wanted to let that tension turbocharge her very real reaction to his nearness. She could almost see sizzling tethers stretching between them, slowly tightening, pulling them together.

Another part of her wanted to scream that this was too much. She didn't know who she was or where she was headed. She didn't know if she was angry or turned on.

She pushed out a hand, palm outward, as if that could hold back the flood of emotion that threatened to swamp her. Then without a word, she turned and walked through the door.

TOM TURNED his truck into the driveway of the Bark Park. In the passenger seat sat his excuse for coming—Clara, his eleven-year-old Labrador retriever. Clara provided his excuse, not his reason. His reason drove the little yellow Neon that was parked next to Jane Connor's house.

"Time for you to do your stuff," he told the dog. "Be cute. Be friendly. Maybe if I have something warm and fuzzy on the end of a leash, these ladies won't be too hard on me."

Jane greeted him as he walked through the door to the office. "Well, lookie who we have here. What brings you all the way out here, Counselor?"

"It's Saturday."

"Yes, it is. All day long."

"So...well, I'm off work. And I've been looking for a good place to board Clara when I go out of town. Being here the other day reminded me. I thought maybe I could get a tour of the place."

Jane looked over the counter at the dog. "Hi, Clara. Is your dad working you on the obedience exercises we taught him?"

The Lab wagged her tail.

Jane turned her attention back to Tom. "It's a long way to drive to kennel your dog. There's a ton of kennels in Prescott."

"Yes. But I really trust you. Clara's getting old, so she needs some special attention. This dog has been with me since my rodeo days. Stuck with me through law school. Helped me study for the bar. Making her comfy is worth driving an hour. And a good boarding kennel is hard to find."

Jane smiled. "I knew there was some reason I liked you, Markham." Then she gave him a canny look. "But I know why you're here. I've been listening to her complain and emote all morning." She came around the counter and knelt down to get at Clara's level. Scratching the dog's ears, she said, "Our Mckenna needs a good dog, doesn't she, Clara? That would make her all better, eh?"

Curled on top of Jane's desk, Titi objected with a loud meow, followed by Mckenna's comment, "That's all right, Titi. Jane thinks the solution to every problem is a good dog."

Both Jane and Tom looked up in surprise, Jane with a

laugh, Tom with a guilty look on his face. Mckenna lounged in the open doorway to the kennel wing. Unruly locks of hair curtained one eye. Her T-shirt showed brown smudges of what Tom hoped was simply dirt. The hems of her blue jeans were wet.

Tom had known Mckenna as a smart, classy, very together woman who never had a hair of her sculpted style out of place. The Mckenna in the doorway bore little resemblance to that woman, other than the chiseled fineness of her features, and even those had softened a bit, along with the sharp angles of her once fashionably twiglike figure. The other Mckenna had been drop-dead gorgeous, a sight to set any man to fantasizing. But he liked this scruffier version better. She was more approachable, more human, and still could knock a man's socks right off his feet.

"I finished the kennels," she announced. "And if any of those pooches decide that they have further business to do, they had just better wait until tomorrow."

"Did you do the cat condos?" Jane asked.

Mckenna closed her eyes in a pained grimace. "Cat condos. Rats!"

"Never mind. Tom wants a tour, to see if he might want to leave Miss Clara here. So why don't you show him the place?"

Mckenna peered around the corner at the dog. "Hi, Clara."

"Go ahead and show Tom around," Jane said, trying to sound innocent. "I'll do the cats."

"Oh, no," Mckenna said, flashing a look at Tom. "I'll do the cats. You take Tom."

"I'd rather you take Tom."

"I'd rather do the cats."

"I'm the boss. I get the cats."

Tom began to feel like a piece of lit dynamite being thrown from one person to another.

"I get the cats," Jane repeated firmly.

Tom began to understand why in disagreements with mastiffs and pit bulls, Jane always won.

Mckenna huffed her surrender. "Okay, then. I guess I get Tom."

"It's nice to feel welcome," Tom commented.

Jane grinned. "Don't mind her. She gets cranky after shoveling shit all morning."

"She should be used to it; after all, she's an attorney."

Jane laughed. Mckenna did not. "Just leave Clara in the office while you look around," Jane said. "I'll keep an eye on her from the cat room."

As Tom followed Mckenna into the kennel wing, she turned and threw bitter words back toward him: "Was an attorney, you mean. These days I shovel a less metaphorical load of shit."

"Well, that's what I came to talk to you about."

She ignored him and assumed the role of a tour guide, pointing to the first aisle of kennels. "As you can see," she said in a tour guide voice, "all the dogs have roomy indoor-outdoor kennels that are absolutely squeaky clean, thanks to your truly."

"I came to apologize." He dangled the prospect before her like a lure. "Believe me, it's not that often that anyone gets to hear me apologize for anything."

She stuck up her nose in a manner very like her old self. "I don't know why you think you owe me an apology."

"Whether it's owed or not, I figured that an apology might get me back in your good graces."

"I can't imagine why you need to be in my good graces. After all, you're the one who's been doing favors for me, not the other way around." The edge in her voice belied her words. She still had her back up over the previous night's fiasco. When the Good Lord handed out stubborn, Mckenna had been first in line.

But Tom was no slacker in the stubborn department,

and he wasn't about to give up. "I want to be in your good graces because . . . because . . ." Because why? Why couldn't he just let it go, dismiss Mckenna from his mind and get rid of at least one complication in his life? Mckenna had stepped on his foolish romantic ambitions long ago, and at this point, he didn't need one single thing from her. But they had forged a friendship of sorts, perhaps born of professional competition and nurtured by mutual respect. Her accident had reminded him how much that friendship meant to him, even if sometimes she did annoy the hell out of him.

So he did want to stay in her good graces. He did want to help her, partly out of guilt—he admitted it. He still felt uneasy about his possible role in her accident. But he also wanted to help her because she was a brand-new Mckenna. Whether or not she liked the new her, Tom did. Or at least thought he might, if he could stay in her life long enough to see the finished version.

"Come on, Mac, give me a break, here. I want to stay in your good graces because, well, because I do. That's all."

She gave him the look that women reserve for men who try to explain their feelings and fail miserably. After aeons of living side by side with men, Tom thought, women should have lowered their expectations in that regard and stopped giving the dirty looks. But they hadn't.

Before he could try to explain further, she led him out of the kennel building, across a narrow pathway, and into a structure that might once have been a garage.

"This is the grooming room," she said in a bored voice. "Note the raised bathtub, grooming table, and cage driers."

"Listen, Mckenna, I *am* sorry about last night. I handled things really badly from start to finish. I shouldn't have just sat you down at a table and quizzed you like some uppity law professor."

Her mouth twitched downward. "It's not your fault that I can't jump-start my brain."

"Your brain is going to fire up just fine one of these days."

She replied with a disbelieving snort, then led the way out of the grooming room to the outside section of the kennel building. "Every dog can come or go, inside or outside, as it pleases. And there's a raised platform in each pen in case the dog wants to lie down off of the gravel. An older girl like Clara would appreciate that."

"And about the other"—it seemed as if they were carrying on two completely different conversations—"I don't have any right to tell you how you should be living your life."

"The watering bowls are automatic. They're heated for when it freezes. Which it did last night. As you can see, fresh water is always available."

He persisted. A man didn't learn to tackle bulls without persistence, and Mckenna couldn't be that much tougher than a bull. "You probably don't remember, which in this case is a good thing, but when I first came to work for BKB, I decided right off that you were about the sexiest woman I'd ever met, and I strutted around trying to impress the hell out of you. I guess I expected you to swoon like some rodeo groupie."

A raised brow in his direction provided the only clue that she heard.

"On the other side is a big play yard, and each dog gets at least two turns a day in it. If it's an amiable dog, it can play with others. If not, it gets the yard to itself."

He sighed. "What I'm trying to say, Mac, is that I have a history of expecting you to be something you aren't. And what you did with your life, or what you do with your life from here on out, isn't any of my business."

She looked at him thoughtfully for a moment, almost speculatively, then continued: "We provide a good quality kibble for the dogs to eat, but many owners prefer to bring their own food."

"So I had no call to get on you about anything, or to sermonize about how you should be living. Okay?"

"Hours are six days a week, Monday through Saturday, and we're open for two hours Sunday afternoon."

He slammed a fist into the open palm of his hand. "Would you quit with the goddamned tour! I'm trying to apologize here! It isn't something that comes naturally to me, so you'd better pay attention. It might be your only chance to get through my guard and land a good, hard slap upside my head."

The speculation in her eyes grew brighter, he thought. Probably at the mention of the slap upside the head.

"That was metaphorically speaking, not an invitation to haul off and slug me just because I'm a jackass."

She stopped her progress along the row of kennels and cocked her head, seeming to consider it. Her expression questioned, then resolved, her face relaxing into a faint smile. "No need to call yourself names. Apology accepted."

"What? No snipes, no sarcasm, no spitfire huffiness?" Very unlike her.

"I said, apology accepted. I guess I should apologize, too. My Swiss cheese memory makes me crazy. And when I get frustrated and cranky, I take it out on whoever is closest. Have I always been that way?"

"Maybe," he admitted cautiously. "Sort of."

"Well, maybe we can call it even, then. I know you were trying to help. I'm beginning to think that nothing but time will help, though." Her mouth pulled downward in dismay. "Heaven knows how much time."

"Maybe you're right, Mac, but immersing yourself in things you used to know can't help but speed along the process. Let's try again, taking a little different slant on this tutoring thing. I have an idea about how to make it work. You might get what you need, and some other folks will get what they need, as well."

Her brows knit suspiciously. "What kind of different slant?"

"You'll have to trust me on this, while I try to make some arrangements. But I really think this might work."

The frown stayed as she searched his face, maybe for hints of another disaster in the making. "All right," she finally said. "I'll stick my toe in the water again."

All right! Tom thought. No need to tell her that what he had in mind was more like jumping in the deep end.

chapter 11

DURING THE next week, Mckenna worked hard enough that she almost forgot to be frustrated or sorry for herself. Monday, Tuesday, and Thursday were her days at McDonald's. She would never be a star player on Mickey D's team, but she survived, with the help of her coworkers. She could now slap a cup under the correct spigot on the beverage dispenser without looking, and usually she managed to make coffee that didn't earn too many complaints from the customers. Usually. She could operate the register without hunting five minutes for the correct entries, and her skills with a bucket and mop were also coming right along.

Mckenna could picture the headlines of her next alma mater newsletter: *Harvard law graduate makes it big at McDonald's.* "I knew this law degree would come in handy somewhere," *Wright declares.*

Every hour behind the counter, however, made her more determined to regain her lost skills. Everyone said she had been a good attorney. No one would ever praise her fast-food skills.

Mckenna badly wanted to be good at something again.

Wednesday afternoon and Saturday she entered a completely different world: the Bark Park. There she felt more comfortable—mostly because of Jane. For all Jane's tough talk, she possessed almost endless patience with dogs, cats, sheep, and friends on the down-and-out.

"You should have been a teacher," Mckenna told her on Wednesday, as Jane showed her how to work the mats out of an Old English sheepdog that had been too-long neglected. "If you can handle this nasty boy, you'd be a natural teaching the little punks in junior high."

Titi sat atop a counter littered with bottles of dog shampoo, grooming implements, and a stack of folded towels. She commented smugly. "Stupid dog. Should learn to groom himself. Doesn't have a tongue?"

As if he understood the insult, the sheepdog whipped around—for the tenth time since they had put him up on the grooming table—and tried to sink his teeth into Jane. Jane grabbed an ultrasensitive part of the dog's anatomy—gently but firmly. "Don't even try it," she warned the sheepdog.

He immediately comprehended. Who said dogs couldn't reason? The massive head swung back, teeth retracted, and he gazed innocently at the wall as if he didn't have a single uncooperative thought in his big fuzzy brain. He even ignored Titi's satisfied smirk.

"I don't think the school administration would approve of my methods of encouraging good manners," Jane said with a chuckle. "Though they should give it a try. It works well with males of all species, and I don't imagine the human species is an exception. Those snotty junior-high boys could use a little discipline in their lives, don't you think?"

Mckenna laughed. "No wonder you don't date."

"You think?" She handed Mckenna a mat splitter. "Try

your hand on the other side. He shouldn't be giving us any more trouble."

Wrinkling her nose, Mckenna picked up a clump of dirty, matted sheepdog hair. Unfortunately, the beast had to be combed out before he could be bathed.

"Speaking of dating," Jane said casually, "how's it going with Tom?"

"Tom and I aren't dating."

Jane snorted. "Yeah, right."

"The first tutoring session was a disaster. I told you about that."

"You know what they say about romance and rocky roads."

"We are *not* dating. I don't think he even likes me."

Jane snorted again.

"We're going to try the tutoring again, though. He's setting up something different, but he won't tell me the details."

"If at first you don't succeed..." She snickered. "That's something I think Tom understands very well."

"What do you mean by that?"

"You figure it out. He's going to a lot of trouble for you, and I don't think it's out of guilt."

The dog whimpered as Mckenna pulled too hard trying to get the mat splitter through a felted mass of fur. "Sorry, Simon."

"He's a keeper, you know."

"Who? Simon?"

"Blockhead. Don't be dense. Tom. Tom's a keeper if I've ever seen one, and I don't often say that about a man."

Mckenna chuckled. "I don't recall him offering to be kept."

"Just give him a chance and watch how fast he jumps at the bait."

"The bait being me, I assume?"

"You're catching on. You could do a lot worse."

Mckenna could think of at least a million reasons why she shouldn't give any man encouragement at this particular time in her life, especially Tom Markham, but she didn't argue. She had learned to take Jane's comments with a grain of salt. Everything that passed through the woman's brain came out of her mouth without a bit of censorship. It made for entertaining conversations, but one couldn't be touchy about what Jane said.

Surprisingly, Mckenna had begun to enjoy working at the Bark Park. Not that cleaning kennels, feeding a pack of drooling, barking dogs, brushing out matted and dirty coats (why did people let their pets get so ratty?), and being with sometimes irascible pet owners was a barrel of laughs. But Mckenna liked dealing with the animals, and she also discovered a knack for managing people. Maybe that came from her buried law experience. Had she been one of those dramatic trial attorneys who could twist a jury around her little finger? she wondered sometimes. Did her talent with words come from instinct, or from a Harvard education?

Wherever the talent came from, she enjoyed using it to deal with the Bark Park's clients. Jane whistled in amazement on Saturday afternoon after listening to Mckenna persuade a cowboy from Camp Verde to have his three-year-old male cattle dog neutered.

"I've been telling Justin for a year that he needed to get that dog fixed, but everytime I brought it up, I swear the man crossed his legs."

"And then you told him to stop empathizing with his dog's testicles?"

"Well..." Jane screwed her face into a guilty grimace. "Not exactly in those words."

Mckenna smiled. "Something more direct? A bit earthier?"

"I think I told him once that they needed to cut off the dog's, not his."

"Jane Connor, golden-tongued queen of Cornville tact."

"Well, hell, I could have trotted out all that stuff about prostate cancer, aggression, and wanderlust if I'd thought about it." Then she grinned. "But you—you enjoy getting into the persuasive mode, pulling out facts and figures, convincing some poor slob that your way of looking at things is the only way. Don't you?"

"You're right," Mckenna confessed. "I do."

"It's the trial lawyer in you."

Mckenna brightened. "Maybe it is. I'm good at that, aren't I?"

"Hell yes. And now that I've got you to deal with these little public-relations issues, I don't need to worry about it, do I? I tell you, Mckenna, I'm feeling really confident about leaving the kennel with you when I go to Tucson."

"Because I'm cheaper than your usual kennel-sitter, I'll bet."

"There is that. But you've got a talent for this business. The dogs like you. The people like you. Even the cats like you. Maybe someday we could expand this place and become partners."

Another headline flashed into Mckenna's mind: *Harvard law graduate cleans up in Cornville. "Scooping poop a step upward from having to put up with lawyer jokes," Wright claims.*

Mckenna chuckled. "I don't think so. Lawyering may involve shoveling a certain amount of shit, but the pay's a lot better. I'm going to get it back, even if I have to pound my head against a wall to get my brain back in order."

"Right. I'm sure there's a less painful way." Jane smirked. "Maybe a whole lot of tutoring from Tom?"

"If he ever calls."

"He'll call. Or you could go to Nell's swami friend in Sedona—the hypnotist."

"The head-pounding idea would probably work better."

Jane grinned. "That leaves you with Tom."

In her time off, what little of it there was, Mckenna

stayed home with Titi and worked on her humble abode. The cat supervised, full of advice on everything from the wallpaper pattern in the kitchen to the kind of bulbs to plant in the flower beds.

"Tasty chickens," Titi said of the wallpaper that Mckenna struggled to apply to the kitchen wall. A wet, heavy strip wanted to wrap around her head. "Fat chickens," the cat commented on the pattern. "What's for dinner?"

And on the garden: "Catnip. Lots of catnip. Toss the gladiolas."

"We are not planting catnip," Mckenna said sternly. "And not only because you don't plant catnip until spring. You would be drunk all the time. You're an addict. Every bit as bad as some drug-head snorting coke."

An almost-memory rushed in then, drowning out Titi's indignant denial. Somewhere in Mckenna's brain a bell rang about drug-heads, coke, and addicts. It was there, just beyond her reach. The frustration made her throw a trowel and shred an unfortunate gladiola bulb before it ever had the chance to live.

In spite of the trowel incident, however, Mckenna discovered an aptitude for growing things. Watching the grass and shrubs she had planted struggle for survival in the desert soil somehow gave her a sense of kinship, almost as if those struggling seedlings, with their blind striving for the sun, represented her new life. Come spring they would be stronger. The struggle wouldn't be so hard. The flower beds would erupt with color, and her shoddy little acre might actually look alive.

And the same might happen to her.

Except that the sun Mckenna strove for wasn't a new life at all, but the old one that crept back day by day in bits and pieces of unconnected, seemingly unimportant details. That life was what she should be striving for. Anything new she might build involved living on a scrubby piece of land in a cramped trailer house, learning the ins and outs of hamburgers and fries, and playing chambermaid for Jane's hairy clients. What kind of life was that for a Harvard law graduate?

By the next Sunday, Tom still had not called to schedule their next tutoring session. Mckenna suspected his enthusiasm had waned along with his sense of guilt. Or maybe the Thanksgiving holiday this past week had delayed his plans. Everything in the Verde Valley had closed down, including McDonald's and the Bark Park. She and Jane had shared a dinner of roast chicken (a turkey, Jane claimed, was way beyond her cooking abilities) and mashed potatoes. Mckenna had half-expected Tom to call, if only to wish them a happy Thanksgiving, but the phone at the Bark Park was silent all day, and her new message machine—she could finally afford phone service—had only a message from Nell in Tucson, telling her about their new house there, Dan's progress with his law studies, and Piggy's latest antics. Apparently Piggy and Dan were engaged in a nightly contest to determine just who would occupy the majority of Nell and Dan's bed. Nell had already surrendered most of her legroom, but Dan still deluded himself that he couldn't be bested by a mere dog.

But no one from Mckenna's barely-remembered family had called on the holiday—more evidence of a relationship that wasn't exactly close. And neither had Tom.

Why did she care if Tom called? Mckenna asked herself. Things were better this way. Exposing herself, or rather, exposing her inadequacies for Tom to witness, embarrassed as well as frustrated her. Perhaps pummeling her brain with his help might encourage her former skills to return, but how stupid he must think she was. Better to let the tutoring idea die. She had a whole law library boxed up and stored beneath the trailer. Why couldn't she just tutor herself?

And yet the thought of not seeing Tom again left the taste of disappointment in her mouth. For all of Sunday morning, she hung out in the trailer, cleaning the refrigerator, mopping the floor, and telling herself that she definitely was not waiting for the phone to ring. By the time noon rolled around, Mckenna was sufficiently fed up with herself to stuff Titi into the cat carrier and load her into the car.

"This is my day off, and we're not sticking around like a pair of losers with nothing better to do," she told the cat.

So the two of them drove off in the Neon to look at their old digs in Oak Creek Canyon. They couldn't get very close, of course, because the gate across the driveway closed them out. But a pull-off along the highway allowed them to stop for a while and gaze through the pine, oak, and juniper at the log-and-glass home across the stream. A few leaves still clung to cottonwood and birch trees, and the scrub oak alongside the house still flamed bright red. The scene was incredibly beautiful.

Sitting sedately beside her, her feline eyes echoing the yearning on Mckenna's face, Titi sighed plaintively. "Want my house back. Sunny spots everywhere. Birds outside windows. Nice, clean carpets."

Mckenna dredged her memory for something about the house that she had loved. She had only moved in three weeks before her accident, Nell had told her, but surely something about such a beautiful place had moved her enough to push through the wall around her memory. Something like Titi's sunny spots.

Only the image of sunlight streaming through the trailer's kitchen window came to mind. She did love the warmth of the kitchen when that cheerful yellow light seemed to make everything glow. The new wallpaper—with Titi's appetizing chickens—brightened up the place and made it look welcoming and almost new.

But why was she thinking about the trailer while standing here looking at her old house? "It's still technically mine," she told Titi, then at a look from the cat, amended the statement. "Ours. It's still technically ours." She hoped the tenants were taking good care of the place. Mckenna really didn't want to sell it. The house, more than anything else, stood as a symbol of her old affluence and style, the high life she only remembered in snatches.

"We're idiots sitting here like this, staring at something I barely remember."

"Speak for yourself," Titi said. "Cats not idiots. Left a catnip mouse there."

Mckenna smiled. "It really takes very little to make you happy. A warm spot in the sun. A catnip mouse."

"Tuna. Don't forget tuna."

Mckenna sighed. "I suppose there's a lesson there."

Titi agreed. "Learn from the cat."

Mckenna pulled onto the highway headed back toward Cornville, the trailer, and their new life.

Once back home, Mckenna suffered a restless need to be doing something. Anything. Her days lately had been filled with unending hustle, and that pace still beat in her veins.

She almost wanted to call Jane and offer to spend the afternoon at the kennel, but Jane had taken Idaho and Shadow to an agility trial in Phoenix, leaving the kennel in the care of Suzy Crider, who had been her kennel-sitter for several years. Mckenna had offered to work while Jane was gone, but Jane had told her to go have some fun.

"You need a break," she had declared. "You're getting that old look about you again."

"What look?"

"Driven. This is the old you leaking through, the never-take-a-day-off attitude that earned you a stroke at the tender age of thirty. You have to put a stake in its heart before it eats you alive—again."

So Jane had driven off to Phoenix with her dogs, Suzy had stationed herself firmly in the kennel office, and Mckenna paced the confines of her trailer house, wondering what one did on a break. This morning, hanging around waiting for Tom to—perhaps, maybe, potentially—call, she had cleaned the refrigerator, vacuumed the floor, and watered the nascent lawn. After that she'd driven to her old house. And now? . . .

The house was clean, the garden weeded, the laundry washed. She had brought home and read the McDonald's employee manual three times already, had written a chatty letter to Nell. She could have unboxed her law books and started reading. Getting through all of them would only take a couple of centuries. Even if she could read them all, would that make her the attorney she had once been, the woman she had once been?

If Tom would call . . . But no, she didn't care if Tom called. She absolutely would not care.

She could go grocery shopping. Yes, that was something she could do. But going out the door, she glanced at her checkbook balance. Grocery shopping was out until payday at McDonald's next week. Good thing she didn't mind macaroni and cheese.

"Stop!" Titi demanded with a wide yawn. She perched on her favorite spot, the top of the television.

"What?"

"Walking, walking. Worrying. Silly girl. Sit. Relax. Lie in the sun."

"Titi, I'm not a cat."

"Right. A cat wouldn't drive off a cliff."

To ponder the logic of that statement was to take the first step toward insanity. But then, someone conversing with a cat might have taken more than one step in that direction already.

"Sit," Titi commanded. "Quit twitching your tail. Slow down. Stretch. Yawn."

"That's fine for a cat. You're supposed to be ornamental and lazy."

Titi jumped onto the floor and rolled tummy topmost

on the carpet. "Not lazy," she said with another toothy yawn. "Smart. Save energy for fun stuff. Pounce on bugs. Chase dust motes in sun. Have fun. Cats don't have blood pressure."

That brought to mind the blood-pressure medication she had stopped taking because she couldn't afford to re-fill the prescription. At first she had been a bit nervous about sending her blood rocketing through the top of her skull again, but she actually had barely noticed the ab-sence. No headaches. No pounding pulse. No ringing in her ears.

Because in spite of all the hard work and uncertainty of the last few weeks, she had slept every night the whole night through without fretting about a case or staying on top at BKB or how to get promoted and moved to the of-fice in Phoenix. Yes, she remembered these things. She re-membered the dread of failing—not so much failing to win a case as failing to live up to her own strict standards of success. She remembered nights at the office when her light was the only one still on. She remembered constantly watching her back to guard against those who might try to advance not through their own merit, but by the discredit-ing of someone else, namely her.

These things had crept back into her recollections with-out her even realizing it. Suddenly, sitting in that spot of sun on the sofa seemed an excellent idea.

When Mckenna sat, Titi jumped down onto the sofa and cuddled up next to her, much as she might with a pa-tient in the hospital. "Get it now. Humans *can* learn."

Just as an experiment, Mckenna lay back, swung her legs onto the couch and pillowed her head on the arm. The cat climbed onto her stomach and curled into a warm vibrating ball of sable fur. Lassitude crept over Mckenna. Her old self shook a scolding finger and pronounced this inactivity a lazy waste of time, but she told her old self to take a hike. For weeks now she hadn't had to rely on medication to get her through the day, nor had she downed a single ounce of alcohol to make herself relax. Her bottle of sleeping pills she hadn't even unpacked from the move.

Mckenna closed her eyes, letting the warmth of the sun and the vibration on her stomach seep through her. Slowly she let go, let herself slide down the warm dark tunnel toward sleep. Her lips eased into a smile. There was something to be said for listening to a cat.

MONDAY, MCKENNA arrived home from her shift at McDonald's to find a dozen roses on her doorstep. The card inside wished her a speedy recovery from Todd Harmon and Buddy Morris. How sweet for a major recording star to remember her. And Morris, as well. When she had met him at the BKB offices before getting sacked, he hadn't impressed her as the type who would make such a gesture.

But the roses were lovely. Their scent surrounded her with luxury.

Another surprise awaited her inside—a message on her phone from human resources at the medical center. She had applied there for work, along with just about every other place in the Verde Valley, but at the time they had no position that fit her particular lack of skills. But Diane Mast, the director of volunteers, had promised to keep an eye out for her.

She checked her watch. The admin offices closed in ten minutes. By some stroke of luck, she had come home just in time.

The woman who answered the phone knew just who Mckenna was. "You're the one with the cat," she said. "My nephew was in here for an appendectomy last week, and all he could talk about was the cat who got up on the bed with him and purred like a buzz saw. Those are his words, 'like a buzz saw.' His mom was really grateful that you came by, because the kid doesn't think hospitals are so scary anymore."

"That's good to know. It's a bummer when a kid has to be in the hospital right before Thanksgiving." Mckenna had almost not found time for the hospital that week. Now she was glad that she had. "I had a message on my machine to call."

The woman put her on hold to check with her boss. Mckenna sat waiting, humming a tune. Lord, when had she taken up humming? She smiled at the recollection of the little five-year-old with the big scared eyes and an incision where his appendix had once been. He refused to sleep, or work in the coloring books his mother had brought him, and the television showed only soaps and news—nothing fit for a five-year-old's consumption. His mom had been at her wit's end, trying to keep him entertained and quiet at the same time.

When he had laid eyes on Titi, the scared look changed into a delighted smile. Titi had played with the kid for almost an hour, with Mckenna standing ready to keep the cat from touching the covered incision. They had played catch the finger, pounce on the string, and cuddle cat—Titi's specialty. She loved to fill the space between a person's body and arm with warm, vibrating cat, snuggling in, closing her eyes, and acting as if she had just walked through the gates of cat paradise. People loved it. The five-year-old had been no exception.

"Mckenna?" The voice belonged to the director of human resources. Mckenna surprised herself by recognizing it. Maybe her brain had finally shifted from first into second gear.

"Molly, hi. I got this message . . ."

"Yes. I'm glad you called back. The volunteer department is losing its secretary, although Cindy is more of a jack-of-all-trades than just a secretary. She's having a baby, you know, due in two weeks, and she's decided to stay at home and be a full-time mom for a while."

"Good for Cindy."

"So what do you think? Want the job? Diane says to give you first shot. You'd be in charge of the chaplains and pet therapy, as well as being Diane's personal slave. Thirty-two hours a week, eight fifty an hour with benefits."

Hallelujah! She snapped it up before Diane and Molly could change their minds.

"Finally!" she crowed to Titi. "A job that doesn't involve animal fat." Although she had grown fond of hamburgers and fries, and she would miss Rick, Charlotte, and the crew that had been so patient and kind with her bumbling. "We're going to McDonald's right now to give notice. And while we're there, we'll celebrate with a Big Mac and fries. And a chocolate shake."

They were just walking out the door when the phone rang once again.

"Ready to get back to work?" Tom asked when she picked up the receiver.

TWO DAYS later, Mckenna knocked once again on Tom's door, more confident now than she had been the last time she had come here. Confident and determined. Last time she had been floundering in a flood of confusion, uncertain of herself, wary of Tom, angry at the nasty trick fate had played on her. Now she had her feet firmly on the ground. Next Monday she started a real job that didn't require her to wear a ball cap and apron. Her brain was slowly opening to let her past trickle through to the present. And she had discovered a capacity to learn new and different things. When her old skills and knowledge finally came flowing back, they would complete a wiser and better person. She would get back her old life plus some, not only regaining what she had before, but this time having the wisdom to appreciate it.

Tom opened the door in jeans, bare feet, and a T-shirt with "Cowboyin'!" scrawled in red across the chest. The nicely broad chest. His attractively shaggy hair looked as though he had just run fingers through the sand-colored waves. And his blue eyes—how could any guy have eyes that bright sky-blue?—crinkled in a welcoming smile.

Mckenna's heart gave an undisciplined thump. When she finally became reacquainted with her old self, she was going to have a few words with Old Mckenna for the way she had frozen out this man when he had still liked her.

She smiled saucily, just to show how her confidence had improved. "Hi, Teach."

"Mac." He grinned as she came inside. "Hear from Jane that you got a fancy new job."

"You're looking at the assistant to the director of volunteers at the Verde Valley Medical Center. I'm going to have my own office, my own desk, my own filing cabinet, and a ton of stuff I'm in charge of." No reason to tell him that the office doubled as a storage closet, the desk was a one by three piece of lumber braced against a wall, and the stuff she was in charge of included mostly files and a pack of volunteers who pretty much came and went as they chose. It was a step up—progress.

Tom gave her a heart-stopping grin. "Top of the heap. That's you."

A new voice chimed in. "Sounds right fancy, hon. Wish I could get me a job like that."

A thirty-something woman leaned against the den doorframe. A Dolly Parton mass of bleached curls crowned her head, and a Dolly Parton figure filled out her gaudy Western shirt. Worn jeans encased her slim hips and legs, ending in a pair of cowboy boots that had obviously never seen the inside of a barn.

But they had seen the inside of a slew of cowboy bars,

Mckenna guessed. This woman had the worn look of someone who had been chasing a good time long and desperately, and had come up shy of anything but hard living.

But for all of that, the woman owned a beautiful smile that softened the hard planes of her face, and dark eyes sparkled with a certain humor that made Mckenna suspect there was more to her than the exterior revealed.

Tom performed the introductions. "Mckenna, this is Sally Morgan. Sally, Mckenna here is the attorney I was telling you about."

The word *attorney* hit Mckenna like a blow, but Tom didn't give her time to clarify or deny.

"Sally has a bit of a problem with her ex-husband. A legal problem."

"Yeah, he's a jackass."

"He's been harassing her. Causing trouble at her work and losing her a couple of jobs."

"I was working over at the paint store on Main Street, and he came in cussin' me up one side and down the other, claimin' I'd whaled on one of the kids. Got me fired. And that's not the first time."

"But Sally can't afford an attorney. So I thought you two could help each other out."

"What?!" Mckenna's blossoming confidence fled. Here was another painful reminder that the fancy law degree hanging on her living-room wall might as well be a blank sheet of paper. As blank as her mind right then. "Tom! You...I..."

"Sally, why don't you go relax in my office for a few minutes while I get Mckenna up to speed. Stop by the kitchen and get yourself a soda if you want."

The moment Sally left the room, Mckenna whirled on Tom, pointing an accusing finger. "It's going to take more than a few minutes to bring me up to speed, buster, and you know it. What the hell is going down here?"

"Don't kick down the barn, Mac. This is a great idea.

There are people in this valley who have legal hassles of all kinds and can't afford a lawyer. So they get you for free, and you learn by researching their problems and helping them out of their difficulties."

"You are insane!" Her finger became a weapon, poking into his chest as a pointed punctuation to her objections. "Did it occur to you that it's not doing these people any favors by giving them a fake attorney who doesn't know jack about the law?"

"You know plenty about the law, kiddo. You just have to dig it out. The best way to learn is to do, and dealing with real people and their problems will motivate you."

"No!" Something close to terror gripped her. "I can't do it, and I won't put these people at risk. Send them to legal aid."

"Legal aid is full to bursting. They might not get their cases looked at for weeks. Or months."

"But—"

"And I will be here to make sure you don't deep-six anyone. I'll be here to help."

In the silence, she withdrew her finger from the dent she had poked in his chest, but she refused to meet his eyes. All the joy of her small accomplishments had evaporated. Surviving Mickey D's, her minor victories at the Bark Park, landing a job at the hospital—they seemed as nothing compared to the challenge that Tom laid before her. For a moment Mckenna wondered, even suspected, that Tom Markham might be indulging himself in some sort of revenge for the way she had treated him in the past. She shot him a look dark with suspicion. But those sky-blue eyes held no hint of a "gotcha," and the easy smile was a challenge, not a smirk. Not even a shadow of a smirk. No one could be that good an actor.

"You can do it," he said in answer to her silence. "I know you, Mac. You've never seen a mountain you couldn't climb, especially when that mountain had anything to do with the law. Shall I tell you an embarrassing truth?"

"What?" she said cautiously.

"I hated it that you were going to defend the Harmon case. Don't get me wrong—we caught Mr. Clean Country-Western with his hand in the cookie jar, but if any lawyer was slick enough and just damned good enough to get him off, it would have been you. I never would have told you, but you had me running scared. You were that good. *Are* that good. You're still you, Mac. Everything is still there. You just have to dig and find it."

He made her want to try. Amazing. He was pretty damned good himself. She managed a faint smile. "Are you this persuasive with juries?"

"Only when I believe in the cause, kiddo. Only when I believe."

It seemed so natural for them to come together in a comforting hug, but the moment that Mckenna came up against that solid chest, she knew more than comfort sped her pulse and sent a sudden melting heat into her loins. She looked up at him, and for a heartbeat she thought he might kiss her. Hoped, perhaps, that he would kiss her? But before the moment came to fruition, Sally's voice from Tom's office brought them back to reality. Reluctant, embarrassed, Mckenna pulled away, and Tom let her go.

"I'll try," Mckenna promised.

"You'll succeed."

AFTER AN hour spent with Sally Morgan, an hour searching through the tomes of law in Tom's office, and yet another hour discussing injunctions and restraining orders with Tom, Mckenna drove home wrung out and limp as a dishrag. But happy. She was helping someone, using the tools of the law to make someone's life easier. It felt good. As an added bonus, the floodgates holding back her lost life seemed to have cracked a bit under the crowbar of her determination. And Tom's determination.

Was it merely guilt that prompted him to tutor her? Mckenna couldn't help but wonder. Or perhaps after all this time, after the old Mckenna had frozen him out, might he still be harboring some desire for her? Certainly in that moment before they had remembered Sally waiting in his office, the sizzle in the air had nearly burned them both.

What would she have done, Mckenna pondered, if he had kissed her? Had she wanted to be kissed?

The answer came to her: yes. Definitely yes. Everytime she saw Tom, she marveled at her old self. How could she have turned her back on those kind blue eyes, or the way the corner of his mouth quirked upward at the beginning of a smile? Not to mention the broad shoulders and muscles that had been sculpted by hard work, not by a personal trainer in some gym.

Nell and Jane had both seemed to think she turned up her nose at his cowboy background and unsophisticated tastes. How lame was that? In fact, his cowboy past gave him depth, Mckenna decided as she drove through the dark, alone with her thoughts. He wasn't just another suit, another pampered upper-crust son who had chosen law school over business or medicine.

Yessir. Driving through the moonless night, Mckenna decided that she liked Tom Markham. More than liked him. And if her old self didn't approve of her new taste in men, then her old self could just lump it. Especially since that old self apparently hadn't done all that well in the man department.

Or had she? Mckenna wondered suddenly. How would she know if there wasn't some guy out there who had been the love of her life, and she simply didn't remember him? That was the problem with a Swiss-cheese memory: you didn't know what things had fallen into the holes. But if such a man existed, surely he would have contacted her by now—it had been well over a month since the accident, after all. Or Nell and Jane would have mentioned him.

Nope. The old Mckenna had probably scared away every man in the state, while the new Mckenna just might have found someone she didn't want to scare away. This amnesia wasn't all bad, after all.

That thought kept her warm during the long drive over Mingus Mountain, through a Cottonwood whose sidewalks had long since been rolled up, and out the highway toward a dark, silent Cornville. She would sleep well tonight, Mckenna thought. Why had she ever needed those sleeping pills that had been in her medicine cabinet?

The house was dark when she pulled into the driveway. Mckenna had thought she'd kept on a light that morning when she left. Poor Titi was alone in the dark, wondering, no doubt, if Mckenna was ever going to come home and feed her.

But when she opened the front door and flipped on a light, no Titi greeted her with complaints about the late dinner hour. What did greet her made Mckenna gasp for breath.

The place had been ransacked.

chapter 12

"TITI! OMIGOD! Titi!"

Mckenna's first thought was for the cat, who had become so much more than just a pet. Had she run terrified out into the night to become coyote bait? Had she been hurt when whoever did this horrible thing trashed her home?

"Titi! Oh, please be here!"

She tore through the kitchen, searching under the table and opening every cupboard. Titi loved to open the cupboard doors with her agile paws and curl up inside, beside the pots and mixing bowls. But tonight the cupboards sheltered no Titi.

"Titi, dammit! Where are you?"

Not under the couch with its cushions all tossed about by the intruder. Not behind the television stand Mckenna had picked up at Wal-Mart and put together herself—though she noted absently that the television had gone missing. Not behind the washer or dryer. Not in the bathtub, or behind the stool, or in the bathroom cupboards.

Then she heard a huffy reply. "Here!"

Mckenna rushed into her bedroom and looked under the bed. "Thank God! Are you all right?"

An indignant diatribe greeted her. "Alone all night! Rude man! Crashed window. Tearing, throwing everything. I told him, 'Go away!' Fierce. Like a tiger. But he kicked me. *Kicked* me! Me! Shouted rude words."

"Are you hurt?" Mckenna gently ran her hands down Titi's rib cage. "No, thank heaven. Everything seems to be okay."

"Not okay!" Titi complained. "Mad. You left me. The man came, and no dinner. Starving."

Mckenna lifted the cat into her arms and cuddled her. "I'll give you double your dinner, you brave cat."

Titi sniffed.

"And tomorrow you can stay with Jane while I go in to work."

Would her humble little home ever feel safe again?

She pacified Titi with a heaping bowl of cat gourmet chicken in gravy, then called the police. She knew better than to touch anything—a remnant of her legal past? Right then, she didn't care about her legal past. She just wanted her security back. She also called Tom. She shouldn't have, because it was almost midnight. If she had to call someone, that someone logically should have been Jane, she realized much later when she had time to reflect. But she called Tom.

"I'm coming over," he said immediately.

"No. Tom, you're an hour away. There's no need. I'm fine."

"How do you know you're fine, sitting there alone in a house that's been broken into for God only knows what reason? I'll be there in forty-five minutes."

"Don't you dare drive those mountain curves so fast!"

"I'll be there."

She hadn't argued with him much, Mckenna admitted as she hung up the phone. Every fiber of her being longed for the comfort of his arms around her, telling her everything would be all right. Just as Titi had needed a cuddle from her, she needed a cuddle from someone bigger and stronger than she was. Somewhere in the night, possibly close by, was someone who had raped her home, all for a nineteen-inch television set and heaven knows what else he had carried away. This place didn't have much worth stealing.

But missing possessions didn't anger her nearly as much as the violation of having her home, her private, personal shelter from the rest of the world, casually invaded and desecrated. It left her feeling violated herself. As if she had no place to run, or hide, or be safe. If your home wasn't safe, what was?

Unlike Titi, who enthusiastically tucked into her dinner, Mckenna would not be comforted by a mere bowl of chicken with gravy.

The sheriff's deputy took almost as long to get to the house as Tom. He arrived first by only ten minutes. Thirtyish, balding, with a physique that suffered from too many donuts, Deputy Raeburn recognized Mckenna at once, even though his face didn't ring a single bell in her memory.

"Well, Mckenna Wright, as I live and die!" He stepped through the door she held open. Looking around him, he raised incredulous brows. "You live here?"

Somehow, Mckenna gathered his disbelief didn't have anything to do with the mess surrounding them.

"Hot-shot lawyer Mckenna Wright lives in a—"

Before he could describe the place as a dump, Mckenna interrupted. "In a place that has been ransacked by parties unknown. I haven't touched anything. The place is pretty much like I found it."

He chuckled softly as he pulled out a pad and pencil. "Mckenna Wright lives in Cornville in a trailer. Wait till I tell the guys."

She wondered what she'd done to this fellow, sometimes in her past, that made him take such delight in her circumstances. Had the old Mckenna offended every man on the face of the planet?

"Anything missing?"

"The television, VCR, and a portable CD player."

"Any jewelry, money, computers?"

She hadn't even thought to check the closet-size second bedroom where she kept her computer. She got up and looked. "Yes, the computer's gone, as well. But they left the monitor and printer."

"Anything else?"

"No." She sighed. "I don't think so. There's not much here to tempt a burglar. I can't imagine why anyone would even bother to break in."

Tom asked the same question when he arrived a few minutes later. Watching him greet the deputy by his first name and exchange a friendly handshake, Mckenna speculated that both men were probably members of the MABMW Club—Men Abused By Mckenna Wright.

"Why would anyone want to rob you?" Tom wondered. "A five-year-old home computer that's next to worthless on any market—black market, flea market, or anything else. A nineteen-inch TV that was how old?"

"Six years."

"Nobody burgles a six-year-old TV that won't even get the HDTV broadcasts."

"Well," Deputy Raeburn said cheerfully. "Somebody did."

Tom frowned at the mess. "It almost looks as if someone was searching for something."

"I can't imagine that I have anything of interest to anyone," Mckenna said with a shake of her head.

The deputy put in his two cents. "Drag any witnesses over the coals lately, Ms. Wright? Piss off anyone who might want to get back at you?"

"What?"

Tom came to her defense. "Back off, Chuck."

"It's a fair question. Ms. Wright here didn't exactly make her name as a legal shark by being nice to folks."

"She does her job. And you need to do yours. Don't you have a report to write and a burglar to find?"

The deputy snapped his notepad shut. "Yeah, well, I doubt we'll ferret this one out. If we do find someone to arrest, he'll just hire some fancy lawyer to get him off, or get him probation, or get him back on the streets so he can break into other folks' homes."

Tom shut him up with a warning glare.

The deputy shrugged. "I doubt we can get a fingerprint team out here before tomorrow. Try not to mess anything up. And we'll do our best. We always do."

Tom gave him a look. "Tomorrow for fingerprinting?"

"Hey, waddya want? It's the middle of the damned night!"

"Nice fellow," Mckenna said once the deputy had left. "I suppose he was one of those witnesses I raked over the coals at one time."

Tom grinned. "Not one time. Lots of times. The local law enforcement officers have a name for you that I won't repeat. No one wants to take the stand for the prosecution when Wright is arguing the defense."

"Great." She felt like crying. Every time she thought her luck was picking up, something happened to bring her down.

"Don't look like that," Tom said. "It's traditional for law enforcement to loathe defense attorneys, and the better the attorneys are at their jobs, the more the police dislike them."

Mckenna sighed. "And I'll bet I really reveled in their animosity, didn't I?"

He chuckled. "You did. To you, it was a badge of honor."

"Never knowing that someday I would be groveling for their help and protection."

"Don't worry about that. The guys around here do their job. In the meantime, you shouldn't stay here tonight."

She sagged, too tired for words. "There's that new motel out on the highway."

"Not a chance, Mac. Pack a toothbrush, your jammies, and your cat. You can camp at my place tonight, or for as long as you need to. Tomorrow morning you can call McDonald's and tell them you need the day off. You look like someone drained all the blood out of you."

"Nice to know I'm so fetching." She tried for her usual sassiness and failed miserably. He told the truth. She felt as though she'd been beaten like an old-fashioned rug, until all the life was pounded from her, just like dust flying into the wind. But the thought of Tom's concern, and of having his comfort for the rest of this scary, nightmarish night, did raise her spirits just a bit—raise her spirits and fill her with a warm sense of security that let her surrender to exhaustion. She fell into an irresistible drowse nearly before they left Cornville, wilting slowly down until her head lolled on Tom's shoulder. Rude, she chided herself foggily, but then Tom shifted and gently lowered her into a more comfortable position with her head pillowed on his hard thigh. So warm. So safe. Before she could truly appreciate how good it felt, she fell asleep.

Mckenna didn't wake until they pulled into Tom's driveway, and then she was groggily embarrassed. "Geez, I'm sorry, Tom. You should have shoved me off."

"Why would I do that? Believe me, it would be my pleasure to serve as your pillow anytime you have need of one." His grin somehow made the embarrassment fade. "Welcome to Hotel Markham. Just watch out for the doorman."

The doorman being Clara, who greeted both Tom and

Mckenna with tail-wagging joy, but hesitated when Titi strolled out of her carrier.

Clara advanced cautiously, sniffing, but Titi would have none of her polite advances. The cat jumped onto the nearest chair and fluffed herself out to twice her normal size.

"Usually she gets on well with dogs," Mckenna said. "She goes to Jane's kennel with me all the time. Though she does consider dogs way beneath her."

"She's just showing old Clara that she's not easy," Tom said with a laugh. "They'll be all right."

On this night, Mckenna felt a bit easy herself. Needy, vulnerable, frazzled, and exhausted—a dangerous combination while spending the night in a hunky guy's home.

"I'll sleep on the couch," Tom offered. "You can have the bed."

The image of them sharing that bed popped uninvited into Mckenna's head. Not a good idea, her common sense warned. "I won't throw you out of your own bed," Mckenna insisted. "I don't mind the sofa. Really."

She stretched from weariness. But perhaps a hint of flirtatiousness, also. She knew the stretch of her sweater across her breasts would draw his attention, and a part of her with no common sense at all had seized control of her brain.

"I don't mind the sofa either."

She could feel his eyes upon her, though, and his voice had roughened to a husky tone.

"I sleep on that couch all the time after falling asleep reading a book. You take the bed."

"No, I would feel guilty," Mckenna insisted. "You sleep in your own bed, Tom."

Titi, who had abandoned hostilities and now rubbed herself against Clara's legs, suggested, "Both on sofa. Cat on the bed."

Mckenna couldn't hold back a sudden bubble of laughter at the cat's disgusted comment.

"What's so funny?"

"Nothing." Except the laughter, once begun, fast became hysteria, running out of control. This whole evening had been too much. Absolutely too much.

Hysteria quickly deteriorated to tears, and even Tom's taking her by the shoulders didn't make her stop.

"Mckenna, don't. Tomorrow morning the world will look better."

She couldn't articulate an answer, even if she'd had one. Through tears she saw both Clara and Titi turn concerned faces her way.

"Okay," Tom conceded softly. "Don't stop." He drew her against his chest, smoothed unruly hair back from her face, and rocked her gently in his arms. "Come on. Let's put you to bed."

His tender care brought a fresh flood of tears and wailing.

"What you need is sleep." He picked her up as if she were a child and carried her into his bedroom. A still-rational corner of her mind reproached her for acting like a spineless, childish ninny, and if Tom had respected her at all, he certainly wouldn't after this display. But still she couldn't stop weeping.

When he laid her on the mattress of the king-size bed, she clung to his arm, at the same time apologizing.

"I'm sorry. I'm really sorry."

"Hey. You're entitled, kiddo."

He managed to free himself and abruptly left. His sudden departure sent a chill over Mckenna's body. But within seconds he came back with a cold washrag and a glass of water.

"Drink up." He held the glass to her lips as if she were helpless, which she pretty much was. Then, after she had obediently taken a few swallows, he sponged her face with the cool rag.

Sniffling, she took the rag from him and finished the job. "Where did you learn to be such a good nursemaid?"

He chuckled and sat on the side of the bed. "I raised my two younger sisters. They each threw a fit at least once a week, over school, boyfriends, or what have you. Half the time I didn't even know what it was about, and maybe they didn't, either. But I learned that the storm has to run its course."

"Where was your mother when your sisters were throwing fits?"

"She died when I was twelve. And my dad didn't handle fatherhood all that well. He was mostly gone."

Embarrassed, she gave him back the cloth. "You're quite a guy, Tom Markham."

He smiled. "That's me. You feeling better now? I'll leave if you want to change into your jammies."

She laughed, and some of the sticky cobwebs cleared away from her brain. "Jammies?"

"What my sister Dora used to call her pajamas."

"I don't think I have the energy to change into my jammies," she said with a smile. Then, when he started to get up, she put a hand on his arm. "Don't go, Tom. More than anything, I don't want to be alone right now."

His eyes warned that she treaded on thin ice, but she plunged ahead. Her mood, her unexpected neediness, made no concessions to good sense.

"I know I'm being a crybaby. But please, just stay here a while and talk."

"Mac, you look too tired to so much as open your mouth, much less carry on a conversation."

"If I go to sleep in the middle of a sentence, then you have my permission to leave."

"Okay. You want a beer?"

"A beer at midnight?"

"Beer goes well with conversation, whatever time it is."

"Then we need beer."

When he came back with two bottles of Budweiser, he settled onto the bed beside her. Sitting back against the headboard, bottle in hand, Mckenna decided that beer did go well at midnight, even though right then there wasn't much conversation going on.

On the other hand, tired as she was, just a few swallows of beer made her feel brave. "Tom? Was I really very awful to you back when you worked at BKB?"

He laughed. "Define 'awful.'"

"That definitely sounds like an attorney." She thought a moment. "Awful as in hurtful, rude..."

"Arrogant, brusque, insensitive, narrow-minded, elitist," he finished for her.

She pinched the bridge of her nose between two fingers, wishing she hadn't asked the question. "That bad, was I?"

"No. Not really. And to tell the truth, you didn't discriminate. Every guy I ever saw you with had to pass your third degree."

"Did we ever...uh...were we ever..."

"An item?"

"Yes, an item. Were we?"

"Nope. Not by a long shot. That was part of my problem, because I wanted us to be."

She took another sip of beer and looked over at him, embarrassment bringing tears close to the surface once again. He smiled down at her with those kind blue eyes. "I was an arrogant jackass, straight from the top mark on the bar exam and thinking I was hot stuff. I figured my great accomplishments and my cowboy charm earned me the right to romance the sexiest woman in town."

"Was I sexy?"

"You were very sexy. You still are. More, even, because a

lot of the sharp edges are gone. I'll be honest, Mac, and tell you that I hope that's one thing you don't get back."

Find out who she really was, Jane had advised. Her true self. Mckenna hoped that her true self, if ever it came to the surface, wasn't someone who could consider a man like Tom Markham beneath her notice.

Somehow they had drifted together on the bed, their faces close. "I don't understand," Mckenna almost whispered, "why I couldn't see back then that you're a nice man."

"I am a very nice man."

It took only a couple of inches of forward motion for their lips to touch. As if some electric circuit had been closed, a current sprang to life between them. But he withdrew, his eyes narrowed on her face. Then he carefully took the beer bottle from her hand and put it with his on the bedside table.

Her eyes widened at the hunger in his gaze, but before she could utter a word, they were kissing once again. His hands cupped her face as they melted down onto the bed, legs tangling to lock their bodies together. His lips plied hers gently, caressing, nibbling, and finally devouring. Mckenna responded in kind. She loved the beer-tinged taste of him, the warm scent of soap and denim and aroused male. His day's growth of beard scraped across her chin and cheeks, but she welcomed it.

She crowded closer to him, instinctively tilting her hips into his. His hand found her breast and squeezed gently. Mckenna nearly lost her mind with the pleasure of that simple basic touch.

The kiss slowed. A space opened between his body and hers, allowing cool air to flow between them. Mckenna didn't want cool air, or a cool head, either. She wanted comfort; she wanted desire; she wanted Tom.

"Mckenna," he whispered against her lips. His voice sounded hoarse with bottled-up passion, but when she would have surged back toward him, he held her in place. "Damn you, woman," he said gently. "You are temptation. Temptation with a capital T."

"Temptation can be a good thing," she sighed. "We could—"

"No, we can't." He spoke softly, even sadly, but his hands held her away from him. "Not that I wouldn't love to, Mac. God knows I've dreamed about having you in just this position, on my bed, tangled up so tight with me that we're almost tied in knots. But I won't take advantage of you when you're shaken up and might jump into bed with anyone who offered a shoulder to cry on."

Mckenna closed her eyes. Some men just took chivalry too far. She sagged into the mattress. "Am I in the habit of jumping into men's beds so casually?"

He smiled down at her. "I can't really say. But you never jumped into mine, so you must have had some discrimination."

At that she had to laugh. "My mistake, obviously." She grabbed a pillow and batted him with it. He retaliated, and before long they were both laughing. But when they settled down, she sobered up fast. "Tom, I don't think I'm jumping into your bed just for a shoulder to cry on." She reached out and touched that broad, muscular shoulder through the warm cotton of his T-shirt.

"If that's true, then there will be a rerun of this episode someday soon, won't there?"

Her lips twitched upward. "Can we do it without the burglary?"

"By all means."

"Good." She sighed, so full of jumbled emotions that she hardly knew what she felt any longer.

He shook out the bed quilt and pulled it over her. "Go to sleep, Mckenna. Tomorrow things will be clearer."

Even before Tom finished tucking the quilt around her,

she had fallen deeply asleep. She didn't move or blink when he passed a hand in front of her face.

Beer will do it every time, he mused. He really ought to get off the bed, take the beer bottles to the trash, wash his face, and try to get some sleep out on the sofa. But he didn't want to move. His eyes stayed glued to Mckenna, his breathing adjusted to her rhythm, and even his heart seemed to beat in time to the steady pulse he saw in her throat.

Mckenna Wright. Damn! This woman wasn't the Mckenna he'd known before. This girl was more open and infinitely easier to hurt. Yet a certain pixie humor shone through, along with a personal honesty that the old Mckenna would have buried for fear of making herself vulnerable.

Not to mention that the old Mckenna wouldn't have been caught dead in his bed, lying there looking winsome and almost innocent, not at all the smooth, hard-hitting woman he had long ago decided any man would be insane to court.

All the time, this Mckenna had been lurking inside the Ice Queen, waiting to get out—the soft spots, the humor, the spontaneous affection. Somehow he had always suspected a woman with a big heart lay beneath the sharkskin armor.

Tom lay back, enjoying the warm feeling of her sleeping next to him. If not for her accident, he never would have gotten to know the real Mckenna Wright, never learned that her kiss could shoot desire clear down through his toes. If not for that accident . . .

Quite a coincidence, he thought, Mckenna's run of bad luck. First she drives off a cliff, then she gets fired, and now some thug breaks into her home. For what? he wondered. She had sold most of her fancy furniture for cash before she had moved, replacing it with inexpensive Goodwill purchases that no one would walk through an open door to steal, much less climb through a window for. True, the thief had taken the usual stuff—the computer, television, VCR, and CD player. But those things were so old that no one would have picked them up from an alley if they'd been left there for the trashman. And he still thought the place had looked as if someone were searching for something.

Maybe his time as a prosecutor had warped his mind toward suspicion, but Tom couldn't help but wonder if Mckenna's accident had really been an accident. Nothing added up. He felt as if he were trying to view a whole puzzle from looking at only a few pieces. Sooner or later, other pieces might drop into place.

As long as they didn't drop like blocks of concrete onto Mckenna's head. Feeling protective, Tom rolled close to her and put an arm across her waist. Her hair smelled like some fruity shampoo, and flyaway tendrils tickled his nose as he tucked her head beneath his chin. He smoothed it back into place with a gentle caress of his hand. Mckenna didn't move.

Tom smiled to himself as he drifted off to sleep, thinking about the golden opportunity he had missed. What a sap he was. What a sentimental sap.

TITI LAY in the bedroom doorway like an old-fashioned ceramic cat doorstop, her feet tucked beneath her, her long tail curving neatly around her body. Comforting Mckenna was supposed to be her job, and the spot next to Mckenna on any bed was hers, as well. But she wasn't truly jealous. No dumb kitten, she could recognize a situation where a cat's comfort didn't quite fit the bill. Humans were strange creatures. Sometimes they needed to cuddle with each other rather than reach for the superior company of a cat. Difficult to understand, but there it was.

And after all, Titi had thought from the beginning that

one of the things Mckenna might need in this time of trouble was a little romance in her life. Not that Titi thought much of romance, but people seemed to like it. Television shows were chock-full of humans panting after each other. Silly twits. And that stuck-up impostor corgi Piggy specialized in matchmaking, as if that made her exceptional. At least, the corgi took credit when any of her providers happened to hit it big in the love department.

Could Titi do less? Letting those two scrunch together on the bed without disturbance might be her contribution to a love story. Maybe.

Still, with Mckenna cuddled up to Tom, where was Titi's comfort? Titi, after all, was the one who had endured the break-in and feared for her life. After such shoddy treatment, she could have used a warm, caring body to sleep with, to purr against. Even a dog would do.

She glared at Clara, who snoozed peacefully on the floor by the foot of the bed. A worthless dog, as far as Titi was concerned. Earlier she had tried to sidle up next to that warm furry side, but Clara had given her a look—a look that proved humans were wrong in thinking dogs good-natured—and then she had stalked off on stiff legs, rumbling under her breath. Okay, so Titi had let the silly dog know she was no patsy when she had first come in, but a cat had to put a paw down firmly right at first or endure being chased here and there like some kind of pathetic mouse. Once she had been sure that the lower orders had gotten the message, Titi had shown her softer side, but it turned out Clara was a dog who held a grudge.

And now that Titi felt the need for consolation, the cur wouldn't give her the time of day. How unlike her master Clara was. Mckenna had in the past treated Tom like a scratching post, but now look at the two of them cuddled up together. Touching. Very touching.

And probably, the cat noted, the bed had room for

three. She walked deliberately to the foot of the bed where Clara lay, sprang nimbly onto the mattress, and let her long tail brush tantalizingly over the dog's face.

Clara growled. Titi snatched her tail out of reach, then let it drop again when Clara lowered her head to the carpet. Clara glared. Titi purred.

Satisfied that she had won, she curled into an open space in the tangle of human legs and feet. From there she gazed with condescension at the dog lying on the floor.

Snub a cat, would she? Dogs were such insensitive clods.

chapter 13

MCKENNA WOKE as gray dawn crept through the windows. A glance at the bedside clock told her the time—a little after six, a late hour for one accustomed to rising at five so she could open at the restaurant. She closed her eyes, trying to remember why on this morning, she didn't feel that she had to climb out of bed.

Then it hit her. This comfy bed wasn't hers, and the warm bulk lying against her back wasn't a pillow. The previous night came flooding back. The burglary—scary. And the almost love scene with Tom—even scarier, in its way.

She had to call work to tell them she wouldn't be in—even after giving notice, she owed them a week. And then she had to meet the police at her trailer. But for right now, nothing said that she couldn't lie here next to Tom, his arm draped across her waist, and enjoy the moment. Last night had been... she searched for the right description. And while she searched, she found a few surprises. Memories. Her dreams had been full of memories.

Startled, half-afraid, she bolted upright, disturbing the

cat, who had been comfortably curled in the bend of her knees.

"What?" Tom mumbled and woke as she sat and rudely discarded his encircling arm.

"Nothing." Mckenna feared this new knowledge of herself would disappear at any moment, like the fragments of a dream. Talking might scare them away.

Tom reached up for her. "Come back down here."

She looked down at him, rumpled and drowsy, his eyes regarding her with the warmth of first waking, before reason flows back into the brain. The temptation to sink down beside him, turn into his strong arms, and enjoy the moment's intimacy almost overwhelmed her. But fear goaded her out of bed.

"I've got to call the restaurant," she said as her feet hit the cool floor. "I've got to get back home."

What she really had to do was concentrate hard on these recollections that had snuck out of hiding while she had slept. If she didn't, they might retreat once again.

She could feel Tom's eyes on her as she tried to brush the wrinkles out of her clothes. His gaze rested heavily, making her self-conscious and awkward. After a long silence, he said, "Okay. I'll go fix us some breakfast."

"Really?" She turned in surprised delight. "You cook?"

"Any idiot can throw a couple of eggs into a skillet."

It wasn't that so much as the idea of him caring enough to do it. Breakfast was a small thing, but most single men thought conversation over eggs and coffee smacked entirely too much of dreaded domesticity, as if any intimacy after getting out of bed came with apron strings attached.

Now where did that come from? Mckenna wondered. The floodgates of her dammed past were beginning to open. The prospect both elated and terrified her.

Tom stumbled to the bathroom. He came out with a wet face and dripping hair. "All yours, my lady."

She laughed at him. "You look as if someone doused

you with a bucket of water. Don't you take the time to dry your face?"

"It'll dry."

"Typical guy!" She felt a dose of that domesticity hit her veins. Grabbing a towel, she wiped a droplet from his cheek, then brushed damp hair out of his eyes. And then, as she looked up into that rugged face, her throat almost closed with emotion. "Thank you, Tom."

He lifted one brow in query. "For bed and breakfast? No problem."

"Yes, for that. But mostly for . . . for being so kind."

Touching her cheek, he gave her a smile that was almost sad. "Anytime, sweetheart. I suspect that not many people have been kind to you in your life." Then he grinned. "Breakfast in fifteen minutes."

Left alone, she went into the bathroom and faced her image. Rumpled from sleep, shadows deepening her eyes, the Mckenna reflected in the mirror differed drastically from who she had been in her dreams. In memory she was smooth, sleek, self-assured, with the sharp edge of ambition etching every feature.

There were her parents. She remembered her father's thin face, his thick, graying hair. Her mother had hair as dark as Mckenna's own, assiduously guarding against gray, Mckenna remembered, with the services of an expensive hairdresser. Kenneth and Ellen Wright. Their memory inspired little warmth in her. Mckenna wondered why. Her mother was a fretter. She remembered now. Had they phoned and gotten the disconnect message? She should call them, but for some reason, the notion met with reluctance.

More memories. There was her first day in law school. What a nightmare that had been. Harvard. The nobody from Evergreen, Colorado, playing with the big boys. Her classmates came from families listed in Who's Who. But she had shown them, graduating number two in her class.

Not being number one had annoyed her. She remembered the chagrin, not much dimmed across the distance of seven years. The embarrassment at not being first in her class stung less once she had aced the Arizona bar examination. Top of the list. It was the only thing that would satisfy her.

Mckenna didn't much care for the anxiety that twisted her stomach at the thought of those rankings. That drive to be the best went far deeper than her ambition to improve her French-fry-serving skills at McDonald's. The visceral satisfaction at making top score on the bar exam included a certain agonized fretting that somewhere around some future corner, another test of her excellence—a trial, a brief, a hearing—might not come out so well.

So this was the very together up-and-coming attorney that everyone had thought so competent and tough-minded. Apparently she had hidden her feet of clay very well. How had she lived thinking the first little failure, the first instance of not being the very best, dimmed her worthiness as a person?

Mckenna closed her eyes on the little frown that knitted her brows. Find your true self, Jane had said. Did she want this to be her true self? Would the woman she had been overtake the woman she wanted to be?

Something brushed up against her legs. "Eat a rotten mouse?" Titi asked. "Look like it."

Mckenna relaxed from a stiff tension that she only just then noticed. "I saw a ghost," she said.

"I see ghosts," the cat informed her cheerfully. "Not so bad."

Never try to have a serious conversation with a cat. But Titi was one of the only ones who knew. "Titi, was I a really screwed-up person?"

The cat jumped to the tile counter and sat primly by the basin. " 'Screwed up'?"

"Screwed up. A total loser."

"Fed me twice a day. Took me to the hospital to play with sick people."

Regular food topped Titi's priority list.

"Not home much," Titi observed. "Didn't lie in the sun. Didn't purr."

"Yeah, I'd guess I wasn't big on purring."

"Are you talking to your cat?" asked Tom as he came through the bedroom door.

Great. Now he would be sure she was insane. She brazened it out. "Of course I am. Who else would I be talking to?"

He stuck his head in the open bathroom door, saw Titi sitting on the counter, and tickled the cat under her chin. "As long as she doesn't talk back." Titi shoved her head beneath his hand, purring, a sly cat smile on her face. Tom stroked her, as demanded. "Breakfast is ready, madam. Come and eat before it gets cold."

As he left, the purring swelled. "Good Tom. Breakfast for me, too."

FOR THE amount of sleep he'd gotten, which wasn't much, Tom felt like a million bucks. For breakfast he made not only bacon and eggs, but pancakes, as well. After breakfast he phoned work and told the receptionist he was taking a personal day, then they climbed into his truck and headed for Cornville.

While he hadn't been sleeping the night before, he had lain beside Mckenna, listening to her even breathing, smiling at the little sounds she made in her sleep. He liked Mckenna without her armor. This was the Mckenna he had tried to pry loose when they had worked side by side at BKB. The prospect of having the armor gone forever, of having her continue to look at him the way she had looked at him the night before, had Tom ready to believe in Santa Claus and fairy godmothers.

But like fairy godmothers and Santa, this stroke of luck might prove too good to be true. She could grow back into the woman whose mantra was ambition. Or, more troubling, she could fall prey to some mischief, some "accident" that might finish the job that driving off a cliff had left incomplete.

Call him paranoid, but Tom thought bad luck had been following Mckenna a little too closely to be chalked up to coincidence. Her accident in Oak Creek Canyon could be explained away. The hour had been late. She had a history of high blood pressure. And the impact to her brain might be either the cause or the result of the crash.

But who would want to break into a scruffy little trailer home in Cornville? Any thief with half a brain would choose a place that looked like it might have something worth stealing. Mckenna's place didn't, and the articles stolen weren't worth the effort to haul away. It didn't add up. The more he thought about it, and he had thought about the subject quite a bit during the nearly sleepless night, the more he thought something smelled fishy.

Suppose whoever broke in had been looking for something that had nothing to do with resale on the black market. Mckenna had been lead defense attorney on a case that would be very high profile once it exploded in the media, and Tom's gut feeling told him that she knew something that he didn't know about the case. Gut feeling was something that had always served him well. Hints from other witnesses, hints he couldn't quite put his finger on, made him uneasy about the case, as well as his own nagging sense that something that should have been there wasn't.

But he had never doubted that if something was missing in the prosecution's case, sharp-eyed, clever Mckenna would have known about it. If that something weren't protected under client confidentiality, then eventually she would have told him, because the rules of discovery demanded it. But if that something would damage her case, revealing it, for Mckenna, would have been like pulling a tooth. She might have put it off, and off.

And just suppose someone who had a vested interest in the case had decided that Mckenna couldn't be allowed to tell whatever it was she knew. Just suppose . . .

The scenario that kept pressing itself upon his mind sounded like a plot from a cheap television mystery. Real-life cases were seldom so convoluted. But sometimes they were. Not often, but sometimes.

This could be one of those times.

Or he could simply be a fool lusting after a woman and imagining life to be more complicated than it was.

Through the ride over the grasslands of Prescott Valley and the winding road up the west side of Mingus Mountain, Tom sensed a tension in the way Mckenna sat and looked ahead at the scenery. She had reason enough to be tense after the night before, he mused. But when she finally spoke, her words dealt with something else entirely.

"Last night," she said, still gazing out the window, "while I slept, I remembered things, in my dreams."

"Excellent."

"Do you think that's possible? That I should start to remember things while I'm asleep?"

"Do the memories seem real?"

"I could swear that they are."

"Then it's possible."

"I remembered my first day at Harvard Law."

"Do you remember what you learned?"

She laughed, and a bit of the tension eased. "I learned not to try for the library computers at three in the afternoon. And that the coffee at a certain snack bar tasted like tar."

"Sounds like a profitable first day."

"I remembered my parents, the details of how they look, what they're like."

"Better and better. Everyone told you that eventually things would start coming back."

Her mouth pulled into a grimace. "But I still can't tell a habeas from a corpus."

"The law will come," he said with a chuckle.

She stared silently into the rising sun. Then, "I wonder why all that stuff started flooding back last night? The shock of seeing my place broken into? Or maybe . . . maybe just relaxing with you, forgetting my problems for a space of time."

Yes, indeed. There on his bed, they had forgotten everything for a space of time. If he had forgotten just a little bit longer, then that little episode on the bed might have had a good deal more significance than it presently did.

He was amazed to see her blush, as if her thoughts followed his exactly.

"I was, uh, very forward last night. I hope that I, that you . . . that you don't think I crawl over every man like that."

He smiled.

After a moment of thought, her eyes widened slightly. "Do I crawl over every man I meet like that?"

Tom laughed. "Not as far as I know. At least, that hasn't been my experience."

She bit her lip, a charming habit of uncertainty that had only appeared since her accident. The old Mckenna had been too sure of herself to show such hesitancy. "I'm sorry," she said abruptly.

"Sorry for what?"

"For treating you like slime. That's what I did when we first met, didn't I?"

"Well, I wouldn't exactly say 'slime.' "

She made a rueful face. "I know I apologized before, but

this is different. This time I remember how I treated you, so it's like, a more specific apology."

"I'm glad I had such importance in your memories."

"Well, you didn't deserve how I treated you, Tom. I was . . . rude and arrogant. And stupid, too. Because you're a first-class guy. I should have been flattered you were interested."

"That's me," he said with a crooked grin. "A first-class guy. At the time I certainly thought so. But like I said before, Mac, I shouldn't have put a move on a big fish when I was such a little minnow."

Her sharp little laugh held a shade of bitterness. "Well, I'm certainly not a big fish now, am I?"

That might just be an invitation, he reflected. Things truly were getting interesting. "I'm going to remind you of this conversation when you're the boss of some prestigious law firm. Or when you're back in your big office at BKB and I saunter over to ask you to dinner. I should have a tape recorder going, so I can play back that part where you said I'm 'a first-class guy.' "

"I'm not likely to forget, Cowboy."

He liked her smile. It was more open than he had ever seen it, unfettered by uncertainty, caution, or the icy reserve she had once cultivated. It wouldn't stay that way, of course. Things, people, times never did. They always changed one way or another.

How great it would be if Mckenna could simply pick and choose what she wanted to retrieve from her old life and leave unwanted baggage behind. And if, then, she would choose him.

The thought startled him. True, he had once had Mckenna in his sights and had gotten blasted by return fire before he could get a shot off. Was he serious about taking aim once again? She drew him all the more because she had lost that polished perfection, had become a softer, gentler version of Mckenna Wright, while at the same time maintaining the strength, determination, and courage that he had always admired.

Not to mention she was still a knockout.

But if he truly wanted to get serious about him and her, he risked a repeat performance of getting blasted if she got up on her high horse again.

As if reading his thoughts, she commented on that very issue. "You know, Tom? I really want my life back. Working with Sally Morgan yesterday gave me a good feeling. A right feeling. Digging through the books to find out how we could help her was not only interesting, but, well, worthwhile. It made me really want to be an attorney again, not just so I can wave good-bye to the minimum-wage jobs, but so I can feel like I'm doing something significant for the people I work with."

He gave her a considering look.

"Does that sound too sappy?" she asked with a little grimace.

"I don't think it's sappy at all. I think it's great you feel that way. What you just said is what the law should be about."

"Yes, well, I think I've remembered why I loved what I did, work-wise. But I'm beginning to almost be afraid of what I was, person-wise. Sometimes I feel as if the old Mckenna is lurking in some cave in the dark of my mind, and someday she's going to come strutting out to move back in. I don't like some of the things I'm remembering about her."

He wanted to focus on her expression, to discover if she spoke sincerely or merely pulled his chain. But he couldn't. They had topped Mingus Mountain and started down the other side over a narrow, winding highway that required his eyes stay locked on the road. He heard a note of real concern in her voice, though, and suddenly he wondered how it would be to lose your whole identity, labor long and hard to build a new one, then have the old you creep out and try to take over the show. Maybe he and Jane and others who were watching Mckenna go through this didn't appreciate the tough bull fate had given her to ride.

When he didn't respond, she switched to the less personal. "This view from up here is so spectacular."

He risked a glance to see her face turned to look off the side of the mountain over the entire expanse of the Verde Valley. The communities of Clarkdale, Cottonwood, and Camp Verde were mere smudges on the valley floor, while Sedona hid itself in the folds of the vermilion escarpment that rose abruptly in the distance. Up above, on the plateau, San Francisco Peaks jutted upward, almost a hundred miles distant.

"I drive this road all the time," she said. "But when you're driving up here, you really can't appreciate the scenery, can you?"

The scenery he wanted to appreciate had nothing to do with vistas of mountain and valley, and everything to do with smooth skin and velvet brown eyes. And the little frown that worried the smooth line of her brows.

"Mckenna, don't you think you have enough things to worry about without imagining your old self staging a coup?"

"Seems silly, doesn't it?"

"You can be whoever you want to be, you know? There's not the old-you and the new you. There's just you. You, now. When old memories come back, maybe they'll bring old habits and prejudices with them, but you always have a choice. In some things maybe you've learned better ways, attitudes you like better than your old ones. It's always your choice."

"You're right."

"And besides, the Mckenna Wright of three months ago was a good person. She's not some snake lurking in the weeds ready to strike."

"Thank you, Tom." She put a hand on his arm, which made concentration on the road more difficult. "I know the old Mckenna did miss something, though, something really good, when she took a pass on you."

He laughed. If that wasn't a go-ahead, then he had never heard one. "Mac, kiddo, she didn't miss a thing. Lucky for her, the main attraction is still in the building."

They drove on in comfortable silence, Tom watching the winding road, Mckenna gazing at the spectacular vista, humming a little tune under her breath. Tom struggled with the pros and cons of adding one more worry to her already long list. He didn't want to. The macho part of him that still followed the rodeo game and sang along to country-western music wanted to somehow wrap her in cotton and protect her. He wanted to declare her *his* woman. His to protect. His to comfort. His in every way.

But she wasn't his woman, and even if she wanted that dubious honor, the Mckenna he knew, both the old and the new, liked handling her own problems. The idea that she needed a man to shield her would never wash. The night before, she had been frightened and needy, and she had turned to him fast enough. But she had wanted him for comfort and distraction, not for running her life.

So after they twisted their way through the little mountain town of Jerome and the road finally stretched out straight and level on the valley floor, he laid his suspicions flat out.

"You know, Mac, I'm beginning to think that you've had too much bad luck lately."

"What do you mean?"

"First you drive off a cliff. You survive that—which you really shouldn't have—and then your house is robbed."

"I don't see any connection."

"Maybe there isn't. But was there any reason for you to drive off the cliff that night? Had you been drinking a lot?"

"I don't remember."

"I was with you for a lot of the night. We were having a few words about the Harmon case at the Rainbow's End. Probably I left not long before you went home. And when I left, you hadn't drunk nearly enough to influence your driving."

"My doctor said I had a stroke—or at least the next best thing."

"But he's not sure about it."

"Well, no. But he said I was bad about taking my blood-pressure medication, and just generally terrible about stress management and everything else. I guess I was a catastrophe waiting to happen. In fact, I think those were his very words right before I got out of the hospital."

"I can certainly believe that was true. But even so, you're...thirty?"

"Yes. And still younger than you."

He grinned at the little stab. "A mere spring chicken. And that's my point. How common is it for a young sprig like yourself to have a stroke, even if you have stress out the kazoo and are the world's worst blood-pressure patient?"

She turned to look out the window, and he saw the muscle of her jaw tighten. "Point taken. But I can't think why anyone in the world would wish me harm. Real harm, I mean. I'm a nobody."

"Now you're a nobody—no offense. But before you were let go from BKB, you led the defense on a case that, while it's a relatively minor drug offense, involves the multimillion-dollar enterprise of a popular icon whose worshipful fans regard him as Mr. Clean, a return to family values, and on and on ad nauseam."

"You surely aren't accusing Todd Harmon—"

"I don't accuse anyone without a load more evidence than just a hunch. I'm just saying be careful. Keep your eyes peeled. Don't leave your doors unlocked. Get a big dog."

She laughed. "Now I know you're joking. A big dog, indeed."

A warning growl from the cat carrier on the crew-cab seat drove home her point.

"Okay. No big dog. Just sharpen the cat's claws."

He turned into the dirt driveway that led to her house. No police car waited for them.

"We're a bit early," Tom said, checking his watch. "When I called the sheriff's office this morning, they said they'd be here about ten."

"Are you going to mention this theory of yours to the police?"

Chuckling, he shook his head. "Hell no. They don't believe me half the time when I do have a pantload of evidence. And by the way, before the fuzz arrives..." He slid his arm along the seat behind her shoulders. "I was real proud of myself last night for not taking advantage of the very hot lady who was scared and tired and maybe had a swallow too many of beer inside her. But now that you have your wits together, kiddo, I consider you fair game."

She gave him one startled look before he bent toward her and took a kiss, but he met softness, a hesitant eagerness, and maybe a hint of desire. She melted against him willingly, opening her mouth to his gentle invasion, sliding her arms around him, giving sweetly, so sweetly, of her warmth. Beneath the sweet warmth lay fire. He could feel it, calling to him, daring him to probe deeper to a fiery core of response.

But now was neither the time nor the place. He simply wanted to serve notice. Well, that, and he had really, really wanted to kiss her. Ever since last night he had burned. Truthfully, the kiss threw fuel on the fire rather than eased it, but oh, having her in his arms, under his mouth, was worth it.

He pulled back, steadying her with his arms. She looked as flustered as he felt.

"Mac, it's going to happen between you and me. You know it. I know it. The only uncertainties are when and where."

She exhaled a forceful breath, as if she'd been running faster than she could breathe.

"It won't happen when you're working over at my place," he told her. "So you don't have to get yourself in a twist when you come over. But it's going to happen. There's this thing between us, like a good taut rope, and it's drawing tighter and tighter everytime we see each other."

She merely swallowed hard. Had his kiss been that good? (He hoped so.) Or could she merely not think of her usual wisecrack riposte? Very unlike his Mac.

Finally, she spoke. "Okay," she breathed with a sigh. "Thanks for the notice."

"Don't mention it."

"You're from the last century, you know that? And I mean the nineteenth, not the twentieth."

He grinned. "Thank you."

And just in time, there came the police.

chapter 14

MCKENNA GRATEFULLY accepted Jane's invitation to move to the kennel for a few days. She didn't have to go back to the restaurant—when she stopped by Thursday afternoon after she was through with the police, they told her she didn't need to bother coming in for her last week. Sorry to leave the friends she had made there, but glad to be shed of the place, she said her good-byes, then packed a duffel bag with some clean clothes and Titi's favorite cat food and headed to the Bark Park.

"Of course you can't stay there alone after what happened!" Jane declared. "Are you certain that you're going to be all right here when I leave for Tucson this weekend?"

"Sure I am. I'm fine. Just a little spooked, is all. Is this the guest room?" She set her duffel bag on the hide-a-bed sofa in Jane's living room.

"Yes, or you can sleep with me if you want. I have a king-size bed."

"You already have two big dogs sleeping with you. You don't need me and a cat."

Titi jumped onto the back of the sofa and gave them a lofty look. "Dogs belong on the floor."

Jane laughed at the cat's tone. "What a meow! I think Titi wants her own bed."

Mckenna smiled. "You're closer than you know."

"You want some tea or something? Girl, you look like someone rode you hard and put you away wet."

"Thanks." Mckenna followed her to the kitchen. "Some tea would be good." She sank down onto a kitchen chair, leaned her elbows on the table, and dropped her weary head into her hands. How glad she was not to be alone back at her trailer. Who would have thought that she was such a wuss?

Jane put a teakettle on the stove to boil and then sat across from her. "Did the cops find anything?"

"Who knows? There's got to be fingerprints everywhere. Mine, yours, Tom's. Maybe they'll get lucky and find a strange set of prints belonging to someone on the National Register of Bad Guys. They dusted for prints here and there and looked at the window where he broke in. I ask you, Jane, who would want to break into my place? It doesn't make sense."

"I don't know, Mckenna. This place has some deadbeats, some real lowlifes. Maybe somebody was hoping to find something worth stealing in your trailer."

"Uh-huh. And a mile up the road are three-hundred-thousand-dollar homes that have everything a thief could hope to find. It just doesn't make sense."

But Tom's theories had begun to make sense, which just went to prove how shaken she was by all of this. Her returning memories, the break-in, Tom's suspicions, and, oh, yes, Tom Markham becoming a genuine object of lust in her mind. Not only her mind. Lust settled in other places, as well.

The kettle whistled. Jane poured hot water in two

mugs—both trophies from obedience trials—and dropped in generic tea bags.

"Here you go." She set one of the mugs in front of Mckenna. "Hot tea cures everything. At least, that's what my mother used to say."

"Thanks," Mckenna said with a sigh. "Tom thinks some-one is targeting me for mayhem. Me specifically."

Jane looked alarmed. "He does?"

"He does."

"I've always thought Tom had a lot on the ball. You should get a dog."

"What is this? A plot against poor Titi? Tom suggested the same thing."

"That just goes to show that the man has his head in the right place. There's nothing makes a person feel more se-cure than a good dog."

"Well, I don't want a dog. I already have a cat who wants to run my life. What I want is all these cobwebs cleared out of my brain. I want to quit bumping into myself unexpect-edly and being surprised at what I see."

Jane heaped a spoonful of sugar into her tea and re-garded Mckenna curiously. "You still want your old life back?"

Mckenna grimaced. "I want the law back. The other night with Tom—and a real client—I realized that it's a part of me. If I don't get it back, well, I've lost an important part of myself."

"I guess I can understand that."

"It doesn't mean that I want to be that woman who thrived on stress and lived on sleeping pills, who spent so little time at home that her own cat barely recognized her. But I need to remember. If I can't deal with the old Mckenna, how can the new Mckenna ever be complete?"

Jane raised her brows. "Heavy."

"Yeah. Welcome to my life."

"Hm." She took a sip of tea, frowned at Shadow, who

was looking hopefully at the hamburgers thawing on the counter, and then shifted her frown to Mckenna. "I have an idea. If you want to really remember your old self, and I mean your really basic old self, why not hop up to Denver and visit your family? I can't believe you haven't done that yet."

Mckenna grimaced, and Jane's eyes widened in distress. "You do remember your family, don't you?"

"Of course I do. Sort of. In fact, I dreamed about them last night, among other things. And this morning I was feeling guilty for not calling them. Still, I get the feeling I didn't stay in touch too well. Maybe for a reason."

"If you dreamed about your family, it's got to be a sign. You're supposed to go see them. You have plenty of time to get ready. I'll be gone a week in Tucson. When I come back—hopefully bragging about Shadow winning High in Trial every day—you can hop in that little car of yours and head north. Just in time for Christmas. Perfect. Shadow! Get your eyes off that hamburger!"

When Jane spoke with the voice of authority, few—people or dogs—could stand against her. Shadow gave the hamburger a rueful look and padded over to sit attentively at Jane's feet, and Mckenna yielded to Jane's logic and realized that she really did need to see family. A visit had been in the back of her mind since she had first gone through her address book and recognized their names. Over the past few weeks, the blank spaces in her memory that were mother and father had filled in with a few details, and then last night, those vivid pictures had come into her dreams.

"Maybe you're right, Jane. I should go to Denver for Christmas."

"You shouldn't have waited this long to see them."

"Every time I reached for the phone to call, my hand stopped halfway there. They don't even know anything is wrong."

Jane gave her a look.

"I just couldn't bring myself to make the call. It would have been like confiding in strangers."

"Weird."

"Did I ever talk about my family, before the accident, I mean? My parents? My sister?"

"I can't say that you ever did. At least to me."

Titi interrupted the conversation by jumping up onto the kitchen table. "Feed the cat," she demanded.

Jane laughed and brushed her off. "Rude pest. Cats, I swear. I don't know why people put up with them. Mckenna, you really should get a dog."

JANE LEFT for Tucson early Saturday morning after giving Mckenna a list of kennel dos and don'ts that covered everything from A to Z and back again.

"You sure you'll be all right?" Jane asked.

"I'll be great. Really. Suzy will be around if I need any help. I have her phone number. Go."

She went, leaving Mckenna and Titi alone with twenty-five dogs, ten cats (not counting her own), and two bunnies. Mckenna felt secure, though. Now that she had a little space between her and the break-in, the idea that the intruder was anything more sinister than a down-and-out thief looking for an easy mark seemed ludicrous. True, the expensive homes up the road offered more lucrative pickings, but they also offered security systems and daunting high walls. Maybe the guy had just been lazy.

Everything perked along smoothly during the weekend. The kennel had nearly a full complement of guests, but hard work didn't bother Mckenna. And during her downtime she became acquainted with Jane's computer. Jane had asked her to research county and state animal laws—a neighbor down the road from the kennel let his two antisocial terriers run free, and Jane wanted to know her legal options in dealing with the problem. Mckenna suspected that Jane knew the pertinent animal laws by heart and simply wanted to add her bit of encouragement in Mckenna's return to the law. But Mckenna willingly went along with the ruse, grateful that she had friends who cared.

While Mckenna worked in the kennel, Titi had the time of her life strutting up and down the aisles between pens, tail high, whiskers erect, lording it over the dogs.

"I like kennels," she told Mckenna, purring. "Dogs are all penned up."

At the time, Mckenna was scooping kibble into half a dozen different bowls and loading them on a wheeled cart. This was her second feeding trip, and she still had two more to go. She was in no mood for Titi's shenanigans. "If you start them barking one more time, *you're* going to be penned up."

"Cages are for dogs, not cats."

"We could change that really fast."

"Cranky."

"Busy," Mckenna snapped.

"Go lie in the sun. Feel better."

That made Mckenna laugh. "Is that your solution for everything?"

"No. Go lie where the hot air comes out of the floor."

"The heating vent. Right." She gave the cat a fond look. "You're right, you know? I need to find a human equivalent of lying in the sun."

"Or where the hot air comes out."

"I'll have to think about that. You might do me some good after all, Titi."

"Of course. Therapy cat." With a smug look on her face, the cat padded off, heading for the Great Dane halfway down aisle one.

"Don't bother the dogs," Mckenna scolded.

Titi gave her an arch look over her shoulder. "Watch

and learn." Then she sprang nimbly to the top of kennel three, where Cato the Great Dane bounced up from where he lay and tried to sniff at the intruder that dared dance on the wire roof of his pen.

"Titi!" Mckenna said sharply. "Get off there."

Titi's whiskers twitched in something very like a smile. "Cranky," she replied, unconcerned. "Cranky, cranky, cranky. Learn to have fun."

"You are not going to have fun if Cato gets hold of you."

"So serious," Titi complained. "Always so serious."

With a flair that rivaled the Great Wallendas, Titi strolled along the top frame of the pen, doing a seductive little dance for Cato's benefit. "Have fun!" She threw Mckenna a kittenish glance. "Live for fun."

"Titi..."

"Be daring." She hissed boldly down at the Dane, who responded with a troubled whine. "Take chances." Her tail flicked into the pen, dangling like a fishing line into dog territory, nearly brushing Cato's nose.

"You little devil!" Mckenna tried to reach for her, but the top of the pen was too high.

Titi whisked the tail out of Cato's domain just as the dog leapt for the bait. "But not too many chances," Titi advised.

Tail aloft, the cat danced along to the next pen, where a puzzled German shepherd watched with a tongue-lolling grin. Titi reached through the wire top and waved her paw in invitation. Mckenna groaned, but the shepherd couldn't quite reach the cat.

"Be bold," Titi continued. "Be entertaining. Be entertained." The dog followed as she sauntered above the pen in tight circles, until finally the circles became so tight the dog nearly turned himself inside out. Titi made a sound very close to laughter.

"Fun is everywhere," she said. "Look. Too serious. Work can be play."

Mckenna found herself smiling, in spite of the annoyance.

"Good!" Titi crowed, dancing a little cat jig on top of the pens. "She smiles."

"Work can be play," Mckenna echoed. "And misbehaving cats can be caged in the other room. Now get down from there before one of those dogs manages to snatch a cat appetizer."

After a final pounce onto a confused cocker spaniel's quarters, Titi jumped across to a shelf and hunkered down beside a sack of Purina. She blinked innocently at Mckenna. "Still cranky," she grumbled.

Mckenna gave her a scratch between the ears. "Go lie in the sun," she advised with a chuckle.

With all the boarding animals to keep her company and Titi at her side, Mckenna couldn't really feel alone. But she was grateful when Tom called every day to check up on her, and Jane, as well. On Sunday, even Nell called.

"Jane called and told me what happened!" Nell exclaimed. "You must have been so upset! Have the police collared the thief?"

"Not yet," Mckenna told her. "There's very little for them to go on."

"Bummer. I should send Piggy to stay with you a while. She's excellent at solving mysteries."

Mckenna laughed, and it felt good to laugh. "Don't bother. Seems to me that Piggy usually causes more trouble than she solves."

"How could you say such a thing?" Nell said with a chuckle. Then her voice grew serious. "Are you sure you're all right? Titi's taking care of you?"

"We're both fine. But, Nell, it really is good to know I have friends like you and Jane."

"You'll call if you need me?"

"I will."

"All right, then. We'll not send in the Piggy squad. For now."

Mckenna laughed again. When she hung up the phone, she wondered if the old Mckenna had appreciated what good friends she had.

On Monday, Suzy Crider came to the kennel to watch things so Mckenna could report to her new job at the hospital. She had spent a few hours with Cindy the week before, so she knew what was expected.

"People skills," Cindy had told her in no uncertain terms. "Dealing with volunteers is different than with employees. The volunteers don't really have to do anything you tell them to." Then her face had brightened. "But I know you have great people skills. I've seen you and Titi with the patients."

People skills. Mckenna was a great persuader at the kennel. She could talk clients into training, spaying, and neutering slicker than a snake-oil salesman. Not to mention the occasional closing argument—usually on whatever legal case was being mentioned on cable news— before an appreciative jury of cats or dogs. Would she do as well with the hospital volunteers?

The first day went smoothly, much due to Titi's help. Diane, her new boss, had suggested that the cat come with her to work.

"That way you can visit patients on your lunch hour, or if you have a break. They really enjoy your Titi, and the staff does, too. She's so loving."

She was. All you had to do was show her a person in need of a cat to pet and she willingly went to work.

Tuesday Mckenna started work on a hospital volunteer website, with the help of a computer guru who worked in administration. When she had to consult with the legal office about photo release forms from the volunteers, she got an unexpected greeting from the legal staff. They knew all about Mckenna Wright the hot-shot attorney, Mckenna

Wright the patient, and the Mckenna Wright who tagged along when Titi did her hospital rounds.

"You mean, you're working at the hospital?" a young woman attorney asked. "Not…not in this office!" As if she suspected someone had kept the secret from her.

"No." Apparently they didn't know about her fall from legal grace. "I'm taking some time off from the law. And I'm helping out in the volunteer department."

The young attorney gave her a quizzical look, but all she said was "Wow!"

Within thirty seconds they had cleared the wording of the release forms, and one of the other attorneys, an older man with white hair and a quiet smile, asked her to look over one of the lawsuits pending against the hospital.

Mckenna sought a graceful way to refuse, but could only stammer that she didn't feel qualified.

He was having none of it. "I know civil law isn't your specialty, but I'd be interested in your opinion. It would be a waste having you here in the office and not hearing what you have to say about it."

So he sat her down at his desk and put a brief in front of her.

"Read the fourth paragraph on the second page. The bit about the assisting physician."

She read. Then she went back and read over the entire brief with an absorption that seemed totally natural. With a shake of her head, she said, "The physician's toast. You know that. And so does he. But the hospital shouldn't bear any liability here. I hope the case is being argued before a judge, not a jury."

"Jury," the hospital attorney said.

"Ouch. In that case, I'm afraid all I can say is 'Good luck.' One never knows what a jury will do."

On her way back to her own storage closet/office, a bolt of adrenaline surged through her veins as she realized she had actually understood the case. Without even thinking about it, once she had let herself sink into the legal details, the salient points, the precedents, the possible strategies of both sides simply were there. She hadn't needed to dig, or strain, or pound her head against a wall to jar her recalcitrant brain. It had all simply appeared.

It was happening, just as the doctor had said it would. Whatever had affected her memory—blood clots, bruises, whatever—she was recovering. Hallelujah!

Back at her desk, Mckenna almost picked up the phone to call Tom. But didn't. Intruding into his workday to shout her excitement over such a minor thing seemed a bit pushy. She tried to tell herself that was the reason. But honesty compelled her to admit that her last encounter with Tom had left her shaken.

It's going to happen between you and me. You know it. I know it. The only uncertainties are when and where.

He had made the statement with such calm certainty. It had sent a shiver down her spine. Not a bad shiver. A sort of helpless, sensuous female shiver—one she wasn't at all sure she was prepared for.

So she needed a bit of distance from Tom Markham. Heaven knew she had enough complications in her life right now without bringing romance into the mix. And a strange romance it would be. Two weeks from now, she might not be the person she was today. As memory returned, along with old habits and attitudes, would Tom still like the woman she could become? And what if that transformed woman turned her nose up at Tom?

Though if she did such a stupid thing, she should be booted sharply in the behind. From where Mckenna currently stood, she couldn't imagine any sane woman turning up her nose at Tom Markham.

Still, she didn't phone Tom to share her small triumph in the legal department. Instead, she snapped on Titi's therapy vest and leash and wandered up to the second-floor patient area to give the patients a cat fix.

The charge nurse greeted her with a smile. The staff of Verde Valley Medical Center had become accustomed to seeing cats, dogs, and Theodore the certified therapy bunny parade through the medical units. "Don't go in twenty-seven. He's contagious. And thirty-two has a compromised immune system, so skip that room. Everyone else is fair game."

They couldn't get started, however, until the staff at the nurse's station said "Hello" to Titi.

"They love me." The cat purred as a nurse scratched behind her ear. "More," she demanded when the scratching stopped. "Don't leave. Pet the cat."

She was equally demanding of the patients. Titi seemed to think she owned the hospital—the hospital, the beds, and the people in the beds. As far as the cat was concerned, the beds were hers. She just loaned them out to sick people who needed them. But because they were hers, she got to nap in them whenever it pleased her. If a patient wanted to pet her and snuggle while she relaxed, all the better. She accepted the attention as her due.

Patients crammed the unit that day, as the influenza season had arrived with gusto. They didn't bother those who appeared to be sleeping. One old gentleman waved them away dismissively, apparently not a cat fan.

"He doesn't know what he's missing," Mckenna comforted her partner. Titi got mortally offended if anyone she met didn't want to pay her homage.

The three-year-old in thirty-four squealed with delight when Titi strutted in, however, and her mother's grin showed equal excitement. Titi endured clumsy but enthusiastic caresses from one pudgy little hand—a cast encased the other arm and hand.

The middle-aged woman in thirty-six purred almost as loudly as Titi when the cat snuggled up against her side. She told them all about the two cats she had at home and how the worst thing about having an appendectomy was not sleeping with her pets.

Then they came to room forty-one, and Mckenna recognized the patient lying in the bed.

"Hello, Doris."

"Mckenna!" Doris's greeting had enthusiasm, if not volume. The elderly woman looked yellow and shrunken, half-sitting in her bed, a fashion magazine in her lap and the television tuned to an all-news channel. "And where is darling Titi?" she demanded.

Mckenna lifted the cat onto the bed. "Titi is right here."

While Doris crooned and petted Titi, Mckenna felt like dancing with excitement. She hadn't seen Doris since before the car accident, yet she remembered her clear as day. The feisty old gal lived at Desert Acres, a nursing-care facility the pet therapy group visited at least once a month. Doris was one of Mckenna's favorites, because the woman adored Titi. And while Titi willingly spread her favors far and wide, she seemed to harbor a special affection for Doris. Perhaps because the woman knew that special place under the chin where a cat always loved to be scratched.

Right now, though, Doris looked very fragile. Her hair, which she always had styled weekly by the Desert Acres beautician, stuck out at odd angles and needed a washing. Lines of pain framed her mouth and dulled eyes that had always shone with a bright and impish light.

And Mckenna remembered all this. But the triumph she might have felt was dulled by the obvious suffering of the woman lying on the bed.

But it took more than discomfort to quench Doris's spirit. "You're looking better than when I last saw you," the old lady observed. "I've always said you would look better with a bit more weight on you. Have you finally found yourself a man?"

Mckenna laughed, but her face did heat a bit. "No man, Doris. If I find a good one, I'll throw him your way."

The patient smiled serenely. "Don't bother, dear. It wouldn't do me any good. I'll not be leaving the hospital this time around."

The unemotional declaration made Mckenna's smile fade.

"Don't look so shocked, dear. I'm a very old lady, and when a person gets this old, death no longer looks like such an enemy. My liver's going. My heart seems to beat only when it damn well pleases. And probably there's parts of me they don't know about that aren't working all that well, either."

Denial was on the tip of Mckenna's tongue, the standard "You'll be out of here in no time," or "Don't be talking like that. You've got years left." But she didn't utter the lies. It was obvious that Doris had gone downhill very fast, and the old lady had accepted her fate with peace. So instead, Mckenna was honest. "Doris, I don't know what to say."

"Oh, you don't have to say anything, dear. You've done enough just bringing Titi here. I'm so grateful to see her again. I've always loved animals, you know. The days that you girls bring your pets to the home are very special to us."

Titi purred loudly enough to vibrate the bed.

"I don't mind dying, really." Doris waved a hand toward the television, where a news commentator talked about the latest political wrangling in Washington, D.C. "And listening to that almost makes me grateful I'm not going to stick around much longer. You young people, you've got to live in a vicious world."

She gave Mckenna a deep old look, then sighed. "Take some advice from an old lady, dear. Don't put off living. Don't delay doing what you want to do, what you should do, until you think the time is ripe. I didn't put anything off, I tell you. And I'm glad of it. I never said, 'I'll do this tomorrow when I have more time,' or 'I'll wait until the money is there,' or 'My friends will still be there next year. I'll go see them then.' Let me tell you, years fly, and before you know it, you're walking with a cane and taking out your teeth at bedtime. Then suddenly you've got an appointment with the man upstairs. I don't mind, because I've done everything I needed to do. Aren't many people who can say that."

"Doris," Mckenna said softly. "You're a remarkable woman."

"Yes, I am," the old lady said with satisfaction. "So many of my friends . . . They didn't take the cruise, didn't make the trip to visit their kids, didn't bother with this or that because it was inconvenient, or expensive, or what have you. A lot of them are passed on, and now they'll never do whatever it was they put off." She squeezed Mckenna's hand. "Don't you do that, dear. You have fun while you're still young and energetic."

Mckenna and Titi stayed with Doris for the rest of the lunch hour, and Mckenna promised to come back for a daily visit, if she could. When she got back to her office, five phone messages called for her attention. Diane had left a note about typing up letters regarding the next volunteer orientation, and one of the chaplains waited for her because he couldn't find the hospital devotional tapes. The work piled up enough to keep her thoughts away from Doris and the slightly eerie feeling that the old woman had unerringly aimed her advice right at the bull's-eye of Mckenna's problems.

The next evening, Mckenna drove over the mountain to Tom's place for what she had come to think of as their double-duty legal aid—aid for those who couldn't afford a lawyer, and aid for Mckenna herself, so she could recover her education-in-hiding, except maybe it wasn't hiding quite as well as it had been the week before.

On the drive over, she reminded herself of her thoughts about needing distance. She smiled to recall Tom's promise that they wouldn't jump each other when she worked at his place. Had he known she would need the reassurance before walking back into his lair? And was she truly nervous, or just seething with anticipation?

Be careful, she warned herself. *Remember that you don't need more complications.*

Then Doris's words echoed in her mind. "Do what you need to do before it's too late." Mckenna imagined herself tottering around with a cane, her teeth in a glass, and still wondering if taking a chance with Tom Markham might have been a good thing after all.

"I need a place to lie in the sun," she told Titi.

The cat opened one eye, not deigning to move from where she was curled on the passenger seat. "Clara?" she asked.

"Yes, you get to harass Clara tonight."

"Good." The eye closed. Apparently, Titi felt that Mckenna had already gotten her dose of advice for the day.

Tom behaved with professional propriety the entire evening, which proved both a disappointment and a relief to Mckenna. Two "clients" took up most of her attention, however. Ruth Morris, a hardworking woman with four children, a husband who had taken off to live with his girlfriend, and a mounting pile of medical bills, believed she had been let go from her job at a local discount store because of her health problems. Soon she would be out both a wage and her health benefits. Jack Heidinger had a neighbor harassing him about his dogs, even though the dogs were quiet and he had only two, one less than the maximum allowed by city zoning.

"This jerk's called the cops on me three times," Jack complained. "Says Toby and Rose are barking. But it's those two boxers down the street that are doing the barking. The other day he threatened to slip my dogs some ground glass in hamburger unless I got rid of 'em. Regular animal hater, he is. And if he hurts my dogs, I'm going over there with a shotgun. I sure am."

How fortunate that Mckenna had just been researching animal law back at the kennel, thanks to Jane.

Mckenna gave Ruth some sympathetic reassurance, then managed to calm Jack out of his vengeful plans, though she acknowledged to herself that if someone had made a similar threat to Titi, she would be tempted to grab the nearest blunt object and teach the offender some manners. She vowed to do more research and put together a plan for both clients. The shelves of law books behind Tom's desk held none of the threat that they had the week before. She already had ideas about where to look for precedents and what solutions would apply.

She didn't finish her research until ten, and discussing her ideas with Tom took another forty-five minutes. By the time she gathered up her handbag and her cat, preparing to leave, exhaustion dragged her down like lead pumped into her veins. But she felt a warm satisfaction from the work, and when Tom said, "I'm proud of you, Mac," his words temporarily banished weariness and made her smile glow.

"It's coming back," she confessed. "I went over to legal at the hospital yesterday, and they asked me to look over a case. I almost felt like I knew what I was doing."

"That's great. Soon you'll be commanding those big fees again."

The remark brought her back down to earth. Were huge fees what this was all about? Had money and status been Old Mckenna's only goals? And were they what the new Mckenna strove for? She didn't think so. Her short time working with Tom had made her realize that the law profession itself, in spite of ever-popular lawyer jokes, was neither sleazy nor self-serving. The law profession was whatever individual lawyers—like Tom, like Gil Bradner—made it, and ultimately, everyone had to decide how they would use their skills.

She wondered if someday, when she looked back upon her life, she would be as peaceful as Doris. Some part of her wanted to tell Tom about Doris and how her conversation had struck a chord inside her. But it was a very personal chord, and for a while, she wanted to keep Doris and her words of wisdom a matter for private contemplation. But there was something she could share with Tom, a decision Doris's admonitions had helped her reach.

"Tom, when Jane comes back, I'm going to Denver to visit my family for Christmas."

He smiled wryly. "You make that sound like you're going to climb Mount Kilimanjaro without a jacket."

She shook her head and laughed. "Well, maybe it won't be that hard. But imagine facing your parents and admitting there's very little you remember about them."

"With my family, that would be a boon. But seriously, Mac, I think it's a great idea. Your memory is coming back in droves. Being with your family, in the place you grew up, can only help."

"I'm only going for a week. Diane was really nice about letting me have the time, but I can't take longer than that."

"When is Jane coming back?"

"Saturday. I plan to leave next Thursday." Uneasy about the whole prospect, she asked, "Did I ever say anything to you about my folks? How we got along? What kind of people they were?"

He shook his head. "We never got that personal, Mac. I can't help you there."

"Yeah. I figured."

"Not that I didn't try to get that personal," he reminded her with a grin. The grin grew wider as he took her handbag out of one of her hands and Titi's leash out of the other. "You really look done in." He stepped closer. "Are you sure you shouldn't bunk here for the night?"

A sudden blossoming of temptation made it hard to remember that she needed some distance. "Is that a proposition?" She tried to make the question sound scolding, but it came out more hopeful than reproving.

"Hell no, it's not a proposition. I did promise not to jump you when you came over to work here. Didn't I?"

"You did."

"So you can sleep here in perfect safety. One of us would use the couch."

That arrangement would last about five minutes, Mckenna thought. She trusted Tom, all right. But trusting herself would be just plain stupid. "I'd better go home. I'm fine to drive. Really. I'll just take the freeway instead of going across the mountain."

"Okay. No pressure. It's good night, then." He had closed the small distance between them, and before she could move, he brushed her lips with a kiss. A brush only. Then a pause, waiting for her to object, to move away. When she didn't (How could she force herself?), he moved in, folding her in his arms, threading his fingers through her hair, gentling her mouth with his own. His scent, his warmth embraced her. She felt herself slipping under the luxurious waves of sensuous abandon.

So much for maintaining distance.

But just as she was on the verge of surrendering, he released her. She struggled to catch her breath, to anchor herself through a flood of feeling still rocketing through her veins. "I thought ... you promised ..."

"Oh, that's not it. Not the big IT. That's just a simple good-night kiss."

She swallowed, trying to appear composed. "It was a good one."

He touched her cheek with his thumb. "Think about it

when you're in Denver. I'm hoping it will make you want to come back."

"Why wouldn't I want to?"

He smiled in a way that made her melt clear through to her bones. "Just come back, Mac. Just come back."

chapter 15

MCKENNA PULLED the Neon over to the curb a half-block away from her parents' home in Evergreen, Colorado. She reached over and unfastened the door of Titi's carrier, and the cat sprang up onto the passenger seat, propped her front paws on the door, and peered out the window. They had a good view of Mckenna's childhood home from this vantage point—the spacious, sloping lawn, winter brown showing through patchy snow, the big porch with its impressive Georgian columns, the two-story brick house. Artfully placed shrubs and conifers didn't soften the imposing facade, the sort of in-your-face "Don't tread on my walkway unless you belong to the country club" look of the place.

"Can a house have an attitude?" Mckenna asked Titi.

Titi dropped down to the seat and yawned. "Dogs there?"

"In my mother's house?" Mckenna laughed at the idea. Amazing how much she had recalled about her mother and father on the nine-hundred-mile drive, when she had nothing better to do than bury herself in memory. "No animal of any kind has ever set paws on my mother's carpet. You'll be lucky if you're not sleeping in the car."

"Kidding, right?"

"Don't worry, if my mom's that persnickety, we'll find a motel."

Mckenna sat in silence for a moment, gathering her courage. Yes, she had remembered some things, but who knew how much she still didn't know about her home, her family, her childhood years? How did she explain to her parents that she was no longer the person they thought she was, the ruthlessly ambitious Harvard-educated attorney with a prestigious job and brilliant future?

Maybe she would be those things again in time. But right now she held down two low-wage jobs, lived in a thirty-year-old mobile home in the middle of nowhere, and carried on conversations with her cat. She wouldn't fill them in on the last part, of course. Her mother likely wouldn't even accept a cat as a houseguest, much less her daughter's confidant.

"All during this visit," she warned Titi, "you are to behave like a cat."

"I am a cat."

"You know what I mean. Just behave."

All innocence, Titi replied, "Cats invented good manners."

Mckenna rolled her eyes.

"Fishbelly face," Titi observed. "Sick?"

Mckenna gritted her teeth. "Not sick. Just nervous."

Titi scratched an ear, then gave Mckenna a chiding look. "Bad idea."

"What's a bad idea?"

"Parents. Kittens leave at eight weeks. Forever."

Mckenna's laugh had a sour note. "That only works for cats and puppies, Titi."

"Good idea. Try?"

"Sorry, Titi, but human families are for life."

"Too bad."

"Yes, maybe. Too bad." Too late for regrets, though. She had driven nine hundred miles, endured a motel room that smelled like stale cigarette smoke and heaven knew what else, and expended four entire tanks of gasoline to get here, so she had to walk up to that oak front door with its fancy cut-glass side panels and face her family. Her parents were expecting her, and if they knew she was sitting half a block away agonizing over a simple family visit, they surely would send for a therapist.

"Lie in the sun," Titi advised.

Mckenna sighed. "The sky is overcast, Titi. There's no sun to lie in." She thought of Doris, who had died in the hospital the day before Mckenna had left. The attending nurse had told Mckenna that the old lady had passed very peacefully, almost happily. When Mckenna's time came, would she be able to face passing on with such assurance of a life bravely, completely lived?

Not if she didn't even have the courage to face her parents and get reacquainted. She could almost hear the old lady's voice in her head, admonishing her to quit cringing and take life by the tail.

"Okay," she replied to Doris's shade. "We'll take my parents by their tails. Here goes."

The woman who answered Mckenna's doorbell ring wasn't her mother, but a short, rotund Hispanic woman with white hair curled close to her head. She was totally unfamiliar, and for a moment Mckenna panicked. Did she have the wrong house? Was her returning memory playing tricks?

Then a voice from the back of the house called out, "Who is it, Carmen? Is it—? It is! Mckenna!"

Mckenna instantly recognized the woman who sailed into the foyer. "Hi, Mom."

Her mother, Mckenna reflected, almost looked younger than she herself did. Not a hint of gray corrupted the glossy black of her hair. Nary a line nor wrinkle dared defile the perfection of her makeup. And for a casual day at home, she wore pressed linen slacks, a soft cashmere sweater, and a lapis choker that certainly hadn't come from Wal-Mart. Her sleek figure showed no concessions to age or gravity.

"Mckenna! Darling! What a lovely surprise that you decided to visit for Christmas! We called at Thanksgiving, you know, and twice since, but you must have been having trouble with your line. The message said you'd been disconnected. I think your phone service must have made an error."

One worry dispelled, Mckenna thought. Nice to know her parents hadn't been frantic at her lack of communication. Nice to know, but disappointing, too.

"Carmen, get her bags, please. Is that your car out front, Mckenna? Is it a rental? What happened to your Beemer? And gracious, if you're going to rent a car to drive all the way from Arizona, why didn't you get something bigger?"

Mckenna didn't have time to insert a word into the stream of comments, but her mother didn't seem to notice. Apparently she didn't expect answers.

"Mckenna, what is . . . oh, my goodness! Is that an animal in that bag you're carrying?"

"It's my cat, Mom. Nefertiti is a genuine certified therapy cat. She's allowed into hospitals and nursing homes, so I thought you might not mind having her in the house."

Her mother drew back a bit. "Well, my goodness. She must be very clean to be all that. I suppose . . . well, of course it's all right. She won't get on the furniture, will she?"

"I brought along her special blanket, and she'll limit herself to that, won't you, Titi?" she said to the carrier.

"Meeer!"

Mckenna shot Titi a surprised look. She sounded

like...a regular cat. Then again, Mckenna had warned her to act normal while at her parents' house.

"Put the bag upstairs, Carmen," Mckenna's mother instructed as Carmen came in with Mckenna's single piece of luggage, a duffel bag. The maid didn't look like she should be lifting anything heavier than a teapot.

"I'll get the bag, Mom." With a suspicious frown at Titi, Mckenna turned her attention back to her mother.

"Let Carmen get it, dear. Goodness, if she can haul the vacuum cleaner up the stairs with no problem, your bag won't bother her a bit. Come into the family room and I'll fix us both a cup of tea. Your father is playing golf, of course. He thought you wouldn't arrive until later. You must have driven very fast, dear, but I suppose the interstate lets you do that these days."

Mckenna and Titi exchanged a glance. Permanent separation from the age of eight weeks was looking better and better.

Mckenna and her mother drank herbal tea while Titi wandered around the family room beneath her hostess's wary gaze.

"She does, uh, tend to her business outside, doesn't she?"

"I'll put a litter box in the bathroom off of my bedroom."

"Ah. Yes, very good, but you'll be staying in the guest room, dear. I knocked out the wall between your bedroom and your sister's and converted the whole into my design studio. I'm working from home now. It's so much more convenient. And business is booming, I'm pleased to say. I've worked very hard at it, and that's the key, isn't it?"

Mckenna tried to remember her mother's profession. Nothing came to mind, and she cursed her hit-and-miss memory.

"I must show you some of my new designs. They would look very good on you. But Mckenna, darling, I do believe you've put on weight. At least, what, five pounds? More? You're not going to become a pudge like your sister, are you? She uses two pregnancies as an excuse, but you know that a woman doesn't have to give in to fat if she has the will to keep herself looking good. Well, not to worry. I'll introduce you to my personal trainer. Kevin is his name, and he's absolutely gorgeous. Fit, too, of course. He'll set you up with a diet that will have those pounds off in no time, and while you're here, we can go to the gym every day. They're even open on Christmas Day. You must have gotten lazy in your workouts, dear. But then, all of us backslide now and then. We're only human, after all."

Did the woman ever stop talking? But at least Mckenna had learned that her mother designed clothing, or at least, that's what she assumed.

"Do you like what we've done to the house?" She led Mckenna from room to room like a tour guide, proudly gesturing to a new painting on the wall, the new tile on the floor. Titi followed behind her, mincing along, hips swaying, tail erect, in a fair imitation of the older woman's manner. The cat glanced over her shoulder with a lofty expression so similar to Ellen Wright's that Mckenna almost succumbed to a fit of the giggles.

"Are you choking, dear?" her mother inquired.

"No. Sorry. I . . . tried to hiccup and cough at the same time. This is nice."

"That ancient brown carpet really had to go, you know. It was at least six years old. And I like this color scheme much better, don't you? And those big cowboy and Western oil paintings that your father so adores—they're in his study where I don't have to look at them. Really, the Western theme is so passé. Why people in Colorado are so fascinated by cowboys and Indians I'll never know."

Mckenna simply smiled and nodded, which seemed all her mother expected. Certainly the mystery of why Old

Mckenna had no use for an ex—rodeo cowboy had been solved.

"Oh, dear, Mckenna, your kitty is headed for the kitchen. Don't let her go in there. She might jump on the counter, and that would never do. Oh, gracious!" she complained as Titi quite deliberately jumped onto a kitchen chair, her expression clearly sending the message that cats went wherever they damn well pleased.

With a frown, Mckenna snatched the cat from the chair. "I think I'll take Titi and go have a little nap, if you don't mind, Mom. It was a long drive."

"Of course," her mother said, with a frosty look at Titi, who smirked from the protection of Mckenna's arms.

The guest room elicited no memories, but then, why should it? Mckenna wouldn't have spent time in here when she was growing up.

"Is the cat going to sleep in its carrier?" her mother called up the stairs to her.

"Sure thing, Mom," Mckenna lied.

Titi huffed. "Cats sleep on beds."

"Of course they do." She shot the cat a concerned look. "What was that 'meow' business when we first came in?"

"What 'meow'? I told your mother that all furniture is for cats."

"I missed that."

Had she missed it, or was she perhaps losing this peculiar talent of understanding Titi? Since the talent rode in on the back of a brain injury, maybe that wasn't a bad thing. The thought gave her hope and made her sad at the same time.

She sat down on the bed, patted the spot beside her in invitation, then reached out to stroke Titi's fur when the cat joined her.

"I would miss speaking to you, my friend, if it ever comes to that."

Titi gave her a look that seemed impossibly wise. "Cats always speak. Words or not. You just need to listen."

Mckenna ruffled Titi's neck fur. "I'll always try to listen."

They slept for an hour, Titi curled in the bend of Mckenna's knees, before a soft knock sounded on the door.

"Miss Mckenna," said Carmen's voice. "Your father is home."

A maid who called her "Miss Mckenna." How quaint.

Mckenna's father, a tall, spare man with a balding head and thin lips, greeted her with open arms when she came down the stairs. His brief hug enfolded her in the familiar scents of his aftershave and hair tonic. "How's my girl, eh? I'm sorry I wasn't here when you got home, but I'd promised eighteen holes to Ralph, and we had to drive down to Denver to find a course free from snow. You know how Ralph is about missing an opportunity for a game."

She didn't know.

"Ralph sends his love, by the way," he told her as they walked into the living room. "He's so proud of you. Hell, you'd think you were his daughter instead of mine. Amy didn't do half as well for herself as you did, you know. A nurse, of all things. Emptying bedpans. You would think a modern woman would want something more. But as long as she's happy, I guess."

Amy—barely remembered. Her best friend in high school. Ralph's daughter.

"It's good to see you, girl," her father said. "You don't get up here to visit nearly enough. What's the use of having a wildly successful daughter if I don't get to show her off once in a while?"

Her mother joined them, a glass of wine in her hand. "It would help if she would call once in a while."

"Well, Ellen, we're all busy. We don't exactly burn up the phone wires ourselves. And speaking of phones"—he turned his attention back to Mckenna—"what was wrong with yours, eh? Tried to call you twice since Thanksgiving. We were getting worried."

"Sorry. I didn't mean to worry you, but I changed numbers. I should have told you sooner."

"Really?" The inquiry contained more indignation than motherly concern.

Two pairs of curious eyes fastened upon her. Mckenna began to think this whole visit had been a mistake. She wanted to go back home, to Cornville, to Jane and her job at the hospital and Tom. Especially to Tom. She sighed. "Dad, Mom, there's a reason for this visit."

They raised brows.

"I mean, a reason other than the Christmas holiday, and of course I wanted to see you. But I need to tell you something."

"You're getting married!" her mother guessed. "Finally. Adam should have told us, that devil. When is the date?"

Who the hell was Adam? But she didn't have time right now to follow a tangent. She wanted to get this over with.

"I'm not getting married."

"You're not getting married?" Her mother was crestfallen. "Well, dear, you're not getting any younger, you know. I had so hoped—"

Her father neatly interrupted. Apparently, he'd gotten good at it over the years. "Mckenna, dear, are we going to need a drink to hear this? How about a martini before dinner? Carmen, make us three martinis. No, make that another glass of Zinfandel for Mrs. Wright."

Mckenna opened her mouth to decline, but then realized a martini might be just what she needed.

Finally they settled, drinks in hand, in the shadow of a huge white-flocked Christmas tree hung with a dazzling display of red balls. With her mother's mouth occupied sipping her wine, Mckenna told them about the recent developments in her life—the accident, the amnesia, the doctor's prognosis, the loss of her job. She left out the part about conversing with a cat, of course.

For a moment after she finished the tale—the edited tale—they stared at her in stunned silence.

The first reaction from her father: "You lost your job with BKB? But...I don't understand how they could let you go. You're one of their top people. A partnership was right around the corner."

Was her career status his greatest concern? Mckenna suffered a pang of disappointment. With an almost inaudible sigh, she explained. "Dad, I was lucky I could find the office, much less do useful work there. I'm not exactly a competent attorney right now, and I was even worse when they fired me. I remembered almost nothing about the law."

Her father scowled, looking as if he still didn't understand. "You are an outstanding attorney. You went to Harvard. If you got a knock on the head, they should have given you more sick leave. They'll be sorry when some other firm snaps you up."

Mckenna sighed and took a sip of her martini. Titi was right. She really needed a place to lie in the sun.

Her mother frowned thoughtfully. "There aren't that many first-rate law firms in Sedona, are there? Who are you working for now, dear?"

"I just started a new job at the local hospital."

Her father grimaced. "Medical lawsuits. Well, there can be big money in that, but I'd say you were on the wrong side to make your fortune."

"I'm not working in the legal department, Dad. I'm the volunteer department secretary." The job had seemed like such an important step up in her fortunes, but the look on her parents' faces relegated that accomplishment to less than nothing.

" 'Secretary'?" her mother whispered, as if the neighbors might hear if she said the word too loud.

"This is outrageous!" her father thundered. "You need to slap BKB with a lawsuit that will blister their hide. They can't let you go because of a temporary disability. They owe you—"

"What, Dad?" It wasn't as if she hadn't thought of suing. But her drop from legal erudition to unemployable ignorance was an embarrassment she didn't care to air for the entertainment of the legal community. "What should I sue them for? My job back? I can't do my job. Money? They gave me a generous severance package."

Her father simmered down, but he grumbled. "It's not right."

"When I'm feeling more confident that I can work in the law again, then maybe ... If I have to. I'll think about it."

Considering her parents' reaction to her job at the hospital, Mckenna decided to leave out the part about working at McDonald's. And certainly she wouldn't tell them that her second job involved picking up dog poop. That might give both of them a heart attack.

She plowed through the next few days with grim determination to learn what she needed to learn and then get the hell out of her parents' house and back to her own life, which, shoddy as it might be, was at least her own. Her mother pestered her to see a therapist, as if a shrink could unlock the secrets in her misbehaving brain.

"My friend Cassandra goes to an excellent man. You remember Cassandra, Mrs. Stone, from the Junior League, don't you?"

Somehow in all that explanation, Mckenna hadn't communicated that she was lucky to remember her parents, much less their friends. Well, maybe "lucky" wasn't the right word.

"He's helped her really understand why her husband divorced her. She's channeled all her anger into opening her new real estate brokerage, and what a success she's been."

"Mom, I'm not going through a divorce. I don't need a therapist."

"But I'm sure he could help clear up your memory, dear. I read somewhere that amnesia can be psychological."

"My memory is coming back. You don't have to worry."

The pressure to see Mrs. Stone's wonderful therapist didn't let up. It hung in there along with exhortations to accompany her mother to the gym, a daily pilgrimage that, with the help of Kevin, the personal trainer, allowed a fifty-five-year-old woman to maintain a figure that would have been envied by many twenty-somethings. Mckenna gave in once—exercise might vent some frustration, she decided—but that one trip convinced her that a walk in the piney hills behind her parents' house would serve her better, both in the venting and the exercise departments.

When her mother wasn't pestering Mckenna about weight loss and psychiatric therapy, she kept busy with social obligations—the committee on this and the project to promote that. Not to mention her twice weekly bridge appointment with a group of friends, and somewhere in between all that she found time for her fashion designs. Her schedule didn't slacken just because Christmas was right around the corner. For the most part, once she understood that Mckenna insisted on refusing her help on any front, she pretty much left her daughter alone, a boon for which that daughter was duly grateful.

She saw even less of her father. He spent hours holed up in his study editing a legal journal—a job he had taken on after his retirement as a superior court judge. He emerged to play golf, eat dinner with the family, and occasionally to watch the news on television. Once he offered to phone a friend, one of the partners in the Phoenix law firm of Statler, Mooney, Urbridge, and Gordon, to get

Mckenna an interview, but she declined, and he gave up. He still didn't quite grasp the significance of her memory loss, Mckenna knew. He was a man of laws and rules, his world cut-and-dried, bound up in a neat package, not of right and wrong, but of legal and illegal. The laws and rules couldn't account for someone who one day was headed for partnership in a prestigious law firm and the next day worked at McDonald's.

Her primary mission on the home front proceeded little better than her family reunion. As she complained to Titi their second night there, "I was counting on going through family photo albums and renewing old memories, but my family doesn't seem to be much on picture-taking. We went to Disneyland when I was a kid—I do remember that. But we didn't even get a picture of Mickey Mouse."

Titi perked up immediately. "Mouse?"

"Not the kind of mouse you'd be interested in. This mouse is six feet tall and wears clothes."

The cat's tail started to bristle out at the very thought. "Kidding?"

Mckenna laughed. Heaven knew she hadn't found much to laugh about since coming home.

She had also thought to discover old friends, relive high school and college days. But apparently old friends were few and far between. Actually, they were downright nonexistent. She did find an old high-school yearbook in a box of her things that her mother had stored in the attic. Leafing through it, she found not one of the sentimental notes that friends write to one another at the end of a school year. Not a single one. Some of the faces pictured there inspired memories: a good-looking guy she had longed to date, but who, she recalled, had never asked her out; the girl who had been her chief rival for the honor of valedictorian; the geeky math whiz who kept professing his love for her and got hurt feelings when she told him to buzz off. And there was Amy, the golf-playing Ralph's daughter, who had gone on to become a nurse. She and Amy had been friends, Mckenna remembered, but their friendship hadn't gone much past eating lunch together and sharing notes in study hall.

She hadn't had time for many friends in school, Mckenna remembered now. Good grades had been her top priority, pleasing her father, who wanted her to make something of herself.

"I shouldn't have come here," she confessed to Titi after spending an hour searching the yearbook. "You were right. Children should be separated from their families as soon as they're old enough to eat solid food."

"Warned you" was the cat's response. She had spent the visit trying to stay out of Ellen Wright's path, because Mckenna's mother imagined germs and cat hair everywhere Titi set a paw, and she was absolutely convinced that the cat would try to climb the Christmas tree.

"Your mother has claws," Titi told Mckenna.

"You don't know the half of it," Mckenna replied. "She also has a therapist and a personal trainer waiting in the wings."

Since Mckenna had come home to visit, her mother felt obliged to drag her to the annual Christmas party at the country club. And she wouldn't take "no" for an answer.

"I have nothing to wear, Mom. I brought only jeans and sweaters."

"Your mother is a fashion designer, dear." She regarded Mckenna with a critical eye. "We'll just let out my blue sheath for you. It's a shame we can't get you down ten pounds or so before Saturday, but I suppose that would be asking too much."

"She looks fine, Ellen," her father said rather sharply. "Leave the girl alone. Women aren't supposed to look like scarecrows."

"Thinner is healthier," his wife proclaimed.

That, Mckenna thought, sounded like a philosophical nugget from the vaunted Kevin.

If her father didn't find her new, plusher figure a matter for concern, he did show a bit of embarrassment about her job status.

"Just don't talk about your 'problems' at the party," he warned her. "I've done a lot of bragging about you, little girl, and this set of people won't understand, you know."

Mckenna was more than willing not to talk about any problems. In fact, she wished she hadn't mentioned them to her parents.

"I didn't pull every string in the world to get you into Harvard, to have people laughing about you working as a—what is it you're doing now?"

As if exchanging BKB for McDonald's had been her idea?

"The hospital, Dad. I work at the hospital."

Good thing she hadn't told them about the kennel.

Mckenna refused to wear her mother's let-out dress to the party. Instead, she splurged money she didn't have and bought a slinky velvet outfit that showed every curve to advantage.

"There's nothing wrong with those extra ten pounds," she told Titi when she modeled the creation before the party. "Do you think Tom would like this?"

The cat voiced an inarticulate meow—not what Mckenna wanted to hear. So Mckenna answered for her. "Tom would love that dress, Mckenna. He likes a little substance to a woman. And besides, you look simply stunning.

"That's what he would think," Mckenna told Titi. "That I look stunning. He likes me just the way I am."

And before coming home, Mckenna hadn't appreciated what a wonderful thing that was.

. . .

BACK IN Arizona, Tom Markham sat in his Prescott office plowing through the interview notes of witnesses in the Harmon case. He had read his notes so many times he could almost recite them word for word, but he didn't intend to leave anything to chance. The case against Todd Harmon was not as firm as he would like. The guy was guilty as sin. No doubt about that. But the truth of guilt or innocence had surprisingly little to do with the outcome of a trial, which depended much more on legal maneuverings, technical minutiae, and the whims of a jury.

Saul Lehrer stuck his head in the doorway of his office. "Going to lunch, Tom?"

"Nah. Brought a bologna sandwich."

"Those things will kill you."

"Donovan will kill me if I don't come up with some magic for the Harmon prelim."

"Yeah. That's coming up, isn't it?"

"January."

"It oughta be cut-and-dried, shouldn't it?"

"Nothing is ever cut-and-dried, Saul."

Saul grinned. "You'll be famous, one way or the other. There's going to be more cameras in that courtroom than at the Country Music Awards."

"Yep. Sure am looking forward to that."

Saul chuckled and left him with his pile of files.

Tom sighed. Everything about this case had turned into a circus. At first Tom had been amazed that the county attorney, John Donovan, had turned it over to him rather than handling it himself. High-profile cases were Donovan's meat and drink. The man was as much politician as he was an attorney.

And of course that, Tom realized later, was exactly why an expendable underling got the case instead of the Big Boss. Bringing a popular celebrity to trial was a touchy thing. Everything was media hype and speculation. Everyone from Delaware to California speculated on the

charges, the evidence, the attorneys, the witnesses—
everything down to and including what kind of underdrawers the defense attorney wore. If Mckenna Wright
had still been arguing the defense, for sure the media
would be speculating on her underdrawers. Especially the
men.

Mckenna. Damn, but he missed her, and she'd been
gone less than a week. He hadn't missed her when he had
left BKB. He had gone weeks without seeing her and
hardly even had her cross his mind. But now, the new
Mckenna—well, she crossed his mind a little too often for
comfort.

He shook his head, yawned, got his bologna sandwich
from the office fridge, and started into business again. A
case like the Harmon affair would be a routine matter if it
didn't involve America's country-western hero. Yesterday
they'd seen a preview of things to come—an inquiry from
one of those television celebrity gossip shows. Things
were going to heat up. Soon the attention of the whole
country could turn toward the lowly hick prosecutors that
were trying to bring a case against America's Boy Next
Door. When that happened, the case could easily blow up
in the prosecution's face. The prosecution being Tom
Markham, the expendable one. Nobody liked to be made
a fool while the television cameras were watching, especially not John Donovan. If Tom didn't make the county
attorney's office look like a shining star of legal erudition,
he would be out of here so fast, the wind of him leaving
would suck the air out of the office.

With a sigh, he read for the fourth time the account of
one of Todd Harmon's party guests, who had admitted
seeing Todd cutting a white powder into snort-sized piles
in the kitchen. And later he had seen Todd offer the drug
to one of the women guests, who also was on the witness
list. Admittedly the witness was drunk out of his mind, but
everyone else at the party had been in the same state. The

lack of sober witnesses—besides the undercover cop, whom juries sometimes chose not to believe—was certainly the weakest point of the prosecution's case.

But wait...He went back to the second paragraph. What was this brief mention of a maid? The maid had probably cleaned up the mess afterward, the guy had said. A maid? A maid was in there somewhere? How had he missed that?

Surely the police had interviewed a maid if she had been in the mix. He walked his fingers through the headings on the witness files. No one had interviewed anyone who possibly could have been a maid. The cops had missed her.

Tom would bet his best pair of boots, though, that Mckenna Wright hadn't missed her. In her days at BKB, Mckenna hadn't missed much of anything, and that sound in his brain was the pieces of a puzzle starting to fall into place.

He needed to talk to Mckenna, Tom decided. He needed to talk to her now, not when she returned days from now. The phone wouldn't do. Wouldn't do at all. If she did know anything about this, the details were no doubt hiding behind that wall that blocked so much of her life before she'd driven off that cliff. It would take some digging to get it out.

And how fortunate for Harmon if Mckenna had found something prejudicial and an accident had prevented her from handing the information over to the prosecution, as she was legally required to do. How fortunate, indeed.

Yessirree. Pieces of the puzzle were meshing all over his brain.

Or was this just his thoroughly-in-lust subconscious providing him with an excuse to check up on Mckenna?

Whichever. Legitimate excuse or lame, it looked as if he was going to Colorado for Christmas.

chapter 16

CHRISTMAS MORNING arrived without much ado in the Wright home. Mckenna and her parents drank hot apple cider and opened presents by the tree. Her mother received a diamond tennis bracelet from her husband, and he got a new putter from his wife. Mckenna gave her parents an *Arizona Highways* coffee-table book of Arizona photos, and her parents gave her a check for a thousand dollars.

"To tide you over until you get back on your feet," her father said.

Very practical, although not full of warm fuzzies. But, as she was learning, her family simply wasn't about warm fuzzies, a reality driven home by a Christmas phone call to her sister in Washington State. Memories of Carla had slowly surfaced since Mckenna had arrived home, but they lacked much emotion. The phone call was similar to the memories—polite, even a bit formal, but lacking warmth. It left Mckenna feeling disappointed and somewhat sad.

That afternoon, Mckenna sat in the family room paging through one of her mother's fashion magazines. Titi curled at her feet. Now and then the cat raised her head and gave Mckenna's lap a longing look, then slid a sly glance toward Ellen Wright's empty chair. The furniture monitor was absent.

"Cats don't belong on the floor," she complained.

Mckenna frowned at her, jerking her head almost imperceptibly toward her father, who sat in an easy chair by the fireplace.

Titi didn't care, obviously, because she continued her complaint. "Cats own the furniture."

Mckenna rolled her eyes.

"Noisy animal," her father commented. "Pretty, though. That coat of hers would make a heck of a fancy fur something-or-other if there were enough of it."

"Maowr!" Titi shot into the air, landed on Mckenna's lap, and sent the judge a sizzling glare. Mckenna hastily wrapped her arms around the cat. "He didn't mean it, Titi."

"Mewr?" Titi regarded her in confusion.

"Yep, she sure does talk a lot," her father said.

This was the third instance of Titi sounding, well, like a cat.

"You've got a mighty strange look on your face, Mckenna. Are you feeling all right?"

"I'm fine, Dad."

Titi brushed her soft head against Mckenna's hand and looked an apology as their eyes met. Mckenna realized she wasn't the only one who would be saddened if the time came when their conversations were no more. And that time seemed to be coming.

"If your mother sees that animal on her new sofa, she'll have a coronary, Mckenna." He snorted. "It was all I could do to keep her from covering every damned piece of furniture with plastic."

Mckenna gave Titi a hug and then put her back onto the floor. "She wasn't on the sofa, she was on my lap."

Her father smiled wryly. "Well, you'd better watch out.

Your mother will try covering you in plastic, as well." He gave her a concerned look. "How is it . . . well, you know . . . going? Are things coming back to you."

"Yes. Slowly, they are. I went up to the high school yesterday and walked around. I remembered a lot of little incidents, a lot of people. The school secretary was there even though it was Christmas Eve. Mrs. Orland. I recognized her, and she remembered me. Amazing."

"You were a star student. Why shouldn't she remember you? People who do well always make an impression."

"I suppose."

He scrutinized her a bit suspiciously. "You seem different than you used to be, Mckenna."

She refused to be embarrassed for that, because she grew more and more certain that the new version of Mckenna improved considerably on the original. So she met her father's eyes without apology. "A lot of my notions of what is necessary to life got toppled, Dad, mostly because I couldn't remember them. Now I've gone and built new patterns, new foundations. I'm not surprised you think I'm different."

"But your doctor thinks it will all come back, that you'll be the same as ever?"

A question that haunted her in more ways than one. "He thinks so."

Apparently her tone didn't convey the certainty her father sought. "You know, Mckenna, I don't often think your mother is right when she goes off on one of her dithers. But I'm beginning to think her idea of your seeing that shrink friend of hers isn't such a bad one."

Great. Nell with her swami and now her parents with their shrink.

"Dad, I don't need a shrink. Honest. I got way overstressed and let things get out of hand, but now I'm learning to keep my stress level under control." With the help of a cat. She gave Titi a subtle wink.

Her father dismissed such assurances with a wave of his hand. "Stress? Bah! Life is stressful. You can't avoid it. And if you want to play with the big boys, especially in the law profession, you can't be namby-pamby and whine about stress. You've got to work hard and make the hard calls, like you've always done, girl."

Mckenna buttoned her lip, with difficulty.

"Stress is just some uptown yuppie excuse for slacking off instead of keeping the old nose to the grindstone. Don't you listen to that nonsense. If you want to be successful, to get ahead in the world, you can't baby yourself with notions about cutting down on stress."

If she had grown up trying to meet both parents' expectations, Mckenna mused, no wonder she had driven herself until her brain exploded.

"So if you need to see a shrink to get your head straightened out, do it. Hell, I'll even pay for it. Then you start living your life again the way it's supposed to be lived." He snorted. "And that doesn't mean answering the phones in some podunk hospital."

The doorbell rang. Saved, Mckenna thought, by the bell.

"I'll get it!" Mckenna sprang from the chair, nearly tripping over Titi in her haste to escape her father's lecture. Carmen had gone to the movies—she had Christmas Day off—and the door was fair game.

Mckenna arrived too late, however. A taxi was pulling away from the curb, and her mother stood in the foyer talking with their caller, a tall, lean man made taller by the battered Stetson on his head. For a moment Mckenna didn't recognize him, so unexpected was the sight. Then she cried out, "Tom!"

He stepped into the foyer, taking his hat from his head and leaving the unruly sandy hair flat and sticking out in odd directions. He looked good enough to kiss, as far as Mckenna was concerned.

"Merry Christmas, Mckenna," he greeted her.

Her mother regarded him with a polite, neutral look.

"Mother, this is Tom Markham. He works in the Yavapai county attorney's office, and he's . . . he's a friend."

Tom grinned at her. He didn't seem a bit intimidated by her mother's scrutiny, but then, he had once made his living riding bulls.

Titi trotted eagerly into the foyer, gave Tom a meow—another of those meows that were nothing more than meows—and rubbed joyously against his legs.

If Mckenna could have rubbed up against him in a like manner, she would have. "Tom, it's wonderful to see you! What a lovely present for Christmas. But what brings you here?"

"Business, actually."

"Oh." Disappointment must have echoed in her voice, because her mother fixed her with a probing look. With deliberate effort, she brightened her tone. "I'm glad you dropped by. How on earth did you find me?"

"Oh, we prosecuting attorneys are prime investigators, you know. No one can get away from us."

Her mother, whose sense of humor was limited to knock-knock jokes, looked horrified.

Mckenna laughed. "Don't worry, Mom. I'm not on Tom's list of suspects. You got the address from Jane, didn't you?"

Tom spread his arms in surrender. "You got me."

"How long will you be in town? Are you working on a case that brings you to Denver?"

He smiled. "I'm working on a case that brings me to you, Mckenna."

THEY WENT for pizza at the Edgewater Inn, a hole-in-the-wall little place with an antique oak bar and booths along one wall, each made into a semiprivate alcove by the carved pine sidepieces to the seats.

"I know this place is a bit of a hike from your folks' house," he said as they walked in, "but I swear they have the best pizza in all of Colorado. I remember it from my rodeo days. Whenever I was anywhere within fifty miles, I would come to this place for pizza and beer. Besides, it's one of the few places open today."

"I don't mind." The farther away from Evergreen, the better, as far as Mckenna was concerned.

They slid into a booth that shielded them somewhat from the talk, laughter, and cigarette smoke coming from the crowd sitting at the bar—other escapees from Christmas, Mckenna guessed. A waiter immediately appeared to take their order—pizza with the works, and two Coors.

"When you're in Colorado," Tom explained, "you have to order Coors. I think it's a state law."

"Don't tell that to my dad. He won't drink anything but imports." She gave Tom a quizzical look. "So . . . what are you doing here, Tom? Are you really here on business, or"—she grinned at him—"could you simply not stand to be without me?"

Something very like chagrin crossed his face and told her she had hit close to the mark. But he dashed that happy notion with his reply. "I actually am here on business. Not to say we all—Jane and I—haven't missed the hell out of you. Jane's having to clean her own kennels."

"She's gotten spoiled." Mckenna was tempted to ask exactly in what way Tom had missed her. But she wasn't up to being quite that bold.

Then an unpleasant thought occurred to her. "Nothing's happened with any of our little project cases, has it? Jack didn't go buy a shotgun to use on his neighbor? Sally's ex didn't get to her?"

"Nothing like that. No. Something has come up in the Harmon case."

The Harmon case. Mckenna shook her head. If she never again heard the name Todd Harmon, it would be too soon. "I really haven't had any stunning revelations, legally speaking, Tom. The only thing I know about Todd Harmon is the title of his latest hit, and I got that off a jukebox in Denny's."

"Well, just listen to this and see if anything rings a bell."

He told her about finding a reference to a maid that had worked the party where Harmon was seen selling drugs. No one had interviewed this maid or had any information about her.

"Maria." The name popped out of Mckenna's mouth.

Tom let loose a whoop of triumph. "I knew that sharp-eyed Mckenna Wright wouldn't let any stone go unturned. Maria! You talked to her?"

Mckenna felt a bit stunned. "I don't know where that name came from, Tom. Really, I don't. It just sort of popped out."

"But it shows the information is in there somewhere." He reached across the table and gently tapped her forehead with a finger. "Right in there."

Some bell had chimed in her head. No doubt about it. But what? Concentration did no good. It just forced the hint of memory back into hiding.

She shook her head. "This is too frustrating! Who knows why I said that name? It might be just my own stereotype that all maids are named Maria. In Arizona, while it's not very politically correct, jumping to the conclusion that the maid was Hispanic and named Maria has a good chance of being true."

"What's the name of your maid in Evergreen?"

She cocked her head curiously. "How did you know we have a maid?"

"I met your parents. No offense, but your mom doesn't look like the kind of woman who cleans her own toilets."

True enough. "The maid's name is Carmen."

"Okay, then. Why didn't the name Carmen come out of your mouth in association with the idea of maid?"

"Good point."

He grinned. "Just call me Sherlock."

"I wouldn't go quite that far."

Their pizza came, set before them in a steaming feast of pepperoni, mushrooms, peppers, onions, olives, and three cheeses. Even the smell of it could add a pound to her hips, Mckenna figured. She thought of her mother's horror if she could see what her daughter was about to ingest.

"Oh, my, this looks wonderful," she said, digging in with a twinge of guilt. Even at the ripe old age of thirty, going against the grain of parental wisdom made her feel slightly wicked, adding yet another bit of spice to the pizza. "It is wonderful," she said around a mouthful of gooey cheese and tomato sauce.

"Told you this was the best pizza in Colorado."

For a few minutes, they ate in comfortable silence. But Mckenna couldn't escape a certain uneasiness about the possibility of her old self knowing about this maid.

"So what makes you think that I got to this maid person, other than the fact I just blurted out a name that may or may not have been hers?"

"Because if anyone had the inside scoop on this case, you did. You never miss details. Never."

"Obsessed with perfection, eh?"

"Sometimes that's not a bad thing."

"If I knew something pertinent to the case, wouldn't I have told you?"

He grimaced, scratched his head, and toyed with a bite of pizza. "Wellll . . . yes and no. If you found out about this person through your own investigation and thought she had something to say, then yes, you would have been required to tell the prosecution. Only things that come directly from your client's mouth to your ears are protected by client-attorney privilege. And I doubt this would have been one of those things."

"Then I would have told you if I'd known anything."

He shrugged, a bit uneasily, Mckenna thought. Her heart sank. "Wouldn't I have?"

He looked up in surprise at her despondent tone. Reaching out, he brushed a crumb of crust from the corner of her mouth. "Don't jump to conclusions about yourself, Mac. You weren't unethical. You always followed the rules, in your own time. You liked to win, and with winning in mind, you sometimes stretched the concept of 'immediate' and 'timely' to suit your own purposes. Everyone does that, though, to some extent. Prosecutors do it to the defense, defense does it to the prosecutors."

She sighed. "After spending the last few days with my father, I can understand why I liked to win. For him, coming in second place isn't an option."

"Most everybody in this country thinks like that."

"Mm. Did I ever mention that I graduated second in my class at Harvard?"

"You did mention that a couple of times during our acquaintance." He grinned. "Like maybe ten or twelve."

She winced. "Were you impressed?"

"Right down to my toes."

"You lie. I don't think things like that impress you."

He laughed. "You want to know what impresses me? You impress me."

"Because I was this take-no-prisoners attorney?"

"No, because you're you, the way you are now."

She felt her face grow warm.

At the sight of her embarrassment, he changed the subject. "So how's the visit with the family going?"

She groaned. "Don't spoil my appetite."

"That good, eh?"

"Well, the visit hasn't made me remember anything important—just annoying incidents from when I was growing up. I'm beginning to wonder if I'm not better off having a semiblank past than tuning into the neuroses that living with my parents must have produced. A few days with my mother has me feeling guilty about eating a slice of pizza. Think what seventeen years of her influence must have done."

"I always wondered how you could live on nothing but lettuce."

"And my dad—he's a retired judge, you know. Lives for the law. The law and golf. He's bragged far and wide about his hot-shot daughter, the up-and-coming attorney. For him a person's worth is entirely defined by accomplishments." Mckenna shook her head. "You should have seen his face when I told him I'm working as a secretary. I didn't have the nerve to tell him about Mickey D's. I've plummeted from favorite daughter to family black sheep. My sister in Washington State is a dental hygienist. My dad used to annoy the hell out of her by throwing my Harvard law degree in her face, but now I'm guessing she's looking pretty good, by comparison."

Tom reached over and took her hand. "Mac, you aren't letting them get to you, are you?"

She shook her head no, but it was a small, uncertain shake.

"You know something? If you never remember the rules of evidence or anything else about the law, you're still worth every bit as much as that Old Mckenna Wright who could quote the criminal code chapter and paragraph."

She eyed him dubiously. "And what if I never remember a maid named Maria?"

His expression turned serious. "I'd just have to shake it out of you, I guess." Then he grinned. "In a nice sort of way."

"You are so full of bull."

"That's what comes from riding bulls for a living."

She laughed, helpless to do otherwise. "Heavens, Tom, I wish I could hop on a plane and go back with you. I wish I hadn't promised my parents a full week's visit. It hasn't had the results I'd hoped for, and I'm getting so cranky even Titi refuses to talk to me."

"Titi's gone silent? That's bad."

Mckenna caught herself too late. When she was with Tom, confidences simply spilled out without censorship. Bad habit.

"I mean, well, you know what I mean. You talk to Clara, right?"

"I do. We have a language all our own. Hers mostly concerns food."

Mckenna smiled, relieved. "Yeah. Titi's big on food, too."

"Speaking of food..." Tom looked longingly at the empty pizza dish. "Want another?"

"Oh, please! It's a wonder you don't weigh four hundred pounds." Then she thought a bit. "Though another pizza would mean I didn't have to go back to Evergreen for another hour or so."

He gave her a look that started a slow sizzle in her blood. "If you insisted, Mac, I could arrange for you to stay away from Evergreen the entire long night."

Temptation raised its seductive head, but she battled it down—mostly because she wasn't quite sure if he was serious or kidding.

"Enticing though the idea is, my mother would have a heart attack if I didn't show up for her Christmas dinner." She sighed. "I guess it really is time to go back to the house."

He silently regarded her over the empty pizza platter, and she could see wheels turning beneath the disarray of sandy hair.

"Okay, then, how about this? I'm going up to Estes Park

tomorrow to visit a buddy. We used to ride rodeo together. Why don't you come with me?"

Her mouth pulled into a doubtful grimace.

"A little minivacation might get rid of those wrinkles forming between your brows."

Her fingers automatically flew to her face to verify the offending lines, then she laughed at her own vanity. "You are so full of it."

"Did it work?"

"Getting away, even for a few hours, might make me more sane. Hell! I'll do it."

"Great. Pick me up at the motel about eight tomorrow morning. If the snow isn't too deep, we'll get on a couple of horses and ride into the mountains behind his place. It's beautiful."

Mckenna bit her lip. "Horses?"

"Yeah, you know. Four legs, hooves, a horsehair tail."

"Do I like to ride horses?"

"Sure you do, Mac." He grinned. "Trust me."

THE NEXT morning, the sun rode high in a frosty blue sky. The town of Estes Park nestled at the entrance to Rocky Mountain National Park, surrounded by some of the world's most spectacular scenery. Mountains crowned with glaciers towered above the town. Cold, pure streams rushed down valleys that once groaned under the burden of ancient ice, and still blue lakes reflected nature's glory like artfully placed mirrors.

"This place is too gorgeous to be real," Mckenna commented as they drove into town. "Are you sure this isn't a Disney production?"

"If it is, they've outdone themselves."

"I can't believe the lake isn't frozen."

"Estes Park is the sunbelt of the Colorado Rockies. This

place gets better weather than almost anyplace in the Front Range."

They wound through town, up narrow streets lined with touristy shops and fudge stores. She should buy Titi a new toy, Mckenna thought, to make up for leaving her behind in the boarding kennel. But they didn't stop, and the road continued to climb. Finally they left behind the purveyors of art, T-shirts, jewelry, and ice cream. The aspen trees were winter bare, but a few golden leaves still stubbornly clung to the naked branches. Ponderosa pine grew dense enough to block the sky, though, and as they climbed, spruce joined the forest. The snow lay thicker here than in town, but the ground still showed in occasional bare spots.

"Gimp believes in privacy," Tom told Mckenna. "He owns a restaurant down in Estes, but he wouldn't be caught dead living in a town. Ah, here's the turnoff."

"Your friend's name is Gimp?"

"Actually, his name is Owen Harvey. You saw a photo of him at my place, I think. Great bulldogger. He got the name Gimp when his horse fell on him during a bulldogging run up in Cheyenne—Frontier Days in the year 1998. Whoa, was that a wild show!"

"Oh, dear! Was he badly crippled?"

"Nah. Broke his leg in two places, is all. It healed up shorter than the other one, but he can still outride any man east of the California shoreline."

A short time later, after being enveloped in a bear hug from Tom's friend Gimp, Mckenna sat drinking coffee while the two old friends relived old times. Not that they left her out of their male bonding party. No, indeed. In fact, they directed most of the storytelling at her—as if she would believe some of the wild tales of bronc- and bullriding, and even wilder tales of after-hours shenanigans.

Gimp did not look like Mckenna's idea of a restaurant owner. A bear of a man with a barrel body, balding head, and ugly but good-natured face, he lumbered rather than walked. And apparently he never saw a stranger. Fifteen minutes after they first walked in, he was teasing Mckenna with the same sharp, affectionate banter he used on Tom, mostly about how a good-looking woman like her managed to get lassoed and hog-tied by an ugly sonofabitch like Tom. The man didn't believe in tact or political correctness, and the volume of his merriment could fill the pine-clad valley that sheltered his home.

But Mckenna liked him enormously.

"How do you know I'm not the one doing the lassoing and hog-tying?" she teased back.

"Because, girl, I credit you with more taste than that. This man doesn't ride a bull any better than he sits a horse. And he can't hold his liquor. Well hell, I remember one time when a mere double six pack with a few chasers of whiskey put him under the table. It was purely a disgrace."

Tom shook his head and laughed. "Oh, man! Those were my wild and stupid days. And I had to ride the next day, too."

Mckenna grinned. "It's nice to know he's not the model of decorum he pretends to be."

"Oh, girl!" Gimp said with relish. "I could tell you stories...."

Tom threw up his hands as if to defend from a blow, but he was laughing. "Enough, Gimp! I promised Mac I'd take her riding. You still have horses in that barn out there?"

"Do I have horses! And you're in luck. The trail up the canyon is pretty clear. I was up there myself two days ago, and it hasn't snowed since then. Do I have horses!" He snorted, then laughed at the idea of any sane person not having horses.

A half hour later Mckenna regarded those horses dubiously. Two of the beasts tossed their heads restlessly in the cold air, blowing steam from their nostrils and pawing the dirt impatiently while Tom and Gimp threw saddles upon their backs and pulled cinches tight. To Mckenna, the horses looked more like the wild steeds that loved to throw rodeo riders high in the air than the nice, quiet, safe plodders that Tom had promised her.

"You two have a good time, you hear?" Gimp slapped one of the horses—a big white monster with spots on its rump—on its arched, muscular neck. "Miss Daisy here will give you a good ride, Mac." Already the man had adopted Tom's favorite nickname for her.

"Miss Daisy? This huge horse is a girl?"

"As sweet a mare as you could ever hope to meet."

The "sweet" girl horse swung her big head around to regard Mckenna with a gimlet eye. Mckenna thought she probably was going to come back from this ride with every bone broken. But she wasn't going to show her yellow streak to Tom.

"Right." She tried to sound confident. "She's ... very pretty."

Gimp and Tom just grinned.

Their host left them to their fun, and Tom handed her the reins to her mount. "Climb up and I'll adjust the stirrups for you."

Miss Daisy's looked high enough to have clouds gathering around her ears. "Do you have a ladder?"

Tom laughed. "I'll give you a leg."

What she needed was a backbone, Mckenna decided. But she allowed Tom to cup her foot in his linked hands and toss her into the saddle. Literally toss, with what Mckenna judged an entirely unnecessary boost to her backside to send her the final distance.

"Comfy?"

"Oh, very." Comfy as one could be while straddling a hard piece of oak covered with a thin layer of leather. "Don't these things come with cushions?"

"Some do. Not in Gimp's tack room, though. Cowboys don't use cushioned saddles."

"Well, of course not. Perish the thought. You know what, Tom Markham? I think you lied to me. I don't think I do know how to ride. That's something a person wouldn't forget, kind of like riding a bicycle. And this horse isn't feeling like any bicycle I ever rode."

She thought his answering chuckle had a wicked edge. "You'll do fine. Gimp is a great trainer. These horses are really well mannered." He wrapped his big hand around her denim-clad calf. Even through the jeans she felt the contact like a warm caress.

"Just bend your leg up this way." He helped her, seeming reluctant to let go, but then gave her calf a pat and turned his attention to business. "Try that." He guided her foot into the dangling stirrup, then rubbed her thigh, as if the pressure of his hand were necessary to keep her leg where it was supposed to be. When their eyes met, Mckenna saw the warm smile there. Lord, how she loved a man who could smile with his eyes alone.

He repeated the process for the other stirrup, and she actually considered suggesting they forget the damned horses and just spend the day in the barn, taking advantage of the soft, warm piles of clean straw. What would Tom say, Mckenna wondered, if she made such a racy proposition. He had warned her that it would happen between them, at the right time, in the right place. IT, rather, the capital IT. No minor little pronoun could describe this promised event.

But this was neither the right time nor the right place, because Mckenna chickened out. Riding the huge Miss Daisy proved less frightening than the prospect of walking down that path of sensual commitment with Tom.

A multitude of trails threaded through the countryside surrounding Gimp's place. Much to Mckenna's relief, Tom chose a trail that wove its way through the valley rather than one that climbed the mountains. Miss Daisy, much to Mckenna's surprise, was a biddable girl, content to follow behind Tom's more lively bay. But her gait, though nothing designed to send her flying into the trees, possessed a rhythm that went forward, back, and side to side in an unpredictable pattern. Mckenna found her hips moving in different directions than her shoulders, her legs swinging back and forth in a motion that was nothing like the picture Tom presented in his saddle. He and his horse seemed to be one beast, in tune, in rhythm, wholly in harmony with each other. Tom's shoulders and back stayed straight, his legs never moved. While Mckenna flopped like an awkward rag doll, Tom rode along as if he were part of his horse.

"How do you *do* that?" Mckenna demanded.

"Do what?" he said, twisting in the saddle and regarding her with a smile.

"Sit so straight. Keep your butt from sliding all over the saddle and your legs from flopping in the breeze."

"You'll get the feel of it after a while."

"Like maybe twenty years!"

He laughed. "Okay, Mac. This nice flat meadow looks suited to a riding lesson. You're on."

"A riding lesson? Oh, no, I didn't mean... You're not going to make me go faster than a walk, are you?"

"Never fear. Tom is here."

"Oh, that's a great comfort. I'm beginning to think I should have stayed home with my cat. If I get killed doing this, who will pick her up from the boarding kennel? She'll never forgive me."

"I'll pick her up. Don't worry."

"Well, if you inherit her, you have to make sure she has a bit of tuna with her cat food each meal. And promise Clara won't harass her."

Tom chuckled. "And who will protect Clara when Titi comes to live with me?"

Mckenna leaned over Miss Daisy's neck. "Oh, heaven! I'm going to die. He admits it."

She didn't die, but only because Tom tied his horse to a tree and mounted behind her on Miss Daisy. When his arms wrapped around her, the expedition suddenly took on a whole new light.

"Now look, you can't just slouch there in the saddle and expect to feel comfortable. Straighten your back."

He brought her up close against him in a posture more akin to his.

"Point your shoulders forward, and just relax."

The patient Miss Daisy walked in a big circle with Tom poking and prodding Mckenna about how to sit and how to move. Soon they had trampled a smooth track in the snow.

"Isn't that easier?" he said, his breath brushing her ear.

That depended on the meaning of "easy." With Tom so close behind her, who cared about the horse?

"Now let your heels drop. That's it. Keep a little leg on your horse. Good, good, and now we're going to trot."

Suddenly things weren't so easy anymore. She bounced and jarred along, until his firm hands upon her waist guided her to move in the proper rhythm. Mckenna decided she might actually like horseback riding as long as Tom was behind her like this.

"I think you're ready to try it on your own."

"What? No, I don't think so. This is great just the way it is. Tom? What are you doing? Don't get off."

"I have my own horse to ride, kiddo. You'll do fine."

His absence allowed the cold breeze to shiver up her spine. But when he swung aboard his bay and smiled at her, she grew warm again.

"Just enjoy yourself, Mac. You're doing fine."

This time, instead of riding in front of her on the trail, he guided his horse to fall in beside Miss Daisy. Knee to knee they rode through broad snowy meadows and crossed rushing streams. Eventually Mckenna did relax and manage to enjoy herself. The cold snap of winter made her feel uniquely alive. The sound of the breeze through the pines sounded like the song of Mother Nature herself.

"This is beautiful," she said with a sigh. "Do you know that all the time I spent growing up in Evergreen, right in the foothills of the Rockies, I never came up here? What a waste to miss all this."

"You were too busy with your head in your schoolbooks, trying to get good grades, right?"

"How did you know?"

"Just figured. This is the life, you know? The smell of pine and fallen leaves and warm horse, the sky so blue it looks like midnight. I miss things like this. I really do."

She looked a question at him. "Why on earth did you decide to become a lawyer? I mean, how far removed from this can you get?"

He shrugged. "I wanted to help people."

"As a prosecutor?" she scoffed.

"You don't think getting the bad guys off the street is helping people?"

"Well, I suppose if you put it that way. But really, how often you able to get the bad guys off the street?"

He laughed. "Now that you're not practicing law, it'll be a hell of a lot more often."

She took a jab at him, which upset Miss Daisy, who apparently preferred to have a more peaceful rider on her back. The horse crow-hopped, sidled sideways, and threw her head in aggravation.

"Watch out for those trees!" Tom warned. Then he winced. "Oops. Too late."

chapter 17

THEY RODE up to Gimp's barn much less briskly than they had left. Mckenna slouched in the bay's saddle. Tom rode behind her, arms around her, hands controlling the reins. Led behind came Miss Daisy, a satisfied look on her equine face.

"I could have ridden back myself, on my own horse," Mckenna complained weakly.

"Of course you could have," Tom agreed. "But just in case Miss Daisy hurt something, we wouldn't want her to be carrying your weight."

It was a lame excuse, and both of them knew it. Miss Daisy was right as rain, friskier now that she had shown her rider a thing or two. "She seemed so calm at first," Mckenna said with a sigh. "The sneaky bitch."

"Women can be like that," Tom said wisely.

"You could get an elbow in your ribs."

"Ha! Just remember what happened the last time you took a swing at me."

Mckenna had to laugh. "I suppose. I'll behave, at least until we're off the horse."

Gimp greeted them at the barn. "Hey, you two. Have fun? What happened, Mac? Miss Daisy dump you?"

"We just had a bit of a misunderstanding."

He tried to look chagrined, but the attempt didn't achieve much credibility. There isn't a cowboy alive who doesn't find a bit of amusement in a horse getting the better of a greenhorn.

"You okay?"

"I'm fine. And Miss Daisy, bless her, sustained no damage at all. She definitely won the argument."

Both men laughed. Tom slid off the bay's hindquarters and came around to help Mckenna from the saddle. She enjoyed his solicitous attention, but as he lifted her down, every muscle complained bitterly. Her feet hit the ground and folded sideways. Her knees felt like water. Someone was driving nails into her back and shoulders. But all that paled beside the agony in her backside.

She gasped as she tried to stand upright. "I'll hand it to you, Tom. This little one-day vacation certainly has made me forget the aggravation of being at home with my parents."

Tom waxed sympathetic. "Ouch! Mac, I'm sorry. I guess we old cowboys just forget that not everyone is accustomed to being on the back of a horse."

"Oh, I'll survive. Actually, I had a good time—up until landing in that thicket. And even after. How else could I have gotten a look at such gorgeous scenery?"

Gimp slapped her on the back, eliciting a groan. "You're a good sport, Mac. But you look all done in. Hey! Why don't you two bunk here tonight? Mac doesn't look like she's up for a two-hour car ride back to Denver. I'll be at the restaurant most of the night, and I plan to sleep in my apartment in Estes. I stay there instead of driving back up here when I work late. What do you say?"

Mckenna's first thought was of her mother's indignation. But hey, since when did she let herself get tangled in apron strings? She would survive the raised maternal eyebrows, the meaningful looks from her father.

Still...

"I have a spa on the back deck," Gimp told her, enticing. "It does wonders for sore muscles."

"You'd feel more like the drive tomorrow morning," Tom urged. His face had assumed a neutral expression. Did he want to stay, or was it a bother? Was he merely being polite? Or might he have an ulterior motive or two?

To hell with speculation, Mckenna decided wearily. "Let's stay. I don't think I can bend enough to get into the car."

She did find the phone and leave a message for her parents before allowing herself to relax. Then she looked around. Gimp had designed the house himself, built it with the help of contractor friends from Denver, and then made it into a home that showed the touch of a man who loved the mountains, fresh air, and open spaces. Logs and glass shaped the structure, and knotty pine colored the interior. The kitchen was Mexican tile, designs both plain and ornate complementing each other in comfortable harmony. The great room encompassed a huge open space, sparsely but comfortably furnished, a huge stone fireplace keeping the room warm, and floor-to-ceiling double-paned windows affording a view of mountains thrusting up into the sky.

In truth, Gimp's place reminded Mckenna of her house in Oak Creek Canyon, now occupied by the yuppie couple with two kids and a terrier, except that this house welcomed a person into its fold with a warmth that the Oak Creek place lacked. Titi, she reflected, would adore the sun coming through the huge windows. The late afternoon painted warm golden squares onto the great-room carpeting. The cat would have been purring in delight.

"This place fits Gimp," Mckenna commented to Tom. "He's a very nice guy."

"He's the best. Except he's out of beer. There's wine here, though. I swear the guy is turning into a wimp."

"All these mountains and horses and—yes, the showcase of rodeo photographs on the walls—has made you backslide into the West's version of a caveman."

" 'Caveman'?" He smiled. "The image that every man secretly longs for. Want some wine? It might take the edge off the soreness."

"Are you sure we should be helping ourselves to his wine cellar?"

Tom laughed. "Gimp might own a fancy restaurant with high prices and imported wine, but the stuff he keeps at home is the five-dollar a gallon kind. I wouldn't worry about it."

Cheap wine or not, it went down smoothly as Mckenna sipped a glass while she sat in Gimp's roomy spa. The water swirled about her in steaming hot currents. The cold air above the water formed dense clouds of steam that obscured all but the vaguest view of the forest and mountains. When Tom walked out onto the deck, he was a mere blur. But he materialized into flesh and bone—bare flesh, bone, and a lot of muscle above Speedo swim trunks—when he mounted the steps and stepped into the hot tub.

The heat and the wine had relaxed Mckenna to the point that it took a moment for her to realize the danger. Then she flailed a bit in embarrassment. "Tom! You can't come in here now!"

"It's plenty big enough for two. Hell, I've been to parties here where five or six have crowded into this thing."

"No. I mean . . . I mean . . ." To hell with delicacy. "Tom, I don't have a bathing suit."

He cocked his head. "You mean, you're buck naked under those bubbles."

"Got it the first time. Congratulations."

"Well, in that case . . ." After a few contortions, the

Speedo went flying and landed with a splat on the cedar deck. "I wouldn't want you to be the only one."

His brash grin took her breath away, and the heat in her cheeks didn't grow hotter just because of the water temperature.

What did a girl say sitting naked in a hot tub with an equally naked man?

He stretched out his long body, laid back, and pillowed his head on folded hands. "Nothing like a spa to relax those sore muscles." His foot brushed against her thigh, causing her to jump nearly out of the water.

"Oops!" he said. "Guess there's not as much room in this thing as I thought."

"Oh, right!" But laughter bubbled in her voice. "You know, being the sophisticated, fast-track sort of woman I am, or was, I'm sure I've been baby-butt naked with a man in a hot tub lots of times."

"Have you?"

"Absolutely. I just can't remember any specific instances. Is there a protocol for this sort of thing? A Miss Manners for spa loungers?"

"Got me. If there were, I'm sure this ol' cowboy wouldn't know about it."

This time his foot grazed her calf. She was beginning to forget all about sore muscles. She lay back, letting the tension ease out of her. If she couldn't draw on past experience, then she would just pretend that she was cool with the sensual heat that was building inside her, with the desire that warmed Tom's eyes, with the prospect of getting high just on the need running through her veins.

"How are you feeling now?" he asked.

She regarded him from heavy-lidded eyes. The steam softened his strong features and curled his hair around his face in thick disarray. With his broad shoulders framed in swirling water, and his hard-muscled arms laid out along the rim of the tub, he could have been some Greek god come to life. Adonis. Was Adonis a god? Was he even Greek? She felt like giggling, but instead, she took another sip of five-dollar per gallon wine.

"I'm feeling...lonely." How bold she felt. "It seems a great distance between over here where I am, and over there where you are."

He smiled and rectified the problem. The water parted around his chest as he flowed toward her. "Better?"

"Much better," she sighed. So relaxed.

"Are you drunk?"

Another sigh. "No, I am not drunk. Not even tipsy. Just tired and relaxed. It seems a very long time since I've been so completely relaxed."

"Good. I wouldn't want anything to be dulled by alcohol."

"Mm." A little frown. "Anything?"

"Anything. Like this."

Suddenly he was very close. Not a hair's distance separated them, making it seem so natural to kiss, just a scant movement forward for both of them. He tasted of wine and spa water, with just a hint of chlorine. His five-o'clock shadow scraped her cheeks, his lips warmed her mouth, his tongue probed gently, answered by her own.

Let up for breath, she smiled. "That was nice."

"I can do better," he said.

Another kiss. She steadied herself by placing her hands on those broad bare shoulders. He caged her against the rim of the tub with an arm on either side. Slowly the kiss deepened. Her arms slid around his neck. His enveloped her, pulling her close, where warm bare skin met, grew warmer. Legs tangled, twined, and hips sealed together. And then...

Water engulfed them as they slipped beneath the surface. They came up laughing and sputtering. "Oh, ouch!" Mckenna yiped.

"What?"

"I hit my butt against the bottom. Sore."

He chuckled. "We'll have to be careful of all your sore spots." And then he reached down to caress the smarting part of her anatomy. Surprised, she jumped—right into his arms—and somehow settled astride his lap, a lap made all the more interesting for not being restrained by clothing. Unembarrassed, he gently checked her first impulse to escape.

"I have an idea," he whispered low.

Oh, heaven, how she hoped his idea was the same as hers!

"Why don't we get out of the tub before we look like prunes..."

That was romantic.

"...and I'll massage every bit of soreness out of those muscles."

Now that had potential! "You would give me a massage?"

"With great pleasure."

"That is the sweetest thing."

"I live to please."

"And you have no ulterior motives?"

"Nothing that you won't like."

She laughed. "Promises, promises!"

He casually stepped out of the tub, taking his time about wrapping a towel around his lean middle. Not before she took note of washboard abs and...other stuff. He obviously had no modesty at all, because he just smiled at her when she peeked.

She, on the other hand, possessed modesty in abundance, and he didn't seem inclined to hand her the towel that lay a good five feet from the tub.

"Coming?" he asked with a grin.

"I'm not climbing out of this tub without that towel."

"What towel?" he asked, feigning innocence.

"That towel."

He shook his head. "Modesty is the citadel of cowardly minds."

"That's a stupid quote. Who said it?"

"I did."

"Ah. Well, try this one. 'Modesty preserves mysteries to delight the imagination.'"

"Hm." He nodded. "Not bad."

"Would you *please* hand me the towel?"

"Compromise. I'll turn my back."

Of course, the man had eyes in the back of his head, but Mckenna reminded herself that she was, probably, an experienced woman, not given to maidenly shyness. She tiptoed from the tub, picked up the towel, and wrapped it firmly around the mysteries. When she told him to turn around, he was smiling like a cat with canary feathers sticking from its mouth. But it was a smile that made her laugh. Had she ever before met someone who so often made her laugh?

Gimp's guest room boasted a queen-size bed with a goose-down comforter that felt like a soft warm cloud.

"Plop yourself down," Tom instructed. "I'm going to fetch something to soothe all your bumps and bruises."

"More wine?" she inquired archly.

"Something better."

He came back within five minutes, but she had wandered close to the boundary of sleep. The feel of the towel disappearing woke her quickly.

"Eek!"

"Don't panic. Your modesty is intact."

Depending on the meaning of intact! The towel lay across her backside, and she lay front side down on the comforter. Then his hands spread warm oil on her back and she began to forget all about modesty. Between good friends, what did it matter?

"What is that?"

"Arnica salve. Great stuff. Herbal. It helps muscle pain but doesn't smell like a gym."

"Smells good. Oh, yes—right there. That feels so good."

Her shoulders relaxed in the care of his wonderful warm hands. Then her back. Then—oh, heaven!—he started on her feet.

"My feet didn't do a lick of work today," she sighed, "but I think they hurt in sympathy with everything else." Was there anything in heaven or earth more wonderful than a foot massage?

"You have the prettiest feet I've ever seen," he told her. "Most people have bumps and lumps, crooked toes, callused heels. Your feet are perfect."

"Mm. Just like the rest of me."

"I won't argue with that."

She chuckled. "I was being facetious."

"I wasn't."

His hands moved to her ankles, fingers tracing the paths between the bones, stretching the tendons that ran to the heel.

"How did you learn to do this?"

"When you ride bulls for a living, you learn."

"You could make big money with this talent."

He shifted attention to her knees. "With such a limited clientele?"

"Hm?"

"Just one." Hands worked upward along her thighs. "You."

She sighed happily. "Just me." Thought had become impossible.

He paused at the barrier of the towel, and she could almost hear him thinking. Somehow it didn't alarm her. She wished he would go for it. But no, he gave the towel a chaste pat and started on her neck.

"Oh, that's good."

His fingers traveled into her hair to gently massage her

scalp, driving her beyond words. Her hair would be full of oil, but she didn't care a bit.

"It's the back that really cops it when you're in the saddle," he said, moving once again to knead the small of her back, put warm pressure where each muscle joined the spine, stretched the flesh over her ribs. And if he brushed the sides of her breasts in passing, it might have been an accident. Or not.

Mckenna didn't really want that brief caress to be an accident. Just to make sure he understood, she took one of his hands and put it exactly where she wanted it. He froze.

"Tom?"

She turned over, managing somehow to keep the towel serving at least part of its purpose. No sense in outing all the mysteries at once.

His eyes shone warmly as he looked down at her. Again, Mckenna placed one of those big masculine hands over her breast, with her much smaller hand on top of his. The sensation made her close her eyes in sheer bliss.

"Now would be a good time," she said in a soft voice. "And here would be a good place. For, you know, IT."

He dropped his own towel and joined her on the bed.

WHEN THE morning sunlight hit Mckenna in the face, waking her from dreamless sleep, she didn't remember where she was. The pines outside the bedroom window glistened, their needles ablaze with the morning. The soft whisper of the furnace sending warm air into the room was the only sound in a peaceful silence. Warmth and comfort surrounded her. She turned her face into the pillow, defying the sunlight to find her there, and drifted back toward sleep.

Then something soft whacked her in the butt.

"Rise and shine, slugabed! Breakfast time!"

She groaned. Now she remembered. "Go away!" she complained into her pillow, but beneath the complaint she wore a smile.

"Not much of a morning person, are we?"

Apparently *he* was. She pulled the down comforter over her head, but his hands came seeking, tickling, which reminded her that she was buck naked. Embarrassment couldn't quite make it through her laughter, though.

"Stop! Aaaagh! Yeeek! That's enough!" She popped her head out of her burrow and wrapped herself regally in the covers. "You have no dignity!"

"Bless you, woman, I believe you're right. I also have no food in my stomach, because I've been waiting for you to get out of bed and make me breakfast."

"You *are* kidding." Then she laughed. Tom wore a bathrobe that came only to his knees and probably could have wrapped twice around him.

He saw the direction of her laughter. "Gimp's robe. What's wrong? You don't like my knees?"

She kept on laughing.

"I could take it off."

She shook her head no, laughter making speech impossible. His poor knees really weren't that funny, but the merriment welled up from inside her, partly due to his appearance, partly to the pure enjoyment of being wakened by a gorgeous man—knees and all—after a night of unrestrained lovemaking. Life this good deserved laughter.

The laughter, however, made her forget herself to the point of loosening her grip on the bedcovers. By the time she noticed that his smile had changed in character, that the warmth in his eyes had heated to desire, it was too late. She sat there exposed from the waist up, rosy from sleep and high spirits.

"Then again," he said in a husky voice, "breakfast could wait a while."

He dropped the robe, completely diverting her attention

from his knees, and came for her. She shrieked, but the cry held no real objection.

"You are a wicked, wicked man," she said, right before his mouth covered hers.

He merely smiled against her lips and proved her right.

THE SUN was much higher in the sky when they finally made it into the kitchen, clean from their showers—or rather, shower, singular, because they had shared the roomy tiled stall.

"Up here in the mountains," Tom had pronounced, "it's good to save water however you can."

Which didn't take into account the long minutes they had let the hot shower rain down upon them when they indulged in things that had nothing to do with washing.

The morning workout had given them both an appetite, but Gimp's larder was stocked only with juice and half a pizza, left over from much too long ago.

"You would think a man who makes his living from food would actually have some in his kitchen," Tom complained.

"Do you realize that we never ate dinner last night?"

He grinned. "We were busy with other things."

"That's so." She felt herself blushing, and covered up by turning back to the subject of food. "It's just as well the cupboard is bare," Mckenna told him. "I can throw frozen waffles in a toaster, but other than that, I'm not much of a cook."

"I am. Here I was going to make you my famous eggs Benedict."

"Is it better than the eggs and bacon you made when I cowered at your place after my trailer got burgled?"

"Way better."

"No kidding? I'm impressed." It wasn't the only thing

that morning that had impressed her. "Is there anything you don't do well?"

"Lots, unfortunately. You'll no doubt discover every one of them in time."

The implication of time—time together, time stretching into the future—made Mckenna smile.

"I know," Tom said. "We'll make Gimp cook us breakfast. His place opened a half hour ago."

They couldn't face the world before coffee, however, and while Tom brewed a pot, Mckenna stripped the sheets from the guest-room bed and put them in the laundry room, where much earlier, before she had awakened, Tom had washed and dried the clothing they'd soiled, thanks to several hours spent on top of a horse. Horseback riding got clothes very dirty, Mckenna had discovered, and her flying dismount into a thicket hadn't helped matters any.

Unfortunately, Tom had washed the clothing in one single load—all of them. Underwear, blue jeans, sweater, his flannel shirt. Her underwear and sweater had emerged a slightly different color than they had gone in, but Mckenna didn't mind. She had found one of the things Tom didn't do all that well, and it made her smile.

He did make a good cup of coffee, however, and they sat at the kitchen table enjoying orange juice and caffeine, sitting there as the sun came through the window, basking in a kind of happiness that required no words. It occurred to Mckenna as she sat there that she had finally followed Titi's often repeated advice. Being with Tom was Mckenna's version of lying in the sun.

THE CHUCK Wagon Restaurant, as Mckenna expected, welcomed diners with a décor of cowboy rustic. Knotty-pine walls displayed photos of Gimp (who else!) roping calves, hanging onto bulls, and in one photo, lying in the dirt wrestling a steer. Other décor included old horseshoes, blacksmith's tongs, a mess kit that looked as though it had been on one too many trail drives, and some genuinely marvelous bronzes of cowboys, horses, and cattle in various combinations of action.

"This really is kind of nice," Mckenna commented as the college-age hostess led them to a booth.

"Gimp does all right. He's a pretty good cook himself, but he hired a better one—an expensive chef from London, would you believe? And that guy's trained all the other cooks who work here."

"The eggs could have been hatched by royal hens in London for the price. No wonder Gimp can afford that house and one in town, as well. Heavens!"

"This is Estes Park—tourist central, even in December. People on vacation are willing to pay premium for good food. And even the breakfasts here are special."

Gimp came out and greeted them heartily. "Hey, Mac. How you feeling this morning?"

"She's ready for another horseback ride," Tom said with a grin.

After her activities the night before, a horseback ride was the last thing she needed. "Too bad we have to get back to the city," she said, kicking Tom under the table.

"Well, hey! Come back anytime. I wish this guy would visit more often, but he's too busy playing lawyer. I've tried to get him into something more respectable, but he's a stubborn cuss. By the way, guys, breakfast is on the house. I'll bet the cupboards were bare at the house, weren't they? How about that? Invite guests to stay, then make them pay for their own food."

They protested, but Gimp insisted. Mckenna didn't protest too loudly, however, because she was in no position to dine at expensive restaurants. Hell, if she hadn't had her McDonald's employee discount, she would have starved rather than put on the pounds since she had tumbled into poverty. And fortunately, the hospital cafeteria was cheap.

However, after a wonderful breakfast of French toast, eggs, and turkey bacon, she made a point of seeking out Gimp on her way back from the ladies' room. He came out of the kitchen and gave her a brotherly slap on the back.

"How was the food, Mac?"

"Wonderful." She couldn't resist. "Worth every penny, even if we had paid."

Gimp laughed. "I love a smart-ass woman."

"Gimp, thank you for everything. For the horses, and letting us spend the night. I swear I was too stiff to move."

He chuckled. "Were you now?"

The implication made her blush, and he slapped her on the back once again, chortling. "Don't pay no mind to me, Mac. You're a hell of a sport. Lord, you can't be the Mckenna Wright that Tom told me about some months ago."

"Yes, that would be me." Sort of, she added silently.

"Boy, did Tom have you pegged wrong." He shook his head without going into details.

Mckenna could just imagine what Tom might have said.

"But I see that he's recognized his stupid mistake. You're good for him, Mac. I can tell."

"We, uh, we just had a few misunderstandings back then. Besides"—she gave him a bright smile—"people change, you know."

Sometimes they required a knock on the head to change. Sometimes they lost their whole lives, then got it back again in spades.

chapter 18

DRIVING HOME from Estes Park, Mckenna felt as though everything in her life had changed. She was charged with laughter; happiness bubbled inside her. A new security, a new warmth, a new sense of joy infused every moment.

When she dropped Tom at his motel in Golden, they had shared a good-bye kiss that warmed her clear down to her toes. "What time does your plane leave tomorrow?" she asked. "I'll give you a ride to the airport."

"That would be great. Why don't you come by the motel about midnight?"

"Midnight? What the heck time does your plane leave?"

"Noon."

"Wicked man!"

His grin made her laugh. Midnight, indeed! Yes, everything had changed.

But when she walked through the front door of her parents' home in Evergreen, it seemed that nothing had changed. She felt like an errant teenager who had broken curfew. No one said anything in reproof—except for Titi,

of course, who had complained all the way from the boarding kennel to the house. But disapproval hung thick in the
air. Apparently the girl who grew up in this house, making
the honor roll every term, ignoring the temptation of adolescent antics in order to make something of herself, of
her future—that girl did not, positively *did not*, gallivant
off and spontaneously spend the night with some hunk,
engaging in activities her parents didn't even want to
imagine.

"Did you have a nice time, dear?" Her mother's inquiry,
delivered during a delicate little hug, dripped censure.

"A very good time." No lie there, except that the good
time could scarcely be described in such tame words.

Her father looked up from ESPN golf to send her a
frown. "Who was that young fellow? That wasn't Adam."

"Adam?" The name they'd mentioned before, when
they thought Mckenna was engaged. A shadow of unease
clouded the green pastures of her future. She was almost
afraid to ask.

"Adam!" her mother interjected. "You know . . . oh, for
heaven's sake, Mckenna. You can't have forgotten Adam."

Apparently she had. "Who the heck is Adam?"

Her father snorted. "If you ask me, she should forget all
this gadding about with Adam and whoever this fellow
is—"

"I introduced you," she reminded her father. "Tom
Markham. He's with the county attorney's office in
Prescott."

Her father harrumphed. "Works for the county attorney? He isn't *the* county attorney?"

"No, but he's a very capable prosecutor." Not that she
remembered that specifically, but Tom did everything ca-
pably, with the possible exception of laundry.

"Well, if you ask me, girl, you should forget these fellows . . ."

Fellows, plural, Mckenna noted. She didn't want to know. She did *not* want to know. But she had to know.

"...and concentrate on getting your head screwed on straight and getting your job back. First things first. You always understood that before."

"Who is Adam?"

"Now, Kenneth," her mother countered, ignoring Mckenna's inquiry. "A young woman needs to pay attention to finding the right husband. Especially at Mckenna's age. She's no spring chicken, you know."

"Bah! She doesn't need to marry. She does plenty well on her own, or she did up until lately."

"Of course she doesn't *need* to marry, dear. In some ways"—and here she fixed her husband with a gimlet eye—"marriage can be a burden to a bright woman. But a single woman past a certain age is at such a social disadvantage. One never wants to invite a single female to a social function, especially an attractive single woman. Because whether or not she is perfectly well behaved, the married women always fear their husbands are eyeing the available one and holding them up in comparison. Very awkward."

"That, my dear, is because they are eyeing the available one. Nothing wrong with that. Just because a man's wearing a wedding ring, it doesn't mean he's dead. Women do the same thing...."

Mckenna's parents continued to debate as if Mckenna weren't in the room. They had forgotten all about the mysterious Adam, so he couldn't be important, she told herself. She would ask about him later, when her parents weren't having such fun sparring. If this Adam were someone significant in her life, he would have contacted her, whether or not he had known about her accident. And surely Jane or Nell would have mentioned him. Wouldn't they?

Yet the thought of Adam bothered her the rest of the afternoon, even though Titi claimed to know nothing about the man.

"Who?" Titi asked when Mckenna posed the question.

"Some guy named Adam. Know him?"

The cat gave her a disdainful stare. "Why know? Cats are nothing. Things to be dumped into kennels." Then she curled into a ball in the middle of Mckenna's bed with her face turned away.

"Don't be huffy, Titi. Would you rather have stayed here, with my mother and father?"

The sable tail lashed back and forth.

"I thought about your advice," Mckenna told her cajolingly. "I found out how to lie in the sun."

"No sun here," Titi complained, still turned sullenly away.

"No sun here. That's for sure. That's why I went with Tom."

"Cats can go, too."

"Not always, sweetie."

"Meeeer! Yowrl maol!"

Mckenna closed her eyes and sighed. Her fickle brain had just shut down the Cat linguistics program again. How long did they have before their conversations were a thing of the past? She sat down on the bed and stroked the cat's sleek back. "That's all right, Titi. I really didn't want to know about Adam, anyway. He's probably no one important."

The afternoon didn't get any better. While Mckenna fixed herself a late lunch in the kitchen, her mother walked in, took one look at the tuna sandwich with mayonnaise and avocado, and nearly had a heart attack.

"Mckenna, don't tell me you're going to eat all that."

"Mother, it's one sandwich."

"Avocado?"

"Is a vegetable." She frowned. "Or is it technically a fruit? Whatever, it's good for you."

"Mayonnaise?"

"What could be healthier? Eggs—"

"And fat!"

"Recent research indicates that we need fat in our diet."

"Nonsense! Mckenna, you're going to weigh a ton and look like a cow."

No wonder she had grown up being the next thing to anorexic, if this was the pressure her mother had applied. And no wonder she had indulged in a rhapsody of eating when all her mother's warnings went into hiding in her brain. She had gained a few pounds, but the last several weeks her weight had stabilized at a number still on the slim side of average. She might no longer look like she could pose for the cover of *Cosmo*, but neither did she belong in a barn.

"Mother, I'm hungry. Just let it go, all right?" Still, her mother's words had an effect, and the first bite of that beautiful sandwich included a salting of guilt.

Her mother heaved a resigned sigh—the one that says, with no words at all, that children are the bane of a parent's existence. "I suppose you're a grown woman, and if you choose to grow into a middle-aged frump, that's your decision."

"You want me to make you a sandwich, Mom? I promise not to use mayonnaise or anything fattening." Or nutritious, either.

"No, dear. Thank you. I just came in here to remind you about the Women's Business League luncheon tomorrow. You did say you'd like to go, and I thought with all your gallivanting about, you might have forgotten."

Oh, yes, the WBL luncheon. She had consented to attend simply to avoid maternal nagging. Mckenna dreaded eating the inevitable institutional rubber salad under her mother's watchful eye, not to mention answering curious questions from a host of silver foxettes. And foxettes they would be, with fashionably coiffed hair, expensive designer clothes, and figures that belied their age. Her mother wouldn't be caught dead lunching with a bunch of comfortable grandmotherly types.

"Yes, Mom. I remember. Noon at the Club."

"All my friends will be so glad to see you," her mother said. "I admit to bragging a good deal about how well you're doing."

"Yes, Mother." She didn't miss the warning to say nothing about her present circumstances. Apparently, her position at the hospital wouldn't impress the ladies of the Women's Business League.

Lying in bed that night, she complained to Titi, who lay curled warmly against her side. "I'm slipping beneath my parents' thumb again, my friend."

Titi raised her head and yawned.

"I feel guilty for every bite I eat. I'm ashamed that I lost my job—like it was my fault! And the warm fuzzies I felt about pulling myself up by the bootstraps are all going cold."

The cat sent her a disgusted look. "Heart beats heavy. Thump, thump. Bad."

"Yeah." Mckenna sighed. "I'd hate to take my blood pressure right now."

"I warned," Titi reminded her. "Kittens leave, eight weeks."

"Well, human family ties last a good deal longer than eight weeks. And if not for my past going into hiding, this would have seemed like a totally normal family visit to me."

"Be brave," Titi urged with another yawn. "Find your own territory. Then lie in the sun."

Mckenna smiled and scratched Titi's ear. What would she do without her own little fuzzy guardian angel to remind her what was important in life? Her smile grew wider as she remembered what her version of lying in the sun had proven to be. Tom. What was she doing fretting in this cold guest bed at her parents' home while he slept just a few miles away in a motel bed, alone?

"Not good," Titi said sleepily.

Mckenna chuckled. "Do you read my mind?"

"What do you think?"

"I think you're one smart cat."

She could have sworn the cat laughed. "Smart. Yes."

A resolutions formed and solidified in Mckenna's mind. It was time for her to be smart, as well.

So the next morning, when she picked up Tom at his motel and opened the Neon's trunk to load his suitcase, he looked bewildered when he saw that the trunk already had luggage in it.

When he looked a question at her, she just shrugged. "I figured I might as well just drive you all the way back to Arizona, if you'd care for the company."

A HUNDRED miles south of Denver on Interstate 25, Tom contemplated the advantages of turning a ninety-minute flight with his knees scrunched against his chest into a sixteen-hour drive with his knees in roughly the same uncomfortable position. Though he had to give Mckenna's little Neon credit. It did have more legroom than a Boeing 737. Even with a plump cat curled on his lap as if she owned it, his long legs still maintained enough blood flow to retain their feeling.

Not that it mattered. If Mckenna had offered to spend two days with him in a cramped space capsule, he would have jumped at the chance. Comfort mattered very little to a man in pursuit of a woman, and since arriving in Colorado, Tom had confessed to himself that he was in serious pursuit.

And that confession had cost him a bit of pride. Setting his sights on Mckenna Wright was a fairly stupid thing to do, and Tom had so far in his life avoided doing anything seriously stupid. Riding bulls didn't count as stupid, because at the time, that risky road had offered the most money to a kid who had graduated high school with football being his strongest subject. Besides, he was damned good at riding bulls, and he had proven once already that he wasn't all that good at running Mckenna to ground.

But like his daddy used to say, during the odd moments when he was around, nothing made a man stupid faster than a beautiful woman.

The hell of it was, Tom's desire for Mckenna had little to do with her being beautiful. The woman sitting beside him driving her little putt-putt down the freeway didn't hold a candle to the Mckenna he had tried his luck with over a year ago. Outwardly, that is. The changed Mckenna had a hell of a lot more going for her than the sleek, manicured, and elegantly-styled attorney intent on clawing her way to a partnership in BKB. She had humor, perspective, guts, and a spontaneity the old Mckenna had lacked.

Not to mention that she'd proven her superior taste in men by climbing into bed with him. He grinned at the memory, perhaps a bit too widely, because out of the corner of her eye, Mckenna flashed him a wary look.

"What are you smiling about?"

"Me? Nothing important. Just sitting here enjoying the scenery."

"There's nothing but plain old grasslands out there."

"I happen to like grasslands. Besides, those mountains in the distance are spectacular. At least, they would be if we were thirty miles closer."

"Right." She smiled.

Probably she was on to him, Tom admitted. But that was all right. He allowed himself to drift back to that most pleasant memory of Mckenna naked in his bed, or technically speaking, Gimp's bed. The important thing was that Tom was the man in it with her.

Not that getting Mckenna into bed—his own or someone

else's—constituted Tom's idea of pursuit. A man could very easily lust after a woman and have no interest in her outside the bedroom—not one of his gender's more endearing qualities, especially to women, but there it was. He wanted a good deal more than a tumble in bed from Mckenna. He didn't yet know how much more. Or maybe he did, and hesitated to admit it to himself. That final commitment loomed in a man's mind as something very scary. Scarier even than a Brahma bull standing seven feet tall.

Especially since Mckenna could at any moment revert to the thorny, nose-in-air legal-eagle Barbie doll that she had been before. The amnesia certainly complicated things. What would happen in a few months, or a few years, if the old Mckenna charged back and carried the day?

"You're awfully quiet over there," Mckenna commented. "Did you decide to join Titi in a nap?"

"Nope. I was thinking about you, actually."

"That crazy woman who kidnapped you on your way to the airport and dragged you into a two-day road trip home?"

"Yup. That's the one. But then, I'm not going to object to a little private time with a gorgeous dame."

"To pick my brain."

"Among other things, one of those other things being a chance to get you alone in a motel room tonight."

She laughed. "Very direct. I like it."

"Direct is the only way. Now that you've got your parents' place behind you, I can ask: Did being there help at all with your memory?"

"Oh, sure. I remembered a lot. My sister Carla and I skating on the lake during the winter. Me modeling for my mother when I was a teenager. Carla was jealous about that. She wanted to model, but stayed pudgy until she was about twenty. Did you know my mother is a fashion designer?"

"Doesn't surprise me, twig woman."

"Mom was actually embarrassed about Carla's weight problem, but she wanted me to make the big time as a model. That wasn't a high enough goal for my dad, though. I do believe, thinking back upon it, that he saw me following in his footsteps to the bench." She sighed. "Carla, brave girl, had the guts to ignore their criticism and do what she wanted with her life. But me, I wanted so badly to be the star they told me I could be. They each felt very strongly about what I should do with my life. Fought about it, even. Now I realize that I tried to please them both." She chuckled. "Be a hot-shot attorney, maybe even a judge, but do it with a *Cosmo* figure in designer clothes."

"You were doing an excellent job of it. But you know what? I like your current figure a lot better, and since I've had a private viewing, I know whereof I speak."

She hit him in the shoulder with the heel of her hand. "You are a nimrod," she laughed.

They stopped in Santa Fe, passing up the chain motels in the sprawling outskirts for the historic La Fonda Hotel on Old Town's central plaza. The plaza dated back to the seventeenth century, when the first colonists from Spain put down their stakes and claimed the land, and its wealth, for their own. The first territorial governor's palace, more hovel than palace by modern standards, still stood at one corner of the plaza. And other buildings on the quadrangle, buildings now occupied by shops and galleries, also dated from that time when the nations of Europe first began their expansion into the New World.

"Have you been here before?" Tom asked as they wandered the plaza.

"Don't remember," she admitted. "But my guess would be no. I can't picture me taking the time to wander through historic buildings, even if they are filled with art, clothes, and jewelry. Heavens! Look at the price on this simple cotton dress."

"Is that high?"

"You don't shop much for women's clothing, do you?"

"Got me there."

"I guess it wouldn't be high compared to, well, the same dress on Rodeo Drive in California. Jeez! To think that once I could have afforded some of this stuff. Look at that bronze. Isn't that stunning? That would look so good in the entryway to the Oak Creek house."

They walked on. Mckenna bought a silver bracelet for Jane—not in a shop, but from a smiling Navajo woman who, along with several others, had jewelry and pottery spread on a blanket in front of the governor's mansion. It was much prettier than the inexpensive price indicated.

"She won't wear it," Mckenna acknowledged, "even though it would look good on her. I don't think I've ever seen her wear any kind of jewelry. You know, Jane could be really pretty if she just took some time with herself and didn't use the same grooming tools on herself as she does on her dogs. Oh, well, it's worth a try, and she'll appreciate the thought."

And in a small gallery she found a framed photo for Nell.

"She's a good amateur photographer herself," Mckenna told Tom. "That's another one of the myriad facts that surface in my brain every day."

He admired the photo. "Nice composition. Look at the light and color."

Mckenna laughed up at him, her eyes merry. "Who would have thought Cowboy Markham would appreciate such a thing."

"Shows what you don't know about me. I love beautiful things."

The look he gave her made her blush, and it was his turn to laugh.

After they walked out of the last shop on the square, Tom presented Mckenna with a silver-and-lapis pendant hanging from a delicate filigree choker.

"You bought this for me?"

"Must be. I certainly didn't buy it for Clara."

"Oh, Tom! It's beautiful."

"I thought it would look good on you. And don't go feeling all awkward about it, because it wasn't that expensive."

She gave him a look that melted his bones. "It's the thought that counts. I know that's an old saw, but it really is true. Besides, it really is lovely."

He fastened the choker around her neck. Beneath the collar of her jacket, her skin felt warm against his cold fingers. Warm, soft silk. She leaned into him as he labored at the small chore, and the light scent of roses made him smile. She had always worn that scent, and he had always liked it. Apparently, it took more than a knock on the head to wipe out a woman's preference in fragrance.

"There," he said, and fingered the pendant that rested in the hollow at the base of her neck. It had warmed against her skin. Lucky pendant. As his fingers brushed against her collarbone, her eyes met his, and a smile touched her lips. She rose on tiptoes to press a soft, chaste kiss to his mouth.

"Thank you, Cowboy."

A flush of desire made him forget the cold snap of the air. And from such an innocent little thank-you kiss, too. He might as well admit it, Tom mused. He was beyond help. May Cupid have mercy on his soul.

They had dinner at the hotel, at La Plazuela, a beautiful enclosed courtyard restaurant that boasted "Nuevo Latino" cuisine.

"Whatever is Nuevo Latino?" she asked with a laugh.

"You got me. Gourmet burritos?"

Actually, the menu offered a wide variety, none of it cheap, but not outrageous, either.

"My treat," Tom told her when he saw her eyeing the less expensive entrees. "The hotel is on me, too. It's only fair, after all. You're providing the car, the cat—"

"The cat?"

"Great lap warmer, that cat is."

"So you provide bed and board? For me *and* the cat."

"Seems fair to me."

"Well, it's not, but I'll let you. And when we get back to the room, I'll tell Titi that it's her job to warm your lap on demand."

"I don't think Titi does anything on demand, does she?" Tom asked with a chuckle.

Mckenna smiled. "She's pretty much the boss of me. But for a good-looking guy . . . Well, she was in your lap all day."

They gave their order to the amiable waiter—fajitas for Mckenna and the combination plate with green chile sauce for Tom. And wine. What was a wonderful dining experience without wine?

Waiting for their food to arrive, Mckenna munched on homemade chips and looked around at the dining room, whose cozy fireplace and hanging plants offered a warm, lush contrast to the snow outside. "Funny to think that not too long ago I could have afforded all this and thought nothing of it. I could have wandered into any of those shops on the plaza and picked out an outfit to buy without even looking at the price. I even could have bought that beautiful bronze sculpture of the cowboy roping the steer."

Tom smiled. "You wouldn't have, though. You didn't used to care that much for cowboys."

She caught the double meaning and grinned. "Yes, well, maybe my taste has improved."

"Those things happen. I know my luck has certainly improved over the past few weeks." Then he grew serious. "Do you still want your old life back, Mckenna?"

She bit her lip. "Maybe. Sort of." Then sighed. "Hell, I don't know, Tom. Sometimes I catch myself liking my new life. The trailer is a bit of a dump, I know, but every bulb buried in the flower bed, every piece of furniture I bargained for at yard sales and the Goodwill, gives me a sense of accomplishment. And the hospital isn't a bad place to work, even though the pay isn't that great. I get to take Titi with me to work and visit the patients, and I tell you, everytime I go into the patient rooms, I become more and more aware of just how lucky I am."

She thought of Doris waiting for death in a hospital bed, proud that she had made the most of the life she had been given. Doris would have cheered at the way Mckenna had taken the bull by the horns and whisked Tom off on a two-day idyll.

The food arrived, and the lull in the conversation gave her time to think. The fajita tasted wonderful, done just right, with the vegetables marinated in something very tasty. A fast hamburger at McDonald's was fine, and so was the hospital cafeteria. Both of them were better than her cooking, that was for sure. But she missed this. Fine food, good wine, a beautiful atmosphere. She stirred her food with her fork, and then shook her head.

"You know, I miss having money. That's shallow of me," Mckenna admitted with a wry smile, "but I remember that I enjoyed nice restaurants. Gourmet food. Beautiful places. And I wish I didn't have to worry about making ends meet. Right now, if an appliance broke or the roof started to leak, I couldn't afford repairs."

"I don't think wanting a secure living is shallow," Tom said.

"Nell—you remember my friend Nell, with the strange little corgi dog named Piggy, don't you?"

"Sure I do."

"Nell lived a hand-to-mouth existence for years, because she wanted to write freelance for the local papers rather than keep a job in the big city, and she never seemed to mind it. I remember having the devil of a time getting her to spend any of that money that Frank Cramer left to her dog." She tilted her head thoughtfully, a smile slowly taking over her whole face. "I *do* remember that! What do you know? It just came to me as naturally as stepping off a curb." Then the smile faded a bit. "I also remember enjoying the law. And working with you on our little projects has made me fall in love with it all over again."

He reached over the table and took her hand. "Mac, I'm glad."

"I want the law back, Tom. I can survive without the status and the money—I've learned that. But I do want the law back."

"You'll get it, Mac. You said it yourself—things are coming back. Soon you'll have a plush corner office somewhere and you'll set about making life miserable for prosecuting attorneys like me. You were very hot stuff, you know." He lifted one brow. "Not only as an attorney."

"Was I really hot stuff?" she asked half-playfully.

"Still are," he confirmed.

"Hot as your enchilada smothered in green chile sauce?"

"Oh, far hotter." He waved a fork at her for emphasis. "And I know what I'm talking about. Personal experience."

A mischievous dimple appeared in her cheek. "I don't suppose . . . no. I don't suppose you'd care to expand on that personal experience?"

"The subject could always use some more exploring."

She gave their empty plates a meaningful look, then raised an inviting brow, rose, and sauntered toward the door. Tom's jaw dropped as he momentarily stared at the oh-so-subtle sway of her hips as she walked away, then he hurriedly signed the check and followed.

"God help me, Mac," he said under his breath, "if you don't stay just the way you are."

WITH HIS broken leg elevated on a stool in front of him, Buddy Morris sat in his study watching the Arizona Cardinals massacre the Oakland Raiders on a cable sports network. He had started to follow the Cards when Todd built that palace of his in Sedona. God knew he spent enough time in that godforsaken state to claim residency, if he wanted to, so he might as well be a Cardinal fan.

Of course, it would help if they knew their way around the game of football better than, say, the Tiny Tot League for athletically dysfunctional five-year-olds. Still, on this particular Sunday night, the Cards were winning 21—7, with only one quarter left in the game. Not that they couldn't screw themselves in the fifteen minutes remaining. They could.

When a beer commercial came on the screen, Buddy hobbled to the kitchen for a Budweiser. It wouldn't have done any good to yell for his wife to fetch it for him, because she was in the living room weeping over some chick flick she had rented at Blockbuster. Thank the stars he had his study as a retreat.

"Is the game over?" she asked as he passed the living room.

"Just starting the fourth quarter."

"That's nice."

Like she cared. He didn't ask if she wanted anything from the kitchen. Crutches and all, he had to fetch his own damned beer, so she could fetch for herself, as well.

He had just gotten comfortable back in his easy chair when his phone rang—not the house phone, which he would have let Gloria deal with, but his private line that rang only in his study.

"Goddammit!" The Raiders were setting up on Arizona's six-yard line, a touchdown coming up, and the goddamned phone rang! Eyes still glued to the television, he snatched the phone off its cradle, glanced at the caller ID, and growled, "This better be good, Jack."

"Hey, Buddy, my man. How are things in Nashville?"

Buddy delayed his answer to watch the Raiders down the ball on Arizona's two-yard line. Second down.

"Jack, I'm involved in something important here. Could you call back tomorrow?"

"Hell, Buddy, how important could it be? It's Sunday night, for chrissakes!"

Buddy groaned as the Raiders ran into the end zone.

"You're watching a game, aren't you, man? If it's the Raiders' game, you don't need to watch to know what's going to happen. Oakland's going to walk all over the Arizona Turkeys."

Now Buddy started to get annoyed. "Jack, what the hell are you doing calling on a Sunday night? Isn't there such a thing as a weekend out there in lala land?"

"Hell, Buddy! Out here in California, every day is a weekend, don'tcha know?"

"Can it, Jack. Just tell me what's up so I can get back to the game and watch the Cardinals stomp all over the Raiders. The score, by the way, is still 21–14. Cards are winning."

Jack chuckled. "Not for long, Buddy boy. But back to business. I didn't want to call tomorrow because on so-called workdays you're harder to track down than Osama."

"You have my cell number."

"Yeah, and all I get there is voice mail. Besides, I wanted to have a little private chat with no chance of secretaries or suchlike eavesdropping. About Todd."

Buddy scowled and thumbed the remote to mute the

television. "What about Todd? Did you catch his concert out there last week?"

"I did. Thanks for sending the tickets. The boy is looking good. Sounding good, too. But I want to know what's going on. Hell, everytime I turn on CNN or Fox News, some talking head is jabbering on about these drug charges, with expert lawyers here and retired judges there all giving their goddamned opinion about the evidence and the case judge and the cops and everything down to the prosecutor's bad haircut and the defense attorney's shapely legs. Hell, man, we have sunk a ton of money in those Pepsi ads. He's supposed to be Mr. Clean. He's supposed to appeal to both the kids and their goddamned parents. He's supposed to be America's boy next door. He's NOT supposed to be on the news every day as some lowlife drug dealer."

Buddy sighed and squeezed the bridge of his nose, trying to relieve the beginnings of a headache. "Todd is not a drug dealer, goddammit, Jack. You know the media. They finally got on to this, and now they're blowing everything out of proportion. We kept this quiet for a while, but this was bound to happen sooner or later.

"But I'll tell you this for sure. This nonsense was a setup from the get-go, and if we do go to trial, the cops and that headline-grabbing county attorney are going to look like fools." He hoped.

"It goddamned better be a setup, Buddy, because Pepsi doesn't want some high-living druggie representing its product to an America that's getting tired of these loose-living yahoos. We're aiming to premiere these ads during the Superbowl broadcast, but if this mess isn't cleared up by then—with your boy still looking like Mr. Clean—then we're pulling them, and you're going to see the mother of all lawsuits, Buddy."

"No worries, Jack. Media babble aside, this case is not going to fly. And it will be cleared up by the Superbowl.

The preliminary hearing is a couple of weeks away, and if we're lucky, Todd won't even be bound over for trial."

"Well, I hope not. I like the kid, personally. Have all his albums. My daughter nearly swoons whenever one of his songs comes on. But I thought I'd give you fair warning. Don't let him mess this up, Buddy. We've all got a lot at stake."

"I hear you, Jack. Don't worry about a thing. I've got it covered."

He hung up just as the Raiders made another touchdown to tie up the game and send it into overtime.

"Goddammit!" he growled. Couldn't any damned thing go right lately? First Todd Harmon, who had more talent than brains. Then Mckenna Wright, whose shoddy trailer wouldn't lend a clue about what she had and what she knew. And now the pissant Arizona Cardinals.

"Goddammit!" Grinding his teeth, Buddy sent a glass paperweight flying into the television screen, which shattered in a shower of glass and angry sparks.

chapter 19

THE NEXT afternoon, they left the freeway behind at Flagstaff and turned onto the two-lane highway that would lead them through Oak Creek Canyon and beyond that, to the Verde Valley and to her little trailer in the middle of nowhere. As they drove through the pine forest south of Flagstaff, Mckenna found herself in no hurry to get home. Perhaps Tom felt the same way, because each time he'd taken the driver's seat on this trip, he had held the little Neon to a sedate observance of the speed limit—not at all his usual driving style. Mckenna had seen him in his noisy diesel pickup truck barreling down the road, if not recklessly, then at least fast enough to help the local highway patrol fill their daily quota.

Just now the Neon toodled down the highway at a conservative fifty-five, and Tom slowed conscientiously for each curve. There were a lot of curves in the road between Flagstaff and Cornville.

"I'm almost sorry for our little road trip to end," Mckenna admitted.

Tom reached over, took her hand, and placed it on his

hard thigh, wrapped in his own. His hands were surprisingly callused for a desk jockey. The vivid memory of those hands exploring, caressing, touching threatened to distract her. How could hands so big and hard become such gentle instruments of loving?

She could go on like this for days, Mckenna mused—happily suspended between Evergreen, the roots of her old life, and Cornville, where she struggled to build a new one. How nice it would be to just drive on. On and on. South to the border, then east to El Paso. Or maybe California would call to them. They could walk the beach and play with the foam that rushed up the sand from the big Pacific breakers. Their room would have an ocean view, and every night they would make love listening to the roar of the surf.

"What are you thinking with that faraway look on your face?" Tom asked.

"Thinking of ways to avoid going back to life as usual." No need to tell him how big a role he played in her fantasy. He would think she was picking out china patterns and planning a honeymoon.

He squeezed her hand. "Life as usual is going to get better, Mac. I know it is."

They were silent as the road wound in hairpin turns to the bottom of Oak Creek Canyon, where Mckenna had once had her palace of log and glass, and still silent as they drove from the southern mouth of the canyon into Sedona, where she had once reigned like a queen at BKB. But their hands still rested together, fingers comfortably entwined. Not until they sped out of Sedona on the highway toward Cottonwood—the site of her current less-than-glamorous job—and Cornville—where waited her less-than-palatial home—did the tension of the real world creep back to buzz along her nerves and speed her pulse.

It wasn't so much that she didn't want to be home, Mckenna realized as Tom swung the Neon into the dirt lane leading to her trailer. The problem nagging at her was that she didn't want to be alone. She didn't want to be without Tom.

Dangerous waters.

Titi woke with a yawn and kneaded Mckenna's lap. "Home?" she asked.

"Home," Mckenna sighed.

Tom turned off the engine. "Yes, indeed, home." He surveyed the place suspiciously.

"It's not that bad," Mckenna objected.

He chuckled. "No. I'm just paranoid, where you're concerned."

"Still think someone's out to get me?" A ridiculous notion. Sort of. She hoped.

"I'll just feel better once the police find the yahoo who broke into your place and verify that he's nothing more than a not-very-bright burglar. Why don't you stay here while I go in and check things out."

She let him do the manly thing, somewhat amused. But how nice it was to have someone care about her, someone strong and kind, who made her feel . . . well, just a little bit cherished.

Titi looked out the car window as Tom disappeared into the trailer, then curled once again in Mckenna's lap. "Tom stay?"

"Don't I wish" was Mckenna's answer, without even thinking about it.

"Good for you. He's your lie in the sun."

"Things aren't as easy for people as for cats," Mckenna said with a sigh.

"Not easy for cats," Titi denied. "Have to take care of people like you."

"Thanks a lot."

"Therapy cat. My job."

Tom appeared in the front doorway, smiling and waving her in. Had she secretly been hoping that something would be wrong? Something that would force her to take refuge once again at his place? No such luck.

And Jane's place was closer, anyway.

"Don't be sad," Titi commented when her paws hit home ground. "You ask. Tom stay. Good."

"Sheesh!" Mckenna grabbed her suitcase and headed for the house. "Now you're a matchmaker?"

"Could be," Titi boasted.

Tom came out to take the suitcase from her hand—the last of the world's practicing chivalrists. "All clear," he said when she walked through the door.

"Heaven! How would you know?"

She had stayed at Jane's for the week after the break-in, and her attempts at straightening the mess left by the burglar, and then the police, hadn't been very serious. The trip to Colorado had occupied most of her attention, and that kiss—that wonderful, mind-numbing kiss—at Tom's place had filled the rest. Cleaning had been at the very bottom of her priorities.

"Well, I can see what I'm going to be doing the rest of the day."

"You want help?"

"I suspect you have better things to do with the rest of your Sunday afternoon than help me stuff my underwear back in drawers and the cracker boxes back in the kitchen cupboard. Besides, isn't your buddy Roger picking you up?"

Tom had arranged for a ride across the mountain to Prescott by calling a friend—another attorney at the county office—who visited his parents in Sedona most weekends.

"Yeah. Rog should be here soon." He glanced out the window regretfully.

How silly were they? Mckenna mused. Mooning like teenagers at being parted for a few days. On Wednesday she would be in Prescott for their regular "legal aid" session.

And yet—it wouldn't be the same, really. These past few days had been just theirs, apart from the world, apart even from their own responsibilities and problems.

"Are you sure you're okay about staying here alone?" Tom said, sounding half-hopeful.

Now that she was back in the mess, the violation of her home, she did feel a bit nervous. But she had too much pride to admit it. "I'll be fine. I have a watch cat, you know."

Titi commented from where she curled on the sofa. "Tom stay?"

"The watch cat doesn't sound too sure about things."

"You obviously don't speak Cat. She said that she'd rip any intruder to pieces."

"Yes." Titi stretched elaborately, spreading her front toes to show her claws. "Tom stay anyway."

"Maybe you should get a big dog, like Jane suggested."

"Titi is likely to rip a dog to pieces, as well."

"Well, then..." He grinned. "The next best thing. You could have a macho cowboy come live with you."

Her heart thumped. He was kidding, of course. He had to be kidding. But the gravity of the frown knitting his brows and the seriousness in those keen blue eyes gave lie to the grin that twisted his mouth. A question lingered between them, thickening the air.

Tom had the courage to state it out loud. "Where are we, Mac? Do you know?"

Instinctively, Mckenna dodged the ball. "Where do you want to be?"

He refused to play that game. "That's not an answer, kiddo."

"Cowboy, I don't know the answer. You, me... There are so many uncertainties. I don't trust my feelings. And why should I? I still can't remember a lot of my past, and I have no idea where my future is going."

"It might be that your future will go where you want it to."

"And suppose the Mckenna Wright in that future isn't the Mckenna Wright who...who was wishing when we drove down the canyon today that we could just keep driving, you and me and Titi, forgetting everything but enjoying each other. Suppose the Mckenna Wright who would gladly, this very minute, drag you back to the bedroom and have her way with you isn't the Mckenna who will be here when my gray matter gets around to falling back into place?"

The shadow in his eyes told her that he had wondered about the same thing.

"How can I commit to a relationship when I don't even know who I am?"

He reached out and touched her cheek. "How about we don't commit to anything until you're comfortable with it, okay? No pressure. No unpacking the toothbrush—"

"Well, you could certainly leave a toothbrush here," she told him with a smile.

He smiled back. "I guess time will tell what we are. Good friends..."

"Friendly lovers," she added.

"Buddies."

"*Muchachos.*"

"Sidekicks."

"Very close sidekicks. You could maybe leave some clean underwear here, as well." She dimpled. "It's a long drive across the mountain. Just in case you wanted to come over and help me review a point of law, or something, and got so tired you had to sleep over."

"Sounds like a plan."

The crunch of her driveway gravel under the tires of a car warned them of Roger's arrival.

"Tom stay?" Titi yowled.

"She doesn't want you to go," Mckenna admitted, "and neither does her mom. But you need to go, before I get myself into trouble."

"Or trouble gets into you."

She laughed. "Wicked man."

He brushed her lips in a light good-bye kiss, but that quick buss turned out to be not nearly enough for either of them. His mouth came down on hers for a second, deeper taste, and she opened to him, taking everything he had to offer. They had plastered themselves together, breast to chest, hip to hip, and he had cupped her buttocks in his hands, lifting her closer to him, when the doorbell rang.

Slowly, reluctantly, they parted.

"Roger," Tom said with a sigh. "He's always on time."

Mckenna tried to catch her breath. "Good for Roger."

Ten minutes later, Mckenna looked around at the mess of her house, feeling hollow and empty now that Tom had climbed into Roger's car and the two of them had headed toward Prescott. How much more confusing could her life get? she wondered.

As if in answer, the phone rang. She picked it up, thinking it was Jane. But it wasn't Jane.

"Mckenna," said a somewhat testy voice. "This is Adam."

Adam?

"HEY, FELLA," Roger said heartily. "What happened? Develop a fear of flying?"

"What?"

"Weren't you supposed to fly back on Friday?"

"Yes, but would you turn down two days in a car with a gorgeous woman for two hours shoehorned into an airline seat, probably next to some widget salesman who weighs four hundred pounds?"

Rodger chuckled. "You have a point. Though calling the Sedona Ice Queen gorgeous is stretching it."

"You think?"

"There's a point where bitchiness subtracts from face and figure, you know? And in Wright's case, the score comes out to just about zero."

Tom bristled. "You don't know her very well, Rog."

"Thank heaven for small favors. I've heard the stories."

"She is one hell of an attorney, and a hell of a woman, to boot. She's sharp, no-nonsense, and no-holds-barred in the courtroom, and maybe outside it, too. But that doesn't make her a bitch."

Roger's brows shot upward. "Whoo-hoo! A quick leap to the lady's defense! Tell me it ain't so, brother! I thought you went to see her because she might 'fess up with some info about Harmon."

"I did. And get that smirk off your face. If I was involved with her, it wouldn't be anyone's business but mine. And hers. She's no longer with BKB. She's not even practicing law right now."

"Yeah, so I heard through the grapevine. So tell me, did you pry anything useful out of her?"

Tom didn't much like the wording of the question, but he answered. "Not really."

"I hear that accident hit her pretty bad. Can she remember anything?"

"She will. It'll just take time."

"The preliminary hearing for Todd Harmon is in two weeks. More time than that?"

"Looks like it. I'm going to start talking to the guests at that party, to find out if they remember anything specific about the maid who was there that night. But this whole thing is probably just a dead end, anyway."

"Just like your trip, eh? How many days wasted, and not a thing to show for it?"

Tom smiled, remembering the way Mckenna had looked, all soft and bemused by their kiss, when he had left her at the trailer. Hardly what he would call a wasted trip.

Roger whistled. "Man, another bachelor bites the dust."

"What?"

"I've seen that look before, brother. You're toast, dead to the brotherhood of free men."

"Bullshit. And don't go starting any rumors."

Roger chuckled wickedly. "Not me, brother. You're going to have enough to worry about. Donovan is on a tear. He thinks the media's trying to paint us as fools." He made a face. " 'Course, they may be right, but if the boss-man loses the next election because of the Harmon case, anyone who touched it is going to find himself out on the street. And that means you, friend."

MCKENNA SPENT her lunch hour the next day at the Bark Park, yelling at Jane. Not that the mess that currently engulfed her was Jane's doing, but she needed somebody to yell at, and Jane was handy.

"A fiancé!" She slapped her hand down on the counter of the kennel office. "A fiancé named Adam! Couldn't you have told me I have a fiancé? Didn't you think that little detail of my life might be important?"

Jane shot her an impatient look, totally unimpressed by the show of temper. "How the hell was I supposed to know you guys were engaged? Do I look like a walking encyclopedia of Mckenna Wright's life?"

"We're supposed to be best friends! What kind of best friends don't talk about their love lives?"

"Look in the mirror, Mckenna."

"You mean, I got engaged to be married, and I never told you or Nell?"

Now Jane looked less sure of her ground, perhaps even a bit guilty. "We knew you'd been dating this Adam guy in Denver, but you never mentioned being that serious. Are you sure he said 'engaged'?"

"Would I imagine that word? No!"

Jane shrugged. "We teased you about him, because your attitude toward men, well, let's say you put just about every guy you met through a third degree that made most guys feel like they were about an inch tall. You didn't think most men were worth the air it took to keep them breathing, so I would be mighty surprised if you really intended to marry this Denver hottie."

Mckenna pounced, her eyes slits of suspicion. "How do you know he's a hottie?"

"Oh, come on, Mckenna. When you went out with a guy, he was a hottie, a lot of times with more looks than depth."

Mckenna collapsed over the counter, tempted to bang her head on the Formica. "Dammit, dammit, dammit! Jane, what am I going to do? I feel as though my old self is some stalker who leaps out at me from behind every corner of my life. I was just gaining some real confidence to get on with my life. Things are coming back to me, even the legal stuff. I'm beginning to feel like a human being. And Tom... Tom and I..."

Jane shot her a sharp look. "Tom and you? Tom Markham and you are an item?"

Mckenna retrieved some of her indignation. "What's wrong with that—other than that I apparently have a fiancé in Denver?"

Jane laughed. "Nothing's wrong. I've always liked Tom, and I could never understand why you wouldn't give him the time of day."

Mckenna smiled wryly. "At this point, I've given the man quite a bit more than the time of day."

Jane couldn't keep the glee from her response. "Hot damn! Good for you! That's what's got you so upset. You finally had the sense to get yourself a decent man and now this lowlife Adam appears to throw a monkey wrench into the works."

"He's gone from a hottie to a lowlife?" Mckenna glared with renewed suspicion. "You said you didn't know him."

"I don't know him. But I know Tom, and most guys are lower than him on the evolutionary scale, if you ask me. And I wonder, when you get back your posh job—and some day you will—and your old hectic life, will you give good old Tom the brush-off?"

Mckenna's jaw dropped. "I wouldn't do that. Would I?" she added with less confidence.

Jane gave her a long look tinged with sympathy. "No. I guess *you* wouldn't. Hell, Mckenna. Sometimes talking to the new you while remembering the old you is damned confusing."

Mckenna managed a weak laugh. "You think *you're* confused!"

"You're remembering more and more?"

"It's like having two people living in my head. I definitely do not remember this Adam guy, though."

"Then he couldn't have been that serious."

"You'd think." Mckenna indulged in a huge sigh, leaning her elbows on the counter. "My parents did mention an Adam, but I just let it whiz right by me. I did ask, sort of. But when they got distracted and didn't answer, I just shut up about it. A coward, that's what I am."

Jane snorted. "All of us are cowards about something. Besides, I would think if you were engaged to this guy, he would have been right by your bedside in the hospital."

"He said he didn't know about the accident."

"It's been three months! He hasn't tried to contact you

in all that time? And now he calls you up out of nowhere? What's with this guy?"

"How should I know?" Mckenna wailed. "Jane, what the hell am I going to do? Adam is coming to Arizona. He insisted. He's flying into Phoenix Wednesday and renting a car. Wednesday night I'm supposed to be at Tom's to work on these legal projects he's gotten me involved in. What am I supposed to tell Tom?"

Jane shook her head in sympathy, but her lips twitched in an urge to laugh. "When you were still at BKB, I guess you had a pretty silver tongue. Hope you still have it, girl, because you're going to need it."

IF FOLKS thought only lawyers cultivated a silver tongue, they had never worked in the volunteer department of a hospital. When Mckenna got back to her storage closet/office—she had begun to call it the "stoffice"—she walked into the middle of a candy striper crisis. Sixteen-year-old Pris had duty in radiology along with seventeen-year-old Tiffany, and the girls spent more time sniping at each other than checking in patients and helping push wheelchairs. So they ended up in Mckenna's office, much like students sent to the principal, where Tiffany claimed that Pris (whom she referred to as "that little slut") had been coming on to her boyfriend the whole semester, and that everytime she opened her mouth she made some sly remark about the hunk in question. For her part, Pris complained that Tiffany thought she was God's gift to the world just because she was a senior at Mingus Union High, and could she help it if the guy was ready to move on to a fresher, younger woman?

Mckenna had no desire to be untangling the problems of two teenagers when she could barely deal with her own troubles. She reassigned Pris to the emergency room and cautioned Tiffany about calling her fellow stripers names like "slut." Where men were concerned, she advised the girl, life was a bitch. Deal with it.

Tiffany's jaw dropped, and then her mouth stretched into a delighted grin. "You're bad!" she said with a giggle.

"You don't know the half of it," Mckenna told her. "Now get on back to radiology."

Remembering that she had her own crisis to deal with, she picked up the phone to call Tom when one of the volunteer chaplains blew into her office. "Mckenna! Thank the Lord you're here."

"Reverend Chatham?"

"You know how we all had to take the TB skin test last week?"

She had been in Colorado last week, but employee health had scheduled her for the next day. The hospital had treated several tuberculosis patients in the last month, so everyone had to be tested for exposure.

"Is there a problem?"

"Mine was positive! Tuberculosis! My God! What do I do now?"

Mckenna needed a good ten minutes to settle the man down, explaining that the test simply indicated exposure, not infection, and a chest X ray would probably prove he was clear of the disease.

"I'll bet they've already scheduled one for you, haven't they?"

"The employee health nurse did mention something about it."

"Well, then, see? I'd suggest you put off any worrying until after the X ray, and likely there's no need to worry at all. Even in the worst case, TB can be cured these days, and the treatment wouldn't cost you a thing since you're a volunteer."

"They didn't go into all of this at employee health."

"Well," she said with a smile. "Now you know."

Relief lit his face. "Now I know. Thanks, Mckenna. I

suppose I should hold off visiting patients until I know for sure, eh?"

"Definitely don't visit any patients. And be sure to let me know the results of that X ray."

He left in a much lighter mood, and Mckenna found herself smiling as she walked down the hall to the pop machine. She had a desk in a storeroom, and a wage that barely paid the rent, but she was beginning to realize that the value of a job wasn't necessarily measured by salary or a corner office.

When you get back your posh job and hectic life... Jane had said, and the edge to her voice had cut with disapproval. Did she want those things back? The house on Oak Creek? The hard-driving job that had dominated all her hours?

Will you give good old Tom the brush-off? Jane had asked.

Mckenna couldn't imagine doing such a thing. Even if she did return to her former profession and someday move back into the log palace on the creek, the sharp edges she had once cultivated would stay in the past. So much of her memory had returned, enough to make her realize that the person she had become wasn't so separate from the person she had once been. The old Mckenna had been freed of the shackles imposed by notions drilled into her when she was too young to resist, and now she had settled into a new mold, with new needs and new ideas of what constituted success. Her past was merging with her present, and she felt almost whole again. Whole enough to see that her past really didn't have to dictate her future.

Very nice, she reflected. Very convincing and logical when she philosophized such things to herself. But Tom might be harder to convince of the insignificance of the past when she told him her fiancé would arrive in Phoenix Wednesday afternoon.

She slid some coins into the pop machine and retrieved a Diet Coke from the dispenser. For the phone call she had to make, she would need all the fizz and caffeine she could get.

When she returned to the stoffice, the phone lurked beside her computer monitor like a squatting toad, taunting her with a chore she dreaded. Maybe she should stroll over to the legal department and ask if she could be of any help there. They had told her to drop in anytime, and she wouldn't mind plowing through some of the files there. Medical case law could be fascinating.

Titi jumped onto the desk, hunkered down beside the phone, and gave Mckenna's hand a swat with her paw. "Tom?" the cat reminded her.

"I thought you were suppose to help me keep my blood pressure down."

"Tom," Titi repeated. "Lie in the sun."

"Okay, okay." Mckenna gave up and picked up the receiver. "But there's not going to be much that's warm and sunny about this."

"Hey, Mac!" He answered the phone with a cheerfulness that made her task all the harder.

"Hey, Cowboy. I hate to say this, but I can't come Wednesday night."

"Got a hot date?"

His teasing, Mckenna mused, would take on a new note when he found out how close he had come to the mark. She decided to take the offensive. Things always hurt less when you barreled into them full steam ahead. Now there was an Old Mckenna thought if she'd ever heard one.

"Mac? You still there?"

"Yes." She shot from the hip. "Does the name Adam Decker mean anything to you?"

A long, pregnant silence told her that it did.

"You knew?" she demanded, not waiting for his answer. "You knew about Adam!"

"I knew you'd been seeing a guy named Adam in

Denver. But you didn't exactly tell me volumes about what was going on."

"I don't believe it! First Nell and Jane, and now you! You all three knew about this Adam fellow, and none of you thought to fill me in. Did it occur to any of you that a phone call from some stranger claiming to be my fiancé might give me another stroke?"

" 'Fiancé'?" No teasing at all in his voice now.

Served him right, Mckenna thought churlishly.

"Fiancé? Hell, if you two were engaged, then you did a good job of cover-up. I asked you point-blank the night of your accident, when we were eating and arguing at the Rainbow's End, and you said the rumors that you were about to tie the knot with this joker were greatly exaggerated."

"Well, maybe I lied. The consensus seems to be that the me before I bashed in my head was a shrew with a knife for a tongue and a rock for a heart."

"Yeah, but you weren't a liar."

That hurt. He didn't have to agree to such an unflattering assessment. She began not to care at all if she hurt his feelings with her news. "Apparently, Cowboy, you didn't know me as well as you thought. According to Adam Decker, he and I have been a done deal for months."

His voice turned huffy. "So then why didn't he show up at your hospital bed? What kind of a guy doesn't drop whatever he's doing to take care of his honey when she's hurt?"

"I guess no one told him I was hurt."

"And he didn't give a thought to your not calling him for weeks on end?"

"I don't know! How am I supposed to know? He calls me out of the blue, says what the hell is up, because he heard I was in Denver and didn't call him. Some guy who plays golf with my father told Adam I had been in town. Adam called my parents, my parents gave him my new phone number, and now we're up to yesterday, when my phone rings and Adam announces that he's goddamned coming to Phoenix Wednesday and will rent a car and be up here by five!"

"Whoa, Mac! Take a breath."

She did. "Like I need this right now?"

A heavy silence said he didn't need this right now, either.

"Tom, I don't remember this guy!"

"You'll remember him when you see him, I'll bet."

"What is that supposed to mean?"

"Nothing other than what I said. You'll remember him."

"I feel as if I've been ambushed by my past again, just when everything seemed to be coming together. My memory is returning in leaps and bounds. I was feeling good about myself. And now this."

"You've got to see this guy and find out the truth, Mac. You owe him that."

She didn't answer. What could she say? That this shouldn't make a difference between them? Of course it made a difference, not only to her relationship with Tom, but to her own perspective on her former self. According to Adam Decker, she had said yes to a guy who didn't show the least bit of curiosity when she didn't call him for weeks on end.

Old Mckenna might have been hell on men, but she sure hadn't expected much of the guy she had promised to marry.

chapter 20

"IF YOU tell me to go lie in the sun one more time, I'm going to lock your fuzzy butt into the bathroom where I don't have to listen to your advice."

Mckenna glared, and from her perch on top of the television set, Titi glared back with the superiority only a cat can manage.

"I mean it," Mckenna warned. "I don't need to be told to mellow out, or relax, or take a catnap, or any of your other feline advice. I'm not in the mood."

Indeed, her mood at the moment didn't permit much beside pacing the small confines of her living room. How she wished that she hadn't thrown out the Valium she had found when packing the Oak Creek house. She could have used a tranquilizer just then. Or maybe two. Two would have produced such a pleasant buzz that she wouldn't have cared if Jack the Ripper were on his way to her door, let alone Adam the surprise fiancé.

"Oh, to have this evening over with!"

Adam had called from his cell phone to tell her he was ten miles from her place and would pick her up for dinner.

Just like that. No "Would you like to have dinner?" or "What would you like to do this evening?" No, indeed. He had decided to take her to dinner, and that was that.

"Eating is good," said Titi, in an attempt to mollify.

"Not when your stomach is tied in knots."

"Hairball?"

Mckenna snorted. "I should be so lucky. That might give me an excuse to get out of this nightmare."

But she couldn't get out of it forever. Tom had said she had to see this mystery man, that she owed him an explanation, a consideration. Damn Tom for his up-front, let-everything-fall-where-it-may attitude. She felt like hiding under the bed and just hoping the problem would go away.

How many other ambushes from the past were waiting around the next corner of her life?

Gravel crunched under the tires of a car pulling into her driveway. Mckenna's stomach lurched. She stared at the door.

Tail twitching, Titi rose, circled, and lay back down in the same spot on top of the television—a loaner from Jane to replace the stolen set. "Don't want to go? Don't go. Cat motto."

Mckenna made a face. "In my next life, I want to be a cat."

"Good choice."

The doorbell rang. Mckenna closed her eyes and took a deep breath. "Here goes."

She opened the door, ready with a greeting that she never uttered, because her jaw fell open too wide for speech.

"Hello, Mckenna. God, it's good to see you."

Oh, my. This was Adam? *This* was Adam!

Forty minutes later, seated at a cozy table at the Heartline Café in Sedona, Mckenna had to admit that her former taste in men hadn't been that bad. Adam Decker's looks would catch any woman's attention. Dark, curly hair. Steel-gray eyes. A noble nose and strong jaw that would grace a Greek hero. Add to that flawless manners, an endearingly quirky smile, and an athlete's body clothed with impeccable taste—modern, not too conservative, but not flashy enough to leave any doubt about his sheer masculinity.

How could any woman have forgotten such a gorgeous specimen? Mckenna could understand forgetting her name, her education, her ambitions and eating habits, but surely it would take a sledgehammer to the brain to make a woman forget Adam Decker.

The moment she had opened the door of her home and seen him standing there on her little porch, bathed in the dingy glow of her porch light and the radiance of his own near perfection, another piece of Mckenna's memory had snapped into place. She remembered Adam, all right. Shared skiing adventures at Breckenridge, Colorado. (She skied? Another memory unearthed!) A weekend in Puerto Penasco. For her, the relationship had begun as a lark, a fun time with a man who was as stylish and handsome as she was stylish and beautiful. Common interests—he also was an attorney, a partner in a prestigious Denver law firm—and common ambitions had made the lark last a while, and then deepen. She also remembered that Adam always drove himself to be the best at everything he did, rise to the top of any company.

In other words, Adam Decker was the masculine equivalent of the old Mckenna Wright. No wonder they had gotten along so well.

"Bring the lady a margarita," he said to the waiter who appeared promptly at their table. "And I'll have a vodka rocks."

So he was the masterful type. Annoying, but she supposed all that perfection had to have a flaw or two.

His eyes—a clear, cool gray—came to rest upon her, his

attention riveted. They hadn't said much on the ride in his rental car—a Caddy. But now she felt the full force of his inquiring scrutiny. She had some explaining to do. A lot of explaining. But then, so did he.

"Mckenna, I can't tell you how relieved I am to see you. When your father told me what happened, I was nearly frantic. You could have been killed, or crippled for life."

Somewhere in his tone she heard a complaint that she hadn't called him. Mckenna sighed and hoped that her margarita would turn out to be super-sized. "I didn't call you because I got my memory knocked right out of my head, Adam. I couldn't even remember my own name, much less anyone else in my address book."

No need to mention that she had deliberately ignored her mother's mention of his name, and that she had been busy cavorting shamelessly with an ex-cowboy lawyer who turned her knees to mush.

"The truth is, Adam, I didn't remember anything about us until I opened the door and saw you standing on my porch. Then it came back to me."

He showed a curious lack of surprise at this avalanche of news.

"Adam?"

He smiled—and was there a hint of guilt in the curve of his lips?

"I know that, Mckenna. Your father told me."

So much for discretion from family members.

"Don't take it as an insult, Adam. There was a big part of my life I didn't remember. A lot of it has returned, but some still hasn't."

"I don't take it as an insult," he said calmly. Then, with eyes slightly narrowed, "You didn't remember me at all?"

"No."

"Not until this evening when I picked you up?"

"It happens like that. A sight, a sound, even a smell will hit me, and then a whole section of my past will come flowing back into my head. Like magic. Lately that's been happening more and more."

He took a sip of his vodka, looking thoughtful rather than upset. Mckenna couldn't help but wonder how Tom would react if he had been wiped from his fiancée's mind. She would be willing to bet that he wouldn't have sat around twiddling his thumbs while someone dear to him didn't call, didn't write, didn't e-mail.

"Adam, why didn't you try to find me? You could have gotten my phone number from directory assistance. Or you could have called BKB. Peggy might not have given out my number, but she would have told me to call you."

He blinked in surprise. "You left BKB?"

Apparently her father had left a lot out of their conversation. "I got fired."

"What? Fired? They fired you?"

"Yes, well, at the time I was pretty miffed, considering that a backstabbing bitch of a corporate climber orchestrated my exit, with a little help from one of the partners who didn't like me much from day one. But then, back in the day I was a bit of a corporate climber myself, and I'm sure the term 'bitch' applied to me, as well."

"That's outrageous! You should have sued, Mckenna."

"I toyed with the notion, but I suppose they had some justification. I wasn't much use to the firm when I couldn't tell a tort from a tart."

He nearly turned green. "You forgot your law education?"

"Every chapter and paragraph."

The reappearance of the waiter saved Adam from finding appropriate words of horror. While they ordered dinner, Mckenna considered the man across from her, comparing him to Tom Markham. They didn't compare any better than apples and oranges. Adam certainly took top honors in the polish department. He oozed sophistication, from his expensive haircut to the toes of his two-hundred-dollar shoes, while Tom's hair probably hadn't seen a barber, much less a stylist, in weeks. Adam wore success and ambition like a proud badge. Tom—well, Tom had plenty of ambition. He had put himself through college and law school riding bulls—no easy task—and had graduated with top honors. Not from an Ivy League school like Harvard or Yale, true. But the University of Arizona law school didn't admit just any bullriding smart-ass cowboy who came along, either.

Adam oozed suaveness. Tom's specialties were roughshod rustic charm, a smart mouth, politically incorrect irreverence, and a stubborn idealism that still believed in the essential justice of the courts.

And Adam, bless him, was getting ready to order for her—some salad entrée with a bit of fish thrown in for protein. Obviously he knew Old Mckenna's eating habits.

"Wait, Adam. Thank you, but I'm really not in a salad mood tonight." And then she ordered for herself.

"Steak?" Adam queried, confused.

"I've developed a taste for beef. When you work at McDonald's, you learn to either love it or hate it."

"McDonald's?"

Poor man. One bombshell right after another.

"I tried to get a job at Wal-Mart, but they wouldn't have me."

He seemed at a loss for words. She might as well have announced employment shoveling manure. Come to think of it, she did have a part-time position doing something very close to that, but telling him would just be cruel, considering his reaction to a perfectly civilized job serving up hamburgers and fries.

Adam shook his head. "Is this a joke?"

"No, actually, it's not. I don't work at Mickey D's anymore, by the way, though I'm forever grateful to them for giving me a job when everyone else turned me away. Now

I'm working at the hospital as an assistant to the director of volunteers."

If she said the word secretary, which was the official title of her position, he probably would implode.

"But, Mckenna, a woman of your skills—"

"My skills were in the law."

"You said your memory was returning."

"It is. That part, too. But slowly."

"So you'll be going back to the law."

"To tell the truth, Adam, I haven't yet decided what I'm going to do. I'm a different person than I was before the accident."

"Yes, well, I can see that." He regarded intently the thick rare steak the waiter set in front of her.

They talked little during the meal, and Mckenna could almost see the mental gears shifting inside Adam's handsome head. He was a nice guy. She had good memories of him, now that those particular memories had seen fit to reveal themselves. If she had remembered him earlier, she might have called upon him for help. Then again, maybe not. A certain reserve had always existed between them, on her part if not his. He had proposed, she remembered. He had proposed more than once, tempting her with prospects of their combined income and ambitions, their common interests and priorities, their spectacular performance together as lovers. Yes, she remembered that, too. And the memory didn't hold a candle to a night spent in Estes Park, Colorado, and another in Santa Fe.

But was she being fair to the man? After all, in a way, she had just met him. And didn't she owe him something for their past history?

"You were hungry," he commented as she finished the last of her dinner.

"Making up for lost time. Somewhere along the way I forgot the desire to fit into a size three." She smiled at him. "Nice of you not to mention the extra padding."

"It looks good on you."

She laughed. "Adam Decker, you are a nice man. And by the way," she said, "you very neatly dodged my question of why you didn't call me in all that time."

He looked embarrassed. "To be truthful, Mckenna, we've always given each other a lot of space, but I had been pressing you for a real commitment. Marriage, or at least a formal engagement. It seemed to me that the harder I pressed, the more you resisted, so I decided to give you some space, to give you a chance to miss me, honestly. And, well"—he looked a bit chagrined—"actually, we had decided to cool it for just a while."

She thought that over for a few minutes, then ventured, "We weren't engaged."

"Well, no. Not exactly."

"In fact"—she extrapolated from his explanation of "cooling it"—"I was in the process of dumping you?"

His face colored. "No. Not at all. Nobody was dumping anyone."

But she had the ball and was running for the goal line. "No wonder you didn't call. I had broken up with you!"

"That's not—"

"And when you found out I had amnesia, you figured I would have forgotten that little detail, and you called and introduced yourself as my fiancé!"

"Well . . ." He grimaced, then pinched the bridge of his nose as if a headache threatened. "Actually, you caught me." Hands raised in surrender, he appeared chastened. "I know, I know. It was a rotten trick. But honestly, Mckenna, it just slipped out during that phone call. Unpremeditated stupidity. We weren't engaged, but we were headed in that direction pretty fast, and we'd both decided to take a breather and consider whether or not to take our relationship to the next level. We were on a hiatus. No one was dumping anyone."

Mckenna didn't know whether to be angry or to laugh.

Embarrassment colored Adam's face, but his words sounded sincere. She supposed she should believe him.

"We had something good, Mckenna."

An unexpected surge of forgotten affection rose as they locked eyes. She recalled that once she had thought those eyes were the sexiest bedroom eyes that any man could possess. "I ought to be mad, but I guess I'm not. Miffed, though. Definitely miffed."

"But you're not telling me to never darken your door again."

She raised a brow. What woman could resist a gorgeous, charming man whose smile could light an entire room? "I'm not going to tell you what to do, Adam. We have a past. Okay. Throwing something away without taking a good look at it first is stupid. But I can't make any promises that we'll ever have what you say we had before."

He raised his glass of vodka in a toast. "To you," he said. "And to us." Before she could comment, he amended, "Forever friends, at least. To us."

They didn't find much to talk about on the drive back to Cornville, but she did invite him in for coffee. It was the only polite thing to do after he had bought her an outrageously expensive dinner at what he assured her had once been her very favorite restaurant.

"You really do live here, eh?" he said, surveying the kitchen with its thirty-year-old linoleum tile, the tiny living room, old shag carpeting, and dark fake wood paneling. Not to mention the boarded-up living-room window she had yet to have repaired.

"Cozy, isn't it?"

By now he knew better than to answer.

Some contrary bee under her bonnet refused to even try putting a good face on it. "Back there is a bedroom, a little second bedroom that I use for my office, and a pretty good-sized bathroom. Except the bathtub leaks. I've been saving to get that fixed."

"Amazing. Actually, considering the circumstances, you've done quite well for yourself. I admire the kind of spirit it takes to come back from what you experienced. But of course, all this is merely temporary."

She handed him a cup of coffee, black, with a teaspoon of sugar stirred in. All this she had remembered.

"Ah, and there's Nefertiti. How's my favorite cat?"

Titi gave him a baleful look from her perch on top of the television, but he didn't seem to notice. He sat—rather gingerly, Mckenna thought—on the Goodwill sofa under the living-room window, and regarded Mckenna thoughtfully. "So where do you go from here?"

"Nowhere, for a while. I've been so busy keeping my head above water, I haven't had time to think much about anything but finding out who I am and where I truly belong."

Tolerantly, he nodded. "Understandable, I guess. But I can help you now. You don't have to do this alone." He patted the sofa beside him. "Come sit, Mckenna. I feel as if I have to yell with you standing way over there in the kitchen."

She moved to oblige him, but Titi blocked her by jumping onto the empty space beside Adam and warning her away with an annoyed meow. Mckenna raised a brow at the cat and got another inarticulate meow as an answer.

"Noisy little thing, isn't she?"

"She always has a lot to say," Mckenna agreed with a sigh, then surrendered and sat in the armchair.

Adam smiled warmly. "Mckenna, you have no idea how much I've missed you. You've been through so much. I hope you'll let me help you through this. I can tell that you're having a hard time. Anyone would. It's times like these when the people who love you need to step in and help."

She leaned back, tired beyond words. "I don't think you know who I've become, Adam. I'm not the woman you knew." She hated this, hated the uncertain, bruised look in his eyes. She shook her head. "I need some time to get myself settled, and you shouldn't have to stick around and try to shore up a woman you no longer know."

"But you'll get back to being yourself in no time, now that your memory is returning."

"I'm not sure that I will." Or want to, she added silently.

"Of course you will. Mckenna, I know you. I know what's inside you. I've never seen anything that could keep you down, any challenge you weren't eager to face. You're smart, and driven, and ambitious. You want the best, and you're not afraid to go after it."

He got up, took her hand, and drew her up to stand facing him. Cupping her chin with a gentle hand, he reminded her. "Not too long ago you thought I was the best."

Then he kissed her, gently, but thoroughly. It was a hell of a kiss, expertly accomplished on his part. Firm, but not too aggressive. Gentle, but not timid. Chaste, but with just the right hint of passion. Obviously, Adam Decker was a world-class kisser. And if memory served, and right then it did, his achievements in lovemaking lived up to the advertisement of his kiss.

Very confusing. As kisses went, this one would score a perfect ten, or at least a 9.9. But when Tom kissed her, no score popped up in her mind, because her mind flew right out of her head, along with anything approaching rationality.

Adam drew back, perhaps sensing the uncertainty of her response. "You're tired," he said by way of excuse. "I should go."

"I am tired," she admitted. Really, she told herself, it was rude comparing Adam's kiss to Tom's. She had once thought she loved Adam, and she still felt something, even through the haze of lost memory. Having her brain rearranged didn't give her the right to discard past relationships as if they were so much trash.

She put on a smile. "I'm sorry if I'm poor company, Adam. It was awfully nice of you to fly down here and make sure I'm all right. I simply have to sort things out in my own time before I can figure out what I want, or even who I am. So just, well, you take care of yourself. Don't tie yourself to past expectations. That's the most honest thing I can say to you."

Adam caressed her cheek with his thumb. "You'll be back, Mckenna. My Mckenna. And I'll help you come back. That's a promise I intend to keep."

One part of her was moved, another part confused.

He smiled, disarming and sincere. "But I promise not to push. And on that note, I'll get out of your hair for tonight, at least."

He picked up the jacket he had laid on the back of the sofa. But as soon as he picked it up, he dropped it. "Oh, God! What is that on the sleeve?"

Mckenna looked, and bit her lip to stifle an entirely inappropriate laugh. "Hairball. Sorry."

Titi returned to her television perch and began licking herself—as cats do—while regarding poor Adam through the yellow slits of her eyes.

Adam tried to suck it up like a man. "These things happen."

He gave Titi a weak smile as he went out the door.

With a huge sigh, Mckenna collapsed on her run-down sofa.

"Meeerrrr?" Titi asked.

Mckenna dropped her face into her hands. "Great. You obviously don't have a problem communicating even when we're not talking. Poor Adam."

"Mowwwr!" Sounded indignant, but unintelligible.

Mckenna sniffed and gave the cat a watery smile. "Okay. You don't like him. But I do, sort of." The old affection breaking through the barriers of her mind, or something new? Adam was a modern Prince Charming straight from the cover of *GQ*. And he wanted her. What female heart wouldn't beat faster? Didn't she owe it to herself to at least consider that forgotten love?

Titi growled.

"More advice on my love life?"

A superior, condescending "Meow."

"Whatever," Mckenna said with a sigh. Feeling sorry for herself and not quite knowing why, she was prepared to indulge herself in a world-class sulk when someone knocked on the door. Adam was back.

Mckenna rolled her eyes toward the heavens and pleaded. "Please no. Haven't I put up with enough for one day?"

But she didn't find Adam standing outside the door.

"I just dropped by to see if you're okay," Tom told her with a guilty look.

Just what she needed. Her old lover had just left amid a flurry of commitments and promises, and now her new lover stood on her doorstep, just "dropping in" from his home fifty miles away. Mckenna found herself growing short on patience.

"You're just dropping by? Come on, Cowboy. Checking up on me?"

"Is that a bad thing?"

"I guess that depends on whether you're looking for burglars or old boyfriends."

"Uh...how about either one?"

She sighed. In a way, she was touched. "Come in. There's not a burglar in sight, and Adam is gone. Want some coffee?"

"Sure." He looked relieved.

While she poured, he made himself at home on the couch. Titi jumped from her perch atop the television to the arm of the couch and from there onto his lap, where she settled down, purring. Mckenna smiled. Titi wasn't subtle in her preferences.

She handed Tom his cup and sat down beside him. "I suppose you want to know how things went with Adam."

Considering, he took a sip of his coffee. "No, I don't think I do. Unless you have an irresistible desire to tell me."

Surprised, she blinked. "Really?"

"I figure that your old boyfriends are your business. And if he manages to light a fire in the present, then I guess that's your business, too." He grinned. "Though I would be tempted to shoot him."

She gave him a look, and the grin turned into a grimace.

"Okay, okay. I'll behave. I just came over to find out how you're holding up. All this can't be easy for you."

Her heart warmed. "Oh, Tom . . . Sometimes this is such a nightmare."

He put his cup on the end table and circled her shoulders with one arm. "You're doing fine, Mac. You just need to take your time and do what's comfortable for you. Don't let anyone put on the pressure." With a wry smile, he added, "Including me. Okay?"

The comfort of his words brought tears to the surface.

"Oh, damn!" She didn't want to cry all over the poor man. Weeping accomplished nothing other than making a woman's eyes all red and puffy. "I hate women who snivel! Don't worry. I'm not going to cry. Really, I'm not. Crying on some man's shoulder is for pathetic losers who can't take care of their own problems, and I don't want to . . . want to . . ."

He pulled her close and settled her head on his shoulder. "Crying isn't for pathetic losers," he said gently. "I know you can take care of your own problems, but sometimes letting it all out makes problems seem easier to bear. So you just go ahead and wet down my shirt."

Mckenna couldn't resist the invitation. She let loose the tears, choking out her confusion and uncertainty, her frustration that every time she saw a light at the end of the tunnel, it turned out to be a locomotive headed her way. He listened to it all, saying nothing, massaging her neck with one hand while the other soothingly rubbed her back—as if she were a child who needed comfort. And like a child, she wanted to curl into him, absorb his warmth, surround herself with his strength, and let him protect her from the world.

But of course she couldn't do that, because she wasn't a child. She was a grown woman, and she had no claim upon him other than as a friend. She needed to be strong, adult, self-reliant. And she would be. She really would be. But only after she allowed herself these few minutes of weakness.

"So..." he finally said, softly. "Did you know him?"

She swiped at her flowing eyes with the back of her hand. "Oh, yes, I knew him. I remembered everything about him." She laughed weakly. "I'm not sure he knew me, though. Poor man."

" 'Poor man'?"

"He wants me back the way I was. Exactly the way I was. And I don't think he understands that the Mckenna he claims to love, belongs to another time, another story"— she smiled—"and certainly to another tax bracket. Oh, goodness! Look what I've done to your shirt."

"A little dampness isn't going to hurt it."

Self-conscious now that the squall of weeping had passed, she drew back from him. He looked almost as unhappy as she felt.

"Mac..." He sighed and took both her hands. "I'll be up front with you about how I feel."

Mckenna wasn't sure she wanted to hear.

"I think we could have something special, and I don't want you to change back into the person you were, even if that's selfish on my part. But I don't want to push." He made a face. "That's not true. I do want to push. I've been going crazy all day thinking about you seeing this damned upstart Adam tonight. But you know, I need to stay out of it, because who you are, what you want"—he hesitated, then gave her a rueful smile—"*who* you want, is your decision, and yours alone. No one can make those choices except you, so don't you let anyone, including me, lean on you."

She bit her lower lip and squeezed his hand.

"And..."

Here it comes, she thought, cringing inside.

"And I think maybe this would be easier for you to handle if I just took a hike for a while. You don't need to have two guys hanging on to you, each with different expectations. If it would help for me to back off temporarily, say the word and I'm gone."

Her brow crinkled. "Are you dumping me?"

He chuckled. "Not for the world."

"You're sure? Because considering everything that's happened, I wouldn't blame you."

"Like I said. Not for the world. When I said that I'm crazy about you, I meant it."

All the single women in the world who complained about the shortage of good men, Mckenna thought, and here she had two vying for her affections. Somehow, though, she couldn't smile at the situation. Neither could she bear the prospect of Tom stepping out of her life.

She squeezed his hands. "You have every right to be tired of this, and every right to go out and find some normal, sane woman who can make you promises about a future that, well, that I can't make right now. But for my part, I'm asking selfishly, Cowboy, don't take that hike."

Tom looked relieved.

"I'm a bit confused. Now that my memory is on a roll, everything is coming back in a mixed-up jumble. Give me some time." She lifted one set of their joined hands and touched his knuckle to her wet cheek. "But don't take that hike."

TITI HUNKERED once again on top of the television and watched Mckenna and Tom as they sat together on the couch, holding hands, talking in low, intense voices. She was a bit miffed that all this human drama, the weeping and consoling, had forced her off of Tom's lap, which, being warm and rather cozy, made a better bed than the top of the television. These people took everything so seriously. Love, jobs, money, more love—these things could be simple, but humans never let anything be simple. She had tried to teach Mckenna, but humans were slow to learn even the most basic truths. They let clutter get in the way.

When Tom finally left, Mckenna turned to Titi as if she expected her to make everything all better, which of course Titi couldn't, in spite of being the superior species. Still, being a dedicated therapy cat, she tried.

"Call Tom back?" Titi suggested.

Mckenna's face fell even lower. "Wouldn't you know that just when I most need someone to talk to, my gray matter slips into noncat mode. Damn! It never rains but what it pours!"

Then she collapsed onto the sofa to pour out enough tears to put any rainstorm to shame. Titi bounded down to her lap, courageously disdaining the danger of getting wet. This night just got uglier and uglier.

Scenes like this made Titi very glad that she was a cat.

chapter 21

THE WEEK dragged on, and Adam stayed, insisting that he stuck around mostly to hit the tourist spots in northern Arizona, but clearly letting Mckenna know that she was the main attraction. He showed up every day at the hospital around lunchtime, until she was sure the cafeteria food would drive him back to Colorado. Thursday evening he took her out to dinner at yet another expensive Sedona eatery that she once had loved—she did remember that, and gave Adam credit for his thoughtfulness—but she now found the place too pretentious and expensive. Friday he came to the house loaded with groceries and made them some of the best spaghetti Mckenna had ever tasted.

"I didn't know you cooked so well," she commented after finishing a plateful and enjoying the mellow red wine he had selected. "And somehow I don't think that's something I forgot."

"That's because I never cooked for you," he admitted. "When we were together, seems like we were always at a ski lodge, or on vacation in Mexico—remember that little hole in the wall in Rocky Point where you got food poisoning?"

"Yes, thank you. And that's one memory I would rather have stayed buried."

He saluted her with a glass of wine. "I rather like this domestic scene, though. You, me, and the cat." He threw a cautious look Titi's way. "Good food, good wine, privacy..."

She knew exactly where he intended to go with that, but she wasn't nearly ready. Everytime she saw him, she felt disloyal to Tom. What's more, Titi's disapproving glare was enough to sour any urge to get romantic. Poor Adam. He deserved better. But still... "This is wonderful, Adam, and I thank you so much for cooking dinner, but this week has been a hard one. If you don't mind, could we call it an early night?"

Like the perfect gentleman that he was, he graciously complied, insisting on cleaning up the dishes before leaving.

"I have a great idea," he told her as he went out the door. "Why don't we drive up to the Grand Canyon tomorrow? It's Saturday, the weather is supposed to be beautiful, and we can spend a whole relaxing day together."

"Sorry, but I have to work."

"On a Saturday?"

"Afraid so. I generally work at Jane's kennel on Saturday, but tomorrow I'm going over to Tom Markham's."

His brows slammed together. "Tom Markham?"

"He's a friend who's trying to help me get back on my feet, legally speaking. Usually I go to his place Wednesday evening, and since I missed our session this last Wednesday, I promised him Saturday."

"All day?"

"He lives over in Prescott, so with the driving, it will be pretty much all day."

"Sunday, then."

"I'm working at the kennel. Jane is taking her dogs to an obedience trial."

He scowled. "Just how many jobs do you have?"

"Just the hospital, really, and then a few hours a week helping Jane—you should meet her, Adam. You'd like her. And then what I call 'legal aid' with Tom."

And there she hit upon the reason for Adam's scowl. "Just who is this Tom person?"

"He works in the county attorney's office. We met when he used to work at BKB."

A hopeful smile. "Elderly and bald?"

An image popped into Mckenna's mind—Tom with thinning hair and wrinkles. But his blue eyes still danced with devilry, and his smile still had that irreverent curl that always made her want to laugh.

The image must have somehow reflected in her eyes, because Adam's scowl deepened. "Ah. I see."

She forced Tom—both present and future—from her mind. "Adam, I'm sorry I can't spend more time with you, but I did warn you that I needed some time to get my life back on track."

He quite deliberately smoothed his frown. "You did, Mckenna. But I worry about you. I have a few more days of vacation that I can spend here. We'll just spend time together whenever your schedule permits."

He placed a finger on her lips to forestall her reply.

"I know this is very complicated for you, and you're not ready to welcome me with open arms. I promised I wouldn't push. And I won't." His lips brushed hers in a light kiss. "Take care."

He left, and Mckenna felt like kicking something. She did like the man. How could she help it? If a computer had created every woman's dream boyfriend, the program would have produced Adam, down to his expensively styled hair, manicured nails, gourmet talent, and gentle persistence.

And there was a spark between them, even though it flickered when thoughts of Tom distracted her. She didn't yet know herself well enough to throw away something she had once valued.

The next morning, as she had told Adam, she drove her little Neon across the mountain to Tom's place. She was getting her confidence back, as far as the law was concerned, and no longer approached these sessions fearing that she would make a fool of herself.

When Tom greeted her at the door, however, she sensed a tension in the taut stretch of his smile. His words tried to mask it, though.

"Howdy, there, Counselor. You already have clients waiting in my office." He handed her a cup of hot coffee, closed the door behind her, and launched into a synopsis of the first case—a single mom with a guardianship problem for her three-year-old.

Mckenna firmly squelched a twinge of disappointment. What had she expected—a fond kiss of greeting at the door, like a husband might give a wife, or a lover might give his lady? This was business, not a date.

"Did Jack Heidinger call about his neighbor problems?" she asked.

"He did, and he's coming in later, armed with the covenants and restrictions for his neighborhood."

"Too bad we can't have covenants against jackass neighbors."

Tom laughed. "Why do you think I live out in the sticks with five acres surrounding me?"

They were off and running, and soon Mckenna became absorbed in the work. Every case they discussed, every point of law she researched, information flowed more freely from the formerly locked up areas of her brain.

Before she knew it, her stomach told her the time for lunch fast approached.

As she toyed with the idea of asking Tom out to the nearest McDonald's—she had a craving for a Big Mac with cheese—the doorbell rang. Wondering if Tom had scheduled someone over the noon hour, she poked her head out of the office to discover who had come in, only to lock eyes with none other than...

"Adam?"

"Hello, Mckenna. I thought I'd drop by and take you to lunch."

Incredible. Persistence was a good thing, but Adam took a good thing too far.

"How...how did you find me way out here?"

"You told me Mr. Markham's name, and from there it wasn't hard to find his address. I'll admit I got lost a couple of times trying to get here. This isn't exactly on the beaten path."

"That's because I like my privacy," Tom interjected sharply.

Uh-oh. "Heavens, Adam, you drove all this way, but—"

"But she's too busy to leave right now."

Adam arched a brow. "What is this? Slave labor?"

If Tom had been a cat, Mckenna thought, his back would be arched and ears pinned back. Adam responded with a challenging stare, eye-to-eye, spine stiffened, shoulders squared.

"Guys, at least let me introduce you before you rip out each other's throats." No sense in trying to pretend they were all friends here. "Tom Markham, Adam Decker. Now, since you're both grown, educated, civilized men, can we back off a bit?"

Tom's mouth curled upward at one corner. Mckenna couldn't decide if it was an attempt at a smile or the beginnings of a snarl. "Now, Mckenna, what have I ever done to give you the impression that I'm civilized?"

Adam drew himself up even more stiffly, if that was possible. "I just came here to pick up my fiancée for lunch."

"Adam," she said firmly, "I am not your fiancée."

He spared her a quick glance. "Perhaps we shouldn't be airing our personal affairs in front of a stranger."

Give her a break! Was Adam really this much of a stodge? And Tom, her gentle Tom, seemed about to revert to a caveman. The gleam in his eye definitely spelled danger.

Tom gestured toward the door. "Mr. Decker, the only stranger I see in this house is you. Now, Mac and I still have work to do, so if you don't mind..."

Taking no note of the muscle twitching in Tom's lean jaw, Adam settled more firmly into place, seeming to grow roots into the foyer floor tile. "All right, Mr. Markham, I'll be straight with you."

"What a relief."

At the drip of sarcasm, Mckenna shot a warning glance toward Tom.

"I did come here to take Mckenna to lunch, but also to find out if you were taking advantage of her... her temporary vulnerability."

"Is that so?"

"Don't try to intimidate me with that narrow-eyed, tough-guy look. I have a history with Mckenna, and I feel responsible for her."

"Adam!" Mckenna cried.

Tom sneered.

"You're a bit late on the uptake, Decker. Where were you when Mac was lying in the hospital? Where were you when she woke up and found her life gone? Resting on all that history between you?"

"Tom! Behave!"

Both men ignored her. They were much too busy locking horns.

"Where I have been and will be is entirely between

Mckenna and myself. Our private business needs no justification to anyone else. Especially not a jump-up junior lawyer on the county payroll. What are your motives here, anyway? Does the county know you're moonlighting out of your home using a former BKB attorney as free labor?"

"Adam, you have no call—"

"Or do you have even lower designs?"

"Adam, that is absolutely enough!" Mckenna stepped between the two men. Tom's fists were clenched hard at his side. Adam's face literally twitched with indignation. "You both sound like junior-high macho wannabes on a testosterone high, and I'm fed up with the both of you."

They glared at each other over her head, Tom looking much like one of the angry bulls he used to ride, Adam riding a wave of indignation that would have mesmerized the most hard-bitten jury.

"Tom!" Mckenna punched him hard on the shoulder. "Climb down off your high horse. If I want to go to lunch with a friend, I certainly will."

Adam's smug satisfaction lasted only long enough for her to poke a sharp finger into his chest. "And you! You have no right to follow me here and spout all this nonsense about responsibility and history and on top of it all accuse Tom of slimy intentions that have never entered his head. He is not some 'jump-up junior lawyer,' and he is not taking advantage of me. But if I want to be taken advantage of, then I damn well will be!"

Adam opened his mouth to defend himself, but not fast enough.

"Right now I would rather stuff you up the tailpipe of your rental Caddy than go to lunch with you." She snorted. "Either of you. If you two want to serve up knuckle sandwiches for lunch, then fine. Go to it. But I'm not sticking around to watch!"

Fuming, she grabbed her jacket off the hall tree,

stormed out the front door, and sent her Neon fishtailing down Tom's driveway in a satisfying spray of gravel.

TWENTY MINUTES from Tom's place, Mckenna pulled into a crowded McDonald's, determined to cool her temper with a Big Mac and fries. The only available table hid in a corner beneath an overgrown hanging fern, but Mckenna didn't mind having the plant hanging over her shoulder. No doubt it would be better company than either of the two men she had just left.

"Jackasses," she muttered as she sat down. Separately they were charming. Together—watch out! Who would have guessed that two grown, intelligent men could act like such morons?

"Oh, my! Look who's here!" came a familiar woman's voice. "Ms. Wright, is that you? Hello!"

Mckenna looked up to find Sally Morgan, the woman she'd met during her first session of legal aid, standing beside her table holding a tray laden with hamburgers, fries, a salad, and a boxed slice of apple pie.

"Sally. Hi. How are you?"

"I'm just fine, thanks to you."

"Sit down, why don't you? I don't think there's a single table open, but there's plenty of room here. If you don't mind a close personal acquaintance with a fern, that is."

"Oh, I couldn't. I got my kids with me." She laughed. "You didn't think I was gonna eat all this junk myself, did you?"

"Your girls are welcome, too." Mckenna quailed a bit when she saw two 'tweens,' one sporting a pierced eyebrow, the other wearing jeans so low-cut they defied the laws of gravity. But she had spoken the invitation. She couldn't very well tell Sally to take a hike.

"Well, you're real generous, Ms. Wright." Sally sat down heavily in the seat across from Mckenna. "Kids," she said, "this here is Ms. Wright. She's the one who helped us get shed of your no-good chicken-ass father."

The girls didn't react to Sally's harsh assessment of their dad. Mckenna figured they were probably used to it. Besides which, the hamburgers and fries had their attention, not their mother. They argued briefly over whose sack of fries was larger and then ran off to explore the attached playground.

"Well, that solves that," Sally said, opening the plastic lid of her salad. "I do love those girls, but it's nice when they're in school all day. On weekends things can get dicey."

"I can imagine." Though she wasn't sure she wanted to.

"You have kids, Ms. Wright?"

"No, I don't. Not even married."

The woman chuckled and speared a cherry tomato. "You've got the right idea there. Man, if I'd known twelve years ago what I know now...Not that I'd give up one minute with those girls of mine, but someday the Good Lord is going to realize Her mistake in setting the rule that a woman needs a man to make a baby."

Mckenna nodded, remembering well the distress on Sally's face when she had come to Tom's house and told the story of her stalker ex-husband.

"I gotta tell you, Ms. Wright..."

"Please call me Mac." Funny how Tom's favorite nickname had grown on her.

"That's cute. Mac. I like it. I gotta tell you, Mac, that you sure gave my life back to me by getting that miserable ex of mine to leave me alone. I always knew the sonofabitch was a chicken-ass, but it's plumb amazing to me that just one little letter from a lawyer could get him off my tail."

"Well, Sally, I'm glad it worked."

"And I got me a new job working up at the Prescott mall, at the auto department in Sears. Hard to imagine, ain't it? Me with my fancy do and long nails, sittin' there with the tires and batteries and whatnot, takin' orders for people's cars to be fixed and all. It's a good job, though, with decent pay, and I'm gonna keep this one, because you-know-who isn't gonna come around and make trouble. Nossir!"

Mckenna felt her spirits lighten just a bit from knowing she had helped improve this woman's life. This was why she loved the law. This was why that part of her old life, at least, had to return.

Sally chuckled. "I guess you and me have the right idea, Mac. A woman's better off on her own, with no men to make trouble. That's what I think."

Mckenna's face must have given her away, because Sally immediately backpedaled. "Uh-oh! I touched a nerve, didn't I, girl?"

"Well . . ."

"You got man troubles, honey? I swear, is there a woman in the world who don't get trampled on by men?"

Mckenna shook her head. "I'm not getting trampled on. Believe me, Sally, as far as I'm concerned, a man had better put on a suit of armor when he's with me, because I'm the one who does the trampling." That, Mckenna thought with surprise, was definitely Old Mckenna talking. And maybe for once, Old Mckenna had the right idea.

"Right on! Give 'em hell, Mac!"

Right. Mckenna sighed.

Sally regarded her from eyes that had seen a grittier side of life than Mckenna had ever imagined. "But you still got man troubles, don't you?"

"Double trouble," Mckenna confided.

"Whoo-hoo! But that's what happens when you're a pretty thing like you are." Sally chortled. "I hope one of 'em is that tall cowboy with the knock-'em-dead blue eyes. Oh, my! Those eyes could plumb push a girl over the edge."

And wasn't that just the truth! "I thought you didn't like men, Sally."

"Oh, well, when you been burned, you learn to keep your distance from the stove, you know? But you bet I can admire from a safe distance."

Mckenna grimaced.

"Oh, now, Mac, don't you look so down in the mouth. Let old Sally give you a piece of advice. I've been around the block a time or two, you know. You did me a big favor in getting rid of Eddie, and now I'll turn around and help you out a little."

"Shoot, then." It wasn't as if she was doing that well on her own.

"Okay. I'll tell you what I learned the hard way. In spite of my shootin' off at the mouth about men being useless chicken-ass turds, there are some nice ones runnin' around out there, and a woman who comes up with one of those in her net, she's doin' herself good, you know?"

Her trouble wasn't in finding a nice guy, Mckenna reflected. Her trouble rested with finding too many of them. But let them within a mile of each other, it seemed, and they did turn into "chicken-ass turds," just as Sally had said.

"And the funny thing," Sally continued, nodding her head wisely, "is that comin' up with one of these prizes don't have much to do with the studly bod or that little hot surge you get when you sometimes look at a man. Oh, yes, girl, I been there, and look what it got me. Eddie! And before that, a man who'd as soon slap me silly as look at me."

"Oh, Sally!"

"Yeah, well, that's how you learn. So you listen to me. You don't look for a man that makes you all melted in your shorts, you hear?"

Mckenna squirmed a bit, and Tom's image came to mind.

"Nossir! You look for a fella that you like. Like with a

capital L. All that hot sweaty stuff isn't what counts in the long haul. You look for considerate."

That was certainly Adam. Considerate to a fault. But so was Tom.

"And you look for stuff you got in common."

Old Mckenna had a ton in common with Adam. That was why the man had been so convenient. It came to Mckenna then that her relationship with Adam had been all about convenience—convenience for her. All for her. He was handsome, smart, considerate, sophisticated, good in bed, and best of all, far away, so she hadn't had to deal with the day-to-day intimacy that might demand something of her that she was afraid to give.

How rude of her! Rude, selfish, and false. And there had been that "hiatus," as Adam had called it, though he downplayed it as a mere breather while they considered the next level in their relationship.

If they had truly been in love, would they have needed a breather?

Then Tom's image came to mind. She certainly didn't want Tom at a distance, and the less breathing space between them, she realized, the better she would like it.

"Of course, it doesn't hurt none if you think the guy is a hunk," Sally went on.

To Mckenna's way of thinking, Tom definitely was a hunk.

"But first you got to be sure he's nice. Nice with a capital N. You hear? That's what I've learned." She made a face. "Not that I've come across any of those nice guys lately. At least, none that haven't already been snapped up."

"I hear you, Sally."

Tom wasn't as nice as Adam. He didn't have the sophisticated manners or the polish. He poked at her demons to make them come out of hiding. He prodded her into trying things that scared her. Once he had indulged in the poor taste of pursuing Old Mckenna, and then he had tried to prick her ego at their every encounter.

But he liked the new Mckenna well enough, she reminded herself. Well enough to puff up like an adder when Adam came sniffing around her.

"So you'd go with Nice, would you?" she reprised.

"Every single time." Sally closed the lid on her empty salad container and yelled for her girls to come off the playground. "Nice first. Hunky second." Then she gave Mckenna a grin that was frankly wicked. "I can tell that cowboy lawyer friend of yours is really Nice, though, Mac, in spite of the obvious fact that no woman in the world would throw that man outta her bed. You take care, y'hear?" She was still grinning as she herded her two daughters out into the parking lot.

Well hell, Mckenna thought. That was no help at all.

MCKENNA STILL nursed a bit of ill will toward the battling bulls the next morning when she showed up at the Bark Park for work. Jane had left early for an obedience trial in Phoenix, and the kennel was all hers. Fortunately, the holiday rush was over. Only fifteen of the kennels and three cat condominiums housed furry guests. But that still meant a load of work.

Mckenna put Titi down in the office. "Don't you go traipsing into the cat room and upset the cats."

Titi sent her an innocent look. "Me?"

They were speaking again, which meant that Mckenna's gray matter still wasn't shooting quite on target, but she had been glad when Titi had greeted her the afternoon before with a complaint about being left home while Mckenna was at Tom's.

"When you learn to not tease Clara, then you can go back with me to Tom's," Mckenna had told her.

Of course, after storming out with her nose in the air,

she might not be invited back to Tom's. Not that she hadn't had justification.

"Stupid dog," Titi had grumbled.

"Because she doesn't like you hissing in her face when she comes over to say 'Hello'?"

"She's a dog," Titi had replied, as if that explained everything. Then with her tail in the air like a long furry finger of disdain, she stalked off to the sofa. "Nap time," she said.

Mckenna had decided that, after the frustrations of the morning, she could use a nap herself. And she had done just that, stretching out on her bed—where she was shortly joined by a warm, comforting cat—and let the tensions ease away in a two-hour snooze.

"Learning," Titi had complimented her just before they both fell asleep.

But today's tasks would leave no time for naps. Jane wouldn't be home until long after the evening feeding, and she had left a note telling Mckenna that three of their canine guests needed a bath and brushing, one cat needed medication—she really didn't look forward to poking a pill past sharp teeth and down a reluctant cat's throat—and a potential client named Barbara would probably drop by to take a look at the kennel. Jane always encouraged people to look the place over before they brought their furry children in for a stay, and Mckenna made a note to leave nothing lying around, such as dirty mops or unemptied poop buckets, that might give the wrong impression of Jane's stellar operation.

She stuck her head through the door to the kennel, and all fifteen canine clients let her know that breakfast was past due.

"Just give me a minute, guys and girls. You've got a pinch hitter here today."

An hour later, the dogs had full tummies and clean kennels, the cats were daintily picking at their morning meal, and Mckenna was deciding between taking a coffee break or bathing the giant schnauzer in kennel five. The coffee break had just about won when the cowbell fastened to the office door clanged.

"Be right with you!" Mckenna called out, then quickly surveyed the kennel area to make sure she had put everything away in case the potential client was the fault-finding sort.

But when she walked into the office, no client greeted her. Instead, Tom Markham leaned on the counter and studied a brochure on dog nutrition.

"Did you know," he asked, waving the brochure vaguely in her direction, "that dogs need antioxidants every bit as much as people do?"

"I knew that," she said, cautiously trying to gauge his mood. Was he angry about her snit the day before? Did he think the old snarky Mckenna had returned?

Maybe the old snarky Mckenna *had* returned. These days Mckenna found it difficult to keep herselves straight.

"How you doing?" he asked, putting the brochure back on the counter.

Suddenly she felt very unapologetic. "Don't you mean, how am I doing with Adam Decker? Did you come all this way to find out if he was keeping me company today at the kennel?"

He scowled. "Hell, Mac! He was the one who tracked you down and acted like he had a leash attached to you."

"And you're doing what here?"

He blew out a disgusted breath and looked at his scuffed cowboy boots. "I came over to apologize," he mumbled.

Had she heard right? "What was that?"

He increased the volume to a near shout. "I came over to apologize!"

Glory be! "Just what are you apologizing for?"

He shrugged. "For being a jerk, I guess. For letting your

jackass ex-boyfriend provoke me into a scene. In my own house, no less." He looked up sharply. "He is your *ex*-boyfriend, isn't he?"

"Don't go there," Mckenna warned. "Not after you just apologized so nicely."

Tom grunted, then looked around with those sharp prosecutorial eyes.

"He's not here, if that's what you're wondering," Mckenna told him. "Honestly, Tom, you're both acting like idiots. What happened to that understanding, patient generosity that made you offer to back off for a while, if that was what I needed?"

He crushed an imaginary speck on the floor with the toe of his boot. The task seemed to capture all his concentration.

"Well?"

"You're right. I probably need to apologize again. But the guy rubs me the wrong way."

"How you feel about him doesn't really matter, does it?" Her temper was starting to rev under an overload of frustration. "How do you think *I* feel? My past is coming back in a convoy of Mack trucks that hit my brain everytime I turn around. Half the time I don't know if I'm Old Mckenna, New Mckenna, or someone in between. I don't know what I want any longer." Her voice rose a notch. "The law is coming back, and now I remember how much I loved the challenge of it, how much I loved the law itself. And I'm really enjoying the legal-aid work. But I enjoy the hospital, too. And I like coming home in the evening without worrying about bringing a briefcase full of work with me. I don't know who I am, or what I want...."

She trailed off in a huff of aggravation, only to find him right there, close enough to kiss, looking down at her with a serious expression.

"Mac, don't. Don't let yourself get all twisted up inside. Things will sort themselves out, if you have patience."

She sighed and let her head drop against his broad chest. "Sorry." He'd spouted the same line of advice as Titi, only more articulately. But she didn't want to kiss Titi. At least, not on the mouth. She couldn't say that about Tom.

He folded her into an embrace, rubbing her back at the same time as he held her close. She found herself wanting to be swept away by the very thing Sally Morgan had warned her against—the heated surge, the down and dirty, hot and sweaty ultimate distraction.

But she couldn't. Not only because Sally was right about lust not being the solution to any problem, but because she really couldn't be intimate with Tom while her relationship with Adam remained unresolved. Dammit! Mckenna really wanted to forget about wisdom and ethics and just melt into Tom's embrace.

Instead, reluctantly, she disentangled herself. He leaned over and kissed the top of her head, his breath warm on her flyaway hair. "I promise not to take Adam by the heels and toss him off a cliff if I run into him again. At least, I'll try not to do that."

"Thank you, Cowboy."

With an obvious reluctance that rather warmed Mckenna's heart, he moved toward the door. Then stopped. "You know, Mac, if I were you, I'd take the bull by the horns at this point."

"You're calling Adam a bull?"

He chuckled. "Hardly. I mean about finding out who you are and what you want. Maybe you should explore going back to the life you led before. See if it still fits."

"What?"

"Why not? Your grasp of the law has come back more than you realize, I think. I'd hire you in a minute."

"You would?"

"I would."

He had a point, Mckenna admitted. Her law education was no longer a closed book. While she had worked and worried, the knowledge had crept back, a little at a time, until now it sat there in her brain, good as new—almost. The realization inspired a surge of sudden confidence— confidence enough, perhaps, to beard the BKB lion in his den.

Up until now, she had been afraid to return to the site of that humiliation, to face former colleagues who had witnessed her downfall, to confront Gil Bradner and his little toady Pat Carter. But now she had reclaimed so much of what she'd lost. Maybe the time had come to repossess some of the chutzpah she had once taken for granted.

Her eyes widened with the reckless brazenness of the notion. Go back to BKB? That was something Old Mckenna would have done. And something New Mckenna needed to do.

She looked at Tom and smiled. Eyes twinkling, he grinned back.

chapter 22

THE NEXT day was Monday, the start of a new week, a good time for a new beginning.

"Except is this the beginning of a new life, which is really nothing more than my old life?" she asked Titi as she explored her closet for a suit that would still fit her. "Or is it insanity?"

Titi hunkered in the geographic center of Mckenna's bed, regarding her with steady, unblinking yellow eyes. "Not good," she proclaimed.

"Necessary," Mckenna countered.

That she could carry on conversations with her cat bore witness that her brain still didn't fire on all cylinders, or perhaps it was firing on extra cylinders. Who knew? The only thing clear to her was that she wasn't the same woman who had been BKB's up-and-coming never-lose-a-case soon-to-be partner.

"I'm also not the woman who once fit into these clothes," she told Titi with a sigh.

"Good," Titi declared.

"Maybe." She took a trim red silk two piece with ebony

buttons off its hanger and, with a shake of her head, threw it onto the bed with the other outfits that had become just a bit too formfitting to be decent. "What sort of grown woman fits into a size three? I ask you! If I get this job back, I'm going to have to spend the first month's pay buying clothes. Maybe the first three months' pay."

"Don't go." Titi sounded worried.

"I need to go," she told the cat.

Her job at the hospital was much more comfortable, dress-code-wise. She could wear khaki slacks and a sweater, and they thought she was dressed up. If this mad storming of BKB worked out, Mckenna was going to miss her job at the hospital, miss Diane, and the people up in legal, whom she had lately been helping out, miss taking Titi to work with her and visiting the patients almost every day. She would miss the friendly staff in the cafeteria that kept pressing cinnamon rolls on her, saying she was too thin, bless their lying hearts. She would miss the nurses and aides and technicians—and yes, even doctors—who came into her stoffice to cuddle Titi and rub her tummy as a short little break in their busy schedules.

"Not good," Titi repeated firmly. "Worry."

Mckenna understood what Titi meant. If she once again entered the legal rat race, would the bathroom medicine cabinet once more overflow with pills for blood pressure, pills for sleeping, pills for staying awake when she should sleep, pills for relaxing when the top of her head threatened to blow like Vesuvius?

"I know better now," she assured both herself and the cat. But did she know better? Could she swim with the sharks and not become one of the school? Or, knowing the habits of Old Mckenna, become the leader of the school?

"I'm not going to think about that," she told Titi. "If I do, I'll drive myself crazy."

Would Tom still like her if she once again honed her sharp edges? Would their friendship survive battles in court? And what about Adam? Would he take this as a sign that Mckenna wanted to return to the way things had once been between them?

"I won't think about that, either," she vowed to Titi. "And this fits." She pirouetted in front of the bedroom's full-length mirror, critically regarding the herringbone wool skirt whose matching blazer lay on the bed. "What do you think?"

"Should grow fur" was the surly answer.

"Big help you are."

"Don't," the cat advised. "Wrong."

"Stop being such a pessimist. I can handle this."

She spoke with more confidence than she felt, but now that she had finally decided she was up to the challenge, backing out would be nothing short of cowardice.

"Don't worry so much."

In answer, Titi got up, flexed her claws a time or two, then stalked over to the blazer that lay on the bed. Before Mckenna realized what the cat was about, Titi took a tiger-ish swipe at the herringbone sleeve and left a swath of tattered wool.

"Titi!"

"Now can't go."

"You little snot!"

"Can't go. Listen to the cat."

Nothing solidified a challenge like a best friend saying something can't be done.

"Watch me!" Mckenna replied.

THE OFFICES that housed Bradner, Kelly, and Bolin hadn't changed. The trees in the courtyard were bare. The employees had swapped cotton and silk for wool and linen. But other than that, the place was the same. It hadn't sunk into a great crater in the ground the day she had left. Or more accurately, had been ejected. A boot in the behind was still a boot in the behind, even if delivered with sympathy and regret. False sympathy and regret, Mckenna reminded herself, as she stood in the parking lot staring at the door of BKB's suite.

Behind the little plaza of offices rose the majestic cliffs and spires of Sedona, bloodred and imposing against a brilliant blue sky. But that spectacular landscape rearing above her was not half as imposing as the unpretentious oak door that led into a different world.

She didn't have to succeed today, Mckenna reminded herself. This foray into her former world was like a shopping trip, trying something on to look at the fit. More important, win or lose, she was proving to the world—and herself—that she was back. That life could mow her down, but she would get up again. And if she failed, at least she wouldn't have wimped out. If she failed, she still had a job—jobs, plural, if one counted her hours at the Bark Park. She still had a life, friends who loved her (not to mention two guys battling for her attention!), food in the cupboard, clients at legal aid—and a cat who tried to run her life.

She glanced at her watch. In an hour, she had to be back at the hospital. A phone call to Diane had netted her a couple of hours of personal leave, but that was all. So she needed to unroot her feet from the parking-lot pavement and do what she had come to do. Her jaw clamped together as a surge of pure tension shot through her. Mckenna Wright, she reminded herself, was the best attorney BKB had ever lured into employment with their perks, pay, and benefits. And she had deserved every perk, every paycheck, and every benefit. The floodgates of her memory had opened—mostly. There was no reason for them not to give her the respect, and the job, she deserved.

Big mistake, Titi said in her head. Mckenna couldn't lose the damned cat even when they were ten miles apart.

"Here I come," she told the closed suite door. "Better get out of my way."

Quiet music played in the lobby. Plush carpeting gave beneath Mckenna's feet. And the smell of Starbucks French roast wafted in from the coffee room. Ah, luxury. She remembered it well.

"Mckenna!" Sherry the receptionist, at her desk as always, greeted her in surprise. "Hello! Don't you look wonderful!"

"Thank you, Sherry. It's good to see you. How are things?"

"Oh, busy as usual." Sherry lowered her voice. "We hired a new guy—he's from Cleveland—but he doesn't hold a candle to you."

Mckenna replied in an equally low voice. "That would be because he's a *guy*. We women just work harder at it."

Sherry nodded and winked. "Ain't it the truth."

Feeling herself slip back into the fast-moving, sharp-talking, never-give-an-inch groove, Mckenna decided she could do this. She really could do this.

"I need a word with Gil, Sherry. Is he in?"

Sherry resumed her receptionist manner. "He is in, but ... do you have an appointment?"

"No." She put on a superior Old Mckenna smile. "When have I ever needed an appointment to see Gil?"

"Well ..." Sherry colored a bit. "Things have changed a little."

"He'll want to talk to me. He did ask me to come in when I felt like getting back in the saddle."

Which wasn't strictly true, but neither was it strictly a lie.

"Sure thing." Sherry knew from experience not to stand in Mckenna's way. "I'll just check. Be a sec, is all."

To Mckenna's surprise, the Great One himself came out to the lobby to greet her.

"Mckenna!" He pulled her into a backslapping embrace

that pounded the breath from her body. "You're looking wonderful, Mckenna. So good of you to stop by and say hello!"

Mckenna gasped for breath. "Hello, Gil," she finally managed to say. "I wonder if I might have a word with you."

"Certainly, certainly! Anything for an old colleague."

In the privacy of his spacious corner office, with its wet bar along one wall and his golf bag leaning across the guest chair, Gilbert Bradner was more wary than jovial. Mckenna wondered if he had leaned the clubs against the chair when Sherry had told him who sought an audience—a subtle warning not to sit and stay a while. She pushed them aside and sat anyway.

"So . . . Mckenna." He perched himself on the corner of his desk, looking at her uneasily. "You're looking great," he said with false joviality. "Fit as a fiddle. Wonderful."

"Thank you, Gil. I'm feeling very well. Just as the doctor said, the effects of my accident were temporary." And not completely gone, but she saw no reason to mention that.

"Oh? Well, that's good, then."

He didn't seem to know what to say, and Mckenna decided to go on the offensive before he recovered from the surprise of her sudden reappearance.

"I feel so well, in fact"—she gave him an innocent smile—"that I decided to drop by and discuss my coming back to work. You did say that we would reconsider my situation once I recovered my health."

"I . . . did?"

"Absolutely, Gil. I remember every word." And he could just worry about her perhaps having taped the conversation. She hadn't, more's the pity, but he didn't need to know that.

"Ah. Well, of course I did. And of course we'll talk. But . . . well, you know, things are so very fluid in a small, aggressive firm like BKB. Did you know we've taken a new partner? Yes, we made Pat Carter partner. She's done absolutely super work, you know."

Mckenna felt the news like a slap in the face. Pat Carter had grabbed the brass ring Mckenna had striven for.

"And she really picked up the reins on the Harmon case when you left."

Left? More like, was tossed out the door like yesterday's trash.

"Pat's a mover, all right," Mckenna agreed neutrally. "But back to *our* situation." She deliberately made that an "our" instead of a "my." Let the man know he was involved, for better or worse. "I realize my injury took everyone by surprise, and perhaps decisions were made that, if given more warning and more thought, wouldn't have been made. Things might have been done differently if everyone"—meaning Gil and Pat—"hadn't been so anxious for instant resolution." A resolution ending in Pat's promotion. "More enlightened alternatives could have been discussed. Something a little more fair. Paid leave, for example. Or sabbatical without cessation of benefits."

Gil's wary expression grew even warier. With good reason. After hearing of Pat's promotion, how she'd been boosted to partnership level on Mckenna's bleeding back, Mckenna was not in a charitable mood.

"Well now, Mckenna . . ." Gil tapped the end of his pen against his desktop in a rapid, nervous little drumbeat. "As I said—"

"I know," she said with a generous smile, "that BKB would want to avoid any appearance of impropriety."

Gil frowned. " 'Impropriety'?"

"Oh, you know," she said casually. "In this day and age, people are so sensitive about possible discrimination due to race, religion, *gender* . . ."

"Mckenna . . ."

"And the government is so picky about businesses

giving a fair shake to employees with disabilities. Even businesses who get no federal funds can get into trouble. But then, you already know that, don't you, because BKB has handled several cases along those lines. As I remember, we helped our clients take their ex-employers to the cleaner, big time."

He harrumphed indignantly, but his complexion had turned the color of paste. "Now, Mckenna, you know there was no impropriety concerning your situation. None at all."

"Of course I do, Gil. BKB would never leave itself open in such a way. If only for the reason that there's at least half a dozen rival law firms who would just love to see you embarrassed. Not to mention fined. Laid flat for damages. That sort of thing. They'd probably take the case just for the fun of raking BKB over the coals. Isn't it a shame that our society these days is so litigious?"

The tapping pen froze in place, and he gave her a hard stare. "Your capabilities of arguing a case have certainly returned. I can see that. And of course BKB would be happy to consider bringing you back on board. But you know I can't commit to anything before consulting with the other partners. Does the front office have your current phone number?"

"They do, but I'll leave it with Peggy, just to be sure." Peggy, bless her, would make sure the number wasn't "lost."

"You do that." His tone had soured a bit since his genial welcome. "It's good to see you, Mckenna. I always knew a little knocking about couldn't keep you down."

You were just hoping it would, Mckenna commented silently.

Gil escorted her out of the office. Probably, Mckenna thought, to make sure she didn't try to recruit allies on her way out. In the hall they almost bumped into a group heading toward Pat Carter's office.

"Mckenna Wright!"

Mckenna recovered smoothly from her surprise. "Mr. Harmon. How nice to see you. And Mr. Morris, also. I read in the papers that your preliminary hearing is next week."

Harmon gave her his famous half-grin. Charming, but not as nice as Tom's, Mckenna thought.

"That's why we're here. Dress-rehearsal time, I guess. You coming back, Mckenna? Going to help me get clear?"

Just to annoy Gil, she spoke as if it was a foregone conclusion. "Vacations can't last forever, you know."

Todd chuckled. "Vacation? What's a vacation?" Then more seriously, with what sounded like genuine concern, "I'm glad to see you looking so good, lady. You all right now?"

"I'm fine, Todd. Thank you for thinking about me." Something ticked in her memory at the sight of him in the flesh and the sound of his voice, coming not from the radio or television, but unfiltered. A tickle of something half-remembered, but so vague she couldn't grasp what it was.

"Did you get the flowers we sent?" Todd asked.

"Oh, yes. The roses were lovely. That was very thoughtful of you. And you, too, Buddy."

The agent gestured that it was nothing, but his eyes had locked upon her with an intensity that made her want to back away a step. "Don't mention it," he said with a tight little smile. "Glad to see you're better."

Pat walked out of her office and put an end to the little reunion. Her brows shot upward. "Mckenna! Well . . . hello."

Mckenna pasted on a smile. "Congratulations on your promotion."

Looking flustered, as if the two of them might suddenly leap for each other's throat, Gil took Mckenna by the arm and politely hurried her toward the lobby. "Pat is doing a bang-up job on the Harmon case," he assured her.

"Glad to hear it. I'll just stop by Peggy's office and leave that number, Gil." She gave him a meaningful look—a look that said he'd damned well better use that phone number. "And I can find my own way out, thank you."

Gil gave a twitch of his mouth that she supposed was an attempt at a smile. "Nice to see you again" was all he said.

Peggy greeted her warmly when she stuck her head through the doorway to her former secretary's cubicle. "Mckenna, Mckenna! I heard you were in the office. What's going on, girl?"

Mckenna laughed, walked in, and dropped into a chair. "I came by to give Gil ulcers. He deserves them."

"Are you coming back to work here, then?"

"Hm." She took off her high heels and rubbed her feet. Had heels always been this uncomfortable, or had a couple of months of freedom turned her feet into sissies? "Well, I certainly pulled out all the stops to bully Gil into hiring me back."

"That's wonderful! Oh, Mckenna. I've missed you so much. I swear you're the only one in this firm, or the only attorney, at least, who's halfway human."

Mckenna grinned. "Only halfway?"

"Well . . ."

They both laughed. But Mckenna's laugh ended on a sigh. "You know, Peggy, I'd forgotten what a shark tank this place is."

"It never changes," Peggy agreed. "I've worked here for ten years, and it hasn't changed a bit. But you know, the big corporations are just as bad. I worked fifteen years for Kramer Microsystems, and they were maybe a little friendlier on the surface, but beneath it, the currents were every bit as cold."

"It's what makes the world tick, I guess. Dog eat dog and the timid be damned."

"I guess. But I tell you, Mckenna, if you ever decide to start your own practice, keep me in mind, will you? I would jump ship here so fast I'd be a mere blur on their radar."

Start her own practice? What a concept. She would end up scraping the bottom of the financial barrel, even more than she already was. But in spite of her twisting Gil's arm, did she really want to come back to this piranha pond?

Mckenna arrived back at the hospital in time to edit the volunteer newsletter and then have a long chat with the events coordinator at the hotel where the annual volunteer awards banquet would be held in February. Then Diane dropped by to talk about the accreditation inspection coming up, always a time of high tension, and to ask if she needed help with the chaplain's reports.

"I can handle it," Mckenna told her boss. "Don't worry."

"Oh, I'm not worried. I had some extra time, is all— something that doesn't happen very often." She looked around the room. "Where's Titi today?"

"Since I had that business to attend to this morning, I left her at the house. I'll hear about it when I get home. That's for sure."

Diane laughed. "Did I tell you about the kitten I got at the Humane Society?"

They talked for a few minutes about the new addition to Diane's household before Diane's pager summoned her to deal with a minor crisis in the public relations office.

Mckenna smiled after her boss left. Her current job and the one she had left behind at BKB were so dissimilar they could be on different planets, and not just because they were worlds apart on the pay scale. The staff at the hospital treated one another like family. They had their share of dustups, misunderstandings, and a black sheep or two, like any family, but on the whole they helped one another out when help was needed, they enjoyed one another's company, and watching your back was not, out of necessity, everyone's main occupation.

All of which brought her back to the question: Did she really want her old life back? If the answer was no—and Mckenna hadn't yet decided that was the case—what would she do with a law education obtained at great expense and no little effort? What would she do with her love of the law?

That night she tried to explain her feelings to Titi, who listened with tail twitching and ears at half-mast. The cat still looked in a mood to shred something.

"You were right," Mckenna admitted. She dropped onto the sofa and kicked off the instruments of torture on her feet. She should have taken a change of shoes to the hospital. But no! She had been so entranced with her slick reflection in the mirror that morning that she hadn't remembered the downside of getting dressed up. "When I started backing good old Gil into a corner, I felt how easy it was, how easy to control the situation, how easy to slip dire implications into statements that never directly say anything you can be called to account for."

Titi didn't say anything. The cat simply looked at her with an expression that made a statement of its own.

"Yeah, yeah. Rub it in. The whole visit—except talking to Peggy—left me feeling like slime. I'm having a hard time remembering why I liked that job so much. Except that I was so good at it." She rubbed her abused feet. "Though that little battle with Gil didn't come quite as second nature as it used to. Maybe because I had to keep sitting on an urge to just come right out and be straightforward about what I wanted and why I thought it was the right thing for both of us." She smiled ruefully. " 'Straightforward' is anathema to lawyers. At least to the kind of law we do at BKB."

"Go back?" Titi asked.

Mckenna bit her lip. "I did use the word 'we' in referring to that hellish place, didn't I?"

Again, Titi just looked at her.

"Maybe not," Mckenna mused aloud. "But it would be nice to hear them ask. Actually, it would be nice to hear them grovel and beg."

NEXT DAY, Adam appeared in the stoffice doorway at lunchtime. Mckenna had neither seen nor talked to him since the blowup at Tom's house. She'd begun to wonder if perhaps he had flown back to Colorado in a huff, but she had put off reflecting on how she might feel if that were the case.

As he stood in her doorway, dressed in tailored gray slacks, Oxford shirt, and a tweed blazer—at least he wasn't wearing a tie!—Mckenna discovered that she was glad to see him. His familiar smile brought an answering smile to her lips.

Hands in the pockets of his slacks, he regarded her a bit warily. "Are you speaking to me yet?"

She considered. "Just barely."

"Are you in the mood to accept an apology?"

"Maybe."

"How about I bribe you with lunch?"

"Not at the cafeteria?"

"I saw a Thai restaurant on Main Street."

"Done deal."

They confined themselves to safe small talk while getting settled at their table at the Mai Thai on Main.

"Who would have thought," Adam commented with a little laugh, "that a little burg like this would have Thai food."

"These little Arizona burgs will surprise you," Mckenna told him.

"But you always wanted out of here. You wanted to go

to the Phoenix office, if I remember correctly, and leave this place behind. Now, just what was your name for the Verde Valley? Uh . . . Podunkville, that's it."

Mckenna did not remember that. And right now she had no desire to battle the traffic, pollution, high housing prices, and noise of any big city.

"From the look on your face, I'd say that's no longer what you want."

"I'm not sure I know what I want." The sympathy on his face made her uneasy. She didn't want sympathy. "Yet," she amended. "I don't know what I want yet. I'll figure it out."

"I know you will. You've always been one of the most focused people I know. It's one of the things I admire about you."

Their food came—a noodle-vegetable casserole and spiced Thai iced tea for Mckenna. Vegetable and chicken rolls for Adam.

"So . . . back to my apology. Was it smooth enough to get me forgiven for hovering over you like a mother hen?"

She smiled. "Probably."

"And . . ."

She could see that he wanted to ask about Tom, but he didn't dare. More credit to him. The man learned fast.

". . . and so we're good. I don't know what came over me."

Adam probably didn't have to try this hard with most women. With looks like his, and intelligence, manners, not to mention a successful, lucrative career, women no doubt fell into line for his attention. Mckenna examined her reaction to that thought. Not much of anything, emotion-wise. Interesting.

He reached across the table and touched her hand. "Mckenna, how much of your memory has returned?"

"Most of it, I think. Not everything. I still get surprises. And . . ." She absolutely could not tell him she still had conversations with her cat, which to her way of thinking, was a pretty good clue that some wires still needed rearranging in the old frontal lobes.

"Mckenna?"

"Huh?" Adam had caught her woolgathering. "Sorry. I'm listening."

He nodded. "I've spent the last couple of days doing some very serious thinking."

Mckenna took a sip of her iced tea while he paused and pinched the bridge of his nose. Something big was coming.

"I have to go back to Denver in a few days. I have cases pending, work piled up past my eyeballs. I probably shouldn't have stayed as long as I have, but the idea of leaving you here, in this situation... Well, I just couldn't make myself do it."

"That's sweet, Adam. But I'm fine. I'm great."

"You're not fine. Even you admit that your recovery isn't yet complete. You're living in something that's little better than a tin can. You're being taken advantage of right and left—no, don't deny it. It's true."

"Adam..."

"I think you should come back to Denver with me, Mckenna. You have family there. And we could take our time about getting reacquainted, getting back what we had before."

"Adam, I..."

"And I think you should get some professional help. See a psychiatrist. Get this amnesia thing taken care of, and get back to being yourself."

She shook her head, but before she could formulate a tactful answer, he took her hand. "Mckenna, you could take your pick of Denver law firms to work at. They would fall all over themselves to hire someone with your credentials. You'd be back in a city, with all those advantages. You would have someone you could rely upon—me. You could get the care you need, and then carry on with life and forget all about this nightmare you've been living." He gave her a winning smile. "I don't pretend not to have a selfish motive in wanting you close by. In wanting you to be flooded with memories of how good we were together. But all thoughts of self-interest aside, how could being close to family, friends, and professional opportunity not be to your advantage?"

There were so many denials she needed to make that none of the crowd could make it past her lips. Adam took her silence for consideration.

"Think on it, Mckenna. Why on earth would you want to stay here?"

"Adam . . ."

"Think on it," he insisted.

They ate the rest of their lunch in a heavy silence. Then he drove her back to the hospital, escorted her to the door of her office, and gave her a brief kiss that somehow carried all the intensity of his supplication.

"I'll call you," he promised. "We'll go out for a nice dinner before I leave."

Mckenna watched him walk away, and wondered. Not for a minute would she consider moving back to Colorado. But as to his other suggestions—the ones that echoed Dr. Estrella's—did she need someone to straighten her out? Was she fooling herself in thinking she could, all by herself, evolve from the person she had been to the person she truly was? Her memory was returning, but instead of bringing peace, it brought confusion.

That evening she took her confusion to Jane on the phone. "Adam wants me to see a shrink," she moaned.

"Don't make it sound like a crime," Jane replied. "Lots of people see shrinks. Sane people. Or at least, fairly sane."

"And move to Denver!"

"Well, there are sane people there, I understand. Though

I gather from listening to you that your parents aren't among them."

"Jane, this isn't a joke."

"I didn't say it was."

"It gets worse! When I'm with Adam, sometimes I feel like a different person. Sometimes I really like him. At the same time, sometimes I feel as if I'm simply remembering a time when I really liked him, and now it's not real."

"Okay, maybe *you* aren't numbered among the sane."

"Jane! Will you be serious?"

"Okay, okay. How dare you be attracted to a drop-dead gorgeous, smart, attentive man—did I leave out rich?"

"He's not rich."

"He's a good deal richer than you and me, girl."

"Okay, he's rich."

"Rich, handsome, attentive. The very idea is just repulsive. What woman would want to lower herself like that?"

"All right, all right. I get your point. But I don't love him. I'm almost sure I don't love him. Maybe the attraction is just left over from before."

"Then tell him good-bye and be done with it. Send him on his way."

"He's hard to say no to. He keeps interrupting."

Jane laughed. "He's a lawyer, isn't he? Get a big dog. Not only to guard your place, but to chase off unwanted suitors. And speaking of such, how's Tom?"

Mckenna heard the prodding in Jane's voice, but she wasn't yet ready to talk about Tom.

"Are you implying that Tom is a big dog or that Tom is an unwanted suitor?"

"You tell me."

Mckenna's turn to laugh. "I'm going to bed. Thanks for the nonadvice."

"Getting a dog is always good advice."

"Tell that to Titi."

"Titi might learn a little humility from a dog."

"Good night, Jane."

She was still chuckling as she climbed into bed, where Titi, as usual, hogged the covers in the geographic center of the mattress.

"No dog," Titi told her sternly. "Tell the phone. No dog."

"Yes, well, if you rip up anymore of my clothes, my cat friend, you could find yourself face-to-face with a bouncing baby puppy. That might keep you in line."

chapter 23

TITI NURSED a grudge as she settled down to sleep, curled warmly into the bend of Mckenna's knees, with her head resting on the extra pillow. Everyone teased Mckenna about the need for a stupid dog, and Mckenna had just better not take them seriously. A dog, indeed! They had absolutely no need for a dog. A dog wouldn't fit in the trailer, for one thing. A dog would take up all the room on the bed—and knowing Mckenna, she would let the creature get away with it, because Mckenna was a sucker. Titi should know. And dogs weren't the heroes that people thought they were. Any thief or villainous skulker could bamboozle a dog with a piece of juicy steak.

A cat, on the other hand, possessed more discrimination. Not that cats had less healthy appetites, but they didn't allow their stomachs to override their brains. A strange hand offering food often hid nefarious motives, and sometimes, sadly, that was true of the familiar hand, as well. Unwary cats could be lured into cat carriers, tubs containing soapy water, and any number of unpleasant situations, just by letting appetite distract from natural caution.

Titi, however, was not one of those gullible felines. Titi was ever alert, ever cautious. A superb watch cat, if she did say so herself. Cats, after all, possessed the courage and instincts befitting the smartest, most beautiful, and most superior creatures on earth. Humans deluded themselves by thinking they ruled the planet. What rubbish! Get a dog! What a joke! Mckenna was safe, and their home was safe, as long as Titi deigned to look after it. She'd been caught off guard once. It wouldn't happen again.

On that self-congratulatory thought, Titi began a soft, rumbling purr, pleased with herself, pleased with life, even pleased with Mckenna. After all, so far, Mckenna hadn't gotten a dog. And most of the time she was smart enough to listen to Titi's advice. Not all of the time, obviously. There was that Adam fellow. Too bad the hairball hadn't driven him off. And today, Mckenna had insisted on galloping off to the place that had nearly destroyed her once before.

But in most ways, Mckenna had become a well-behaved pet. She didn't run around anymore as if someone had lit her tail on fire. Smiling had almost become a habit. Evenings at home she spent lying on the sofa paying attention to Titi instead of wasting her time on work.

Giving advice was becoming more difficult, though, because sometimes Mckenna couldn't understand. Whatever brain blip had granted her the privilege of understanding Cat was flickering on and off like a bad lightbulb. Soon, Titi figured, it would go out completely. Titi would miss their conversations. Cats, after all, had lots to say, and having someone actually listen was a nice change.

Still, the responsibility of being Mckenna's tutor was a heavy one. She had been an unlikely student, needing so much attitude adjustment. Perhaps that was why Heaven had made sure that Titi had drawn Mckenna as a special project (and Titi was absolutely sure that one did not achieve therapy status without being specially touched from above. Animals—especially cats—had a direct pipeline to the spiritual realms). Titi had been up to the challenge. Just look at the incredible job she had done, now almost complete. She deserved an award of merit, at least, and maybe a new fleecy cat bed, her own catnip garden, a cupboard filled with tuna...

Drifting on warm thoughts of all the lovely rewards she deserved, Titi floated off toward sleep. Deep, warm, wonderful sleep—the thing cats did better than anything else. Lying limp, relaxed down to her very bones, paws and whiskers twitching slightly as cat dreams wafted through her slumber. Peaceful. Content. Flaccid.

Then suddenly she woke. One eye cracked open, piercing the dark of the room to find everything as it should be. Her nose twitched to a scent. A scent that shouldn't be in Titi's house.

Silently, she got up and jumped off the bed. A noise made her ears prick forward. A very small noise. But a cat's ears were just as superior as everything else about her.

Titi slunk her way through the hallway toward the noise, past the bathroom, past the washer and dryer, past the little closet Mckenna called a second bedroom. And there in the living room, near the window that now had its boards hanging, was a black, man-shaped shadow gliding almost as silently as Titi toward the hallway. Titi smelled danger, evil intentions—a beast in the shape of man.

For a moment, in spite of her brave ruminations this very evening, she hesitated. Under the bed would make a very good hiding place. The villain would never find her. If she huddled beneath the bed, he couldn't kick her. He might take their new television set, and maybe even the cans of tuna and cat food in the cupboard. But all that could be replaced.

Titi could not be replaced.

Then she remembered. Mckenna slept in the bedroom, and Mckenna would not fit under the bed. Mckenna could not be replaced.

So this was it: Titi's moment. The hair on her back and tail bristled. She didn't let herself think about getting kicked, or thrown against the wall, or trampled. This poor intruder was never going to get the chance to do any of those things, because this was a job for Supercat!

With a mighty yowl, Titi leapt. The man screamed as her claws went through his jacket and into his arm. And then Titi found herself flying across the room, bouncing off the sofa, hitting the end table, and dropping to the floor without a bit of her usual grace. Heavy footsteps shook the trailer as the intruder, abandoning all attempts at stealth, charged toward the bedroom—and Mckenna. Mckenna's alarmed cry pierced the silence.

Titi got up, shook, and wobbled dizzily toward the hallway. Thumps, grunts, shouts, and a crash came from the bedroom. Titi reached the door in time to see Mckenna fight off her assailant by pounding him over the head with her alarm clock. The intruder used some words that Titi didn't understand, but they sounded very bad. The villain twisted the timely weapon from Mckenna's hand and flung it against the wall. Then he likewise flung Mckenna against the wall, where she hit the paneling and slid limply down to the floor. The man raised a hand, and in that hand he had a pistol.

Titi knew very well what a pistol did. After all, she had logged a lot of hours watching television, and television was very educational. So she knew that what a pistol did would not be good at all for poor Mckenna, flattened helplessly against the wall, shaking her head and looking befuddled.

Titi jumped right from where she stood, and with a mighty leap landed on the villain's back, clawing at his neck. He shrieked. The sound woke Mckenna from her confusion, but Titi wasn't about to let her handle the situation. After all, Mckenna didn't have claws, and her teeth were puny things compared to a cat's beautiful fangs—fangs that were useful, too, as the intruder discovered. He screamed again, trying to beat at his back with both arms, dropping his gun, stumbling against the bed.

Suddenly light flooded the room. Mckenna leaned against the wall, one hand on the light switch. Titi had little time to note her appearance other than a wide swath of blood painting the side of her face. As the savior of the day, she was too busy trying to conquer the bad guy, who bucked like a bronco and had come near to crushing her a couple of times as he slammed backward into a wall.

Then, like a vengeful Amazon, Mckenna grabbed the metal-based bedside lamp and swung it at the intruder's head. It connected like a bat smashing into a baseball. The man dropped without a sound and sprawled facedown on the bed. Mckenna dropped also, but only to her knees. Her face, what part of it wasn't crimson with blood, had turned green. She swayed, slowing oozing toward the floor. But not before she knocked the phone receiver off its cradle and dialed 911.

MCKENNA WOKE to the glare of lights stinging her eyes. Familiar hospital odors assaulted her. She tried to raise her head from where she lay and immediately regretted it as pain shot from her skull down to her toes.

"Lie still, Mac."

Tom's voice. Where was he? A big, warm hand closed over hers.

"I'm right here." His face swam into view. He attempted a smile, but couldn't quite pull it off. The stretch of his mouth, the fire in his eyes—he looked ready to kill someone. "You're all right, but you're in the emergency room. Do you remember what happened?"

Before she could answer, the curtain swept aside and in bustled a doctor who was certainly not Dr. Estrella. Mckenna knew this doctor from pet therapy visits to the emergency room. She, Jane, and Nell had frequently joked that if not for the stethoscope hanging around his neck, Dr. Eugene Timms could have been mistaken for a high-school freshman.

"We're awake, are we?" he said cheerily. "Mr. Markham, if you'll just give us a minute?"

Tom squeezed Mckenna's hand, then left. Mckenna wanted him back. But what was he doing here, anyway? Wasn't it the middle of the night? Unlike the last time she had awakened in the hospital, she remembered everything—the thug, the terrifying attack, her brave Titi turning into a pint-sized tiger.

"My cat?" she queried as Timms poked here and there. "Do you know anything about what happened to Titi?"

"Right now I'm more concerned about you," Timms said in the condescending tone doctors too often used with patients. Someone who looked as if he still used pimple cream didn't have a chance of pulling it off, though.

"Knock it off, Eugene. I want to know about Titi."

"Ah-ah. How many fingers do you see?"

"Three."

"Now?"

"Two."

"Good." He shone a light in her eyes. "Headache?"

"Whopper. Really, Eugene, will you go ask Tom about Titi?"

"I'll call him in and you can ask him yourself. Jane is here also, in the waiting room. They can keep you company while you wait."

"What am I waiting for?"

"That laceration on your head needs stitches, but it will be a few minutes before I can get Dr. Bonner in here. He did a residency at Johns Hopkins in plastic surgery, you know. Lucky for you he's on duty tonight."

Tom came back in. Jane was with him.

"Titi?" Mckenna asked anxiously.

"You mean, the attack cat?" Jane chuckled. "Forget my advice about getting a big dog. You don't need one. She'll be fine. I took her in to Oak Creek Animal Clinic—they even waived the emergency fee, under the circumstances. She has one broken rib, a sprained shoulder, and a few bruises. Believe me, the other guy came out a lot worse. I wouldn't be surprised if he's got the docs working on him, as well. All those claw marks." She shuddered theatrically. "Give me a nice simple dog bite any day."

The enormity of the vicious attack settled on Mckenna in a sudden trembling, a tightening of her throat, an urge to throw up. Tears flooded her eyes. "I don't understand. What was that man after? I don't have anything..." She trailed off in a sob.

Jane squeezed Mckenna's hand, sent a meaningful look at Tom, and put on an encouraging face. "I'm going to get you some nice hot tea. There's nothing for soothing the soul like tea."

Without waiting for Mckenna's response, she backed out through the curtain.

"Mckenna, you—" Tom bit down on whatever he wanted to say, took a deep breath, and raised her hand to his lips for a soft kiss on her knuckles. "Right now you just need to take it easy. Later we can talk about what happened." He produced a tissue from the pocket of his jeans and dabbed at the tears running down her face.

"Is it still the middle of the night?" Mckenna quavered, trying to push panic to the back of her mind, to be dealt with later.

"It is that. Midnight, in fact."

"What...what on earth are you doing here at this time of night?"

"Where else would I be?" He grinned, then, a familiar wicked grin that almost made her want to smile. "The hospital called Jane, since they knew you two were such friends, and Jane called me. They weren't going to let me in to be with you, but I told them I was your fiancé."

Her heart thumped at that.

"After all, you had one fiancé you didn't know about. Another couldn't hurt that much. And Jane backed me up."

All she could do was squeeze his hand. Then Jane pushed aside the curtain, a steaming cup in her hand. She looked at Mckenna, looked at the Styrofoam cup, and said, "Oops! That's right. You're not supposed to raise your head. Guess I'll have to drink this myself."

After Dr. Bonner stitched Mckenna's head, he turned her back over to the boy doctor, who wanted to admit her to the hospital. She adamantly refused.

"You have a concussion and bruised ribs," Timms told her.

"I am not spending one more night in this hospital. I spend my days here. That's enough."

"But you need to be watched."

"Relax, Eugene. My brain should be used to this sort of thing by now."

In the end, she signed herself out against doctor's orders. Jane and Tom drove her home, propped shakily in the passenger seat of Jane's Chevy van. The new day was still an infant. To the east, the moon cast eerie shadows along Sedona's looming cliffs. Though Mckenna felt as if she had aged a lifetime since she had unsuspectingly climbed into bed that night, tomorrow still seemed a long way off.

They stopped by the Bark Park to pick up Titi. She greeted them indignantly, obviously miffed at being left behind, but she curled warmly against Mckenna on the drive home. She made no answer to everyone's praise for her bravery in foiling the attacker. Limp and exhausted, she fell asleep in Mckenna's lap.

Home again, Mckenna saw that someone, probably the police, had replaced the boards that the intruder had pried from the living-room window. Boards weren't enough, Mckenna thought. Neither was new window glass. She wanted steel walls around her—steel walls a foot thick. Then maybe she would feel safe.

After only a few minutes, Jane gave Mckenna a gentle hug and took off for her own place. She apologized for not staying, but the kennel had no one to mind it.

"Of course you have to go home," Mckenna told her. "I'm fine. Really, I'm fine."

A lie, of course. She wasn't fine at all.

"I called Nell, by the way. She'll call tomorrow, or today, rather. It's morning, isn't it? I barely restrained her from hopping in her car at one A.M. to come to your rescue."

"She shouldn't worry," Mckenna said, trying for bravado.

"Of course she should worry. We all worry." Jane gave Mckenna a reassuring smile. "I'll call later to make sure you're behaving."

Jane made her exit, and Mckenna found herself alone with Tom and Titi. Tom showed no inclination to follow Jane's example and depart. In fact, he looked about as immovable as Mount Rushmore when he dropped onto the living-room sofa. "Someone needs to keep an eye on you tonight," he declared.

Mckenna didn't argue. She didn't want to be alone. Every shadow seemed to hold someone or something that might jump out at her. Every small noise was the footstep of a villain lurking just outside. Twice now her home had been violated. Would she ever feel safe again?

She must have looked as lost as she felt, because Tom came loose from the sofa and in three long strides stood beside her in the kitchen. He put his hands on her shoulders and gently massaged. "Hey, kiddo. Are you okay?"

She took a deep, shaky breath.

"How about some tea? You never got to drink that tea in the hospital, and according to Jane, it's a miracle worker."

"Do you want some?" she asked in a shaky voice. "There's some decaffeinated in the cupboard."

"I'll fix some for both of us. You sit down." He guided her firmly to the sofa. "This has got to be the height of domesticity," he commented as he set water on to boil and found a tin of decaffeinated tea bags. "Drinking tea together while we chat. Very homey."

She tried to smile, but couldn't quite make it. " 'Chat'?"

"Yes, chat. You really need to get some sleep, but before we tuck you in, we need to talk."

Heaven have mercy! Talking was the last thing she was up for.

"Mac, this can't be coincidence, you know. First a burglary, despite the fact that any self-respecting burglar already has way more expensive stuff than what you have in here. Now some goon breaks in and attacks you. This guy wasn't sneaking around looking for the sterling silver, you know. He was after you. And if not for Fang over there"— he nodded to where Titi had resumed her throne on top of the television—"he might very well have gotten you."

Yes, this was really making her feel a lot better. She lowered her aching head into her hands. She didn't give up that dubious refuge until Tom sat down beside her and wrapped her hand around a cup of tea.

"Mac, this has to be about the Harmon case. I feel it in my gut, and my gut is hardly ever wrong."

She tried a grin. "That's why you get the big bucks in the county attorney's office."

"Damned straight."

She shook her head, immediately regretting it. "I guess

what you say is logical, Tom, but I just can't imagine Todd Harmon behind stuff like this. I saw him when I went to BKB. Did I tell you? He seemed really happy to see me. Genuinely friendly. He sent me roses when I got hurt, you know?"

"Mac, the man is an entertainer. A performer. He can act."

This time she kept her head still. "No. I have better instincts about people than that. He might have sold coke to some friends. I don't know about that, because a lot of the things that happened in the last few weeks before the accident are still fuzzy. But I don't think he would send some gorilla out to attack me."

"To kill you," Tom said in all seriousness. "That man wanted to kill you, Mac."

All the courage seemed to flow right out of her, like air from a balloon. "He wanted to kill me," she echoed shakily.

"Mac, you need to go someplace safe until we find out what's going on, someplace where no one but a trusted few know where you are."

She felt so tired. Far too tired to deal with this right now. "I don't know what to do. Maybe it's just coincidence. Anything else is so melodramatic. I don't even want to think about it right now."

He touched her cheek and took pity. "You need to sleep."

Indeed, she did. But the thought of facing her bedroom after what had happened just a few hours ago filled her with dread.

Tom read the look on her face. "How about I take a snooze right alongside you?"

" 'A snooze'?"

"Sure. I'll trust you to keep your hands off me, for now."

"Is that so?"

"That's so. For now." His slow, lazy grin warmed her.

"See how trusting I am? After all, I know what a hot mama you are."

She caught her breath. "Oh, ouch! Please don't make me laugh."

He kissed her forehead, careful of the bandage that covered the stitches above her ear. "Sleep, Mac. Just sleep."

Strangely enough, when she curled up on her bed with Tom on one side of her and Titi on the other, the nightmare that had lingered there, waiting for her, simply faded away.

MCKENNA REFUSED to take the day off work. She did go in late, and almost immediately, her closet office filled with the curious and the sympathetic. Anyone unfortunate enough to become a patient at the hospital where she works has no secrets from the staff.

"Where's Titi?" a cat-loving nurse asked.

"She's recuperating at home. Poor baby has a sprained shoulder and broken rib. But she'll heal fast."

"You mean, the guy hurt your cat?" This from one of the housekeepers. Plainly it was understandable for an intruder to attack the homeowner, but laying a finger on one of the furry set didn't wash.

"He didn't hurt her nearly as much as she hurt him, believe me. Titi was quite the tiger."

"Titi? Sweet little Titi, who purrs on command for the patients?" The nurse didn't believe her.

"Titi seems to feel very strongly about guys who climb through a window at night while she's trying to sleep."

They all laughed. One of the doctors cautioned her to drop by emergency and have her bandage changed. A nurse asked her sympathetically if she had someone to stay with her until she felt better. The cafeteria manager brought her a bagel with cream cheese. And one of the volunteer chaplains offered his services if she felt in need of spiritual counseling.

The sympathethic crowd trailed in and out of the stoffice all morning, making any attempt at work close to futile. She might as well have given in to Tom's plea for her to call in sick and spend the day with Jane. If he hadn't had to go to work himself, the man would have hog-tied her like a calf and sat on her to keep her in bed.

But he had gone to work, reluctantly, and she had dragged herself into the hospital. The faster she resumed her normal routine, Mckenna figured, the faster she would feel like herself again.

Now if she could just stop jumping at every noise, trying to see into every shadow, finding villainous intentions on every stranger's face. Heaven help her, but she had bought into Tom's theory that someone wanted her either very hurt or very dead. She didn't want to believe it, but her gut reacted to her series of misfortunes in a manner very like Tom's. One disaster was an accident. Two might be a coincidence. But three? . . .

The phone rang, inspiring a jump that almost sent her out of her chair.

"Oops!" her current sympathizer—the volunteer who ran the gift shop—got up from her chair. "You've got work. I'll run along."

Mckenna hadn't heard a word the woman had spoken for the past five minutes, so hard had she been pondering.

The caller was Nell. "Mckenna!" she scolded, as if her life falling apart had been Mckenna's idea. "Are you all right?"

"Fine. I'm fine."

"No, you're not. I hear it in your voice. Piggy and I are coming."

"You don't need to, Nell. But thanks. I'm fine."

"You know, Piggy's really a very good protection dog.

She may not look like much, but she has a great record of foiling the bad guys."

"I know that, but really, Nell, everything here is under control." Ten minutes of persuasion convinced Nell that she didn't need to drop everything and run to Mckenna's aid. "But I'm grateful," Mckenna told her.

"You've got some serious stuff going on," Nell said. "Any ideas?"

"Right now, not a clue."

"Hm. I'm going to e-mail you an article I wrote. Promise to read it."

"What is it?"

"Just promise."

"Okay, okay," Mckenna agreed wearily. "I promise."

"And if you need me, call. Promise."

"You know I will."

"Hardheaded woman," Nell chided. But her voice swelled with affection. "Take care."

Mckenna had scarcely set down the phone when it rang again. The voice on the phone identified himself as Deputy Kevin Nielson. Kevin Nielson was one of the few lawmen in the Verde Valley who would give her the time of day, because she had defended his son, pro bono, in a juvenile case where the kid had simply been stupid, not criminal, and his buddies had tried to hang their own criminality on him.

"Ms. Wright," he started without preamble. "The guy we carried out of your place last night has squealed like a pig."

"He's alive, then."

She had been worried that the heavy lamp might have put a permanent crater in the man's skull. Not very worried, though.

"He's alive and squawking. I thought you should know that this guy isn't just a local thug trying for a few perverted thrills. He's a hired bad guy from Phoenix. He's working for someone who apparently wants you off the planet."

A chill went down her spine. "Who is he working for?"

"Well, unfortunately, he claims to not know the name. And I believe him. Like I said, he's spilling his guts. You know, that cat of yours could be enlisted in psychological warfare. Being brought down by a police dog is sort of a macho thing for some of these guys. But I'll tell you, getting shredded by a cat really drives the stuffing right out of a man."

"She was trying to defend me."

"I know. I'd want that cat on my side any day of the week. I think she's great. But anyway, this guy is shaken right out of his mind, and he's talking out of fear that we're going to turn him back over to the cat. So anyway, I think he's telling the truth here. He doesn't know the guy's name, and he never met with him in person. But on the phone, the guy had just a touch of an accent, maybe from Texas or somewhere in the South, he said."

A Southern accent. Nashville. Todd Harmon or Buddy Morris. Tom had pegged it. She knew something damaging in the Harmon case, something she hadn't remembered, or if she remembered it, the significance hadn't occurred to her.

"Anyway," the deputy continued. "Know anyone with an accent who might want you knocked off?"

"Todd Harmon or Buddy Morris. Morris is Todd Harmon's agent and business manager."

A hesitation, then "Todd Harmon? The country-western star who's up on drug charges?"

"The very same."

"Are you sure?"

She didn't blame him for not wanting to tackle such a big name on such flimsy evidence. Yavapai County already had to shoulder all the bad publicity from the Harmon rap. They would need more than a Southern accent to haul anyone into the police station in handcuffs. That was the reasonable part of her talking. Another part, scared and cringing, wanted to shout at him to arrest whoever had her in the crosshairs, to keep her safe, to let her know that she no longer had to look over her shoulder or be afraid of the night.

The reasonable part won, just barely. In an almost steady voice, she said, "Listen, Deputy Nielson, thank you for letting me know. I need to do some hard thinking about this, and maybe I can come up with something that will make sense. And if I do, I'll be in touch."

"Yeah, well, in the meantime, keep that cat close. She's better than a German shepherd or Doberman. That's for sure."

Mckenna hung up the phone and tried to slow the racing of her heart. Todd Harmon? She couldn't believe it. Buddy Morris? A very intense fellow, judging from their few meetings since her accident. If she knew something that would harm his golden goose, would Morris stoop to murder?

Hard to believe. People you knew and did business with, who said "Hi" to you in restaurants . . . Heaven above! A memory popped into her head—Buddy Morris talking to her at the Rainbow's End, just before she had gotten into her car and driven up the canyon toward home. Could he have had something to do with her car accident?

No. Not likely. But . . . maybe. At this point, nothing seemed impossible. Guys who sent you roses and get-well cards, then turned around and tried to kill you. Why? Because she knew something dangerous, as Tom believed she did? What the hell did she know?

"Hey, Mckenna."

She raised her head to see Diane standing in the doorway to the stoffice.

"You look like death warmed over. Worse even than you looked an hour ago."

Mckenna tried to smile.

"Are you sure you shouldn't take a couple of days off?"

"Thanks, Diane, but I've missed too much work already, for one reason or another."

"You really do look terrible. In fact, maybe you should go down to emergency and have one of the docs take a look at you."

"I'm fine," she lied. Her injuries didn't bother her right now nearly as much as Deputy Nielson's revelations.

"Well. Okay. How did your talk with BKB go the other day? I hate to lose you, but you were up-front about that when you first came on board. We all knew that you'd want to return to the law once you recovered your memory."

Mckenna shook her head. If she had recovered absolutely everything, she wouldn't be neck-deep in this mystery. She sighed. "I'm not sure I want to go back to BKB. It went okay when I went over there, but right now I don't know what I'm going to do."

Diane took in the expression on Mckenna's face and clucked sympathetically. "You go home if you need to, Mckenna. Get some rest. Much as we love you, we can do without you here for a few hours."

With a little wave, Diane left. Mckenna decided she was right. She wasn't doing anything useful here.

Before she left, though, she went on-line to find out what treasure Nell had sent her way. Her mailbox was full of work-related messages, but Mckenna ignored those for now. At the end of the list was mail from Nell—a message with an attachment.

You said not until you were desperate, Nell wrote. *Are you desperate yet?*

Frowning, Mckenna opened the attachment. It was an

article Nell had written two years ago about Dr. George Cantrell, licensed hypnotist.

Nell's pet swami.

How desperate was she now? Mckenna wondered. The answer came to her immediately. Pretty damned desperate.

chapter 24

THE HYPNOTIST was not a typical Sedona swami—Mckenna's term for the numerous psychics, mediums, cult leaders, and other New Age gurus that made the "holy ground" of Sedona their home. Dr. Cantrell worked in a very swank office in Sedona. The nameplate on the door of his suite was brass, highly polished, very professional. Dr. George Cantrell, it announced, along with a number of impressive initials after his name, of which PhD was the only one she recognized.

Mckenna took a moment to gather her courage before going in. She wished Tom were beside her, holding her hand. But no, if she told Tom about what Kevin Nielson had said, he would probably finagle a way to lock her in jail for her own safety.

And what would Adam say if she filled him in on recent events? Adam, who had kept his promise not to pressure her while she considered his suggestion that she return to Denver with him. Adam would have a fit. He would have a fit about the attack and would use it as a tool to bludgeon her into seeking safety with him. Bless him, he really did care about her. She knew it, and she remembered having quite an infatuation for him. On some level, she still cared about him. Certainly she didn't want to see him hurt.

Strange that she would feel so concerned for the men in her life. Not too long ago, she had regarded men as mere accessories to be tried on and discarded at will. She remembered that now. She had thought them bothersome nuisances with motives that were always suspect. Yet they had flocked to her and endured the humiliation she put them through.

But this woolgathering wasn't solving the problem at hand. And if she didn't do just that, dealing with the Tom and Adam problem simply wouldn't be an issue, because the way things were going lately, she could very well become an item in the local obituaries. Taking her courage into her hands, she opened the door and walked into a reception area that looked like any upscale doctor's office.

Dr. Cantrell didn't keep her waiting, but ushered her into the back office less than five minutes after she arrived. An ordinary-looking guy in jeans and a sweater—his nod, apparently, to the casual Sedona lifestyle—there was nothing New Age or swami-ish about him. He was clean-shaven and well-trimmed, with glasses perched on his rather beakish nose and a sparkle of humor in his eyes.

"My friend Nell recommended I talk to you," Mckenna explained when she took a seat in his office. "But, well, I don't know that . . . well, that I've ever considered . . ." She trailed off, embarrassed.

He chuckled. "A little nervous about hypnotism, are we?"

"I . . . uh . . . wouldn't think that *you* are."

He laughed. "You've never been hypnotized, I take it?"

"No."

"Suspect that it's all flimflam trickery?"

"Oh, I wouldn't say that."

He raised a brow.

"Okay," she admitted. "I have my doubts. No offense intended. It's just that I'm a very practical person."

"No offense taken, I assure you. Did you read Nell's piece about me? She was very thorough in explaining how hypnotism works."

"She sent it to me. I skimmed it. But, well, let's just say I'm a skeptic."

He smiled tolerantly. "If I could spend two or three hours talking to you about the science behind hypnotism, you would find it eminently practical. But I take it from our phone conversation that time is an issue?"

"It certainly is if you charge by the hour."

Again he laughed. She liked his laugh. It seemed open and honest, and it put her more at ease.

"All right, then, why don't you tell me what's going on, Mckenna? Just why does our mutual friend Nell think you need hypnotherapy? Does it have anything to do with that bandage stuck to the side of your head?"

"Well . . . yes."

She explained in as few words as possible. Even to her the situation seemed incredible and complex, and she hardly expected a stranger to take her seriously. But he did. The thoughtful furrows in his brow etched deeper as she recited her problems. And when she finished, he looked at her as if she were a particularly interesting subject presented for dissection.

"So . . . This legal case you were involved in seems to be the crux of the matter."

"Right now, it seems that way."

"Do you remember anything about the time you spent on the case?"

"I do. I remember the details of the charges, my interviews with Harmon and his agent, Buddy Morris—"

"But you don't remember anything that might make you a danger to the defense of the case."

"No. I *was* the defense. I was on their side before I

cracked my head, lost my memory, and got fired by BKB. That's why this whole thing doesn't make sense."

"The attorney who took over the case . . ."

"Pat Carter."

"She has all the information you had?"

"By now I would hope that she has more. She has all my files, and she should have picked up where I left off."

He looked puzzled. "As far as you are concerned, your memory has returned."

"Even my law education. In fact, I'm thinking of going back into practice. But it's very frustrating that one important piece of information refuses to come back. Or maybe it was never in my head in the first place, and I'm barking up the wrong tree."

"Hm. Maybe, or . . ." Again with the dissection look. "You know, Mckenna, maybe there's a piece of information you're not remembering because you don't want to remember it."

She made a face. "No. I really, really want to remember whatever this is."

"That's your conscious mind speaking. But to a large degree, the mind is ruled by the subconscious. It might be that the missing link, whatever it is, returned right along with the rest of your memories, but your subconscious caught it in, well, a filter of sorts, because it was something that had caused you grief, or fear, or some other such unpleasantness."

"In spite of what I want?"

"Again, that's your conscious speaking. The subconscious, I'm afraid, has a mind of its own."

"Great. Just great."

He smiled. "But that's where hypnosis comes in. Hypnosis allows us to connect with the subconscious and get it to work for us instead of against us. Let me tell you what we're going to do."

He explained the procedure. Mckenna hadn't expected

hypnosis to be so humdrum. No spinning spirals, no swinging watches—just talk, and relaxation. It sounded so implausible.

"I really don't think this will work for me," Mckenna said.

He nodded. "No harm in trying, is there? You won't feel like you're going to sleep or anything nearly that dramatic. Many people in deep trances don't even realize they're hypnotized. In fact, you'll be awake, and fully in control of yourself."

She tried to smile. "You're not going to make me cluck like a chicken or hop around on one leg, are you?"

"Only if you want to do those things."

She managed a small laugh.

"No chicken clucking," he promised. "We'll just dig around in your mind a little and see if we can get your conscious and subconscious speaking to each other."

Somehow, the notion didn't seem all that comforting. And not for a minute did Mckenna think this voodoo would actually work. But desperation called for desperate measures. At the very least it would get Nell off her back.

"All right," Mckenna said. "Let's give it a try."

MCKENNA LEFT Dr. Cantrell's office unconvinced that anything of note had happened to her. True, she felt amazingly relaxed, even now. And when the good doctor had counted backward from ten, asking her to come more awake as he progressed, she'd had the sensation of swimming upward from some deep well of lassitude, finally breaking the surface as he reached zero. Very odd. But she had been awake the whole session, going along with his instructions mostly to be polite. And certainly no great revelations had come upon her. The doctor had merely suggested that she take her time and remember details of the Harmon case and any circumstances surrounding it, and that anything that came to her wouldn't upset or scare her, but would simply slip into place as another part of a past that she needed to set in order.

On the whole, she was disappointed. Dr. Cantrell seemed to be a nice guy, professional, dedicated, and all that. And maybe this hypnotism thing worked on people who were susceptible to suggestion. But Mckenna suspected that her subconscious, like the rest of her, cultivated the stubbornness of a Missouri mule.

When she got home, her answering machine had three phone messages from Tom, and two from Adam. Tom's first message asked how she felt, and would she like to go out for pizza that evening? His second message told her he had to work that night, and he wanted her to consider spending the night with Jane. His third message apologized if he was being pushy, and he didn't want to hover around her like another fellow he wouldn't mention, but that if she didn't want to go to Jane's, maybe he should drive across the mountain and stay with her after he was done at work.

Mckenna smiled as she listened to the messages. He really was pushy, bless him. Pushy as the bulls he used to ride. But somehow his hovering made her feel a bit warmer inside.

Adam's messages struck a similar tone, first calling her attention to the fact that he was not hovering, that he was giving her time to consider his suggestion, and then telling her he had delayed his return to Denver once again, and could they have dinner and talk the next day?

Mckenna allowed herself to reflect upon the prospect of moving to Denver. Now that her Harvard law degree was more than just a piece of paper, she could no doubt find a good job there. After all, returning to law practice didn't require her to put up with BKB. She could find a reputable firm in Denver. Her father would swell with pride. Adam would be there, handsome, charming, and eager to make her happy.

And maybe Buddy Morris or Todd Harmon or whoever else wished her ill would leave her alone.

Maybe.

But she could think about Denver and Adam later.

She called Tom at his office.

"Are you okay?" His worry made the question sound like a demand.

"I'm fine."

"Are you going to spend the night with Jane? I don't like the idea of your being alone there."

"I'm not going to spend the rest of my life hiding behind my friends for fear that the bogeyman is going to leap from the night and get me. I'm fine. Remember, I have an attack cat."

He made a rude sound. "Your attack cat has a sprained shoulder and broken rib. How is Titi feeling, by the way?"

"She thanks you for caring. Right now she's sleeping in the middle of my bed, under the afghan."

"You'll call me if you need anything?"

"I need about ten hours of sleep. Can you arrange that?"

He chuckled. "Only if I let you get off the phone. I get the hint."

"I knew you would." A smile came unbidden to curve her mouth and warm her heart. "Tom...thank you. I..." She almost said something foolish like "I love you," but she caught herself in time. He had never asked for that kind of commitment, and she was still dangling Adam on a line. "I really am grateful for your help."

"Don't mention it." His voice was heavy with something unspoken, and Mckenna wondered if it might be the very thing she hadn't said. And how would she react if he had said it? Did she know herself, her new self, well enough to know?

And there was the catch right there. She didn't quite have her head straight. She had come far down the road, but hadn't yet arrived at complete recovery. Until she did, was it fair to Tom to make a declaration that implied a certainty she didn't always feel? Was it fair to Adam to close the door between them? Was it fair not to, when she felt more certain every day that Tom was her future? Where was the sharp, decisive Mckenna who had once scared the snot out of every police officer the prosecution had put in the witness box? Not here. Not inside her. Maybe that Mckenna had just been a show she put on all along.

When she picked up the phone to call Adam, she found that she couldn't do it. Not because she didn't want to talk to him, but because she didn't know what to say.

Tomorrow would do, she decided. She would talk to Adam tomorrow. And on that thought, she joined Titi in bed.

"How are you feeling?" she asked Titi. "Better?"

Titi cracked open one eye, purred, then shut the eye again.

Mckenna stroked her softly. "Brave Titi. Are we not speaking again?"

The cat hadn't said anything since Mckenna had come home from the hospital. Maybe this time the Cat linguistics program had shut down for good. Maybe that was the price of having all the pieces of her brain snap into place.

It would be a steep price, Mckenna admitted. Hard to believe that everyone else in the world managed their lives without a cat keeping them on the straight and narrow.

"We'll still talk," she assured the cat. "A little thing like a language barrier can't come between you and me."

Titi sighed out a faint purr, but didn't open her eyes.

As soon as Mckenna's head hit the pillow, she slept, even though the hour was early. Titi's wandering around the bed trying to find the warmest, most comfortable spot didn't wake her, as it sometimes did. The mournful cries of a pack of coyotes hunting in the nearby ravines didn't make her stir, nor did the moonlight streaming through the break in the curtains.

In fact, she didn't open her eyes until the first dim light of morning made Titi think about her empty stomach. She gave Mckenna the usual wake-up call of standing on her chest and poking a nose in her face.

"Good morning," Mckenna greeted the cat in a sleepy voice.

Titi purred, butted her head against Mckenna's chin, and started kneading her collarbone.

"Oh, all right. I suppose it's time to rise and shine. I see we both survived the night."

Mckenna had stumbled to the bathroom before she remembered the dream. Or was it a dream? It was all so clear, as if a spotlight had suddenly illuminated some hidden dark corner of her mind. It had been there all the time, she simply hadn't seen it.

Hooray for hypnosis. She owed Nell and Dr. Cantrell an apology. It had worked, after all.

Overwhelmed by the suddenness, the certainty, of her knowledge, Mckenna grabbed shakily for the edge of the bathtub and sat down. Tom had been right. There *was* a maid, and her name was indeed Maria, the name Mckenna had blurted out on Tom's first inquiry. How could she have forgotten? She had interviewed Maria as a mere matter of course, not realizing until a few minutes into the interview that this witness was going to damage her client beyond saving, and that she was legally obligated to inform prosecutor Tom Markham of the maid's relevant testimony. And Tom Markham, being a prosecutor who seldom missed a shot, was going to drill Todd Harmon right between the eyes with it.

Mckenna also recalled the war that had raged inside her when she'd tried to persuade Todd to request a plea deal with the county attorney. The country-western idol had told her confidently that Maria was in Mexico, and no one would find her there, tempting Mckenna with almost certain victory if she just kept her mouth shut about Maria's existence.

No wonder she hadn't wanted to remember such a thing. Mckenna had wanted so badly to go along with Harmon, to win the case at all costs, even the cost of her ethics. That oh-so-tempting conversation had taken place the very afternoon of her car accident, she remembered. She had sat at a table that night with Tom Markham, at the Rainbow's End Steakhouse, and not given him the information she owed him, even though they had discussed the case. That had been Friday. Monday she would have called his office and filled him in, Mckenna told herself. She knew she would have. But then her car had gone off an embankment, and Todd Harmon and the rest of her life had gotten shoved behind a locked door that only now had completely opened.

And who had known she was headed up the canyon just then? Not Todd Harmon, but Buddy Morris. He had been talking to her in Rainbow's End just before she had left. Had Morris somehow arranged for her accident? When she had survived, had he hired someone to search her house for interview notes that she might have taken home? When he had seen her back at BKB, supposedly with all her memories once again intact, had he panicked and decided to get rid of her once and for all, before she told Pat Carter or Tom Markham what she knew?

All speculation. Maybe pure silliness. How would she ever know?

"Damn!" she said to herself. "Damn me for a fool." She had to tell Tom about Maria, but how would he ever find Maria in Mexico? And if he couldn't find her, she couldn't testify. In a court of law, hearsay didn't convict anyone.

She suffered a wave of disappointment, of regret. She actually liked Todd Harmon. Had almost every album he'd ever cut. She didn't relish the idea of his conviction. Even less did she like the idea that he or Morris might have wanted her out of the picture just so she couldn't pass along that damning bit of information.

Mckenna groaned. It was too early in the morning for this kind of revelation. She wet a washrag in the sink and pressed it to her face. Then another memory blossomed—a dark night driving up the winding highway through Oak Creek Canyon, heading home after a frustrating and guilt-ridden session at the Rainbow's End with Tom. She'd had a pounding headache, but the sudden glare of light that rushed toward her hadn't been an explosion in her head. They were headlights. High-beam headlights, coming straight for her. Blinded, she had swerved. The world had fallen out from under her. And then... nothing.

A chill of remembered fear traveled down Mckenna's spine. Accident? Or attempted murder? Would she ever know?

"Okay," she muttered, trying to pull her scattered wits back together. She needed to call Dr. Cantrell and tell him he was a miracle worker. She needed to call Tom and tell him what she had remembered. And Jane—she would call Jane and gloat that the old Mckenna hadn't needed a new lifestyle, after all. No stroke had sent her off that cliff, just a reckless driver with bright headlights—though, in a way, that image was scarier than the idea of a stroke.

Mckenna looked at the little travel clock on the bathroom counter. Six-thirty. Too early to call anyone quite yet.

"Titi," she called to the cat, who was still curled on the bed. "Time for breakfast." She felt shaky and overwhelmed, but also liberated. Somehow she had to find out the truth behind all her speculation. What would sharp, cagey, bold Old Mckenna have done?

Titi wandered into the kitchen, meowed a complaint, and gave Mckenna an indignant look.

"What do you think of all this?" Mckenna asked the cat.

Titi stared pointedly at the can of cat food on the kitchen counter.

"I'm on my own, huh?"

The cat answered by brushing affectionately against Mckenna's legs, and then staring once again at her canned breakfast, as if to reassure Mckenna that no, she wasn't alone, but even in times of crisis, both cats and people needed to eat.

"Okay," Mckenna told her with a chuckle. "I get the message."

She had just long enough to feed Titi and drop a couple of eggs into a skillet before the cascade of her memory sent yet another tidbit her way.

"I took notes! Of course!" She had taken notes during the interview with Todd Harmon's maid—notes including Maria's home residence in Mexico, where her parents and sister and cousins lived. And after her frustrating conversation with Todd that Friday afternoon, she had slipped those notes into a file, and put the file into her briefcase. More important, as always, she'd taken the briefcase with her when she had left the office. It had been in the car when they had gone off that cliff.

Where was that briefcase now? Had it been destroyed when her BMW hit that tree? Mckenna hoped not. The car hadn't burned. It had been towed, totaled by the insurance company, and probably junked. What had survived the accident was in a box that her insurance agent had delivered to her right after she got out of the hospital. A cardboard box. She hadn't opened it. Where was it? She had moved since then. What would she have done with it when she moved?

The smell of burning eggs brought her back to the present.

"Oh, damn! Yuck!"

The eggs were beyond saving. She dumped them into

the sink and ran water into the skillet, which set it steaming like a boiler.

"No time to eat," she told Titi. "I have to find that box and find out if those notes are there."

Titi gave her a jaundiced look. There was always time to eat, the look insisted.

"No! This is important! We need that box. Where did I put it?"

Just then, yet another complication presented itself. The crunch of gravel in the driveway heralded a visitor. Seconds later, a knock on the door accompanied Adam's voice. "Mckenna!" he demanded. "Are you home?"

Unmindful that she was still in the sweatpants and T-shirt that she'd slept in, Mckenna answered the door. "Of course I'm home. It's not even seven in the morning!"

That didn't faze him. "You didn't return my calls. I was imagining all sorts of things that might have happened...shit! What is that bandage on your head? What did you do?"

"I...we..."

"Tell me!"

"Someone broke in night before last and attacked me."

"And you didn't tell me?" He seemed to grow taller with indignation.

"I...well, there was the hospital, and then...well, work, and...I went to a hypnotist. And now...oh, forget the details!" She grabbed his arm and pulled him inside. "You need to help me look for a box."

He stared hard. "Mckenna, you're talking crazy." He wrinkled his nose. "What is that smell?"

"Burned eggs. I'm not talking crazy. I'll explain while we look, Adam. But you need to help me find this cardboard box, about two feet on a side. Sealed with brown packing tape."

Titi wandered over and voiced an ominous meow.

Adam looked askance as the cat jumped onto the arm of the couch and stared at him. "What's with the cat?"

"She's recently discovered that she can take physical action against those who displease me. So do as I say, Adam."

After another chary glance at Titi, he did.

They started in Mckenna's bedroom, tearing the closet apart, looking in every corner. Then they moved to the hall linen closet, the kitchen pantry, the shelves in the mudroom, and then, finally, Mckenna opened the access door to the dark area beneath the trailer.

"You surely aren't desperate enough to crawl around in there!" Adam declared.

"Yes, I think I am."

"Just what's in this box that is so important?"

"Evidence, Adam. You should appreciate that. I think my briefcase is in that box, and in my briefcase is an address that might make all the difference in the Todd Harmon trial. It's a piece of my memory that just now fell into place, but what I don't remember is where the box is. I know the briefcase was in my Beemer when I wrecked it, so logic says it's in the box of stuff they retrieved from the car. But I haven't seen the box since I moved out of the house in Oak Creek."

"Could you have left it there?"

"No. I moved everything out before the renters moved in."

"Very important address, eh?"

"Yes."

Peering into the dark underworld, he sighed. "I'll bet there's black widows in there."

"Most probably. I'll get a flashlight and some gloves."

Mckenna ended up being the one to search beneath the trailer, where she remembered storing some of the bulkier things from the Oak Creek house. Adam nobly offered to go, but the offer dripped so of martyrdom that Mckenna knew she would have to pay and pay and pay unless she did the chore herself.

In the end, his attempt at martyrdom and her impatient plunge into the spider-infested catacombs made no difference. The boxes in the crawl space were clearly marked. One contained garden tools. Two others were full of law books. The last was a mishmash of pencils, pens, sticky notes, a stapler, and other miscellaneous office supplies. When she emerged, covered in dust and cobwebs, all she could do was curse.

"I know it's here," she insisted. "I just know it. I wouldn't have trashed that stuff, even though I never opened the box to see what survived the wreck. I know it's here."

They found the box, finally, in the closet of the little guest room—scarcely more than a closet itself—built onto the garage. Anxiously, Mckenna sliced the packing tape and emptied the contents: a plastic insulated coffee cup, five CDs, a folder full of maintenance receipts, a roll of paper towels, and her briefcase—soft, supple, hand-tooled leather. An expensive briefcase for a very expensive attorney.

Inside the briefcase were several files. One was labeled "Harmon," and had a file number neatly printed beside the label.

"Bingo," Mckenna crowed. "Things are finally falling into place."

She sat on the rag rug—the guest room's only furnishing—and read while Adam leaned against a wall. Like a movie playing in her mind, the contents of the notes came to life. She could see Maria's face, hear her voice—and her reluctance to admit she had seen anything while she had been working at Todd Harmon's celebrity get-together. She had liked her boss. He treated her well. And Maria had been an illegal immigrant. The last thing she'd wanted to do was bring herself to the attention of the authorities.

But Mckenna had pulled the tale out of her and written it down. Not that scribbled interview notes were admissible evidence. Certainly not. But she had also scribbled down Maria's place of residence in Mexico. It was her father's residence, actually, but from there, Maria would be easy enough to trace.

"I have to get this to Tom right away," Mckenna told Adam. "And omigod, look at the time. I was due at work thirty minutes ago. I have to call Diane and tell her what's going on."

"Wait a minute!" Adam grabbed her hand and lifted her to her feet. "This information is going to make the prosecution's case?"

"That's what I figure."

"Mckenna, are you sure about this? You need to think carefully before making up your mind what to do with it."

Mckenna didn't understand. "The only thing to do with it is give it to Tom."

"Come on into the trailer," Adam invited. "Let's get a cup of coffee and talk about this. Markham has survived months without knowing about this. He can wait another few minutes."

She conceded the point, but only because Adam had been a good sport about helping her find the notes.

While Mckenna called in late to work and poured coffee, Adam digested the notes. "You're right," he admitted. "This woman's testimony could make the prosecution's case."

Not to mention that it could inspire someone to get her out of the way.

"But think," Adam cautioned. "No one on the prosecution team knows about Maria Oranto. No one will know if you don't give them this information."

Mckenna's eyes narrowed. "Why wouldn't I give it to them?"

He rolled his eyes. "Mckenna, think. This is just a minor drug charge, but it could deep-six Mr. Clean Country's career. BKB has a rep for winning cases like this—high-profile celebrity cases. A loss isn't going to do their business any good. You could have a quiet talk with the partner up in the Sedona office—what's his name?"

"Gilbert Bradner."

"Yes. Him. Show him what you have, and demand your job back, with a raise, with a partnership. Then, once you have your reputation well established once again—say, in six months—sell out the partnership, take your reputation, and move back to Denver. Firms would be falling all over themselves to hire you on. You could write your own ticket."

"Adam, that's not ethical."

"Don't pick at straws. This is a minor case. Who cares if Todd Harmon, superstar, is spreading around a little coke to his friends? All these entertainment types do it. This case doesn't amount to a hill of beans in terms of anything but BKB's reputation, and yours. You can have your life back, Mckenna. In Denver. We could have the life we always intended to have together."

Mckenna opened her mouth for a tart reply, but Adam shushed her with an imperious hand. "Don't say it. You know I'm right, Mckenna, so don't say you have to strictly toe the line about this. You're smarter than that."

"I wasn't going to say that," she said quietly.

"Good. You just think about what I said, Mckenna. Look around you at this dump you live in, the nothing job you're so worried about showing up late to. What kind of life is this? You could come back to Denver now and get a decent job, but how much better to present yourself to the Denver law community riding on a wave of triumph. Eh?"

He tapped a finger against the notes in her hand. "Those are a ticket to an easier future. Think about it." He leaned over and pecked her on the forehead. "Just think about it, my love."

chapter 25

FOR LONG minutes after the door closed behind Adam, Mckenna stood in the middle of her kitchen and stared out the window. Titi jumped onto the kitchen counter and stared right along with her.

"He's right, you know? In a very sort of cynical way," Mckenna finally said to the cat.

Titi looked at her silently, then flexed her whiskers and—if a cat can be said to have brows—arched one brow inquisitively. Mckenna realized then that she and her cat had a language of their own that had nothing to do with words.

"He is right," she repeated. "The Harmon case is insignificant in the grand scheme of things—except, of course, to the media. And these few pages of notes would win me my job back in a split second. Gil might even take the Harmon case away from Pat and give it back to me. I could win."

"Meeeewr?"

"I know. Tom is good, bless him. But the legal system

stacks the odds against the prosecution. If I kept these notes to myself, I'd wipe the courtroom floor with him."

"Moowrrr!"

"The media would make me the legal darling of the moment. Adam is right. I could write my own ticket. This would earn me that all-important partnership."

Somewhere deep inside her lay the desire to take Adam's advice, and the realization that she was tempted nearly knocked her off her feet. Heart pounding, she dropped into a kitchen chair.

Mckenna longed to win, to shine. The longing was almost a pain inside her. That Friday night at the Rainbow's End, she hadn't managed to tell Tom about Maria. But she would have the following Monday. She had truly intended to tell him.

Even so, the temptation to find a way around the necessity had nearly choked her, just as it rose up again in her now.

And just as before, she wouldn't give in. Now resistance was easier, because she knew there was more to Mckenna Wright than just winning.

Titi wove a dance around Mckenna's legs, then paused to look up with a worried expression. Mckenna bent down to stroke her soft fur. "Old Mckenna just won't give up."

Then the truth hit her. Adam and his advice had made her realize something: a revelation—frightening, and at the same time liberating.

She didn't have to worry about Old Mckenna ambushing her new life, because Old Mckenna sat right here, right in this kitchen chair in this trailer house. She *was* Old Mckenna.

The thought took her breath away. She was Old Mckenna. Her memory and skills were intact. Whatever injury had short-circuited her memory had healed, and anything she had tried to hide from herself, Dr. Cantrell's magic and her own persistence had ferreted out.

Here she was: the whole ball of wax. The Original. The Unforgettable. Mckenna Wright Version 1.0.

On impulse, she got up and ran down the hall to the bathroom. Flipping on the light, she took a good look at herself in the mirror. Compared to the Mckenna of September, Mckenna of January presented quite a mess. Still in baggy sweatpants and wrinkled T-shirt, she was about as far from cool and sophisticated as a woman could get. Her hair had been trimmed, at least, but the discount stylist couldn't produce anything like the high-end hair designer she had once patronized in Sedona. She hadn't had a facial since her accident. Her face reflected the stress and anxiety of the last few days, and the cosmetics she had bought at Wal-Mart certainly weren't up to hiding the lines that had started to fan out from the corners of her eyes. Probably a makeup artist in Hollywood couldn't erase those lines. And Mckenna wasn't sure she wanted to hide them. They had been earned three times over in the past few months.

"Hello, Mckenna," she said to her reflection. "Welcome back."

"Meeerrrrr!" A warm, soft brush against her legs made her smile.

"Don't worry, Titi. I'm not exactly as I was. I've learned a few lessons."

Over the past few months, her memories had first trickled back, then flowed, then flooded. Now she remembered everything about the person she had been—her worries, her ambitions, what drove her, what annoyed her, what frightened her. But she also recalled everything she had endured during the last few months, everything she had discovered about what she could be, what she should be. And in the mirror, looking out at her through familiar dark brown eyes, were both her old self and someone new, as well.

Most important, she knew who Mckenna Wright was,

and she knew what she wanted. And damn! She was going to get it. No. Not it. Him. She was going to get him.

But first, she had two problems to deal with. Mckenna gave her reflection a smile.

"Watch out, world. I'm back."

THE FIRST problem posed the biggest challenge, both difficult and scary. So Mckenna tackled it first. There wasn't much to be done, really, just a simple phone call. That phone call would involve sticking her neck out far enough for her head to get cut off, but it was a call she had to make—either that or live with the knowledge that her courage had gotten scrambled right along with her brains.

"Nielson here," said the masculine voice on the other end of the line.

"Detective Nielson, this is Mckenna Wright."

"Hey, Ms. Wright. I was going to call you today. The judge is letting us hold Bruner without bail."

"Bruner?"

He chuckled. "The fellow who ran into your cat the other night. George Bruner."

"Oh." That was one way to put it, Mckenna supposed. It carried less scary baggage than calling him the jerk who tried to bash her brains out. "That's good, then. Is Tom Markham prosecuting this case?"

"Nope. Roger Corey. Markham excused himself. Said he was personally involved."

She could almost hear Nielson's eyebrows lift over the phone. *Personally involved.* Mckenna smiled.

"But Corey's a go-getter. He'll nail the guy. Don't worry."

"I'm not worried about Bruner." She worried about the man who had hired Bruner, though. "The one I want to talk about is Bruner's boss, the guy with the Southern drawl."

"Yeah?" Nielson's voice grew cautious.

"I've been sitting here playing connect the dots, and some new data has come into play. Let me tell you what I have."

She did, and her recitation of her theories met with silence on Nielson's end of the line.

"It's damned suspicious," he agreed. "The guy could have beat you up the canyon and doubled back to drive you off the road. And he knows where you live, so he could have arranged for both break-ins. Plus, he's got a motive. But it's still all circumstantial. This is a guy with money and mucho connections. If we haul him in without something pretty concrete, he'll kill us with a lawsuit. You, too, probably. But you know that, being in the business, so to speak."

Mckenna's revitalized legal-eagle brain began to crank out ideas. She chose the easiest. "How about if you give Buddy Morris a call and have Georgy boy identify the voice over the phone? That's not a verdict clincher, but it would be enough to bring him in and launch an investigation."

"Not bad. You have the man's phone number?"

Mckenna chuckled. "All four of them—home, office, cell, and private line. I have Todd Harmon's various contact numbers as well, and if your guy can't identify Morris, we'll give him a crack at Todd. But I think Morris is our guy. He was the one who knew I was driving up the canyon that night, and I have a hunch that he's the kind who rolls over anyone who might get in his way. Evidence aside, my hunches are almost always on target."

Nielson laughed. "And don't we cops just know it. Glad you're on the side of the angels this time, Ms. Wright. And welcome back. Are you going back to work at BKB?"

She smiled. "Don't think so."

"What are you going to do? If I'm not being too nosy."

Her smile grew. "You'd be surprised at what I'm going to do."

So would Adam Decker, Mckenna thought with just a hint of satisfaction. But she suspected Tom Markham wouldn't be surprised at all.

One down, Mckenna thought as she hung up the phone, one to go. For the next task she needed to borrow Jane's computer.

Ninety minutes later, she knocked on the door of Adam Decker's room in Los Abrigados, one of Sedona's premier resorts. As she looked around at the fountains and lush landscaping, she wondered with a twinge of regret if she would ever again be able to afford so much as a day's retreat to such a place.

It wasn't much of a twinge, though. Other things, she had discovered, were more important.

"Mckenna! Hey! You're just in time to go to brunch. I just managed to wash off all the cobwebs from our search."

Cobwebs? She had been the one rooting around beneath the trailer, so how did Adam rate complaining about cobwebs? Still, the wet, curly hair and freshly scrubbed skin looked as if he had indeed scoured away all trace of her ugly little trailer.

"Hey, Adam. Actually, I don't really have time for brunch. I just came by to say thank you."

Adam grinned. He did have a very winning grin, she noted.

"So you've thought it out and come around to the smart way of thinking, have you? No need to thank me, Mckenna. You've been under a lot of strain, sweetheart, and it's no wonder you're still a bit slow on the uptake. Come in, come in."

She accepted the invitation. What she had to say was best said in private. The room was big and beautifully appointed, though the bed was unmade and the furniture cluttered with dirty clothes, a couple of Evian bottles, and an empty pizza box.

He saw her eyes take in the mess. "I need a wife to keep me in line, obviously."

"Good thing for you they have maid service here," she replied.

His smile didn't waver.

"Listen, Adam," she began resolutely. "I brought you a present."

"Mckenna, you don't have to—"

She stopped him with an imperious hand. "Wait." Then she took an envelope from her jacket pocket and handed it to him.

Obviously puzzled, he extracted the folded paper from the envelope and read. "A flight reservation?"

"My gift to you."

His smile faded, then crooked wryly upward. "One way, I notice. Tomorrow morning, bright and early."

"I figured giving you a ticket would convince you that I meant it this time. I'm sorry, Adam, I know we had something in the past, but I'm a different person now."

He raised a brow. "No hope? You're still not quite yourself, you know."

She chuckled and shook her head. "That's what I thanked you for, Adam. When you pointed out the advantages of keeping those notes to myself, I got to thinking on it and—I'll admit it—really wanting to do just that. Then I realized that there is no more old me and new me. There's just *me*. Everything has come back, but what I learned in the present means I'm not quite the same person I was in the past, if you know what I mean. Everyone grows as they live their lives, but I guess I was just stubborn enough to need a knock on the head for the process to work."

Adam put the computer flight confirmation back into

the envelope with a rueful sigh. "We did have something. It was worth a try. You know, if you—"

"I won't. But I'm flattered." She stood on tiptoe to press a kiss to his jaw. "Good-bye, Adam. Have a nice flight."

"Kind of like 'Have a nice life'?"

Mckenna merely smiled and, with a little wave, walked out the door. Her heart felt ten pounds lighter. Now for the most important foray of the day.

THE PHONE on Tom's desk buzzed, and he reluctantly set aside the file he studied.

"Mr. Markham!" said an effusive voice on the line. "This is Colter Gaines of KTVK in Phoenix. How's it going?"

"It's going fine, Mr. Gaines." It would be going better, however, if he didn't keep getting these calls from the media.

"Good, good. Look, I know you're busy, but we'd like to set up an interview with you, to air on our news magazine Friday night. Doable?"

"I don't think so. Right now I have very little time."

"I understand that, Mr. Markham. But you realize that Buddy Morris and Todd Harmon have been on the local as well as national news almost every night for the last week, and so has Pat Carter. CNN ran a taped interview with Todd that must have had every country music fan in tears. Wouldn't you like to get out your side of the case?"

Tom chuckled. "Our side of the case will get plenty of airing at the preliminary hearing, which is next week, as I'm sure you know. And I think that's the appropriate place for it to be presented. Don't you?"

"Yes, but the public has a right to—"

"The public will get plenty of chances to entertain themselves with Mr. Harmon's story, I assure you. Come trial time, twelve of the public will have a front-row seat.

And I'm sure the rest of the country will be watching live coverage. Or, if the judge is smart and doesn't let the cameras in the courtroom, news anchors like you will be bending their ears nightly, complete with sketches, verbatim accounts of testimony, and speculation by every legal expert in the country."

"I take it that's a 'no' to the interview."

"You're a perceptive guy, Colter. Listen, I'm not trying to be a jerk here. But running around giving interviews is a distraction I don't need right now. You might ask John Donovan, though. The county attorney is fond of making television appearances."

"Good idea. I'll do just that."

Tom grimaced as he set down the phone. He hoped his boss didn't make any statements they couldn't back up in court. At times, Donovan was more politician than attorney, and he had a politician's love for spin.

Tom picked up the file he had set aside, then put it down again. His stomach was telling him that lunchtime had arrived about thirty minutes ago. Lunch. The whole morning had passed, and he'd managed to think about Mckenna only about fifty times. Not too bad. Better than last night, when worrying about her had robbed him of sleep—which he dearly needed.

Why the hell didn't he just call her? Call her and get firm. Tell her to forget staying alone until this cursed Harmon case was history, one way or another. Tell her to chuck any ideas she had about this Adam Decker fellow and admit that she was in love with Tom. Tell her to get her curvaceous little self over to his place so he could kiss any notion of another man right out of her befuddled head. Tell her that he loved her, that he wanted her to love him, that they had a future together if only they would grab for it.

That was a lot of telling. Dammit. With a sigh, he drummed the end of a pencil on his desk in a tattoo of frustration. He didn't call Mckenna because he had promised, like a fool, not to put on the pressure, to let her find her own way, make her own decisions. He couldn't hog-tie her and make her do what he wanted her to do, even when she drove him crazy by staying alone when someone out there wanted her hide, even when he wanted to seduce her into telling him that she loved him, not some slick upstart yuppie from Denver. Giving Mckenna the space she needed was the right thing to do, Tom reminded himself. Right for her. Right for him. Just right, goddammit!

He pinched the bridge of his nose, then leaned back in his chair and stared at the water stains on the ceiling. Damn but his insides churned with a hell of a battle. Mr. Sensitive jousting with Mr. Macho. Mr. Politically Correct with Mr. Take-Charge.

Mckenna wasn't a woman who took well to a man coming on too strong, he reminded himself.

On the other hand, Tom had never been a man who sat back and refused to fight for what he wanted. Dammit. He didn't need this right now. He had a preliminary hearing coming up—one whose verdict might well go against him. He had the media crawling all over him, and a boss who would be all too willing to hang him out to dry if he didn't make the county attorney's operation here look like gold. He didn't need to be obsessing over Mckenna Wright.

So suck it up, he told himself. He loved the woman, so he should fight for her. If he managed to win her, sooner or later she was going to tumble to the fact that he wasn't exactly Mr. PC Sensitive, anyway, so he might as well let her know up front that those bulls he'd once ridden couldn't compete with him at being hardheaded.

Five minutes later, he banged the phone back into its cradle with unnecessary force. He had not found Mckenna at the hospital. Her voice mail had picked up with a businesslike little message about his call being important to her—it had damned tootin' better be important to her!

He'd hung up and called Diane, who had told him Mckenna had taken a personal day.

Instantly concerned—what the hell could have happened to her now?—he had called her home. This time a cheery little message told him to please leave a message after the beep. He felt like taking that damned beep and . . . well, frustration and outright anxiety were getting the better of him. Where the hell was she?

Suddenly, he knew right where she was. He looked up, scowling, and saw her leaning against the frame of his office doorway. She wore neatly pressed blue jeans, a slinky-looking sweater, and an impish little smile curling the corners of her mouth.

"Mckenna!"

She twitched a brow. "Howdy, Cowboy."

"You look . . . good?"

"Don't sound so surprised. It's not flattering."

"I didn't mean that like it sounded." Oh, yeah, he was cool. That sort of talk was going to sweep the woman right off her feet and into his arms. "I mean, it's no surprise that you look good. You always look good. But today you look, well, extra good."

It was true. Her eyes sparkled with a certain glint. The angle of her chin shouted confidence. Her hand rested on her hip with just a touch of sassiness. Suddenly he recognized the change. Old Mckenna had come back, but not completely. Her smile lacked the arrogance. A softness around the eyes revealed the heart inside.

"What happened to you?" he asked warily.

"Nothing too dramatic. I'll tell you when we have some time. But first I think you should read this." She tossed a file folder onto his desk. He opened it to find several pages of handwritten script, hodgepodge, some places barely legible, the pages torn from a yellow legal pad.

"Sorry about the handwriting. I was in a hurry. Read."

He did. And then read again. A smile grew on his face. "Hot damn!"

"I thought you might feel that way. You'd better get busy, Cowboy. That prelim is only, what, a week away?"

Then she turned toward the door, smiling in the full knowledge of what she'd given him.

"Wait! Don't go yet! We need to talk. Come to lunch with me."

"Don't worry," she said with a smile. "No way I'm leaving until I say what I came to say." She closed the door, then looked at him with an expression that mingled bravado with uncertainty, catching her lower lip momentarily between her teeth, and then drawing herself up straighter.

"I'm back," she declared.

He didn't pretend to not understand. "So I see."

"I've been back a while, but it really didn't hit me before this morning, when I found those notes, and"—here she hesitated—"and I was actually tempted to, well, do the wrong thing instead of the right thing." She grimaced. "What does that make me?"

"Human?" he speculated. "Like the rest of us."

That earned him a grin. "Very human. But"—her eyes lit with a smile—"I know who I am now, warts and all. And I can handle it. I'm not afraid of the old Mckenna anymore, because she's me, and she's smarter than she used to be." She darted him a look from beneath the dark curtain of her eyelashes, a look that started his blood running. "I'm way smarter about some things, Cowboy."

Tom couldn't resist. He came around the desk toward her, but playfully, she backed off. "We're doing closing arguments, here, Mr. Markham, so don't get out of order."

He gave her a quizzical look.

"I just had a talk with Adam."

Tom clenched his jaw.

"I gave him a plane ticket home. One way. I figured it was the only way I could convince him."

Tom released a long breath. "Sounds right. What do I get?"

She grinned. "Me. Warts and all."

For a moment he couldn't breathe.

Her face clouded. "If you want me, that is. There are a lot of warts, you know."

"I love all your warts, Mac."

She smiled, suddenly and irresistibly radiant, and walked into his waiting arms. "Have I told you lately that I love you?"

epilogue

NELL DROPPED her burden onto the floor with a re-lieved grunt. "Man, is it hot outside! And it's only April. Prescott isn't supposed to be this hot in April."

"It's not hot," Jane told her. "It's just that the slave driver here is making us work up a sweat with all this heaving and toting."

"I'm heaving and toting, too," Mckenna assured them. "What? Do you think it's time for an iced-tea break?"

"Most definitely," Nell declared. "What's in those boxes, anyway?"

"Law books," Mckenna confessed.

"You mean to tell us they haven't put them on CD yet?" Nell demanded.

Mckenna chuckled. "They're more impressive this way."

"There are only a few more boxes," Jane said. "We'll survive." She looked around. "Where are you going to put them?"

"Tom has promised to build me bookshelves. All along that wall."

"Hm." Jane gave grudging approval as she looked around the office space Mckenna had just leased. "This isn't half-bad, for a hole in the wall. Industrial gray carpeting. Industrial beige walls. Industrial gray metal desk. Where did you get that thing?"

"Goodwill," Mckenna admitted. "Along with one office chair, only slightly stained, and two fiberglass chairs that look like they came from the nearest school cafeteria. Fifty bucks for the lot. Don't say it," she warned Nell. "I know you offered to furnish this place, you disgustingly rich woman you, and don't think I don't appreciate the thought, but this is something I want to do myself, from scratch, so when I'm fabulously successful and a regular guest on Oprah and Larry King, I can say I fought my way up from the bottom."

"My dog is the one who's disgustingly rich, not me. But I don't suppose you would let Piggy furnish the place, either," Nell said.

"Nope." Mckenna sent a smile Piggy's way. "Don't be offended, Pig, but this is just something I have to do myself. When Gil begged me to come back and work for BKB," she added with a wicked grin, "and I threw his offer back in his face, I realized that this time I had to things on my own. No help, no compromises. This is something I have to do all my way.

"Now, how about that iced tea? There's a cafe just next door. That's the advantage of having a law office in a strip mall."

"And what shall we do with the children while we drink iced tea?" Nell asked.

All three of them looked at the animals scattered like throw rugs around the office. Idaho and Shadow lay side by side along one wall. The redoubtable Piggy had curled her pudgy little sausage-shaped body to fit into the office chair. (Piggy did not believe that dogs, especially and specifically dogs named Piggy, belonged on the floor.) And Titi hunkered in a sphinx pose, paws tucked neatly beneath her, in the geographic center of the gray metal Goodwill desk.

"Leave them here," Jane proposed. "The air-conditioning is on. They're all in the mood for a nap, anyway."

The animals didn't argue, except for Piggy, who gave them a look as they left. No doubt she had heard the word "cafe"—translation, food—and thought she should be included.

Next door, the friends slipped into a booth and ordered iced tea and pie all around.

"I can't believe you're deserting the Verde Valley," Nell said to Mckenna.

"Twaddle!" Mckenna scoffed. "Prescott is just an hour's drive from Cornville, Cottonwood, Sedona, and anywhere else in the valley. Besides"—her eyes sparkled—"I have good reason."

Jane smirked. "Six foot two and a hundred and ninety pounds of good reason."

"Which reminds me," Nell said. "Speaking of men, Dan wants me to ask Tom about the chances of an internship in the county attorney's office. We're coming back here after Dan graduates, you know. It's two years away, but I guess all the students try to spend their summers interning in whatever area of law they'd someday like to work in."

"He'll never make his fortune as a county attorney," Mckenna said.

"The papa of a very rich corgi doesn't need to worry about his fortune," Jane pointed out.

"Oh, yeah. I keep forgetting that Piggy's rich, famous, and funding northern Arizona's new pet therapy network, with Jane's help."

"Piggy's money, my expertise," Jane said. "Someone had to take charge now that Nell just *had* to follow her husband to Tucson. Mckenna isn't the only one who's deserted the Verde Valley."

They all laughed. Then their pie came. There's no better distraction than apple pie à la mode.

"On a more serious note," Jane continued as she scraped the last of her pie from the plate, "did you see this morning's *Arizona Republic*?"

"No," Nell and Mckenna both answered. "Why?"

"The entertainment section features your favorite ex-client. This you've gotta see." She went to the newspaper dispenser by the cash register and dropped a couple of quarters into the slot. When she came back, she set the entertainment section in front of Mckenna. A color picture of none other than Todd Harmon splashed the first page.

"Good old Todd," Mckenna said softly. "You know, I did sort of like him."

"Coke and all, eh?" Jane's tone was caustic.

Mckenna gave a half-shrug with one shoulder.

"Read the interview," Jane told her.

Todd Harmon had a May concert scheduled in Phoenix, just three weeks away, and the newspaper had given him major space and a very upbeat interview. They did touch on his recent legal difficulties, however—his plea deal with the Yavapai county attorney, probation, rehab, and community service.

"How sweet," Mckenna noted, only half-sarcastically. "He apologizes to his fans, his family, and his friends for letting them down. Admits he had a problem. Urges young people not to be fooled by the so-called glamour of drugs."

"I don't think drugs are glamorous," Jane said darkly.

"I think he's very courageous to own up to his mistakes," Nell said. "After all, he didn't know what Buddy Morris had in mind."

"The interview gets around to that, too," Mckenna told them, "though from the 'poor betrayed Todd' tone, you'd think it was Harmon that Morris sent over a cliff, or Harmon who had his house ransacked and his life almost snuffed out by a hired tough."

"At least that slimeball won't be coming back," Nell gloated. "What's the usual sentence for attempted murder?"

Mckenna grimaced. "I hope it seems like forever to him. He's not going to like the pen. Ironic, isn't it, that Pat Carter is handling his case? She doesn't stand a chance, poor baby, not once I get on the witness stand. I'm going to wipe the courtroom floor with her. And when she loses this case on top of the Harmon debacle, she can just about kiss her future at BKB good-bye."

"Poor baby," Jane and Nell echoed in unison, then grinned.

Mckenna grinned along with them. "God, am I glad not to be working at BKB any longer."

"Yeah," Jane agreed. "Being poor is much more fun."

Mckenna scowled. "You were the one who told me to find my true self."

"I meant it. And I wasn't being snide when I said being poor is more fun. Now you can start from the beginning, choose your own clients, build a law practice based on who needs defending rather than who has the most money and highest profile. And I think it's cool that you're leaving time for the charity cases like the ones you and Tom worked on."

"We call it *pro bono*," Mckenna corrected. "Not charity."

"Well, whatever you call it, it's cool."

"I think it's cool, too," Nell added.

"What's cool?" asked a masculine voice.

None of them had noticed Tom walk through the door. "How do you move so silently in those clunky cowboy boots?" Mckenna demanded.

He grinned. "Practice. Sometimes it pays to sneak up on ladies without giving them warning. What's cool? Are you talking about me?"

Jane snorted. "Isn't that just like a man?" But a smile played around her mouth. She gave Nell a meaningful look. "I have to get back over the mountain to the kennel. Don't you have somewhere you have to be?"

Nell took the hint. "I need to pick up some stuff at the mall. Mckenna, is it okay if I leave Piggy in your office for an hour or so?"

"Be my guest," Mckenna said.

"Charge the dog rent," Jane advised, getting up. "She can afford it. See you both tomorrow. Mckenna, you want me to show up at Tom's place early tomorrow morning, hog-tie him, and throw him in my van?"

Mckenna laughed. "I don't think that will be necessary." She gave Tom a gimlet eye. "Will it?"

He made a rude sound and dropped into the booth that Jane and Nell had just vacated. "I think we've just been purposefully left alone together," he commented as the two women went out the door.

"They're trying to be thoughtful," Mckenna told him.

"And it's much appreciated." He reached over the table and took her hand. "Seems like I haven't had a moment alone with you in days."

An impish glint lit her eyes. "I have some free time tomorrow, if you'd like to take advantage of it."

"Do you, now?" He raised her hand and rubbed the knuckles against his cheek. "Don't have much planned for tomorrow?"

She shrugged. "Not unless you consider our wedding a big deal."

"It so happens that I do." He smiled. "A very big deal. A permanent deal, through floods, fights, rivalry, and even that damned classical music you insist on playing. A very big, very permanent deal. Do you?"

"I do." Tomorrow she would say those very words in church.

Tom grinned, leaned over the table, and kissed her.

• • •

TITI STILL sat in the very center of Mckenna's new desk, where she could survey her entire new domain by moving only her head. She savored the quiet satisfaction of a job well done. Not every cat could have pulled it off—a difficult subject, difficult circumstances, and a sneaky, murderous villain thrown in just to make things more interesting. No, not many cats could have handled Mckenna's problems. But Titi wasn't just any cat. Therapy cats laid claim to special powers. Mysterious powers. Powers no other creature possessed.

As if reading Titi's thoughts, Piggy, still curled peacefully on the chair behind the desk, opened one eye and regarded Titi with ill-disguised contempt. Titi responded with an annoyed twitch of her whiskers. Arrogant dog. Piggy thought she was so special because she had a human soul hidden within that scruffy corgi suit. Oh, yes. Titi knew very well what manner of creature Piggy was. Cats are much too smart to be fooled by appearances. Piggy thought her human soul made her special, but Titi knew better. Titi was the one who was special. Her soul, pristine cat in its original mint condition, didn't need the redemption Piggy worked so hard to earn. Titi did her job simply out of superior understanding.

And just look what that understanding had accomplished. Mckenna was on the road to a happy life, thanks to Titi's advice. The bad guys were demolished, thanks to Titi's courage and ferocity. And Titi was moving to a much nicer house with plenty of sunny spots to nap in.

The only downside was that they would be moving in with Clara, who regarded all cats as something to lick, nudge, and generally annoy. But she figured that before long she could teach Clara her place, probably faster than Mckenna would be able to teach Tom Markham *his* place—which might be never. Clara wasn't as hardheaded as her master. And Mckenna wasn't quite as sneaky as Titi.

After all, Titi reflected smugly. Cats rule.

about the author

EMILY CARMICHAEL, the award-winning author of more than twenty novels and novellas, has won praise for both her historical and contemporary romances. She currently lives in her native state of Arizona with her husband and a houseful of dogs.

If you howled at Nell's adventures in

Gone To The Dogs

And cheered for McKenna in

The Cat's Meow

You'll love Jane's story,
on sale in summer 2005.

Read on for a sneak preview of

A New Leash on Life . . .

A New Leash on Life

on sale June 28, 2005

THE DOG days of summer had begun in earnest—the true dog days, that is. Dog shows. Obedience trials. Agility trials, hunting tests, herding trials, tracking tests, and so on, all summer long. Not that these activities didn't pop up during the winter months. They did. But the true frenzy blossomed with the spring flowers, new grass, and tender green leaves. As the Midwest and East began to thaw and the desert dwellers of the West turned on their air conditioning, dog fanciers everywhere planned their dog show itineraries, packed collars, leashes, dog brushes, and dog chow, and looked forward to summer competition and fun.

June in Arizona brought soaring temperatures in the desert and a thaw of the last snow in the mountains. In those same mountains, the first dog show of the season took place among the pines of Flagstaff, where competitors gasped for oxygen in the seven-thousand-foot elevation. One of these people gasping for air stood at the entrances to Ring Twelve, but her rapid breathing came from a case of nerves, not lack of oxygen. She was accustomed to the thin air. She was also accustomed to the tension of waiting to compete, but that didn't make the wait any easier.

Fun, Jane Connor reminded herself as she stood with her dog Shadow waiting to go into the obedience ring. *This is fun. Fun, fun, fun.*

Of course it was fun. Dogs were the love of Jane's life. In fact, they *were* her life—her livelihood and her recreation. More than a hobby, dog training and handling were the things she did best. Competition was her life's blood, and winning was to her soul like air was to her lungs.

All in good fun, of course.

"This is fun," she said quietly to the alert young golden retriever sitting in perfect heel position at her left side. Shadow looked up at her with a doggy smile on his face. Her dark brown eyes seemed to laugh.

The judge in Ring Twelve was taking his own time about filling out paperwork. The ring steward had called Jane's number a good five minutes ago for this run-off—the American Kennel Club's version of a tie-breaker for a class placement. This would be a performance where any bobble or hesitation could spell defeat, and waiting at the gate built tension to an almost sickening level. Jane could feel her focus slipping, minute by minutre. Couldn't these people be a little more on the ball?

Finally, the judge finished writing and looked up at Jane with a smile. "Number two-five-one?"

Jane made the effort to return the smile. "Yes, sir, Two-five-one."

"Good. Come on in, please."

Quietly she commanded Shadow to watch her, then stepped into the ring and surrendered the dog's leash to a ring steward.

"You are tied for a placement in this class," the judge told her, as if she didn't already know. Earlier that morning she and Shadow had done a bang-up job in Utility class, the highest level of obedience competition. She and Shadow needed a high placement in the class to earn points toward Shadow's obedience championship title. Today he really did deserve those points, because his earlier performance in the class had been nothing short of flawless. Hand signals, scent discrimination, retrieving, jumping—he'd done it all with style and enthusiasm. The judge hadn't specified, but Jane suspected this was a run-off for first place.

"This will be a heel-off-lead exercise," the judge explained. "Are you ready?"

Jane took a deep breath. Glancing down at Shadow, she checked that the dog's attention was riveted on her. "Ready!" she declared.

"Forward," the judge ordered.

They marched around the ring at the judge's direction, performing the peculiar dance of the obedience competition ring. Forward, halt, fast, slow, left turn, right turn, and more of the same choreography—no vocal commands allowed in Utility class, only hand signals. They moved together like experienced dance partners, never missing a beat.

If the dog faltered a bit in one turn, lagging just a hair, it was still only a sliver away from perfection. And his final slide into a sit might have been just a tad crooked. But all in all it was a superior performance, especially considering that the wind was wreaking noisy havoc with all the tents and canopies on the show grounds, threatening to turn them into kites, and worse still, a kid with popcorn sat not five feet from the ring, his aromatic bag of buttery treats held right at golden retriever nose level.

"Awesome!" Jenny Sachs clapped Jane on the shoulder as she left the ring. "Good going, Jane."

Jenny had been standing at ringside with the other Utility exhibitors awaiting the presentation of awards and scores. This morning Jenny's little Sheltie had flunked the class when he had knocked the bar from a jump, but Jenny didn't seem to mind the zero score. She always seemed to have fun—win, place, or lose. Sometimes Jane wished she had Jenny's carefree attitude.

"You think it was good?" Jane asked Jenny.

"Excellent! Really."

"There was a little lag on the about turn."

"Half point, if the judge saw it at all. Uh-oh!" Jenny's voice dropped ominously. "Look who you're up against."

While Jane had been in the ring, the steward had called her run-off competition, who was now walking into the ring, a big smile on his face, a tiny black and white dog at his side. This dog had earned the same score as Shadow in the Utility class? Amazing.

"A papillon, of all dogs!" Jane scoffed. "Give me a break!"

"This pap is very good," Jenny warned. "I watched her at the Albuquerque trials last month. It's just disgusting that a dog can be so cute and so smart at the same time."

Jane made a face.

"Well, Shadow too," Jenny revised. "Shadow's as cute as a bug."

Now Shadow looked disgusted.

"I mean, handsome. Shadow is handsome. Gorgeous. Oh my! Get a load of that heeling."

Jane watched with a sinking heart. The papillon pranced at the man's left side like an animated dust bunny, not budging an inch from perfection no matter what the handler did. She looked like a gremlin wind-up toy with her delicately fringed butterfly-wing ears, her toothpick legs, and her perkily curled tail.

The man in the ring was not as accomplished as his dog, however. His handling did not show the practiced perfection of an experienced competitor. With such a small dog he should have shortened the length of his stride and taken more care to keep his big feet out of the little pap's way. His turns were not quite square, and he stopped too fast when the judge gave the order to halt. All of that should have put the little dog at a disadvantage, but instead, she compensated for his small blunders, adjusting herself flawlessly to the difficult pace and folding herself into a precisely straight sit when her master stopped.

The best part of the performance, Jane had to admit, was that the peculiar pair seemed to have such a good time together. The man positively beamed when he looked down at his little toy-sized dog, and the dog's little jaws gaped in a tiny self-satisfied grin. They were truly an example of what dog sport was all about, a pleasure for any obedience trainer to watch—unless that trainer happened to be in direct competition with all that perfection.

"Wow!" Jenny exclaimed. "Did you see that?"

"I did," Jane growled.

"Your handling was way better."

"You don't get points for handling."

"Well . . . I think you probably won."

"Not a chance." Jane tried to sound casual. "That little papillon deserved to win." She glanced ruefully down at Shadow, who gave her a tongue-lolling grin. Unlike Jane, Shadow didn't seem to care who won.

Jane's prediction was right on the money. Five minutes later she stood in the ring with six other qualifying exhibitors. Twenty dogs had been entered in Utility class, but only these few had earned the minimum score required to pass. Jane pasted a smile on her face while she accepted second place, applauding with the others as the little papillon and her handler soaked up the glory of first-place, along with the obedience championship points the win afforded them. Jane tried to be gracious. She shook the man's hand and offered congratulations, thanked the judge, then marched out of the ring with her dignity hanging by a thread.

As Jane stopped at ringside to give Shadow a consolation pat on the head, a pint-sized girl with a bobbing ponytail brushed past her and bounded into the ring like an undisciplined puppy. She headed straight for the man holding the big blue rosette. The kid pulled up just short of crashing into the guy, then bounced up and down, clapping her hands and grinning from ear to ear. The guy's daughter, Jane assumed. Expecting the rest of the fellow's family to come crashing along the same path, she hastened to move away from the gate area and head for a safe retreat.

"Losing builds character," she told Shadow when they reached the relative privacy of her shade canopy. "It's an opportunity for us to show good sportsmanship, you know. You did your best, big guy, and so did I. That's the important thing."

Shadow pretty much ignored the lecture as he went into his portable exercise pen, slurped a few mouthfuls of water, and curled up on his dog bed for a nap in the shade provided by tarps hung from the sides of the canopy.

"Fine. Be like that. You don't want to discuss it? Well, neither do I."

Jane had been on top of the heap for a long time. Ever since she had started training and competing with dogs as a teenager back in Wisconsin, she'd been a natural. She'd started out with a German shepherd, then had taken top honors with a Sheltie. In her mid-twenties, she'd gathered titles and blue ribbons in both obedience and herding trials with her border collie Idaho, who now lived a life of retired ease at the Bark Park, Jane's kennel and training business in Arizona.

And then had come young Shadow, now eighteen months old and well on his way to earning his obedience trial championship.

"You'd be a lot closer to a championship today if you hadn't let that little sissy dog squeeze in front of you." she told the golden retriever.

Shadow opened one lackadaisical eye, then shut it. Jane snorted in disgust. She had gotten too accustomed to being the best. Sinking back into the pile of also-rans took some getting used to. Not that she intended to stay there. Dropping into a canvas folding chair, she took off her ball cap and scrubbed her hands through a bad case of hat hair. Hopeless, Jane knew. Her mop of red frizz was far less disciplined than her dogs. Not that she really cared. As far as Jane was concerned, an act of Congress couldn't make her look like anything besides what she was—a horse-faced, frizz-headed woman rapidly closing on middle age. Sometimes she looked at herself in the mirror and wondered if a little more attention to femininity might be worth the trouble. But the answers always came up negative. Jane had more important things to worry about—like running a business, making a living, and winning competitions.

But not today, obviously. With a sigh, she scraped the thick mass of her hair into a ponytail and fastened it with a rubber band.

"Hi, there!"

Jane jumped at the greeting, looking up to find herself confronted by none other than the conqueror of Utility class and his little mouse of a dog. Both of them had just popped around the corner of her enclosed canopy. Jane's face grew warm. She hoped he hadn't heard her earlier crack about "that little sissy dog."

"Uh . . . hi." She tried to smile but was only half successful.

"Absolutely gorgeous golden retriever."

"He thinks so."

"Does he?"

Jane stood, surprised to find that the guy topped her own five-foot-ten by at least four inches. When she had seen him in the obedience ring, she'd been so wrapped up in losing that she hadn't noticed.

Awakened by the arrival of an admirer, Shadow got off his bed and wriggled his way to the near side of the ex-pen—wriggled because his tail worked so hard that the rest of him wagged back and forth as well. The man laughed.

He had a combustible laugh, Jane noted. It was one of those sounds that could spread like a wildfire, making everyone around him want to laugh also. But Jane just smiled. She hadn't really noticed much about the fellow during his victorious performance in the run-off. The dis-gustingly perfect little dog had captured all her atten-tion—that and the man's less than perfect handling.

But she noticed him now. He was a man, she admitted, that women couldn't help but notice. While not exactly a hunk, he had an open, amiable face that probably made grannies want to pinch his cheeks. His black hair lay in a conservative trim that might have been a bit nerdy, but somehow fit him. Dark, deep-set eyes sparkled with good humor. Khaki slacks and a sweater didn't exactly show off his physique, but his shoulders stretched from here to there very nicely, and he had enough height to place Jane at a disadvantage.

"My name's Cole Forrester, by the way, and this"—he glanced at the little papillon who sat politely at his side—"is Dobby. We wanted to stop by and say what a nice job you two did in the ring today."

"Jane Connor," Jane said by way of introduction. "And Shadow." Shadow waved his tail at the sound of his name. "Did you say the pap's name is Dopey?"

He laughed. "Not Dopey. Dobby. My daughter named her after the house elf character in the Harry Potter series."

"Ah."

"I saw you and Shadow in Open today and again in Utility," Cole said amiably. "Really nice performances."

The fellow was simply trying to be a gracious winner,

Jane reminded herself. Still, the compliment sounded a bit condescending to her. As if she needed condescension from some dork whose dog had to save him from a bunch of amateurish handling mistakes. But then, she might be a bit sensitive on that score.

So she labored to be polite. "Thank you," she said. "She's a cute papillon. Did you show her in Open as well as Utility?" Open class was one level below Utility, and most truly competitive dogs showed in both classes. "I didn't see you there."

"We were in the ring early. Didn't qualify. Dobby got up on the down-stay. Got distracted by a kid screaming at ringside."

"Oh. That's too bad. It's hard to prepare a dog for something like that." Jane managed to stifle a smug grin. "Your Dobby does very well," she said generously, "for a toy breed." This time the condescension was in her own voice.

If he noticed, he didn't take offense. "Yeah. I've noticed not too many toys are in competition. Dobby's my first try at this. Actually, she's my first ever dog."

His first ever dog. Criminy! Not only beaten, but beaten by a novice handler. How humiliating.

"Well, congratulations on your win." She could be gracious, if she tried hard enough.

Shadow gave a soft woof, not loud enough to be misinterpreted as rude, but just a reminder that he deserved a bit of attention. Dobby's ears—easily the biggest appendages she owned—perked in the golden's direction. Cautiously she eased forward and poked her little nose through the wire exercise pen, just a millimeter or so, but enough to extend a friendly invitation to become acquainted. Shadow responded in kind, carefully touching his nose to hers.

Apparently satisfied that the big golden retriever posed

no threat, Dobby squeaked out a little bark and commenced a delighted little dance. Shadow answered with a considerably more substantial bark. He bowed, his tail waving in friendly anticipation of a romp.

"Sorry, Shadow," Jane said. "You're too big to play with her."

"She's a flirt," Cole admitted. "Never gets intimidated by the size of the competition. Dobby's willing to take 'em all on, both in play and in the ring."

If that wasn't a direct challenge, Jane had never heard one. "Dobby should remember that tiny little morsels like her get gobbled up by the competition if they're not careful."

Cole's smile acknowledged the comeback, and his eyes made a quick survey of Jane that made her want to straighten the wild red ringlets of her hair and hide her chapped lips beneath some lip balm. His gaze infused the air with a peculiar sort of tension that was more than the acknowledgment of rivalry. Not a big tension. Just a tiny current of electricity.

Cole Forrester's wife should keep the guy on a leash, Jane decided primly. That electricity of his should be confined to home. And evidently his little Dobby had a similar current of her own. Shadow vibrated with pure joy when the papillon sidled up to his ex-pen and batted her eyes in an almost human fashion.

All very entertaining, Jane acknowledged wryly, but she wished Cole Forrester and his teacup-size wonder dog would move on. She wanted to shop the vendors to find Shadow a toy as a reward for winning Open, and Idaho needed a toy as well—compensation for getting stuck with Jane's friend Mckenna while Shadow had fun at the shows.

"Anyway," Cole said, "I just wanted to pay our respects."

His smile hinted at the devil. "It's always a good idea to size up the competition, don't you think?"

"Never hurts," Jane said with slightly raised brow. "It's going to be a long summer. Hope the little mouse there has some staying power."

"I guess we'll find out."

His hundred-watt smile matched the combustible laugh, Jane noted, and it was much too confident for someone with a bad case of beginner's luck.

"I think from here we're going to hit some agility trials," he told her. "So we'll be out of the obedience people's hair for a while."

"Glad to hear that," Jane tried to keep the relief from her voice. "Not that it wasn't fun competing against you."

"Likewise," he replied, then called to his little mouse. "Dobby, if you lean any harder against that pen, you're going to push it over. Come back here. We need to get going."

Dobby obediently peeled herself off Shadow's ex-pen, and giving Shadow a last longing look—which the golden reciprocated in full measure—trotted back to her master.

"She falls in love with anything male with four legs. Constantly."

A dangerous problem for any female, four-legged or two-legged. Jane herself had never seen the need for such silliness.

"Nice meeting you," she lied as Cole left. *Just don't come back for a while.* Bad enough to go down in defeat to a pipsqueak dog without having the pipsqueak's married owner sending those little electric tingles through her veins.

Shadow whuffed longingly after the departing Dobby.

"Forget it," Jane advised. "She's not your type. Though he's—I mean *she's* interesing, I'll confess." Picking up a leash, she dangled it temptingly in front of Shadow. "You want to go shopping? Get a new toy?"

Shadow promptly lifted a supplicating paw.

"Okay, then." She snapped the leash to his collar and opened the pen. "We'll forget all about that silly dog." *And her master with the nice laugh and the poor handling technique.* Jane grinned and shook her head. "Losing turns me into such a bitch. Shame on me. Bad Jane."

Don't miss out on enthralling romances from

Christina Skye

❖

__0440-20929-3	THE BLACK ROSE	$5.99/$7.99 in Canada
__0440-20864-5	THE RUBY	$6.50/$9.99
__0440-21644-3	COME THE NIGHT	$6.99/$10.99
__0440-21647-8	COME THE DAWN	$5.99/$7.99
__0440-23571-5	2000 KISSES	$6.99/$9.99
__0440-23575-8	GOING OVERBOARD	$6.99/$9.99
__0440-23578-2	MY SPY	$6.99/$9.99
__0440-23759-9	HOT PURSUIT	$6.99/$10.99
__0440-23760-2	CODE NAME: NANNY	$6.99/$10.99
__0440-23761-0	CODE NAME: PRINCESS	$6.99/$10.99

Please enclose check or money order only, no cash or CODs. Shipping & handling costs $5.50 U.S. mail, $7.50 UPS. New York and Tennessee residents must remit applicable sales tax. Canadian residents must remit applicable GST and provincial taxes. Please allow 4 – 6 weeks for delivery. All orders are subject to availability. This offer subject to change without notice. Please call 1-800-726-0600 for further information.

Bantam Dell Publishing Group, Inc.
Attn: Customer Service
400 Hahn Road
Westminster, MD 21157

TOTAL AMT $_____
SHIPPING & HANDLING $_____
SALES TAX (NY, TN) $_____

TOTAL ENCLOSED $_____

Name_____

Address_____

City/State/Zip_____

Daytime Phone (_____)_____

CS ROM 11/0

With *Marilyn Pappano*

sometimes miracles do happen . . . .

Some Enchanted Season
____0553-57982-7 $5.99/$7.99 in Canada

Father to Be
__0553-57985-1 $6.99/$10.99

First Kiss
__0553-58231-3 $6.99/$10.99

Getting Lucky
__0553-58232-1 $6.50/$9.99

Heaven on Earth
__0440-23714-9 $6.50/$9.99

Cabin Fever
__0440-24118-9 $6.50/$9.99

Small Wonders
__0440-24119-7 $6.50/$9.99

Please enclose check or money order only, no cash or CODs. Shipping & handling costs: $5.50 U.S. mail, $7.50 UPS. New York and Tennessee residents must remit applicable sales tax. Canadian residents must remit applicable GST and provincial taxes. Please allow 4 – 6 weeks for delivery. All orders are subject to availability. This offer subject to change without notice. Please call 1-800-726-0600 for further information.

Bantam Dell Publishing Group, Inc.
Attn: Customer Service
400 Hahn Road
Westminster, MD 21157

TOTAL AMT $_____
SHIPPING & HANDLING $_____
SALES TAX (NY, TN) $_____

TOTAL ENCLOSED $_____

Name _____

Address _____

City/State/Zip _____

Daytime Phone (_____) _____

Anything can ❚❚❚❚❚❚❚ *helor and*
a beautifu ❚❚❚❚❚❚❚ *ife"....*

W/S
11/11
5/13/15

CONNIE LANE

don't miss
REINVENTING ROMEO

He's a sexy tycoon with a hit man on his trail.
She's the FBI agent hired to keep him alive.
Now they just have to stay alive long enough
to realize that they're made for each other....

_____23593-6 $5.99/$8.99 in Canada

Also by Connie Lane :

_____23596-0 **ROMANCING RILEY** $5.99/$8.99 in Canada

_____23746-7 **GUILTY LITTLE SECRETS** $5.99/$8.99

_____23747-5 **DIRTY LITTLE LIES** $6.50/$9.99

ROM 11/04